THE PROPHET
OF MARATHON

Bob Waldner

Publisher's Note: This is a work of fiction. Names, characters, organizations,
places, events and incidents are either the products of the author's imagina-
tion or are used in a fictitious manner. Locales and public names are sometimes used for atmospheric purposes. Any resemblance to actual persons,
living or dead, or to businesses, companies, events, institutions, or locales is
entirely coincidental.

Book Layout ©2013 BookDesignTemplates.com

Cover design by LimelightBookCovers.com

The Prophet of Marathon/ Bob Waldner -- 1st ed.
ISBN: 1517706785
ISBN-13: 978-1517706784

To my father, who passed away too soon. He was a good man.

ACKNOWLEDGMENTS

If anyone had asked me three years ago whether I planned on writing a second novel, I would have laughed. Just finishing my first one had been hard enough, and once that goal was realized, it felt more like an end than a beginning. I had told the story I'd wanted to tell, and said the things I'd wanted to say. I sent my manuscript out into the literary universe and waited.

And then I waited some more. The pace of publishing has accelerated since the Nineteenth Century, but only a little. Someone still has to read all those manuscripts, after all, whether they're delivered via Pony Express or zapped through cyberspace. For those of us who have grown accustomed to the immediacy of the modern world in our other pursuits, mustering the patience to wait for a response from a literary agent is a mighty big ask.

When I looked to more experienced writers for guidance, they all offered the same advice: start working on your next book. Sensible enough, I suppose, but only if you have another one in the pipeline. I didn't, so I told myself that my turn as an author was complete and tried to get on with the business of lawyering.

The longer I stayed away from writing, though, the more I came to understand that it was more than just the waiting that was bugging me. After allowing my mind to spend so many hours wandering around a fictional world, the idea of permanently confining it to the real one was hard to swallow. I needed a new project. After some pondering, I decided to write a story that was set in the Florida Keys. I dove in and everything else came into focus around that.

I was about halfway through the first draft of *The Prophet of Marathon* when I released *Peripheral Involvement*. As one would expect, this was a watershed moment in my writing career. A part of my life that I had theretofore kept hidden became public overnight, and it was terrifying. As good as I felt about my book, I had to confront the possibility that the rest of the world might take a considerably dimmer view of my efforts.

I doubt that I would have gone on to finish this novel without the support and encouragement that I received from the readers of *Peripheral Involvement.* There is nothing more satisfying for me as an author than seeing others engaged with my work. To everyone that took the time to leave a review, or drop me a note, or simply read the book, you have my deepest gratitude.

In dedicating *Peripheral Involvement* to my wife, Erinn, I said that I'd be lost without her, and that remains the truest thing I've ever written. It was her enthusiasm that drove *The Prophet of Marathon* forward, and her keen editorial eye that fixed its defects. Her support makes everything possible for me, and I can never thank her enough.

Many thanks, also, to my mother, Peg Waldner, my sister, Karen Williams, and my aunt, Louise Sieminski. They have been squarely in my corner my whole life, and it's no different when it comes to my writing.

I very much appreciate the help of Ted Callahan, Phillips Johnston and Brandon Holder, each of whom took the time to read and comment on earlier versions of this story. I am proud to call you gentlemen my friends.

It's impossible to acknowledge everyone individually here, but there is one other person that I want to mention. Julia Blankertz was my law school classmate and my friend. She was one of the first people to read *Peripheral Involvement,* and one of the first to review it. She called me to brainstorm about ways to spread the word, and she relentlessly championed my work to anyone who would listen.

Like everyone else who knew her, I was shocked to hear of her sudden passing earlier this year. When she and I last spoke, I thanked her for her support, but I am certain that I failed to convey how much it meant. The idea that I might not get another chance to do so never occurred to me. I know that saying it here is a poor substitute, but it's the only way I have left. Thank you, Julia.

Finally, I want to thank my daughters, Maureen and Maddie, for continuing to inspire me. As I watch them grow, I become more and more convinced that their achievements will far outstrip my own. They are writing their own stories already, and I am in awe of their insight and creativity. If my literary adventures serve to embolden them in some small way, then all of this will have been time well spent.

I hope that you enjoy the book!

Bob Waldner
New York
November, 2015

"Fathers, provoke not your children to anger, lest they be discouraged."

— Colossians 3:21

Chapter One

The whole thing was the government's fault. I know that's not exactly an original sentiment these days, but I'm not talking about abortion, or guns, or any of the other shit that gets people bent out of shape on talk radio shows every afternoon. For me, it was much more personal than that. They took away my livelihood.

On April 15, 2011, the Department of Justice shut down online poker in the United States. A lot of folks were pretty pissed off, but I'm guessing that it wasn't really that big of a deal for most of them. I suppose that it made it harder to chase the pipe dream of parlaying a thirty-nine dollar satellite buy-in into a huge payday at the World Series. Some guys probably had to find new hobbies. People bitched about it for a while, and then got on with their lives.

My situation was a bit more complicated. By 2011, online poker had been my full-time job for more than three years. When they blew it all up, it was like they personally handed me a pink slip. Even worse, actually, because there was no notice, no severance package, nothing to cushion the blow. I couldn't even withdraw the cash that I'd already won.

I'm sure that the administration's lawyers weren't thinking about guys like me back then. They were just enforcing the laws, and if they thought they were hurting anybody, it was the shady offshore operators who ran the gambling sites. No one was looking to put the players in jail. I guess that was fair enough, but it didn't change the fact that I was out of a job.

That's what I mean when I say that everything was the government's fault. If they hadn't ended my poker career, I would have been happy to stay up north. I never would have come down to the Keys, and I never would have gotten involved with John Wainwright, or his daughter. Maybe I'd have become a big-time card player and won millions playing tournaments on TV. Maybe I'd have met a nice girl and settled down. But that's not how things worked out. Fucking bureaucratic assholes....

Chapter Two

I met John Wainwright about three months after I moved to Marathon, in a lawyer's office in the strip mall across the Overseas Highway from the airport. He was a handsome man, every bit of six feet tall, with an air of fitness about him and a closely cropped patch of white hair covering his head. I guessed that he was around the same age as my father. His khaki trousers and plain white dress shirt fit him nicely. Compared to the other old men shuffling around town in their lounge wear, he looked positively dashing.

His arrival took me by surprise. The lawyer was out to lunch, and so was our receptionist/secretary/paralegal, so I was the only one there at the time. It wasn't a busy practice, and we didn't get many walk-ins. I was just about to head outside for a cigarette when I heard the door open, so I slid my lighter back into my pocket and walked around the corner to see who was there. I saw Wainwright standing in the doorway, looking around as if he were trying to guess whether anyone was home. I greeted him as I entered the room. "Good afternoon."

"Good afternoon," he replied in a rich, deep voice, as he shut the door behind him.

He turned to face me, and I sensed that he was sizing me up. That went on long enough to make me uncomfortable, so I finally spoke. "Can I, uh... can I help you with something?"

He smiled and extended his hand. "John Wainwright," he announced. I gripped his hand firmly and told him my name, and we exchanged the usual pleasantries before he went on. "I was hoping that we might discuss..."

I interrupted him before he could finish his sentence. "I'm sorry, Mr. Wainwright, but I'm... uh... not a lawyer. I mean, I think you probably want to talk to Mr. Baker." I made a show of checking my watch. "He should be back after lunch."

A look of amusement crossed the old man's face. "Lunch, huh?" he asked, and when I nodded, he started laughing. "Well," he chuckled, "if you want to call a pint of bourbon and a handful of ice cubes 'lunch,' then I reckon that's true enough." I smiled awkwardly and shrugged, trying to figure out how I was supposed to reply to that, but he spared me. "My apologies," he went on. "I shouldn't have said that." He smiled again before adding, "I've known Bob Baker for years." I noticed that his Southern accent seemed to be thickening with each word that left his lips.

Relieved, I exhaled and tried to flash him a knowing look. I'd only been working for Baker for about two months, but I'd already figured out that he was a drunk. Hell, I'd met him in a bar, lamenting our lots over Wild Turkey and ginger ale. I told him that I needed to find a way to make some cash, and he said that I could help him out with a few things. When I showed up at his office the next day, it took him a few minutes to remember who I was, but he held up his end of the bargain. He operated at the very bottom of the legal barrel: nasty divorces, phantom injuries, and shady insurance claims, and he put me to work on some real lowlife shit. I followed various scumbags around town and took pictures of them, usually while they screwed women that weren't their wives or played pick-up basketball after they'd told their insurance companies that they weren't able to walk. At first, I had a tough time with it, and I had to keep reminding myself that it was just a temporary gig. I was absolutely sure that I'd sort myself out quickly and move on.

Baker paid me by the job, usually a couple hundred bucks each time, in cash. It was all off the books. I'm pretty sure that you're supposed to have some sort of license to do private investigation work, but both of us were OK with bending the rules. He got incriminating pictures for his cases at a cut rate, and I made more cash than I would have if I'd been waiting tables at Applebee's. Also, to be honest, I found myself getting off on the voyeuristic aspect of it all. There was something unexpectedly compelling about watching the high school football coach bang the school nurse in a motel room while their respective spouses were home watching *Wheel of Fortune*. I'm not saying that I wanted to do it forever, but I have to admit that it hadn't taken long for me to get more comfortable with it than I ever thought I would.

Wainwright spoke again. "I'm not actually looking to see Bob today. I was hoping that maybe you could help me out."

I hesitated for few seconds before stammering out a reply. "I don't think that I'm the guy you wanna talk to. I don't, uh... really... work here... officially. I just sort of help Mr. Baker out sometimes...."

He smiled and nodded. "That's exactly what I'm looking for. Just a little help. A little unofficial help."

"Well, I, uh..." Before I was able to say anything else, the door opened and Baker's secretary, Annie, returned from lunch, clutching her Diet Coke in one hand. She looked surprised to see anyone else in the office, but she walked right past us and took her place at her desk on the other side of the room without saying a word. I turned back to Wainwright to continue our conversation, but he ended it before I could say anything else.

"Tell you what... if you want to talk some more, why don't you stop by my place tonight. Say, seven o'clock?" While he spoke, he reached into his back pocket and pulled out a card, which he handed to me. On it was his name, along with an address in Grassy Key, maybe fifteen minutes outside of town. While I was reading it, he leaned in and added in a low voice, "Of course, there'll be some cash in it for you." Without waiting for my response, he turned and walked out the door. I stood there for another minute or so, running my fingers over the card and trying to make sense of what had just happened, before I went outside and finally had that cigarette.

Chapter Three

Moving to the Keys wasn't the first thing I'd thought of doing once I figured out that I wouldn't be able to keep playing poker in my living room. After the government shut down those web sites, it took me a few days to understand what had happened. I kept trying to log on to PokerStars, but every time I did, the only thing that popped up on my screen was an ominous-sounding notice which began, "This domain name has been seized by the F.B.I. pursuant to an arrest warrant..." The message went on to cite the various federal statutes that one would violate if one were to engage in the business of conducting, financing, managing, supervising, directing, or owning all or part of an illegal gambling enterprise. After seeing it enough times, I finally got it through my head that the situation wasn't going to fix itself, and I tried to figure out what to do next.

Right away, I decided to pursue the most obvious avenue that I could see, which was to keep playing poker. The government had only closed the online arena; there were still plenty of places to play the old-fashioned way, with people you could see and cards you could touch. I didn't live that far from Atlantic City, and all of the casinos down there had perfectly legal poker rooms. The newer places in Philadelphia were adding them as well, and even the Indian joints in Connecticut were close enough. I also remembered that, back when I'd lived in New York, there had been a number of card rooms scattered around Manhattan. Those weren't sanctioned by the state, and I figured that the ones I'd known were long gone, but I was pretty sure that I could find their replacements if I asked the right people. I imagined cruising around the tri-state area in search of the juiciest games, kind of like a real-life version of Matt Damon's character in *Rounders*, minus the life-threatening debts to the Russian mob. I was thrilled to give it a try.

My enthusiasm for this plan lasted all of one day. I woke up early and drove to Atlantic City, where I spent nineteen hours playing a series of $1-$3 No-Limit Hold 'Em games at the Borgata. I did OK, money-wise, but the experience revealed a number of drawbacks to live play that I hadn't taken into account. First of all, there was the radical difference in the pace of the game. Online poker moves quickly; you don't have to wait for dealers to shuffle cards, players are forced to act within thirty seconds, and empty seats are filled instantly. In real life, all of those little delays add up to a considerable amount of dead time. Poker is a game in which a good player might expect to have an advantage over his opponents, but that advantage will generally be small. In order for it to translate into significant profits, it needs to be applied to a large number of hands. When I played on the internet, not only was each table dealing many more hands per hour than they would in a casino, but I also had the ability to play multiple tables simultaneously. Even after one day, it was clear that I was going to have to play higher-stakes games if I was going to have a chance at making anywhere near as much money in person as I did online.

That led me to think about the quality of the opposition that I'd be facing. It stood to reason that higher-stakes games would be tougher to beat, so I was hesitant to move in that direction. Even at the lower levels, the standard of play at the Borgata was higher than what I'd seen on PokerStars. Novices who watched poker on TV and wanted to give it a try might have been willing to turn on their computer and throw away a few hundred bucks, but they were less likely to get in their cars and drive to the shore in order to try it out. Not having guys like that at the table definitely took away some of my edge.

Those were real concerns, but if they were the only issues I had with live poker, I might have been able to work around them. I could have gotten used to the slower pace, and I probably could have discovered venues that offered combinations of stakes and difficulty that I would have found profitable enough. But even if I had managed to sort all of that out, there was no way around the single biggest problem with playing poker with real, live people, which is the simple fact that poker players are a bunch of assholes. Paranoid, abrasive, petty, defensive... sitting with them was like taking a crash course in antisocial personality disorders. I understand that psychological warfare is a legitimate element of poker, and if you can get your opponents flustered or angry, they're likely to make mistakes that you can exploit. Certain well-known players employ these tactics with great success, which is part of the problem; everybody watches those guys on TV and wants to imitate them. If I ever play against a famous pro and he starts giving me shit, it might well get into my head and affect my game. When that stream of disparagement comes from a middle-aged deadbeat who can't get over the fact that I had the audacity to outdraw his pocket jacks, it's just annoying.

Spending that one day in Atlantic City with those people was enough to show me that I would never to be able to do it on a full-time basis. It was funny, because most of their bullshit wasn't even directed at me. I kept quiet and did my own thing, and I managed not to draw much fire from my table mates. Even so, the amount of arguing, sniping and general unpleasantness was enough to render the whole atmosphere toxic. As I drove home late that night, I realized that enduring it for any length of time would have defeated the whole purpose of playing poker for a living. If I'd wanted to spend long hours surrounded by rude people looking to second-guess everything I did, I would have just become a corporate lawyer and at least gotten a regular paycheck out of it.

Once I abandoned the idea of taking my poker career from the internet into the real world, I thought about getting another "straight" job. In the eight years since I'd gotten out of college, I'd worked for a bank, taught SAT prep courses to high-school kids, and then, after a two-year spell tending bar, worked in sales for a pharmaceutical company. Actually, at that point, my parents still believed that I had that last job. I figured that they wouldn't have appreciated hearing that I'd given it up to become a gambler, so I never mentioned it. They seemed happy that I wasn't living in their house or using their money to pay my bills, and they didn't ask a ton of questions about my situation. It wasn't all that difficult to maintain the fiction.

I spent the next few weeks combing job listings and sending resumes, but I wasn't able to attract so much as a nibble. Given that I was thirty years old, had no marketable skills whatsoever, and hadn't ever stayed in a job, other than bartending, for more than a year, I suppose I shouldn't have been surprised by the market's lack of enthusiasm for my candidacy. As time passed and my already-paltry cash reserves started to dwindle, I got desperate and started looking into restaurant and retail openings. As awful as those prospects seemed, they were more appealing than going to my parents with my hat in my hand. I was prepared to do almost anything to avoid that.

It was ironic, then, that I was spared having to go down that road by a call from my father. He called me on a Saturday, about six weeks into my fruitless search for new employment. It actually wasn't the first time I'd spoken with him since my poker income had dried up, but nothing interesting had come out of our earlier conversations.

Given my circumstances, I wasn't particularly enthused at the prospect of talking to him, but I still answered quickly when I saw his number pop up on my phone. "Hey, Dad. How you doin'?"

"Good. I'm good. How are you?"

"I'm, uh, hangin' in there."

"Everything OK at work?"

I paused before replying, searching for a way to convey the fact that things were not OK without letting slip that I was referring to an entirely different job than the one he was asking about. In the end, I never got the chance to say anything, because my father stuck to the game plan that he'd been following for three decades and went on without waiting to hear my answer. "I'm asking because of the article in the *Times* this morning. Did you read it?"

"Nope."

"Well," he said, sounding slightly annoyed, "you really should take a look. There was a lengthy piece in the business section about layoffs in the pharmaceutical industry in New Jersey. They mentioned your company by name. I just wanted to make sure you were OK."

My first instinct was to give him the usual bullshit and tell him that everything was fine with my make-believe job, but as I opened my mouth to reply, it occurred to me that maybe this was an opportunity to come (sort of) clean. There didn't seem to be any point in telling him the whole truth, but sooner or later my parents were going to find out that I wasn't hawking cholesterol medicine anymore. Given the news in the press, they wouldn't question an imaginary layoff ending my pretend career in pharmaceutical sales. It seemed like the perfect way to clue them in to my current situation without having to explain too much.

I must have dithered for too long while I was pondering all of this, because the next thing that came through the receiver was my father's impatient voice: "You still there?"

"Uh, yeah... Sorry. Got distracted. What were you saying?"

He exhaled theatrically. "The layoffs... Your company..."

"Right. Of course," I replied. I took a deep breath and continued. "I was, uh, actually gonna call you and Mom over the weekend. They came and talked to me the other day. Looks like I'm out."

"I'm really sorry to hear that. I was afraid when I saw the article. Tough times in that business, it seems." He sounded genuinely deflated. I was tempted to tell him not to worry about it, but I let him go on. "It's too bad. I was thinking that maybe you'd finally found a home. You were there for what... around four years, right?"

"Yeah... just about four years."

"Did they at least give you some sort of severance package?"

"Uh, yeah. A small package." I was trying to keep my answers as short and as vague as I could.

"Good. That's good."

"Uh huh."

He hesitated for a moment before moving on to the next question, the one that I knew was coming. "So," he began, "do you have any sense of what you're going to do next?"

"I'm working on figuring that out now."

He seemed to be waiting for me to say something more, but once he figured out that I wasn't going to elaborate, he continued. "I was thinking that maybe we could think about your next move together...."

That was a conversation that I definitely didn't want to have, so I tried to deflect his suggestion as diplomatically as I could. "Thanks, but... you know, uh, this just happened... I'd really like to take a little time to process before we try to figure out next steps, OK?"

He was persistent. "I'm just worried. You've been out of school for a few years now and your career hasn't really gotten going..."

I wasn't in the mood for the full recap of my disappointing adult life, so I interrupted him. "OK. Sure. Let's talk. Can I call you in your office sometime next week?" I had no intention of doing that, but I needed to change the topic. To make sure that he didn't come back to it, I tried to steer in a different direction by adding, "How's Mom doing?"

It worked. "You know your mother. She's always got some project or another," he laughed.

"Stuff with the charity?"

"Charities, plural, is more like it. I feel like we're always gearing up for some sort of event. Actually, come to think of it, are you around next week? You wanna go to the Sloan-Kettering fundraiser with her?"

It was my turn to laugh. "That's more your department, I think."

He sighed. "Yeah, that's what she says as well, but I've got to make some time to get down to Florida and I'm just not sure when..."

I cut him off. "Florida?"

"Yeah. I still haven't finished with your grandfather's estate. You know that house he had in the Keys?"

"Uh huh." I remembered that my grandfather had owned a house down there, but he'd been dead for more than a year, and I had just assumed that my father had already sold it. Since none of the proceeds were headed my way, I hadn't bothered to keep tabs on the situation.

My father went on. "Probating the will took a while, and there were some hang-ups with the transfer of title. Bottom line is that I haven't gotten around to selling it yet, and last month I got a tax bill for the place. I need to go down to Marathon and get everything sorted out so I can get it off our books."

He went on for a few more minutes, complaining about the co-lossal waste of time and money that the whole thing had been. The gist of the story seemed to be that my grandfather had been bitten by the deep sea fishing bug and bought the place on a whim, but had only used it a few times before losing interest, or something like that. By that point, I wasn't really paying attention anymore; I was too busy scheming, and when my father paused, I jumped in.

"So, uh, all of this gives me an idea. Maybe I can go down to Florida and help you out."

"I don't know if that's..."

I went on before he could object. "Look, I have some free time now. And I know that you're really busy. I could take care of this for you."

The initial silence with which this proposal was greeted prepared me for the dismissive response that followed a few seconds later. "I don't think that it's the best idea for you take a vacation to Florida at this point."

Eager to cut him off before he could gain steam, I corrected him. "It's not a vacation. I'd just be working on the house... for you."

"I really think that you should focus on finding another position."

"Dad... look... I could really use a couple of weeks to clear my head, and you just said that you don't have time deal with this. Seems like this would be perfect for both of us. When's the last time anyone's even been in that place?"

"It's been a while. After Grandpa died, I had a realtor go over there, but they didn't do much."

"That's exactly what I'm saying. One of us should spend a little time down there. I could go through Grandpa's stuff, clean it all up, and get it squared away for listing."

Once again, there was silence on the other end of the phone, but my sense was that he was considering giving in rather than thinking up another way to say "no." I wondered if his hesitation was rooted in any real concern about my career, or if he was just afraid that I'd fuck things up in Florida. I figured that it was some combination of the two, but I was betting that his desire to avoid inconveniencing himself would outweigh his misgivings. Sure enough, when he spoke again, it was clear that he'd talked himself into it. "I don't want this to drag on forever, you understand?"

"Of course."

"I'm serious. I'm not in the business of putting you up in Florida long-term. I expect you back in a couple of weeks, tops."

"OK..."

"I absolutely need to have this place sold by the end of the summer, so please let the realtor know that when you meet with her."

"Will do."

"Call my office on Monday. You can get the realtor's name and number from Janet. I'll ask her to book a plane ticket for you as well."

"Actually, I figured I'd drive. Might want to have my car down there, you know?"

"Just rent one."

"I'd really rather drive. More chance to clear my head."

"Suit yourself. Call me on Monday and I'll give you all of the info." I imagined him shaking his head as he spoke, like he always did when he was convinced that I was about to do something stupid and he'd exhausted his appetite for counseling me against it.

"Uh... Dad?"

"Yes?"

"I was wondering if I could get, uh... a little cash, maybe? To get me down there?"

He sighed. "That's fine. Just stop by the house when you get a chance. You should see your mother before you go, anyhow."

"OK. I'll come by tomorrow. Talk to you then."

Before I could hang up, he added one last thing. "When you get back, we're still going to have that talk about finding you another job."

"Great," was all I said before ending our call.

Chapter Four

That conversation with my dad weighed heavily on my mind as I drove out toward Wainwright's place in Grassy Key that night, particularly the part where he told me that he expected me to come home after a few weeks. I felt like I could actually hear his voice, just as clearly as if he'd been in the car beside me, saying that he wasn't in the business of giving me a free place to stay in the Keys. Needless to say, he was less than pleased that I was still in Marathon three months after he'd delivered that message.

His angst was amplified by the fact that Labor Day had come and gone and Grandpa's house was still on the market. That certainly wasn't my fault; I'd actually held up my end of our bargain on that front. I mean, I may have wasted a few days on the beach here and there, but mostly I'd worked hard at getting the place in shape. It only took a couple of days to go through everything that my grandfather had left behind, which amounted to very little beyond the functional necessities that one would have expected to find in a vacation home: linens, flatware, casual clothing, that sort of thing. Given that he died a very rich man after a long career as a partner at a venerable investment banking house in New York, I was disappointed not to have found anything more valuable, or at least more interesting, but it seemed like my father hadn't exaggerated about how little time the old man had actually spent there.

After going through everything, my intention had been to repaint the whole house, but after spending a few days in the midsummer humidity, I wrote that idea off and settled for a thorough room-by-room cleaning. I was pretty proud of how much I accomplished in those few weeks, and the realtor seemed optimistic when we brought the listing online in the middle of July. A few prospective buyers came to see it right away, but we got only one lowball offer that my father dismissed out of hand, without even deigning to counter. The last showing had been in late August, and the realtor was pressuring us to lower the asking price. Dad wanted to stay at $1.6 million, so we waited.

Deep down, I think my father understood that the delay hadn't been my fault, but the fact that I was still down there was clearly driving him nuts. I knew that, but I was living in a million-dollar house overlooking the Atlantic Ocean for free. I didn't see any reason to give that up until I really had to. Besides, I'd skipped out on my lease in New Jersey, so it wasn't like I had anywhere else to go.

Beyond what I'd brought with me in my car, all of my stuff was in a storage locker outside of Trenton. I'd been playing straight with my dad when I told him that I just wanted to go to Marathon for a couple of weeks and help him with the house. I always thought that I might stretch it out a bit, but my intention had been to head back north by the end of the summer, at the latest. Once I got down there, though, I found that I really liked it, even if I couldn't put my finger on exactly what it was that appealed to me. In a lot of ways, it wasn't all that different from the other places I'd lived. It had the usual as-

sortment of fast food joints and big box stores, and the local high
school looked like every other high school that I'd ever seen, except
for the fact that it was painted teal. When you drove down U.S. 1,
you felt like you were driving through a typical American town,
until you got to Seven Mile Bridge and found yourself surrounded
by water. I think I was fascinated by the incongruity of finding all of
the trappings of the modern world set up on this string of tiny is-
lands sandwiched between the Gulf of Mexico and the Atlantic
Ocean.

Or maybe I just really dug living in that house for free. My
grandfather had spent his life making money, and here I was, looking out at the sea through his bedroom window and enjoying the
fruits of his labors more completely than he'd ever taken time to. I'm
sure that wasn't lost on my father, either, as he spent his summer
busting his ass in Lower Manhattan while I was lounging on the
beach. He always seemed to feel that it was necessary to remind me
that I was getting a free ride, but it really wasn't. I may have been
short on work ethic, but I had a full ration of self-awareness. I understood perfectly well that I was coasting, and I was OK with it. In
fact, I welcomed it. I also understood that it was temporary, and I
was prepared to move on to something else once the situation played
itself out. Uncertainty didn't trouble me. Maybe that was the real
difference between my father and me. For forty years, he'd always
known exactly where his next paycheck was coming from. He'd
probably figured out what he was going to do with his life when he
was still in elementary school. I think it was hard for him to understand why anyone wouldn't want to do the same.

Once I decided that I wanted to try to stick around, I spent some
time looking for a job. It didn't take long to figure out that Marathon

wasn't exactly a hotbed of economic activity. There seemed to be two industries in the Keys: tourism and fishing. Some entrepreneurial locals combined the two and took the tourists fishing. There didn't seem to be much else on offer, so I was feeling pretty lucky about having stumbled into Bob Baker's sordid world of adulterers and insurance cheats. Even so, I didn't want to live in that world forever. As the summer ended, I started feeling more pressure to figure something out. I knew that the house would sell, sooner or later. Even if it didn't, I sensed that that my dad might have been one good temper tantrum away from hopping on a plane and dragging me home by my ear.

Finding a steady source of income was critical to my plans. The more respectable that job turned out to be, the easier it would be to sell my parents on the idea of my permanent relocation to Florida, but that was a secondary concern. As long as I made enough money to pay my own bills, I would be able to ignore their views on my career, which was all that I was really worried about.

I didn't think that taking Wainwright up on his invitation that night would lead to any sort of long-term solution, but I wasn't in any position to turn my nose up at his offer. My logic was pretty straightforward: the more cash I had, the more time it would buy me once I got kicked out of my grandfather's place. The money that I was making with Baker helped, but I was spending it as quickly as I earned it. I figured that whatever I could get from Wainwright could go straight into my rainy-day fund. Since a downpour looked inevitable, I never stopped to consider the wisdom of continuing my conversation with the old man. It was a no-brainer. Once he mentioned cash, I was always going to hear him out.

I wasn't nervous at all as I headed out toward Grassy Key. In hindsight, maybe I should have been; I was going to a complete stranger's house to discuss something that he clearly didn't want to mention in public, and that fact alone probably should have raised some sort of red flag. At least some of my cavalier attitude was probably a natural result of my size. I'm about six foot four, and probably still a solid two-twenty or two-twenty-five. Not a lot of people intimidated me; Wainwright certainly didn't. I guess I was naïve, but I was sure that the old guy wasn't going to throw anything at me that I couldn't handle.

I just assumed that he was looking to get some dirt on his wife, or his ex-wife, or one of his business partners. I figured that Baker had probably told him about the kind of stuff that I'd been doing, and he wanted to cut a deal with me directly. That would have explained why he'd clammed up once the secretary returned, and why he wanted to move our conversation away from Baker's office. My only real concern was that Baker might have been talking a little too much. I appreciated the additional business, but I didn't want too many people to find out what I was up to. I wasn't sure what kind of trouble I could get in for doing that kind of stuff without a P.I. license, and I really didn't want to find out.

I drove up Sombrero Beach Road until I hit U.S. 1, and then I took a right and headed toward the airport. About ten minutes up the road, I swung left onto Guava Avenue and then right onto Morton Street. I reached a dead end without finding Wainwright's address, but when I went back for a second pass, I saw the number on a small mailbox that was almost completely obscured by an overgrown bush. I couldn't see his house from the road. The mailbox stood next to a dirt path that had been cut through a dense cluster of tropical trees. I wasn't entirely sure if it was meant to be a driveway or a footpath, but it looked just about wide enough for my car, so I gingerly steered down it, happy that it was still light outside.

After I'd gone about a hundred yards, the path widened a bit and I saw the house in front of me. It was a big, old-looking place, set up on stilts like most of the houses in that part of the world. I parked near the bottom of a staircase and made my way up to the front door. As I knocked, I glanced at my watch and saw that it was about ten minutes past seven.

I was taken aback when the door opened to reveal a beautiful young woman with dark hair. She couldn't have been more than five feet tall, and every part of her was tiny, except for her breasts. Confounded by the sight of her, I just stood there and stared at her chest while I tried to marshal the words to explain myself. Before I could, she smiled and greeted me in a soft voice. "He's out on the verandah. He's expecting you," she said, before turning and walking away from the door. After a few steps, she seemed to notice that I wasn't following, so she paused and gestured for me to come along. I stepped inside and closed the door behind me.

As I walked through the front room, I noticed a photograph on the wall to my left. It showed what appeared to be a younger version of Wainwright standing with his arm around Ronald Reagan. I would have studied it longer, but I noticed that my escort had already gone on to the next room. As I hurried to catch up with her, I took a quick look at my surroundings. The décor was tasteful enough, and the furnishings looked to be of good quality, but everything seemed a bit worn and dated.

When we passed through the sliding glass door that led to the verandah, I saw Wainwright's white hair rising above the back of the rocking chair from which he was watching the sun set over the Gulf of Mexico. He stood and turned to greet me before offering me the chair beside his. We both sat down, and after he thanked me for coming, he offered me a glass of iced tea.

"Sounds good, thank you," I replied.

"Just so you know, I take my tea very sweet," he cautioned.

I smiled. "That's how I like it."

"Good. I don't trust anyone who drinks unsweet tea." He nodded to the young woman, who promptly went back into the house, presumably to fetch our refreshments.

Once she'd gone, I ventured an observation. "She seems like a lovely girl."

Wainwright nodded. "Indeed she is."

"Is she, uh... your daughter?"

"No," was all he said in reply, but his lack of further explanation spoke volumes about their relationship. I suppressed the instinct to give him a knowing nod of approval and instead stared straight out at the horizon. The sun had just about disappeared, but it had left behind a residue of orange and yellow streaks that contrasted beautifully against the blue hues of the sky and the sea. "This," said Wainwright, as he made a sweeping gesture toward the Gulf, "never gets old."

"No doubt," I replied. "Stunning." Just then, the young woman returned with our drinks. I couldn't help but imagine her and the old man in bed together, and I looked straight down at the floor while she handed me my glass, as if avoiding eye contact would better conceal the depravity of my thoughts. As she turned away, I glanced up and mumbled a quick, "Thank you," in her direction. After she'd gone back inside, I decided to try to change the subject. "I couldn't

help but notice on my way in, that picture in the hall. Is that you...
with President Reagan?"

Wainwright nodded as he took a sip of his tea. "That's from the
'84 campaign, in Jacksonville. Feels like another lifetime...." His
voice trailed off and his eyes narrowed. When he continued, I detected, for the first time since I'd met him, a trace of uncertainty in
his voice. "Did you look me up before you came over here? On your
computer?"

"Nope." The thought had never occurred to me.

He stared hard at me for a few seconds, and I felt like he was trying to decide whether I was telling the truth. Then he broke into a
smile and chuckled, "Well, I reckon you will now."

Intrigued, I waited for him to say more. When he didn't, I tried
to nudge him. "So, it would be worth my time to Google 'John
Wainwright?'"

He shrugged. "Depends on how much you value your time." He
paused before going on. "Let's just say that I've had a few ups and
downs, just like any other man my age."

"I'm all ears."

He laughed again. "No, no. I wouldn't want to spoil your fun tonight. You've got a nice little research project to look forward to
when you get home."

I was mildly annoyed by his unwillingness to share, but I let it go.
At the time, I didn't think he'd turn out to be that interesting. I noticed a glass ashtray perched on the table across from where we were
sitting. "You mind if I smoke?" I asked as I gestured toward it.

"Feel free," he replied with a shrug.

I walked over to the railing to light up, and exhaled my first few drags into the gathering darkness before I turned back to face my host. "So, you wanted to discuss some business, right?" I offered.

Wainwright straightened up in his chair, and launched right into his proposal, which was quite simple. He wanted me to return to his house on Saturday morning, pick up an item, and deliver it to a hotel in Miami. A gentleman would meet me at the hotel, where he would pay me cash in exchange for the item. I would then bring the cash back to Wainwright. For my trouble, I would receive one thousand dollars.

When Wainwright presented it in his smooth, even voice, he made it sound like an entirely harmless diversion, the easiest money that anyone would ever make. I was tempted to agree on the spot, but the whole thing was just sketchy enough to give me pause. My family's business acumen had mostly been lost on me, but one lesson I had successfully taken on board was that there was no such thing as a free lunch. I had a bunch of questions, but they all centered on discovering why anyone would want to pay me so much to perform such a seemingly innocuous task.

Rather than ask Wainwright straight away, I took a moment to try to figure it out on my own. As I did so, it occurred to me that my confusion was entirely attributable to the price that he'd quoted me. If he'd offered two or three hundred bucks, it would have been a signal that all was above board; if he had offered ten grand, I would have assumed that he wanted me to roll to South Beach with a trunk full of cocaine. But a thousand dollars couldn't be right. He was either overpaying for something mundane, or underpaying for something dangerous. I needed to figure out which it was.

I took a sip of tea and began with the most obvious question. "Mind if I ask you exactly what it is you want me to deliver?"

The old man sat back in his chair and swirled his tea around his glass before replying. "A trinket. An interesting trinket."

"Uh huh. I'm sure it's interesting, but I was hoping that you might be a little more specific…"

He interrupted me, and his tone grew colder. "I hoped that my thousand dollars might buy me a respite from questions like these."

I took another pull from my smoke before answering. "I appreciate that, but there are certain risks I'm not prepared to take for a thousand bucks." He looked confused, so I went on. "You know… like, if I were to have something in my car that might get me sent to prison if I got pulled over."

"You're talking about drugs?!" he exclaimed, as if it had never occurred to him that anyone would think of such a thing. When I nodded, he continued. "No, Lord no. No drugs. Is that what you wanted to know?"

"That's a start, but drugs aren't the only thing I'm worried about."

Wainwright sighed. "It's not drugs. It's not guns. It's not moonshine. Nothing illegal, OK?"

I extinguished my cigarette in the ashtray and sat back down. "That's good," I said. "But then I have to ask you, why the thousand bucks? And why me?"

For once, he gave me a straight answer. "The money is meant to ensure your discretion. Bob Baker assures me that you're discreet. And reliable. He's not wrong, is he?"

"No. He's absolutely right, so much so that you can trust me with the whole story."

"Are you saying that you won't do it unless I tell you exactly what it is that I need delivered?"

"That's right."

He rocked silently for a few moments before continuing. "You do need the money, don't you?"

I shrugged. "Like I said, I need to understand what I'm getting myself into."

"So, if I made it, say, two thousand, that wouldn't change your mind?"

"Actually, it would probably make me even more nervous."

"Uh huh," he muttered as he rocked slowly in his chair. "I *could* get someone else to do it."

I stood up and set my glass down on the table. "Thanks for the tea, then."

"You're leaving?" He seemed incredulous.

"Not sure there's much else to talk about."

"Sit down," he commanded. When I didn't comply instantly, he repeated himself in a milder tone, and added, "Would you like some more tea?" When I still hesitated, he clarified his intentions. "It's a long story."

Surprised that I'd managed to win our battle of wills so quickly, I declined a refill but sat down next to him and invited him to go on. He spun a fantastic yarn, which began in eighteenth century London, where his ancestor, George Wainwright, was a prosperous merchant who had two sons. The oldest, Edward, followed his father into the family business (and, according to his descendant, ruined it). The youngest, William, like so many others in his situation, went to sea. His father's money secured him a midshipman's berth in a frigate, which was dispatched to patrol the West Indies sometime in the

1740's. The ship's captain was a brutal tyrant, even by the standards of the day, and some months after leaving England, the crew mutinied, murdered him and took the ship. Having irrevocably exiled themselves from their homeland, they turned to piracy. Initially, they had some success, most notably the taking of two Spanish treasure galleons that had separated from their convoy en route from Veracruz to Havana. Not long after securing those prizes, they ran into a squadron of English warships and were captured, but not before they'd managed to stash their haul somewhere along the east coast of Florida.

The mutineers were taken to Charleston in chains to answer for their crimes, William Wainwright among them, and the Royal Navy's justice proved swift and uncompromising. The officers and several other men adjudged to have been ringleaders were all hanged in White Point Garden, while the rest were flogged within inches of their lives and then sent off to Halifax to be re-assigned to other ships.

Curiously, though, William Wainwright had somehow managed to separate himself from his shipmates before their trial, and he was not among those punished. According to Wainwright family lore, he escaped the noose by bribing a group of colonial officials. In exchange for his promise to lead them to the hidden Spanish treasure, they expunged his name from the list of captured mutineers and allowed him to start a new life. About two years later, he bought a farm near what's now Valdosta, Georgia, and lived out his days as a gentleman planter.

The old man paused, and I reached into my pocket for another cigarette. I held the pack out to offer him one, but he waved me away with a curt, "I don't smoke." After I lit up, he asked me, "So, do you believe any of this?"

I shrugged. "No reason not to believe it, is there? I mean, somebody's great-great-great-great... however many greats... grandfather had to have been a pirate, right? Why not yours?"

He shook his head. "I never believed it, and I've been hearing that story as long as I can remember. It's been passed down through the generations, along with that farm near Valdosta. I grew up there, you know."

I nodded. My family had its own origin story, which my parents used primarily as a tool to humble me, citing the achievements of our forbearers as yet another standard to which I continually failed to measure up. I understood that it becomes impossible to separate myth from history once enough time passes.

I started to say something to that effect, but Wainwright cut me off. "I said that I never believed that story when I was growing up, but I believe it now. About fifteen years ago, I sold the old farm. It was terribly upsetting. Like I said, that place had been in my family for more than two hundred years..." He paused, and I got the impression that it pained him to depict himself as the despoiler of his children's inheritance, but he quickly went on. "Anyway, when I sold it, I had to go through everything. You wouldn't believe the amount of stuff that accumulates over six or seven generations."

"I bet."

"In one of the bedrooms, I stumbled upon a secret compartment, hidden in the wall behind a bookcase..."

I jumped to the logical conclusion and interjected, "Where you found the treasure?"

"What was left of it, anyway. I assume that William was forced to give most of it away in order to get himself out of trouble, but he must have kept some back for himself. He would have used part of it to buy the farm, and maybe stashed the rest."

I still wasn't one hundred percent sure that I believed him, but I couldn't deny that it was a fascinating tale. "How much did you find?" I asked.

"A few dozen pieces. Some old coins, some more like jewelry or ornaments. I've been selling them to private collectors, one at a time."

"So that's what you want me to take to Miami? A piece of treasure?"

"Exactly," he replied, smiling. "Does that make you feel better?"

"Uh... yeah, I guess. A little. I honestly don't know what to make of all of this."

"Will you do it?"

"Can I think about it?"

"Sure. Take your time."

"Is there a number where I can call you?"

He shook his head. "I don't care much for talking on the phone. Tell you what... just come back here on Saturday morning at nine o'clock if you're interested. If you don't show up, then I'll know you're out."

He rose from his chair and extended his hand toward me, which I shook as I stood up and mumbled, "OK." The young woman reappeared and led me back to the front door, and I headed back to my grandfather's house.

Chapter Five

Of course, I returned to Grassy Key that Saturday morning, just as Wainwright had asked. After hearing that story, I couldn't stay away, probably for the same reason that boys still like to read *Treasure Island*. There is something unquestionably compelling about tales of the sea, and pirates, and buried treasure. The chance to play a part in a story that began two hundred and fifty years before my birth was just too tempting to pass up.

That's not to say that I didn't have questions. I had a few about the treasure, and the particulars of the transaction in which I was to participate, but I was more interested in asking Wainwright about his past. I had indeed Googled him after getting back from my visit to his house, and I was shocked by what I found. His story pre-dated the internet, but I was still able to tap into a pretty rich vein of information once I started looking.

He turned out to be a fascinating character. I discovered very little about his youth, save that he'd been raised in comfortable circumstances on his family's farm in southern Georgia. From there, he went to the university in Athens, where he stayed long enough to pick up both his undergraduate and law degrees. By all accounts, he was a fine student, and he landed a position as a commercial litigator with a well-respected firm in Atlanta. He spent the mid-1970's there, and looked to be on his way to a successful legal career until his parents passed away within three months of each other in 1977.

I was unable to glean much about what happened next. He returned to Valdosta, but I couldn't tell if he continued practicing law. Whatever else he did, he seemed to develop a passion for religion over the next couple of years. Or maybe he'd always been devout. The details of the start of his spiritual journey weren't spelled out in any of the articles I read, but by the end of 1980, he had started his own church, preaching every Sunday in an outbuilding on the farm that he'd converted for the purpose.

His sermons quickly became a local phenomenon, attracting bigger and bigger crowds as the weeks passed. A few of his parishioners helped to expand his makeshift house of worship, and his most devoted followers began living with him in the farmhouse while they did the work. Before long, the family farm was transformed into a residential compound, inhabited by a growing number of believers eager to live as a community under the guidance of the man that some of them were already calling a prophet.

By early 1983, he'd formed a new legal entity, Wainwright World Ministries, Inc., and he had begun broadcasting his sermons on a local television station. This enabled him to reach an even wider audience, most notably in the greater Jacksonville area. As evidenced by the photograph on his wall, by 1984 he was a significant enough figure to have been targeted by the Reagan campaign as part of their outreach to evangelical leaders. He was only thirty-five years old, but people were calling him the next Billy Graham. He went to prayer breakfasts with the governor of Georgia, and Jerry Falwell called him to discuss tactics for the Moral Majority. It seemed only a matter of time before he took his place on the national stage.

All of those plans collapsed spectacularly once a young investigative reporter from the *Florida Times-Union* named Jerry Barnes published a five-part exposé about life on the Wainwright compound. According to Barnes, what had started as a small collection of men living almost monastically while they built Wainwright's church had evolved into a sprawling encampment of seekers. I struggled to imagine what the place must have been like. The evangelical revival had been a *fait accompli* for as long as I could remember, and I'd embraced certain stereotypes about the members of that community. Barnes' depiction of the farm didn't gel with my preconceptions; it sounded like a hippie commune that had swapped its Grateful Dead bootlegs for a stack of hymnals. Instead of dope, the inhabitants were high on Jesus.

The people that Barnes described sure didn't sound like the evangelicals that I'd been watching on Fox News for the last ten years. The "culture wars" hadn't fully cranked up by that point, and there was no Tea Party. Hell, Reagan himself was in the process of raising everybody's taxes. As part of the first wave, Wainwright's converts were so fired up about being born again that they hadn't yet had a chance to become vocal champions of supply-side economics.

That's not to say that there wasn't a political aspect to the movement, even then. I tried to remind myself that Wainwright's flock had just emerged from the 1970's. The Cold War hadn't yet been won, and Vietnam and Iran had shaken their faith in American hegemony. Civil rights, immigration and globalization were changing their jobs, their schools and their communities in ways that surely convinced them that God was turning His back on them. When

Wainwright, with all of his charisma and eloquence, offered to show them the way back into the Lord's good graces, his words fell on receptive ears. Embracing the righteous path would save them not just in the next world, but also in this one.

The farm was abuzz with the work of salvation. Each week's main event, of course, was a Sunday service, which always centered around one of Wainwright's sermons. These often ran for ninety minutes or more, and were broadcast around the region on television. He received such plaudits for his oration that I really wanted to see him in action myself, but I was unable to find any examples on You Tube. Judging from the number of people that he'd attracted to his movement, I had to believe that his preaching was as good as advertised.

Spiritual development wasn't confined to Sunday mornings. The farm's inhabitants enjoyed a steady stream of bible studies, prayer meetings and hymns, all of which were woven into days filled with simple, honest work. Some members of the congregation planted and harvested the fields, while others tended livestock. Still others framed new houses and an elementary school. A few of the women were in charge of cooking communal meals. More than one person told Barnes that they were building a new, self-sustaining Zion, a place where they could find shelter from the wickedness of the world. They also hoped that it would act as a beacon to the righteous who would, by coming together and embracing the principles they found on display there, eventually drive that wickedness from their country. They seemed to be striving toward a sort of variation on the Jeffersonian ideal, trying to build a nation of pious subsistence farmers.

It wasn't long before Zion revealed itself as Babylon. Reading about it after the fact, I was struck by how inevitable it all seemed. At the end of the day, the only thing that had held the community together was the force of Wainwright's personality. If you'd asked them, I'm sure that his followers would have said that they were feasting on the Word of the Lord, but they really subsisted on a steady diet of John Wainwright. They loved him not only for his preaching, but also for having invited them to transform his farm into their shining city on a hill. Their admiration for him was further bolstered by the fact that he shared in their labors. He would regularly milk cows, hammer nails, and peel potatoes right alongside the humblest members of his flock. No one could question his commitment to the common cause.

Unsurprisingly, the cocktail of Wainwright's inspirational message, charismatic leadership and good looks proved appealing to certain female members of his church, and they began to make themselves available to him. The articles didn't say whether, or for how long, he resisted the temptations of the flesh, but by the time Barnes' articles were published, Wainwright was allegedly carrying on with a dozen of his parishioners. One of the twelve, Coleen Beaufort, told Barnes the whole story. According to her, the big farmhouse had been transformed into a harem, with the minister conducting group prayer sessions for women before visiting them for private spiritual counseling. By the end, Wainwright was allegedly "counseling" as many as three women each night. The tipping point for Coleen came when he asked the women to meet with him in pairs rather than individually. Apparently, whatever scriptural justifications he'd provided for that had failed to assuage her jealousy and guilt, and she regaled the newspaper man with all of the lurid details. Once Barnes started asking around, he apparently found more than enough corroboration to make him comfortable with running the story.

After the piece was published, everything unraveled in short order. Wainwright tried a half-hearted denial, and then a tearful apology, but neither did much to stem the tide of followers flowing steadily away from him. Most of them simply found their way into new churches, much as they had drifted into Wainwright's a few years before. Georgia was lousy with preachers, so there was little reason to expect anyone to suffer along with him. It was much easier to move on to the next guy and get one's Good News from an untarnished vessel.

As Wainwright's congregation evaporated, so did his influence in the broader world. The TV station stopped airing his sermons, and Jerry Falwell sought advice elsewhere. The governor never invited him back to pray over pancakes and grits, and the people he'd met from the Reagan campaign professed not to remember him.

All of that must have been hard for him to stomach, but I'm sure it was nothing compared to how he must have felt about the actions of those closest to him. He might have expected that his most intimate confidants, the guys who had helped build his church, would have offered their support, but they turned on him as soon as things went sideways. Wainwright spent the rest of the Eighties in litigation against his former followers. Two women slapped him with paternity suits, while the men complained of having been duped into donating their time, money and labor to a fraudulent cause. Everyone seemed convinced that the church had a substantial amount of cash squirreled away, but no one was ever able to get their hands on it. My impression was that the enterprise wasn't nearly as flush as those opportunistic plaintiffs had hoped.

As best as I could tell, none of their lawsuits resulted in judgments against Wainwright, but the process of dealing with them more or less ruined him financially anyway. His corporation filed for bankruptcy in 1988, and by the mid-1990's he'd been forced to sell the farm, which is why I found him in the Keys. There was no indication that he'd preached in public since.

All of those facts were still swirling around my head when I knocked on his door that Saturday morning. This time the old man answered it himself. I followed him along the same path I'd taken on my first visit, but instead of leading me out to the verandah, he made a right turn before we got to the back door. After walking down a short hallway, we reached what appeared to be his office. Wainwright paused at the door as I entered the room, and then he closed it behind me. He gestured toward a black leather armchair that faced an oversized wooden desk. Once I took my seat, he walked around and sat opposite me in a high-backed chair.

There were a few moments of awkward silence before Wainwright began. "I'm glad that you weren't put off by what you read." He paused before going on. "You did read about me, didn't you?"

I nodded. "Uh huh," was all I said.

He leaned forward and rested his elbows on the desk. "I bet you have a ton of questions, don't you?"

"Yes," I replied, and I squirmed to the edge of my seat while I tried to figure out which one to ask him first.

Before I could organize my thoughts sufficiently to go down that road, he held his hand up to stop me, and said, "There'll be plenty of time to talk about all of that, but not now." He made a show of checking his watch. "You've got to get on the road soon, after all."

I sunk back into my chair and tried to hide my disappointment. This was supposed to be a business meeting, after all. The man was paying me well, and he wanted his task completed. "Understood," I replied. "Can we talk about how this is going to go?"

"Before we get to that, there is one question that I'd like to ask you." He paused to await my acquiescence, which I indicated with a shrug, and then he continued. "Do you fear God?"

Taken aback, I tried to compose a response. "I, uh... I'm not much for religion."

"So you don't believe in God?"

I shrugged again. "No, I guess not."

"But that's not what I asked. Believing in Him and fearing Him aren't the same thing, are they?"

As eager as I was to learn more about the state of Wainwright's soul, I found that I had no appetite to discuss my own views on the Almighty. "Alright. Then my answer is 'no'."

"No?"

"No, I don't fear God."

"You don't?" he asked again, as if he were genuinely puzzled by my answer.

"Nope. Do you?" I sneered, annoyed by his persistence. When I posed this last question, he looked as if I'd just taken a piss on his shoes. The mixture of offense and shock evident in his expression would have been comical but for the awkwardness of it being directed at me from such close range. Almost immediately, I found myself stammering out an apology. "I'm, uh... sorry. I know that you're... you were... a minister. I shouldn't have..."

Before I could finish, he shook his head and broke in in a soft voice. "You must think I'm an awful person... that my whole life was a lie." He looked down at the floor. "I suppose that I can't blame you for that, after the things you read." He paused for a few moments before looking me in the eye again. "I have prayed every day for the past twenty-seven years for the Lord to show me a way to serve Him once again."

It was my turn to look at the floor. "I really am sorry. It's just that after reading all of that stuff, I was wondering what you were all about."

"Because I'm a sinner, you wanted to know if anything I ever did was real, right?" he asked, gently.

"Yeah, well... it was quite a story."

He sat up straight and his chair and began to recite. "As it is written, there is none righteous, no, not one: There is none that understandeth, there is none that seeketh after God... For all have sinned, and come short of the glory of God."

I nodded. "So Paul told the Romans, at least."

Wainwright raised his eyebrows. "For a guy that doesn't believe in God, you seem pretty familiar with His scriptures."

"I never said I was ignorant. Just unconvinced."

He stared at me for a few seconds, as if he was trying to figure out what he thought of me, before he suddenly snapped back to the matter at hand. "You really do need to get going. You know your way around Miami Beach?"

"Yeah, pretty well."

"You know the Raleigh Hotel?"

I smiled. "Yeah. I've actually stayed there once or twice."

"Good. This'll be easy, then. Just take the package to room 302 at the Raleigh. Someone will be waiting for you there. You give him the package, he'll give you the money, and you'll bring it back here. Any questions?"

"That's it?"

"That's it."

I pressed him a bit. "Nothing else I need to know? Anything I should watch out for? Should I be worried about the guy I'm meeting?" I was all for simplicity, but this seemed way too easy.

The old man looked me up and down and laughed. "I reckon that he'll be more afraid of you than you will be of him."

"Good," was all I could think to say. Before I could ask another question, Wainwright opened one of the desk drawers and pulled out a gold medallion, about twice the size of a silver dollar. He passed it to me, and I examined the intricate designs that were etched into the metal on both sides. "Beautiful," I remarked as I handed it back to him. "This is what I'm delivering to Miami?"

"Yes. Room 302 at the Raleigh. Got it?" He dropped the medallion into a small manila envelope and placed it on the desk in front of me.

I picked it up and shoved it into my pocket. "Uh huh. Room 302. Anything else?"

"Don't lose the money on your way back."

"I'll do my best not to."

"I have every confidence in you," he said as he rose from his desk. I stood up as well, and he walked me to the door and watched as I got into my car and drove off. I had officially gone into business with John Wainwright.

Chapter Six

I wish I could say that my trip to Miami that day had been more interesting. It would have made for a much better story if I had found a Russian gangster or an Arab sheikh waiting for me in South Beach. As I imagined it, we might have conducted our business like a couple of Cold War spies, under the watchful eyes of bodyguards with menacing bulges under their jackets. I even daydreamed about some of the snappy dialogue I could have engaged in. I wanted to be like Sam Spade bantering with Gutman and Cairo at the end of the movie.

The reality of my experience was nowhere near as compelling as the fantasy I'd cooked up during the three-hour drive from Marathon to South Beach. When I finally arrived at the Raleigh Hotel and knocked on the door to room 302, it was answered not by a dashing international man of mystery but by a doughy, middle-aged fellow wearing a wrinkled golf shirt. He radiated weariness, and seemed completely disinterested in the whole affair. When he saw me standing in the doorway, he mumbled, "You Wainwright's new guy?"

"Yes," I answered in a firm voice.

"Uh huh," was all he said as he turned away. He didn't invite me in, but I followed him anyway and shut the door behind me. I watched as he reached into a brown leather satchel that was sitting on the bed, pulled out a medium-sized white envelope and handed it to me without saying a word. I opened it and saw fifteen small stacks of one hundred-dollar bills, each bound by a yellow wrapper with "$2000" written on it. I stood fondling the money awkwardly for a few seconds before I reached into my pocket and gave him the envelope containing the medallion. Neither of us had spoken since our initial exchange.

The rumpled little man barely glanced at the package before he shoved it, unopened, into the bag from which he'd taken the cash. He then turned back to face me and extended his arms in front of him with his palms up. "Anything else?" he asked, seemingly surprised that I was still there.

"Don't you, uh... don't you even want to look at it?"

His lips curled into the thinnest of smiles as he shook his head. "We know that John is a man who keeps his promises."

I waited for him to say more, but after a few seconds, I realized that he wasn't going to. I started to leave, but before I made it to the door, I stopped and spun back around. "You know, I really would feel better if I counted this before I left. I hope that doesn't offend you, but..."

He cut me off. "Suit yourself," he replied with a shrug.

I marched over to the desk in the corner of the room and quickly counted twenty bills in each pile, shoving them back into their yellow wrappers as I finished. Satisfied, I stuffed the envelope into my pants and turned back to face my host, who was watching me with a bemused expression.

"All set?" he asked, with a trace of condescension in his voice.

"I guess so."

"See you soon, then."

I wasn't quite sure what to make of that last statement, so I let it pass without a response. I thought about offering him my hand to shake, but he'd already turned away, so I walked out of the room without looking back.

Once I got to my car, I considered doing something in Miami before heading home. It seemed a shame to come all that way without at least stopping for a Cuban sandwich, but it occurred to me that strolling down Calle Ocho with Wainwright's thirty grand hanging out of my shorts probably wouldn't have been the brightest idea. Leaving it in the car didn't seem any smarter, so I reluctantly drove straight out of town and got on the highway. I didn't stop to eat until I found a Wendy's in Florida City, where I ate in the parking lot after ordering from the drive-through window. The cash remained safely on me the whole time.

It was late afternoon when I got back to Wainwright's place, where I was once again greeted by his attractive young companion. I tried to make eye contact with her, but she turned away quickly, so I settled for an eyeful from behind as I followed her to his office. I found the old man seated at his desk, and when I appeared in the doorway, he snatched up the papers that he'd been reading and shoved them into a drawer. "Back already?" he asked. My arrival seemed to take him by surprise.

As I stepped into the room, I heard John's hostess shut the door behind me. I went straight to the same chair that I'd occupied earlier that day. "Yup," I answered as I sat down.

"Everything go OK? No problems?"

I pulled out the white envelope and set it on the desk in front of him. "Piece of cake," I said with a smile. "Your buyer was a very trusting fellow."

I saw a look of confusion flash across his face, but he gathered himself quickly. "How do you mean?" he asked.

"He didn't even open the envelope... didn't look at the piece at all... just gave me the cash straight away. When I asked him about it, he said something about knowing that you would keep your word."

Wainwright leaned forward in his chair. "Did he say anything else?"

"Nope. The guy barely opened his mouth."

Wainwright grinned. "Well, he was right about me. I always keep my promises." With that, he pulled one of the stacks out of the envelope, removed the wrapper, and quickly counted off ten bills. As he pushed them across the desk in my direction, he added, "I believe that was our arrangement, correct?"

I nodded and said, "Thanks," as I picked up my cut and slid it into my wallet. After a moment's silence, I tried to steer the conversation back to the events of the day. "So, you don't think it was strange that he didn't seem interested in seeing the medallion? I mean, thirty grand is a lot of money, right? For all he knew, I could have been giving him the prize from a box of Cracker Jacks."

Wainwright shrugged. "I've been dealing with those guys for quite a while. They understand that they'll always get exactly what they pay for."

I noticed that he mentioned doing business with more than one person, and I remembered that the man at the hotel had done the same. I started to ask Wainwright whether the guy I'd met was part of a group, or whether he was acting as somebody's representative, but before I could finish, Wainwright stood up and interrupted me. "Sorry to cut you off, but I have to run. Elizabeth will show you out." He'd barely finished his sentence before he'd walked right past me and out of the room, taking his twenty-nine thousand dollars with him. I followed him into the hall, but found my path blocked by the young woman.

I called after Wainwright. "I'd like to continue this conversation. Or maybe there's something else I can help you with? Can we talk some more?"

"I'll contact you soon," he replied from around the corner.

I wasn't sure if he meant that we'd continue that particular discussion, or if there was another job on offer. There seemed to be no way to find out without bowling over poor Elizabeth and following the old man, so I let him go. I took a second to confirm that my money was secure in my wallet before letting her know that I was ready to leave. "I hope to see you again," I told her, truthfully, as we reached the front door, trying again to look her in the eyes as I spoke.

She smiled. "I'm sure you will."

Chapter Seven

I spent the next few days obsessing over that smile. Was it just a polite smile, or something more? A dismissal, or an invitation? How could I find a way to talk to her when Wainwright wasn't around? These were the questions that occupied my mind, when my mind wasn't busy imagining her stripping out of her sundress and wrapping her body around me. I didn't know anything about her, other than her first name, but that only made her more attractive. Without inconvenient facts to get in my way, I was free to imagine her exactly as I wanted her to be. In my fantasies, she was brilliant, adventurous and insatiable.

I thought it was funny that my infatuation with her didn't seem to kick in until I'd seen her a second time. I suppose that I'd been too preoccupied with trying to figure out Wainwright's story to give much thought to a pretty face. Since Wainwright had been close-mouthed about his past, and my trip to Miami had turned out to be somewhat of a damp squib, my attention naturally shifted to the other interesting thing that I'd found in Grassy Key.

That's not to say that I'd lost interest in Wainwright. I still had a million questions, and I was dying to sit down with him again. Besides, he'd just given me the easiest thousand dollars that anyone could ever expect to make. If nothing else, I wanted to ensure I was around the next time he decided to start giving away free money.

The following week seemed to pass unbelievably slowly. Baker asked me to tail a housewife to see if I could catch her cheating on her husband, but after three days, all I was able to report back to him was that she had a Starbucks addiction and bought her groceries at Publix. I snapped one or two pictures of her in the cereal aisle there, just to show Baker that I'd actually tried, and he gave me two hundred bucks for my trouble. He never came back to the office after lunch on Thursday, so I assumed he'd gone off to drown his disappointment at my failure to help him make any money that week.

With little else to divert my attention, I found myself checking my phone every fifteen minutes, longing for a call from Wainwright. Unfortunately, the only person who tried to contact me was my father, and he was persistent. He called every day, until I finally rang him back on Thursday night. Our conversation was predictably uncomfortable, and I mostly just listened while he ran through a list of grievances. Several of these were presented in the form of questions, but he didn't seem particularly interested in hearing my answers to any of them. He was concerned, in some order, about the house not being sold, me continuing to live in it, and my crippling lack of ambition. In an effort to calm him down, I mentioned that I'd started working for a lawyer, but that proved to be a mistake, because he interpreted it to mean that I was interested in going to law school. He promised to talk to a few of the big-shot attorneys that handled his deals and come back to me with advice about the admissions process and opportunities to work for their firms in New York. I wasn't looking forward to continuing that conversation, but at least it got him to hang up without evicting me from the house and ordering me to come home.

By Friday night, I had descended into what I recognized as a depressive funk. I was starting to think that maybe my father was right about me. I was thirty years old, and I didn't have a proper job, a proper home, or a significant other. My only friends in Marathon were a drunk and a disgraced televangelist, and I was lusting after a woman that I'd seen only twice and to whom I'd spoken less than ten words. I had assumed that she was Wainwright's mistress, but I'd been trying to talk myself into believing that she was just his Girl Friday. Either way, I imagined that the old man wouldn't have been happy if I'd pursued her. I figured that going down that road would have left me with just one friend in the Keys, and a world in which Bob Baker was my only friend was indeed depressing to contemplate. Besides, I liked Wainwright, and I felt guilty for even thinking about making him into a cuckold.

In an effort to lighten my mood, I decided to pay a visit to my favorite local restaurant. It was basically just a take-out window set up on one of the docks at a marina on the Gulf side of town. They offered whatever the fishermen had caught that day, and they'd cook it up however you wanted. That night I ordered the grouper, blackened with Cajun spices. It was absolutely delicious, but eating it at a picnic table by myself while I watched a group of young children feeding the tarpon from the pier, did nothing to alleviate my sense of isolation. About halfway through my meal the children left, and the marina was quiet save for the sound of the waves lapping against the hulls of the fishing boats tied up nearby.

It was dark by the time I finished, and I lingered on the dock for a smoke before wandering back toward the gravel parking lot. I shuffled along, looking down and kicking stones as I went, so I didn't notice that there was a man leaning against my car until I was about twenty feet away from him. It was Wainwright, and when I got close enough to make out the details of his features, I could see that he was smiling.

As I approached, he stood up straight and greeted me. "I was beginning to think that you had sailed off on one of those boats."

Still shocked at him having appeared in that parking lot, seemingly out of nowhere, I could only mumble, "Just eating some fish," in reply.

"Don't look so surprised," he admonished me. "I told you I'd be in touch. You didn't take me for a liar, did you?"

"Uh, no, of course not. I just figured you'd call..."

"I told you I don't like to use the phone."

"So I see. But how did you find me here? Have you been following me?" The thought troubled me, even though I'd been following unwitting citizens around Marathon at Baker's behest for months.

He laughed. "You sound paranoid."

"It's not paranoia if someone's actually following you, is it?"

"I guess not, but I can assure you that there's nothing sinister here. I spoke to Bob Baker. He said that you ate here a lot, so I took a look. I was going to go straight to your house, but I spotted your car and decided to wait for you."

I kicked at the gravel. "So you found Bob, huh? I haven't seen him since yesterday morning. Figured he was on a bender."

Without missing a beat, Wainwright replied, "He's not hard to find, if you know where to look."

I nodded. The old man was smooth, but I wasn't really buying his explanation. Even so, I decided not to press my questions any further. I was more interested in seeing what was coming next. "Well, here we are," I said as I extended my arms as if to embrace the empty parking lot.

Wainwright took his cue. "First, I just wanted to thank you for your help the other day, and to say that I'm sorry for walking out so abruptly in the middle of our conversation. I hadn't expected you quite that early, and I had something urgent that I needed to attend to."

I held up my right hand to stop him. "No need to apologize. It's fine."

He paused for a few seconds before continuing. "Good. Glad to hear it. Does that mean that you'd be interested in helping me out again?"

"Maybe," I replied, trying not to sound overeager, but certain that my demeanor was giving me away.

"Are you free this weekend?"

I nodded. "Yeah, pretty much."

"Do you remember Elizabeth?"

I looked straight down at the ground and pawed at the loose pebbles with my right foot. I was pretty sure that I was blushing, but I hoped that the darkness would conceal that fact from Wainwright. I don't imagine that my attempt at masking my interest was particularly effective, but I tried to answer as nonchalantly as I could. "She's the woman I met at your house, right?"

"That's her. I was sure you'd remember. Most men do."

"I'm sure."

"Well, she has an... appointment... tomorrow night. I was hoping that you would give her a ride."

I was, of course, absolutely thrilled at the prospect of spending some time alone with my new crush, and it took some restraint to keep myself from blurting out an unqualified acceptance of Wainwright's offer. I had to remind myself that the old man's request was probably motivated by interests other than my love life, and that I should at least try to figure out what was going on before I jumped into it. "And where, exactly, would I be taking her?"

"Georgia," he replied, casually. "Just across the Florida/Georgia line on I-75. I can give you the details when you pick her up tomorrow."

I shook my head. "That's a hell of a ride."

"I'll make it worth your while, of course."

"I dunno... I mean, that's gotta be, what, like six hundred miles?"

"Probably more like five hundred, but it's a ways, yeah."

"And she's meeting someone there?"

"She's going to spend some time with a friend."

I was afraid to ask if the "friend" in question was male or female. The possibility of it being the former made the whole idea much less appealing. Driving all day in order to deliver my girl into the arms of another man wasn't what I'd had in mind. I understood, though, that as significant as that issue may have been to me, there was no way to raise it to Wainwright without revealing my interest in Elizabeth. For all I knew, she was his lover, and I really didn't want to stir that pot. Instead, I settled on a less interesting question. "So, uh, how much are we talkin' here?"

"How's five hundred sound?"

Honestly, I probably would have done it for a case of beer and some gas money, but I tried to take a tough stance. "Well," I muttered, "it sounds like a pay cut. The going rate for my services last week was a grand, and Georgia's a long way from here."

"You'll have the pleasure of Elizabeth's company this time."

"Uh huh. But this is gonna wreck my whole weekend."

He tilted his head back and forth for a few seconds before replying. "Fine. Seven-fifty, but that's as I high as I'll go."

I believed him. I pretended to think about it for a moment, and then offered him my hand and said, "Deal."

"See you in the morning, then," he replied as we shook. "Around eight o'clock." With that, he turned and started walking toward the docks. He didn't seem to have a car anywhere nearby.

"Hey!" I called after him. "You need a lift somewhere?"

He waved me away. "No, thank you. I'm good. I'm gonna go down by the water for a bit before I head home."

I watched him disappear into the darkness, and then made the short drive from the Gulf to the Atlantic so that I could take up my station on the deck of my grandfather's house. I sat out there for a few hours, staring into the moonless night while I smoked and listened to the crash of the surf against the shore. It was a strange sensation, being so close to a thing as vast as the sea, and hearing its relentless, stirring energy, but not being able to see it.

My encounter with Wainwright had snapped me out of my depression, but it pushed me too far in the opposite direction. My thoughts raced beyond my control. Of course, I was excited about the idea of spending some time with Elizabeth, but she wasn't the focal point of my thinking. Instead, I devoted my energy to trying to figure out what it was that Wainwright wanted with me. There had to be more to it than him just needing an errand boy. That alone wouldn't explain why he'd taken such an interest in a complete stranger. If he felt like I was uniquely qualified in some respect, I would have loved to have heard about it, seeing as how the rest of the world seemed not to think much of my talents.

Hours of contemplation yielded no revelations, so I went inside and tried to go to bed. The change of venue failed to quiet my mind, and I lied there, awake, for God knows how long. Eventually, I gave up trying to analyze Wainwright, and I finally drifted off to sleep, dreaming about how much fun it would be to share my bed with Elizabeth.

Chapter Eight

When I arrived at Wainwright's the following day, I found three cars already sitting in front of the house. In the spot where I had parked on my two previous visits, there was a black Suburban. On one side of it, I saw a grey Mercedes, and on the other, a dark blue Chrysler. I pulled up behind the massive SUV and started walking toward the stairs, but before I could get there, the front door opened and Elizabeth emerged, with Wainwright close behind. They were each carrying a large suitcase, so I climbed halfway up to meet Elizabeth and took hers the rest of way. By the time I had wedged it into the trunk of my car, Wainwright was standing next to me, lifting the other bag and setting it alongside its companion.

When I turned to face him after slamming the trunk shut, he already had his wallet out and was counting off Ben Franklins. He handed me eight of them along with directions to my destination, and when he saw the puzzled look on my face, he announced, "I gave you an extra fifty for your expenses."

For a fleeting moment, I considered asking for a little more. I'd thought about it the night before, and this trip was going to cost me more than fifty bucks. I was going to burn more than that in gas alone, and I would need a hotel along the way as well. If Wainwright was willing to cover my expenses, it seemed reasonable to account for all of them. On the other hand, I'd already reconciled myself to taking the costs out of my end, and his demeanor didn't invite further negotiation. I figured that a night at a Motel 6 in North Florida wouldn't eat too deeply into my profits, so I decided to let it go, and just said, "Thanks," as I put the money into my pocket.

I walked around to the driver's side of my car and waited while Wainwright spoke with Elizabeth, who hadn't moved from her spot at the bottom of the stairs. I couldn't hear their conversation, but it looked as if the old man was doing his best to comfort her. After they talked for a few moments, they knelt beside one another and prayed together. Staring at them felt intrusive, so I tried looking off into the trees instead. Finally, they got back to their feet and embraced, and Wainwright kissed her gently on her forehead before she walked over to my car and got in.

Once we'd pulled out of the driveway and started heading north, I tried engaging her in conversation, but that proved more difficult than I'd hoped. I couldn't tell whether she was sad, or just pensive, or merely disinclined to confide in a stranger. Whatever her emotional state, it wasn't conducive to building our relationship.

That's not to say that she was completely antisocial. We were in that car for hours, so our sporadic bits of conversation, when taken in the aggregate, actually revealed a fair amount about her life. I learned that she was twenty-three and had been born and raised in the Keys. She went by "Liz," but Wainwright always called her by her given name. Her parents had divorced when she was eight, but otherwise she'd enjoyed a normal, middle-class upbringing. She'd started college at a small school in South Florida whose name I didn't recognize, but dropped out before finishing her first year. She and Wainwright weren't lovers and they didn't live together. They'd known each other for about three years and had become quite close, to the point where she was often at his house and did whatever she could to assist him in his work.

I found all of that quite interesting, but whenever I tried to probe a bit deeper, she parried my inquiries with a stream of platitudes and generalities. When I tried asking about her relationship with Wainwright, I heard about how much he had "taught" her, "helped" her and "guided" her, but she never explained how or in what context, exactly, he'd done any of these things. It was the same when I focused more on Wainwright himself; he was a "minister," a "teacher," and a "great man," among other things, but, after riding with her for nine hours, I couldn't have told you anything specific about his brand of Christianity, other than that it was based on the "Word of the Lord" and the "True Gospel."

My efforts to get to know my passenger were stymied by the fact that she was unwilling to volunteer so much as a single scrap of information. She answered when I questioned her, but when I stopped asking, she stopped talking. She didn't even ask the reciprocal questions that one would have expected in a conversation between strangers looking to break the ice. Her lack of interest in me was offputting, and the effort required to sustain our conversation wore on me as the hours ticked by. We stopped for lunch near Port St. Lucie and, after that, I was content to leave her alone for a while and listen to music as I drove.

I sensed that she was unimpressed with the Grateful Dead bootlegs and punk rock standards that streamed from my Ipod, but she never said as much, so I didn't offer to change my listening habits for her benefit. I tried to forget about all of the stuff that I wanted her to tell me and to let myself dwell only on her physical beauty, in the hope of recapturing the feelings I'd had for her only just the day before. It didn't work. She looked great, certainly, but there wasn't the slightest hint of chemistry between us. Even if there had been, I'd noticed how heavy her suitcase had been when I loaded it into the car. I tried to convince myself that it was for the best that we weren't hitting it off. If she was going away for a long time, there wasn't much point in trying to spark a romance between us.

Over the remainder of our trip, I made a few more attempts to engage with her, but each was more half-hearted than the last, and none proved particularly productive. She was especially cagey when I asked her where she was headed and whom she was meeting, saying only that she planned to stay for a while and that she trusted that God was leading her on the right path. By the time we hit Georgia, I was feeling relief at the idea of parting ways with her.

The instructions that Wainwright had given me directed us to a truck stop not far beyond the state line, where I was supposed to find a silver Lincoln in the last row of the parking lot. It was there, as promised, so I pulled into the space next to it and cut my engine. I'd noticed that Liz had grown more and more anxious as our trip neared its end, and as we pulled into the truck stop, she couldn't stop fidgeting. Once I parked, I turned toward her and saw that she'd lowered her eyes and folded her hands in her lap; it took me a moment to realize that she was praying, quite earnestly from the look of it. Not wanting to interrupt her communion with the Almighty, I sat as still as I could with my hands resting on the steering wheel and waited. No one had gotten out of the silver Lincoln. After a minute, she seemed to compose herself, and she gave me a quick nod. "You all right?" I ventured, in as gentle a tone as I could muster. She nodded again, and I reached for my door and said, "OK," as I started to open it. Before I stepped out of the car, I stopped and turned toward her again. "You know... you don't have to do anything you don't wanna do. I mean, I'm still not sure what the hell is going on here, but I'm telling you that you don't have to do it. Just say the word and I'll take you back to Marathon... or wherever."

She reached over and took me by the hand. "Thank you," was all she said, and I felt like it was the most sincere thing that had come out of her mouth all day. As soon as those words left her lips, though, she released my hand, opened her door, and stepped out into the parking lot. I followed her lead, and we both stared silently at the Lincoln for a moment before I moved around to the back of the car and started unloading her bags.

While I was doing that, the trunk of the Lincoln popped open, and someone got out of the driver's side door. As I transferred her luggage from one car to the other, I heard a man's voice exchanging greetings with Liz. By the time I shut the trunk, she was already climbing into his passenger seat, and I could see the driver heading back around the front of his car. I walked the other way so as to meet him before he had a chance to get in.

I was waiting by his door when he turned the corner, and I was flabbergasted when I recognized him as the doughy little man that I'd met at the Raleigh Hotel the week before. As shocked as I was to see him, he seemed completely unfazed by my presence. I'm not sure that he would have even acknowledged me if I hadn't been blocking his path. "Hey!" I blurted out. "I remember you! From Miami..."

"Uh huh," he replied, as he continued inching toward his door.

"So... you remember me?" I prodded.

"Yup."

"Kinda strange, running into you again, isn't it?" I asked, as I made a point of leaning against his car with all of my weight.

He frowned, as that last gesture had made it clear that I didn't intend to let him leave without talking. "Small world, I guess," he mumbled. "Now, if you wouldn't mind, we really should be on our way."

I didn't budge. "First you gotta tell me what's going on here."

He just shrugged, and reached for the door handle. I grabbed him roughly by his arm and looked down at him. I was a good seven or eight inches taller than he was, and I was doing my best to look menacing. "I asked you a question."

His expression darkened as he looked up at me, and then down at my hand on his arm. "You should talk to Wainwright," he said, right before he surprised me by jerking free of my grasp, with more force than I would have given him credit for being able to produce. He repeated his instruction to "take it up with Wainwright" as he again reached for the door of the Lincoln with his freshly liberated hand.

If I had been a character in a movie, I imagine that I would have thrown him to the ground and had it out with him right then and there. I would have given him a good beating and driven off into the sunset with a grateful Liz, and our relationship would have blossomed. In reality, without a script or a cue card to guide you, it's hard to identify the proper time to cross the line into violence. Everything happened so quickly, and my mind was flooded with what seemed like a million thoughts. I was trying to discern the connection between the two jobs I'd gotten from Wainwright, and speculating about the role of the strange man that I'd encountered on both of them. In hindsight, I feel like I should have gotten physical with him, even if it had only served to delay him for a few extra minutes. One or two more questions might have yielded some interesting answers. The thought certainly crossed my mind as I stood there, but instead of lashing out, I subtly, maybe even unconsciously, acquiesced to his departure. I didn't really move out of his way; rather, I just shifted my weight and turned slightly, just enough to allow him to grab that door handle. In a flash, he was in the car, the engine was on, and he was pulling away.

I stood there for a few seconds, dumbfounded by everything that had just transpired, before it occurred to me that I should try to follow the silver Lincoln. By the time I got back into my car, though, they'd already disappeared from sight. My best guess was that they would have gotten back onto the highway and continued north, so I did the same. I drove as fast as I dared, in hopes of catching up to them, but after twenty minutes of weaving through the northbound lanes of I-75 at ninety-five miles per hour, I realized that it was hopeless. For all I knew, they'd headed south, or taken a back road. As the adrenaline from my encounter dissipated, I realized that I was much more likely to get into a wreck, or pulled over, than I was ever going to be to find Elizabeth. Deflated, I pulled off at the next exit and started heading back toward Florida.

Chapter Nine

I wound up back at the same truck stop where I'd dropped Liz, sitting on a stool next to a group of long-haul drivers and trying to clear my head. It was clear that the only person who could answer any of my questions was Wainwright. Under normal circumstances, I simply would have called him, but I didn't have his number, and a quick search of the white pages via mobile internet yielded nothing. He'd mentioned his aversion to telephony twice in the short time I'd known him, so I couldn't be sure that he even owned a phone. If I was going to have a conversation with him, it was going to have to be in person.

After sucking down three cups of coffee and a half-dozen cigarettes, I decided to drive through the night, straight to Wainwright's door. It seemed to make sense at the time. I knew that I wouldn't be able to relax until I talked to him, and it wasn't like I had anything better to do.

I made it as far as Ocala before I changed my mind. It occurred to me that dragging the old man out of bed in the middle of the night probably wouldn't be the best way to get an explanation out of him. Even if he would have proven amenable to having a discussion at four in the morning, I was sure that I wouldn't have been in any condition to hear what he had to say. Feeling dazed after twelve hours behind the wheel, I interrupted my journey and grabbed a room at a Super 8 just off the interstate.

I didn't get to Wainwright's place until about half past three on Sunday afternoon. I'd driven there directly from Ocala, with only a quick lunch break and a couple of pit stops along the way. His driveway was empty when I pulled in, and the house seemed very quiet. I was afraid that he wouldn't be home, and as I climbed the stairs, I resolved to wait there until he returned, no matter how long it took. It never came to that, though, as he answered my knock within moments. As usual, he was nattily attired in a blue oxford and pressed khakis, and freshly shaven. I was sporting a four-day beard and wearing the same clothes that he'd seen me in the day before, but at least I'd showered at the Super 8 that morning. He greeted me cordially. "Back already, eh?"

I stormed into the house without waiting for an invitation, saying only, "We need to talk," as I brushed past him. I was already halfway down the hall toward his office by the time he shut the door and turned to follow me.

If he was put off by my insistence, he didn't show it. "Of course, of course," he murmured. "You seem a bit troubled." When we reached his office, he offered me a seat and asked, "What's on your mind?"

I remained standing. "You gotta tell me what's going on here," I demanded.

He looked back at me with a furrowed brow. "I'm, uh, not sure what you mean…"

"That guy! I'm talking about that guy! Who is he?"

The old man shook his head. "I'm afraid I'm still not following you."

I was sure that he was playing dumb, and it took all of my self-control to prevent myself from grabbing him and shaking him until he started talking. I inhaled deeply, and tried to stay as calm as I could. "It was the same guy. The guy that met us in the parking lot in Georgia was the same guy that bought the medallion at the Raleigh Hotel last week."

Wainwright's expression remained unchanged. The only reaction that I perceived from him after my revelation was a muted "Hmm."

"Who is he?" I asked again, my voice rising.

Wainwright shrugged. "He's nobody... just a guy that works for another guy. Don't waste your energy worrying about him. He's not important."

Hearing that did nothing to calm me down. "Don't you see why I might find it strange," I countered, "to find the same man in both places?"

"It just so happens that Elizabeth was going to see the same fellow that bought the medallion... not all that crazy, is it?"

"Can you tell me who that is?"

"A friend of mine."

"Care to elaborate on that?"

"A friend of mine who wishes to remain anonymous. That's why he sent his... representative... to meet you."

Frustrated, I shifted the focus of my questions. "And what about Liz? What, exactly, is her relationship with your friend?"

"What if I told you that he was her grandfather?"

I eyeballed him for a moment before answering. "I'd say you were full of shit."

He mockingly affected the air of someone who'd been wounded. "Well, that's a very uncharitable thing to say."

I wasn't in the mood for his banter. "Is he? Are you telling me that he's her grandfather?"

"No," he replied, before standing and walking across the room. He reached up and took a pair of tumblers from a shelf near the window, and asked, "Do you want a drink?"

"I just want some answers."

He ignored me and grabbed a bottle of Blanton's. He poured two glasses, one of which he handed to me. "Do you want some ice? If so, I can go to the kitchen and..."

"Neat is fine," I told him as I took my drink and sat down, "but I still want to know..."

He cut me off. "Can I ask you something?"

I shook my head. "I'd rather finish..."

He blew straight through my refusal and continued. "What are you doing here?"

"I think my questions have been pretty clear."

"No... I mean, what are you doing in Florida? What brings a guy like you down to the Keys?"

I stared back at him dumbly for what seemed like an eternity, in part out of frustration at his refusal to engage in the conversation that I desperately wanted to have, but mostly because I couldn't answer for myself. If I could have explained what I was doing down there, I wouldn't have had to dodge all those phone calls from my father. What the fuck was I supposed to say? Eventually, I sputtered out a cliché about how I was just tryin' to make a livin'.

"Uh huh," was all that Wainwright said as he set his drink on the desk in front of him. I watched him reach into a drawer and pull out a small stack of papers. He spent a few moments pawing through them before going on. "I've done a little research myself... I mean, I figured that since you knew so much about me, it was only fair that I learned one or two things about you. I hope that doesn't bother you."

That was the last thing I'd expected to hear, but I tried to feign disinterest. "I've got nothing to hide."

He chuckled. "Everyone's got something to hide."

"Some of us more than others," I shot back.

He ignored this last comment, and began shuffling his papers again, clearly trying to convey the impression that he was holding all of my secrets in his hands. For all I knew, he was. After an uncomfortable pause, he muttered, seemingly to no one in particular, "I can't figure you out."

"I'm not complicated."

"Oh, but you are," he laughed. "You're a very complicated fellow indeed."

"How so?" I asked. Even though I could see that Wainwright was purposefully misdirecting our conversation and trying to get me to lose focus on what I'd come for, his tactics were still effective. I felt myself getting drawn in, wanting to hear what he'd discovered and what he made of my life.

I watched as he picked up his glass and swirled the contents around for a few seconds before taking a sip. His deliberateness was maddening, and when he finally spoke, he once again presented me with a question I hadn't expected. "Are you ashamed of your family?"

Confused, I stammered out a reply. "No. Of course not. Why would you think...? If anything, I imagine it's the other way around."

"But you're the kind of guy that doesn't want people thinking you got a free ride, right? I mean, your father is a very successful man, but you're not looking for a handout."

I shook my head. "I don't give a shit about what other people think. And I'd be quite happy to take money from my father, or anyone else willing to give it to me. As far as I know, though, he's not planning on writing me a check any time soon."

"So, you're not the kind of guy who's uncomfortable with coming from a wealthy family?"

"Nope. It's nice being rich. I'd like to be rich again."

"Interesting," he replied as he raised his glass to his lips for another sip.

"Interesting that I'd rather be rich than poor? I'm guessing that's a pretty common sentiment."

"Interesting that you say that, but then you seem to have devoted all of your energy to putting distance between you and your parents, and their money."

I disagreed with his assessment, and I started to tell him so. "I wouldn't say that my goal has been to..."

He interrupted me before I could finish. "You got kicked out of boarding school...St. Paul's... when you were sixteen, right?"

"Technically, I withdrew."

"They caught you making LSD in the chemistry lab."

I corrected him again. "Attempting to make LSD. I didn't actually wind up with any real acid."

"So that's why they let you withdraw instead of just expelling you? Or did it have something to do with your father and grandfather being prominent alumni?"

"My great-grandfather, too," I added. "I would have been the fourth generation to graduate from the school. I guess I broke our little streak."

He went on. "And even after all of that, you managed to pop up at Hotchkiss the following year. I wonder how they were able to see their way clear to let you in after a stunt like that."

"I'm guessing that you already know about my mother's family connections there, right?"

He nodded. "Indeed. Your mother's family is quite prominent in New York, aren't they? I've heard that they go all the way back to the original Dutch settlers."

"Uh huh. They're the real deal, straight outta the Social Register."

"Which didn't exactly hurt you with the admissions committee at Princeton, did it?"

"I'm sure it helped. I was a pretty good lacrosse player, too. And contrary to what you might think, I'm not an idiot."

He started to laugh. "I certainly don't take you for an idiot. And I remember hearing something about lacrosse. How long did your career at Princeton last? A week? Two?"

"Something like that," I muttered.

"What happened there?"

For once, it seemed like he might not have already known the answer to his question. All I said was, "The coach and I had a bit of a personal conflict." I decided to leave it at that, rather than relate the details of how I'd stormed out of a team meeting after telling my coach to go fuck himself.

"I bet the school was upset about that," he ventured.

"That team went to the NCAA finals twice in a row, and won one of them. I'd say they managed OK without me."

He shrugged. "So you just stuck around and studied philosophy?"

"Yup."

He pulled a sheet from his pile and studied it for a few seconds. "Your transcript is fascinating."

I leaned forward to take a look, and he handed me the paper. Sure enough, it was an official copy of my undergraduate transcript, complete with the university's raised seal. "How the hell did you get this?" I murmured, more confused than anything else.

"I just wrote to the registrar at Princeton and asked for it."

"That's it? They just sent it to you, just like that?"

"I might have signed your name on the request, but, yes, that's pretty much it."

I suppose that I should have been outraged to learn about this violation of my privacy, but I found myself unable to muster the indignation that the situation seemed to merit. Instead, I just tossed the transcript back across the desk and complimented him on his resourcefulness.

I sensed that he was hesitant to continue, but once he saw that I wasn't about to fly into a rage, he went on with his review of my academic record. "What really struck me was how you managed to do so poorly in your easiest courses..." He began reading off the lowlights of my college career: "Intro to Art History... C-minus... Intro to Sociology... C... something called, 'Computers in our World...' C. There are a few others, but then I see..."

"Don't forget the C-minus in freshman Biology... although, to be fair, that one was actually sorta hard."

He ignored my interjection. "But I see that you did remarkably well in a bunch of classes that sound much harder... A's in all these high-level philosophy and mathematics courses. How do you explain that?"

"Like I said, I like to think that I'm not an idiot. At least not all of the time."

He paused for a second before re-raising the question he'd started with. "So, again, I'm wondering... what are you doing down here? We don't see a lot of guys with your pedigree wandering around the mangrove swamps."

I took a sip of my bourbon. "You oughta get together with my father. You guys would get along pretty well, I think."

"He can't figure you out, either?"

"And he's been at it longer than you."

He pressed his question again. "So... what *are* you doing here?"

"The market for philosophers is pretty thin up north," I joked. "Thought maybe I'd have better luck down here."

The old man leaned forward in his chair, drawing closer to me. "You want to know what I think?" he asked, in a quiet voice.

"I'm on the edge of my seat," I replied, telling the truth and mocking him at the same time.

He didn't allow my levity to detract from the earnestness of his next pronouncement. "I believe that God has sent you to me."

"Oh."

"Of course, you're not even willing to entertain that possibility, are you? It doesn't fit into your worldview, so it's a joke to you, right? But hear me out."

"I never said I wasn't listening."

"Look... you're... adrift. You've got lots of talent, but no focus... no purpose. I have a vision. The Lord has shown me what I need to do, but I need help in order to realize it. It makes all the sense in the world for Him to have brought us together, here and now. Don't you see it?"

I put my drink down on the desk and looked him in the eye. "Are you trying to offer me a job?"

"Oh, much more than that... I'm offering you a vocation."

I hesitated for a moment before answering, while I tried to come up with a polite way to let him know that I wasn't interested. No one had ever asked me to work for God, and I didn't want to seem like I was dismissing his proposition lightly. I tried to couch my demurral in practical terms. "I'm, uh, flattered that you would think of me... but, uh... right now... I think I need to try to find a more... permanent position... something with a steady paycheck."

"You're worried about money?" he asked.

"My family's rich, not me," I reminded him. "Like I said, I don't expect them to start sending me checks."

"Yes, but I've given you, what, eighteen hundred bucks for two days of work so far?"

"Well... yeah... but I wasn't sure that we were talking about that kind of thing. Are you saying that you'll pay me like that all the time?"

The old man shrugged. "There will always be chances to make money. If it makes you feel better, you can find yourself another job as well... or keep going with Bob Baker. A man can do more than one thing at a time, you know."

"So, you're just asking me to help you out... on the side?"

"No. I'm saying you can make money on the side, if you want, but you should primarily devote yourself to the Lord's work, as we all should."

I was doing my best to stay respectful, but I couldn't help myself. "Of course," I sneered, "because money is the root of all evil, right?" Wainwright shook his head. "Common mistake, but that's not what Paul wrote. He actually said..."

"The love of money is the root of all evil," I interjected, before adding, "In his first epistle to Timothy, I think."

He looked surprised, but quickly regained his composure. "Money is neither good nor bad, in and of itself. We all need a certain amount of it in order to function. I'm not asking you to become a monk." As an afterthought, he added, "I forgot about your knack for Bible quotes." His face brightened. "You've already started your journey into the Scriptures. Now, you just need to open your mind and let God's Word guide you on your path through life."

He stared at me, waiting for my reply, and I stared back at him in silence, feeling that discomfort that I think all atheists experience whenever they discuss God with a believer. Part of me wanted to challenge him on a fundamental level, in order to demonstrate that I wasn't a weak-minded yokel that he could lead around by the nose simply by tossing crumbs from the New Testament in my direction. I'd already told him that I was unconvinced by the teachings of his religion. Surely, he couldn't have expected me to drop everything and follow him just because he characterized his plans for me as divinely inspired. At the very least, I thought that it would have been reasonable to ask him for a few more details about whatever communication from God had led him to believe that I had a role to play in His scheme.

My desire to argue was tempered, though, by my natural inclination to avoid insulting another man. No matter how I presented my misgivings, it would have been impossible to express them without implying a negative judgment on everything that he held dear. When you're sitting across from someone, it's no easy thing to dismiss the one certainty around which they've structured their entire existence as an elaborate myth.

The task was made even more challenging by the fact that I had much less confidence in my convictions than Wainwright had in his. In hindsight, given what I already knew about him, I suppose that I should have questioned his sincerity a bit more than I did. As I sat in that room and looked him in the eye, though, I didn't doubt that he believed everything that he was telling me. He definitely still had whatever quality it was that had enabled him to amass such a devoted congregation so quickly all those years before. As much as I wanted to see myself as more sophisticated than the followers that Barnes had described in his articles, I have to admit that I, too, was susceptible to his persuasions.

My vulnerability was enhanced by the incoherence of my own beliefs. When I walked out of Princeton, everything had seemed so clear. The Judeo-Christian God was merely the most enduring vestige of ancient man's attempts to impose order on the chaos that surrounded him, no more based in reality than the Greeks' personification of thunder and lightning. "Original Sin" was a handy way of avoiding responsibility for one's actions, and the teachings of Jesus an effective tool employed by plutocrats to persuade the masses to accept economic and political subjugation during their time on earth.

A steady diet of existentialist literature had eroded whatever religious foundation I'd developed in Sunday school, and replaced it with an elegantly simple worldview. There is no meaning, or purpose, inherent in anything, beyond that which we choose to assign to it. In an absurd world, we are endowed with complete personal freedom and, correspondingly, complete personal responsibility. Awareness of that responsibility, along with the inevitability of our death, consigns us to a perpetual state of angst. In the end, we all die alone.

As I'd gotten older, these ideas, that I'd once found so novel and powerful, had begun to lose their sway. I began to understand that, just like every other philosophical trend, existentialism was a product of a specific time and place. The world that I inhabited was much different than the Europe of Sartre, or Nietzsche, or Kierkegaard. As the horrors of the mid-twentieth century recessed into history, the world actually seemed to be growing less absurd, and it occurred to me that there could be more to life than nausea. Maybe I just told myself that because I wanted it to be true. Whatever the reason, when I met Wainwright, I was probably more open to the idea of the existence of a higher power than I'd been at any time since childhood.

None of that meant that I was prepared to embrace Christianity, or to start following Wainwright. All I'm saying is that it made it harder to shut the entire conversation down by telling him, straight out, that I was an atheist. Even so, I felt compelled to share that fact before he expended any more energy trying to recruit me to his cause. I tried to present it as gently as I could. "Look... again... I appreciate the offer, but I'm just not sure that I'm the right person for this sort of thing."

"The Scriptures are full of examples of the Lord calling on those who felt unprepared to hear what He had to say. Before Paul set out on the road to Damascus, do you think he would have imagined himself doing what he went on to do?"

"I understand, but… all I'm saying is that thirty percent of the country are standing by, right now, waiting for a mission from God. If you need help, I don't think you'll have any trouble finding it."

Wainwright started laughing. "You know, you sound exactly like your grandfather. He said pretty much that exact same thing when I first started talking to…"

"Wait," I interjected, as I leaned forward in my chair. "You knew my grandfather?"

"Of course," he replied, still laughing. "How do you think I knew all of that stuff about you and your family?"

Thoroughly confused by this latest revelation, I mumbled incoherently. "I don't know… I, uh, thought… I figured… you looked it up somewhere."

He shook his head. "Not all information comes from a computer."

"So… my grandfather was working with you?"

He paused for a beat before answering. "Your grandfather came to faith only at the very end of his earthly journey. Just like you, he had many doubts that he needed to overcome. Once he did, he was very excited about our project, and I'm certain that he would have helped. Unfortunately, the Lord called him home before he had a chance." After another moment, he added, "I suspect that he would have been pleased by the idea of you picking up where he left off. He was very fond of you, you know."

I made a face. "He told you that, huh?"

Wainwright nodded. "Many times. He talked about you quite a bit."

"Huh."

"What? You don't believe me?"

"It's not that," I replied, shaking my head. "It's just that my grand-father wasn't really the warm and fuzzy type, you know?"

He shrugged. "In my experience, people often get sentimental when they sense that the end is near, and they think a lot about what they're leaving behind. We talked many times about what he wanted to leave to you."

I forced a laugh. "And he chose, 'none of the above' in the end, right?"

"That wasn't his idea."

I had no idea what to make of any of what I was hearing. I had, of course, noticed that my grandfather's will made no provision for me whatsoever, but I hadn't read all that much into it. My under-standing had always been that his money would be split between my father and my uncle, so it wasn't like I'd been expecting a windfall. I had thought that he might leave me something personal, like one of the antique watches that he collected but, like I said, he wasn't much for touching gestures. Until that moment, I hadn't given my lack of a bequest much thought, but once Wainwright made his cryptic asser-tion, I wanted to hear more. "What do you mean by that?" I prompt-ed him.

The old man shook his head. "I've said more than I should have already. It's not my place to... You should talk to your father."

"C'mon! You can't throw something like that out there and then decide not to talk about it!"

"I'm sorry, I shouldn't have..."

"Man, don't give me that bullshit. If you've got something you want to tell me, then tell me."

"Talk to your father."

I looked down at the ground, and muttered, almost inaudibly, ""Cause that always goes so fucking well..."

"What was that?" Wainwright asked.

I waved him away with a curt, "Forget it." Thoughts were caroming around my mind like billiard balls. I had come there to discuss Liz and the mysterious man I'd left her with, but somehow we'd wound up talking about my grandfather. His involvement with Wainwright came as a shock, but it did explain my host's intimate familiarity with my family's history. I looked back up at the old man, who seemed to be waiting for me to say something more, but I wasn't sure if we were still talking about my grandfather, or whatever project for which Wainwright was trying to recruit me, or if he was about to swing the conversation in yet another completely new direction. The more we talked, the more muddled my understanding became. As eager as I'd been to confront him, I found myself wanting nothing more than to get out of that place so that I could find some time and space to clear my head.

I watched as Wainwright opened one of his desk drawers and began pulling out documents. "I'll show you," he announced, "what we're trying to build... what I'm asking you to be a part of." Realizing that I was still completely ignorant of the nature of his work, I leaned forward, curious to get some color on his mysterious undertaking. He had only just started setting papers on the desk, though, when he suddenly stopped and looked at his watch. "I'm so sorry... I just remembered that I'm leading a Bible study in about fifteen minutes. Why don't you stick around and participate, and we can continue this once everyone else leaves?" As he spoke, he carefully returned his papers to the drawer, without ever having shown me any of them.

I had no appetite whatsoever to participate in Wainwright's Bible study, and it seemed the perfect opportunity to make my escape. I offered up some generic excuses about having been on the road for two days and having things to do at home, and he walked me to the door. Before I left, he made me promise to return and speak with him again. It wasn't until I got all the way back out to the Overseas Highway that I remembered that I hadn't ever found out what had happened to Liz.

Chapter Ten

I took a long shower when I got back from Wainwright's, with the water as hot as I could bear. As I leaned against the marble wall, I tried to let the moist heat permeate my skull in the hope that it would somehow bind all of my loose thoughts into coherent, actionable conclusions. It didn't work, at least not completely, but at least my muscles benefited from some relaxation after having spent the better part of two days on the road.

Once I'd shaved and dressed, I grabbed my phone and headed out to the deck. I hadn't come up with any new insights about anything that I'd heard from Wainwright, but it seemed pretty clear that my next step was going to have to be a call to my dad. That wasn't something that I was particularly keen to initiate, but I needed to ask him about my grandfather. I took a few minutes to smoke a cigarette and watch the waves crash onto the beach before I picked up the phone and dialed.

My mother answered, and I tried not to sound anxious when I greeted her. "Hi Mom. How ya doin'?"

"Hello, Malcolm. It's good to hear from you. Everything OK down there?"

My mother was the only person on earth that called me by my real first name. At some point early on in my life I'd decided to use my middle name instead. Introducing myself as "James" rather than as "Malcolm" just seemed easier, so I ran with it. When I signed things, it was always as "M. James Bennett." A few of my friends in college found out and called me "M.J." or "Mr. X" (as in, Malcolm X) or "Big X" (combining the Malcolm X reference with an elegant homage to *The Great Escape*), but I'm sure that most people had no idea that my name was anything other than "James."

Since my mother had issued me my name, I suppose that she felt entitled to use it whether I liked it or not, and she always did. Even though she'd been consistent on this point throughout my life, I still winced a bit every time I heard her say it. This time was no exception, but I had long since given up trying to get her to call me anything else, so I shook it off and went on. "Things are fine, thanks. You?"

She sighed. "So much to do these days! Always running around..."

My mother's activity levels had always been a great mystery to me. Not that I doubted that she was busy. As long as I could remember, her schedule had always been full. I just couldn't figure out why that was the case. She had never had a job. I was her only child, and I hadn't lived in her house for more than a few weeks at a stretch since she'd sent me off to boarding school when I was fourteen. Even before that, there had always been a phalanx of housekeepers and nannies on hand to shield her from the domestic drudgery that drives most housewives to despair. All of her efforts were devoted to social ends, which I guess is a testament to exactly how much work old-school, formal socializing actually is. In her world, people didn't just casually meet up, grab a beer, and shoot the shit. Everything is planned and choreographed, right down to the smallest detail. Sometimes I wondered how anyone would manage to throw those grand events once her generation faded away. It seemed a dying art, although I expected that there were plenty of women my age standing ready to pick up her mantle. I just didn't travel in those circles anymore.

She was still talking, going on about a dinner that she was organizing to raise money to find a cure for some horrible genetic heart defect. I was happy to hear that she was devoting her energy to such a worthy cause, but I confess that I let my mind wander while she related the details of the catering arrangements. I knew better than to try to stop her, though. I intended to let her talk until she ran out of steam before I asked her to put my father on the line.

Before that happened, she regained my attention by shifting the direction of the conversation toward my future. "So, Malcolm, your father told me that you were thinking of going to law school."

"I haven't really decided anything yet."

"I think it's a wonderful idea. I actually met the Dean of Columbia Law School last month. His sister lives in the same building as my cousin, over on Park... lovely man. When you get back up here you should have coffee with him. I'm sure he can give you some advice about..."

"I'm, uh, not quite ready to go back up there."

"And your father does a lot of work with... which firm? I can't quite recall the name, but you remember John Wells, right? I know that he'd be happy to sit down with you..."

"Mom!"

"Yes, Malcolm?"

"Look, I appreciate all of that, but I never said that I wanted to go to law school."

"But your father told me that you and he discussed it, and that you would be back here soon."

"The only thing I told Dad was that I've been doing a little work for an attorney down here. I'm sorry if he jumped to conclusions based on that."

"You're not on your way home, then?"

"Not just yet. I'm planning on staying down here a bit longer."

There was an awkward pause before she continued. "Your father is going to be very upset. He's under the impression that you'll be back here next week."

"Next week! I never said anything like that. How did he get that idea?"

"I assumed he heard it from you."

"Is he there? Can I talk to him?"

"Actually, he's at the club today. Playing golf."

By "the club," she meant Winged Foot, a fact that had always rubbed me the wrong way. It wasn't that I begrudged him his privilege or anything like that. What bothered me was the fact that he didn't even enjoy the game. Golfers all over the country would have given anything to be able to play that storied course, and there was my dad, not appreciating it at all. For him, playing golf was a strictly utilitarian exercise. It was good for his business to socialize with certain people from time to time, and those people liked to play golf at private clubs in Westchester County. If those people had preferred to meet at the dentist's office instead of on the links, my father would have found the most exclusive dental practice around and cheerfully had his gums scraped twice a month. I'm not sure he'd have gotten any less out of it.

I was annoyed that he wasn't available to answer my questions, but I knew that there was no way to reach him while he was on the course. I exhaled and asked my mother to tell him to give me a call once he got home. "You can tell him that I've got a couple of questions that I need to ask him."

I was completely unprepared for her reply. "Why don't you just wait until tomorrow? You can ask him once he gets down there."

"Down... here?"

"Didn't he tell you? He's flying down in the morning, with someone who's interested in buying the house."

"I didn't know that."

"You really should be better about returning his calls. I know that he's been trying to reach you."

"Sorry. I was out of town for a couple of days."

"Well, he'll be there tomorrow."

"OK. I guess I'll talk to him when he gets here."

I desperately wanted to end our conversation, but it dragged on for a few more minutes before my mother finally said good-bye. As soon as I hung up with her, I checked my messages. Sure enough, my father had called twice the day before and once that morning. I'd actually noticed his calls while I was on the road, but I'd blown them off without listening to his voicemails, assuming that they wouldn't yield anything new or interesting. As it turned out, he was bringing some hedge fund mogul down to look at the house. He wanted me to get the place looking presentable, and to make sure that I was around to let them in. By the third message, he sounded quite perturbed that I'd failed to acknowledge the first two.

My immediate reaction was one of despair, as it seemed likely that my run of rent-free oceanfront living was about to come to an end, and I was no closer to figuring out what to do next than I'd been when I first came to Marathon. I countered these feelings by reminding myself that I hadn't expected to stay there forever, and that I'd always managed to get by. Eventually, I convinced myself that things would all work out, somehow, and I found myself almost looking forward to my father's visit. If nothing else, I'd have a chance to ask him those questions about my grandfather.

I spent the rest of the evening tidying up the house as best as I could. I wouldn't call it a professional scrubbing, but I used cleaning products in every room, and by the time I was done, the place looked and smelled fresh enough. It was a small thing, but it was worth doing if it left my father with one less stone to sling at me. I was quite sure that he still had more than enough.

Chapter Eleven

I didn't know that you could get car service in Marathon until my father and his prospective buyer rolled up to my grandfather's house in a black Town Car, just like the ones that line the curbs outside of the big banks and law firms every evening in Manhattan. They arrived right on schedule, a few minutes past noon. Punctuality is one of the benefits of flying private. Convenience is another. The closest available commercial flights would have deposited them in Miami or Key West, but they were able to touch down at the airfield just up the road, about ten minutes away.

I opened the door as they walked up the driveway. Neither of them was carrying any luggage, so I deduced that this was a day trip for them. My father greeted me warmly, so much so that I doubted his sincerity. I figured that he wanted to make it look good while his guest was watching.

After releasing me from his embrace, he introduced me to his companion, a fellow by the name of Burt. He told me his last name as well, but I didn't catch it. Apparently, the two of them had worked on some telecom deals together before Burt had gone on to start his own shop. I knew that my father didn't have his own plane, so whatever Burt was doing, it must have been going pretty well for him.

I gave them a quick tour of the place, during which I learned that Burt was a passionate angler and was looking for a home in the Keys to use as a base for deep-sea sport fishing. He waxed eloquently about the joys of landing blue marlin and tarpon, but the details were mostly lost on me. Despite having been in Marathon for months, I'd never taken to the local pastime. I suppose that to people who live busy, stressful lives, going out on the open water and sitting idly for hours on end must seem like a wonderful escape from the world. For those of us who already have a surplus of downtime built into our daily schedules, though, it's just a prescription for boredom and sunburn.

Our walk-through lasted only ten or fifteen minutes. I did my best to point out all of the house's desirable features, but I got the impression that Burt wasn't paying much attention to my sales pitch. I was pretty sure that his decision to buy the place was based solely on its location. If any of the details didn't suit him, he certainly had the means to change them. A guy like that gave as little thought to remodeling an entire room as the average person did to buying a new throw pillow for their couch.

Once we completed our circuit, we wound up back in the living room and I grabbed beers for each of us. The conversation quickly turned toward the particulars of the transaction between my father and Burt. After a few minutes, I realized that I was superfluous, and I quietly slipped out to the deck to smoke. It seemed better than being made to feel like a child while the grown-ups discussed money.

About twenty minutes later, I heard the door open behind me and I turned to see my father coming out to the deck, alone. I greeted him with a quick smile and a nod. He looked at the ashtray, half-full of spent cigarettes, and just shook his head. "I don't understand why you still smoke."

I guess that's not such an unusual comment for a father to make to his son. In most cases, I imagine that it would be motivated by sincere concern for the son's health. I'm sure that my dad was trying to convey that as well, but, coming from him, I was pretty sure that it was an honest question more than anything else. Every decision that he made, every action that he took, was the product of a cost / benefit analysis. The phrase, "just for the hell of it," was decidedly not a part of his vocabulary. As far as I could tell, he rarely, if ever, did anything that didn't advance his interests in some tangible way. Trying to explain smoking to a guy like that would have been the height of futility, so I brushed off his comment and tried to change the subject. "Just haven't gotten around to quitting yet, I guess. Where's Burt?"

He gestured back toward the house. "He had to make a few calls. He'll be a few minutes."

"Is he going to...?"

My father answered before I could finish. "Yes. We're all set."

"For one point six?" I might have been overstepping my bounds, but my extended residence in the house made me feel as if I had a vested interest in whatever deal he'd struck.

"One point five four," he answered with a slight smile. "I had to make him feel like he got at least a little bit of a deal. Besides, he did fly us down here today."

I tipped my beer in his direction. "Congrats."

"It's a relief to be done with it."

Knowing that it would get under his skin, I lit another cigarette. "When will the sale close?"

He let my smoking pass without further comment. "We've agreed on thirty days."

"Uh huh."

"You don't have to move out tomorrow, but the clock's ticking."

I nodded and simply said, "OK."

"I heard that you spoke with your mother yesterday." I nodded again, and he went on. "She tells me that you're not ready to come home yet."

"I'm thinking about staying down here a bit longer."

"I don't think that Burt will let you stay here."

"No, I don't expect that he will."

He paused as if to invite me to explain my plan, but seeing as how I didn't have one, I just stared out at the ocean and took another drag from my cigarette. After a few seconds, he continued. "I was thinking that you might want to start preparing for the next LSAT. From what I understand, a good score on the test can make up for..."

I cut him off. "Dad... I don't think that I'm gonna go to law school."

"OK... well... what's your next move, then? Back into sales?"

I shook my head. "Still trying to figure it out."

He frowned. "You've been trying to figure it out since you were twenty-two. By the time I was your age, I was about to become a managing director at the bank."

I leaned forward in my chair and tapped my cigarette over the ashtray. "I guess that I'm not quite as ambitious as you were."

"It's not about me," he snapped. A second later, he added, in a milder tone, "I'm just worried about you."

I was tempted to remind him that I wasn't the one who had drawn the comparison between our two careers, but I held my tongue. "I'm sorry that I've never wanted to follow you into the family business."

He laughed. "You think that's what this is about?"

"Isn't it? I mean, you're at the bank, Grandpa was at the bank..."

"Don't get me wrong... I'd have loved it if you'd wanted to do it, but if I gave you the wrong idea by encouraging you, I'm sorry. I just wanted to help you, the way my father helped me when I was starting out."

In all the years that we'd been going round and round about my career, we'd never had such an honest conversation, and I was determined to keep it going. "Grandpa helped you out, huh?"

"Of course. I mean, I was always good at my job. I worked hard. But a lot of smart guys work hard and don't advance so quickly. Some never advance at all. It certainly helps when your father runs the bank."

I shook my head as I stubbed out my cigarette. "Unless you don't want to be a banker."

I perceived a trace of exasperation seeping into his voice when he answered. "I... and your mother... both of us... we've always stood ready to help you however we could. Hell, we're not just ready to, we *want* to."

"I'm sorry that I never wanted what you want."

"But you do want *something*, right? You want to be a writer? An artist? A mountain climber? I don't care what it is, but you need to pick something and start getting good at it."

Just then, the door to the house opened and Burt blustered onto the deck. "What's good to eat around here?" he queried both of us in a booming voice. "Let's grab a little lunch before we head back to the City. I'm starving."

My father pushed his chair back from the table as if to follow him immediately, but I raised my hand. "Uh, Burt... would you mind giving us few more minutes here?"

The look of mild shock on his face betrayed the fact that he wasn't accustomed to people doing anything other than enthusiastically embracing his suggestions, but he responded gracefully enough. "Sure," he mumbled, "I'll, uh, wait inside," before disappearing back into the house.

When I turned back to my father, I could tell that he was anxious to follow his buyer out the door. I sensed that our window of open discussion was about to shut, if it hadn't already, but I was determined to take the opportunity to ask the questions that were on my mind. "Actually, Dad, there's something else I wanted to talk to you about, as long as you're here."

"Sure."

"I was just wondering... Was Grandpa a religious man?"

The sudden change of direction seemed to throw my father off, and he took a second before answering. "No. Not particularly. I never knew him to be especially religious."

"Not at all?"

"No more than usual, I guess. He went to church on Christmas and Easter... maybe a random Sunday here and there... gave a little money... is that what you're asking?"

"He was Episcopalian, right? All the way 'til the end?"

My father rolled his eyes. "Of course he was. What else would he be?" A moment later, he added, "Where is all of this coming from?"

"Did he, uh, ever mention a man named John Wainwright?"

"No," he answered, without hesitation. "Never heard of him. What's this about?"

I rubbed my forehead with my right hand. "Well, I met this guy, Wainwright, recently, down here. He's a minister of some sort, or at least he used to be. Yesterday, he told me that he knew Grandpa, and that Grandpa had found religion before he died, or something like that."

He shook his head. "He never mentioned anything about it to me. And it's not like he spent a lot of time down here." His eyes narrowed. "How do you know this Wainwright guy, anyway?"

Not wanting to go into the details of my dealings with Wainwright, I ignored his question and said, "I don't doubt that he knew Grandpa, at least a little."

"What makes you say that?"

"He, uh... he knew some things. About us. Things he wouldn't have known unless someone in our family had told him."

I could see the concern on his face as he absorbed what I was telling him. He leaned in closer, as if to bid me to conspire with him. "Be careful," he cautioned me in a low voice. "This guy is probably trying to play you somehow... trying to get his hands on some money."

"You think so?"

"Think about it. It doesn't take much digging to figure out that your grandfather was quite well off. Suddenly, a stranger pops up and says he's a minister and that Grandpa secretly came to Jesus right before he died? It all seems very convenient, doesn't it?"

I shrugged. "But he hasn't asked me for anything." I thought about mentioning the fact that Wainwright had actually been paying me, but I thought better of it.

"He most likely wouldn't ask up front. You said that he just told you this yesterday, right?"

"Yup."

"Be careful," he repeated, whereupon I immediately broke into laughter. "Something funny?" he asked, looking annoyed.

"Well, if it's money he's after, he's talking to the wrong guy, isn't he?"

"I'm serious, James. Unfortunately, people look at families like ours and think that they can…"

I cut him off. "I'm serious, too, Dad." I held my arms out. "Look around. None of this is mine. None of it at all."

"Are you complaining about not having enough money?" he asked, hotly. "Because there's something you can do about that. It's called getting a goddamned job."

I held up my hands. "Take it easy. That's not what I was saying. I was just laughing about the idea of Wainwright running a con on me. The best scam in the world is no good if the mark doesn't have anything worth taking, right? Just thought it was a little funny."

"It's not."

"OK," I said, as I reached for another cigarette. "I wasn't trying to piss you off."

"Fine," he said, as he looked at his watch and started to slide his chair away from the table again. "If that's all, we should probably join Burt…"

"Actually, there's one other thing."

"What is it?"

"Did, uh, Grandpa ever talk about me?"

My father looked confused by the question. "Of course he did. You were his grandson and he loved you very much."

"Of course, of course," I replied, nodding. "I never doubted that. I was just wondering... if he'd ever talked about the idea of maybe including me in his will."

"Did Mr. Wainwright tell you that, too?" he scoffed.

"Yeah, he mentioned something about it when we were talking yesterday."

"What, exactly, did he say?" I watched him shift in his seat, and I sensed that he was getting uncomfortable. Another glance at his watch suggested that he was anxious about making Burt wait, but it seemed like my questions were putting him off as well. I started to relate the substance of what Wainwright had told me, but before I could get very far, he interrupted me. "None of that matters now. The only thing we have to go by is what was actually in his will."

"I know what his will said. And what it didn't say." After hesitating for a beat, I pressed the issue. "What I want to know is whether you and he ever talked about including anything for me."

He sat in silence for a few moments, staring down at the back of his right hand while he scratched it with the fingernails on his left. Suddenly, he looked up at me and said, "We did."

I'm not sure why he decided to tell me the truth. It would have been much easier to simply deny it. I guess he still thought that I was complaining about not having any money, and he wanted to make a point. Whatever the reason behind his decision to share, I immediately pushed him for more. "And?"

"And what? He came to me, a few months before he died, and told me that he was considering leaving you a bequest. I told him that I didn't think it was such a great idea. He agreed, and we dropped it. There's nothing more to say."

It was one thing to understand, in the abstract, that I wasn't entitled to any of my grandfather's money. It was quite another to sit across the table from my dad and learn that he was the one who'd made the case against me. I shook my head. "You couldn't just leave it alone, huh?"

His tone grew sharper. "Grow up, James! Your grandfather asked me for my opinion, and I gave it to him. I know that you understand perfectly well why I advised him against handing you a sizeable chunk of money."

I understood, but it didn't make me feel any better. "Of course," I sneered, "it was for my own good. You kept every last dime for yourself for my benefit, right? I suppose I should thank you."

"Whatever Grandpa was considering leaving to you went to charity instead."

"Is that supposed to make me feel better?"

He sighed. "James, someday your mother and I will be gone, and whatever we have left will be yours. It may be next week, for all we know. It may be another thirty years. If you want to hold off on doing anything with your life and just keep marking time while you wait for that day to come, that's up to you." He stood up and started moving toward the house.

"So, we're done talking?" I asked, still seated in my chair.

"I don't think there's much else to say, is there?" he replied as he slid the glass door open. Before he went inside, he paused. "Do you want to come to lunch with me and Burt?"

I shook my head. "I think I'll pass."

"Well, call me when you're ready to come home." He went into the house, and a few moments later I heard him and Burt leave through front door. Just like that, I was alone in Marathon again.

Chapter Twelve

I spent the next few days vacillating between being angry with my family, and then feeling guilty about it. How could I really have expected a man like my father to advocate for something that would have only encouraged me to continue coasting through life? In what twisted universe did I deserve my grandfather's money more than whatever charitable organization had wound up with it? The answers to these questions were obvious, and they confirmed that my dad had acted appropriately when he'd counseled the old man against leaving me any part of his fortune.

Unfortunately, understanding that I hadn't deserved the money didn't make me feel any better about not having it. I'd been around wealthy people long enough to know that being worthy wasn't a prerequisite for material success. If it were, then teachers would drive Rolls Royces while the dissolute descendants of nineteenth-century tycoons lived in trailer parks. I knew dozens of people who lived comfortable lives primarily because they had gotten lucky, either on the day they were born or sometime along the way. I'm sure that there were a few truly self-made men and women out there, but, in my experience, they were a pretty rare breed.

I never learned how much money my grandfather had considered earmarking for me. Even a modest amount would have gone a long way toward improving my position, but there's a mighty big difference between a few thousand bucks and a number with six zeros. I knew, roughly, what my grandfather had been worth, so I just assumed that whatever sum he'd had in mind had been on the larger side. He wouldn't have seen five or ten grand as significant enough to have even been worth discussing with my dad.

So, whether or not it had any basis in reality, I was operating under the assumption that my father was directly responsible for me not receiving a life-changing inheritance. I had seen other guys catch good breaks, and, but for his meddling, this could have been mine. I resented the fact that he continued to treat me like a child even though I was thirty years old. So what if I'd never done anything that made him want to run out and brag to his buddies at the Yale Club? With the exception of those few rent-free months in Marathon, I'd been paying my own way since college. That should have counted for something. I had always maintained that the day he started putting food on my table would be the day that he got to tell me what to do. Until then, if I wanted to make a living by playing cards, or snapping dirty pictures, that was my business. And if my grandfather had been inclined to enable me, then that should have been his choice to make as well.

Deep down, I knew that my indignation was far from righteous, but it was still tempting to wallow in it. I reached for the phone more than once over those next few days, intending to continue the dialogue with my father. On some level, though, I understood that he'd been right when he'd concluded that there was nothing left to say, and I never actually made the call. Instead, I just continued to stew while I started looking for a new place to live.

I quickly discovered that the market for inexpensive rental properties in Marathon was extremely limited. Single-family houses far outnumbered apartments, and landlords were looking for tourists who would rent by the week and pay top dollar. I went to see a widow who had advertised a room for rent, but that arrangement seemed too intimate. After living like a king in my grandfather's place, I just couldn't get my head around being confined to a spare room in a strange old lady's house. I also checked out a couple of the more modest homes that I'd seen listed, but I wasn't able to negotiate affordable terms on any of them. Three days after my dad's departure, my future remained very cloudy.

Knowing that I still had almost four full weeks before Burt would put me out, I tried not to lose heart, but those initial forays into the housing market didn't yield much cause for optimism. In an effort to raise my spirits, I visited the same tavern where I'd first met Bob Baker. It wasn't exactly what I'd call a festive establishment, but I'd had one or two good nights there during my sojourn in Marathon. I thought that the possibility of teaming up with one or two upbeat drinking buddies made it worth the trip.

Even such a modest goal proved beyond my reach that night, as the only people I found in the bar were a pair of surly bikers and a particularly feeble-looking group of old fishermen. I tried making small talk with the bartender, but that pathetic crowd seemed to have sapped his energy as well. After three bourbons, I decided that I'd better off drinking by myself, so I paid my tab and headed home.

I'd long since exhausted the stash of premium whiskies that my grandfather had left behind, but the prosaic alternatives with which

I'd replaced them were satisfying enough when paired with the sea air and the view from his deck. I took a bottle out there, along with a glass and a bucket of ice, and started knocking them back. After an hour or so, I found myself feeling much more at ease with the idea of my impending eviction. I'll be the first to admit that excessive drinking doesn't solve anything in the long term, but anyone who says that there's no place for it is full of shit. Sometimes you just need to let yourself out of your own head for a few hours. Maybe some people can manage that without the assistance of alcohol or drugs, but I'm not one of them.

I'm not sure what time it was when I finally made my way back into the house. As I stumbled toward my bedroom, I noticed an envelope lying on the floor of the foyer, as if someone had slid it under the front door. I wasn't sure whether I'd missed it when I'd gotten home from the bar, or if it had been delivered while I'd been outside. I guess it didn't matter. The intense spinning sensation that I experienced when I bent over to pick it up pointed out how drunk I actually was, but I managed to complete the maneuver without falling on my face. When I got myself upright and steady again, I tore open the envelope and found a short, handwritten note inside. All it said was: "Please meet me at the American Legion Hall on Sunday at 10 A.M. - J.W."

As straightforward as that message was, I found myself staring at it dumbly while my booze-addled brain struggled to discern its meaning. Eventually, I gave up and threw it on the table before staggering upstairs. I slept fully clothed with my belt buckled, but at least I kicked off my shoes before I passed out.

Chapter Thirteen

It was about five minutes after ten when I pulled into the parking lot of American Legion Post 154 the following Sunday morning. I was surprised to find it full of cars, to the point that I had trouble finding a spot. After a couple of passes up and down the rows, I parked about as far away from the building as it was possible to get without leaving the property. I lit a cigarette and wandered slowly toward the door.

I had no idea what I was about to walk into. When I woke up the morning after finding Wainwright's note, I had no memory of it whatsoever. It was only the sight of the envelope sitting on my dining room table that triggered any recollection of that portion of the previous evening, and it was all very hazy. If I hadn't been holding the paper in my hand, I likely would have attributed the whole thing to a drunken delusion and quickly forgotten about it. Finding it after the effects of the liquor had faded forced me to acknowledge it as real.

As I sat and stared at the note while sipping strong, black coffee, I reflected on my last meeting with Wainwright. Since my father's visit, I'd shunted any thoughts of the old preacher aside so that I could devote all of my mental bandwidth to scrutinizing my relationship with my family. Of course, Wainwright's description of my father's role in determining my grandfather's legacy had proved completely accurate, and that had certainly enhanced the old man's credibility in my eyes. I was intrigued by the prospect of speaking with him again.

So it was without hesitation that I complied with the instructions contained in his note. After a few more fruitless days of house hunting, I was itching for a new development to present itself. I had high hopes when I walked into that American Legion hall.

I was completely unprepared for what I found on the other side of the double doors that separated the entryway from the main room. I've always been lousy at estimating the size of a crowd, but there must have been at least four hundred people in there, arranged in rows of folding chairs that covered almost all of the available floor space. They were all sitting quietly and staring at the front of the room, and I quickly discovered that the focal point of their attention was Wainwright.

He cut a striking figure at the head of the assembly, standing on an elevated podium behind a microphone that was positioned as high as it could reach so that he could speak into it without having to bend down. He wore a plain, black robe, which contrasted starkly against his fair skin and snowy white hair. Even from a distance, he looked ten feet tall.

In the midst of such a large gathering, my belated arrival attracted no notice whatsoever. I lingered in the doorway for a few moments before heading for the back of the hall, where I found one of the few remaining empty seats. After I sat down, I spent a few minutes looking around and trying to figure out what was going on.

The composition of the crowd didn't reveal much. They were almost all white, but otherwise they looked to be a diverse bunch. I saw men and women, young families and old folks, all listening intently to the minister on the dais.

I quickly found myself mesmerized by the old man as well. It's difficult to describe the way that he delivered his sermon, and to convey how powerful it seemed to those of us that heard it. The archetype of the southern evangelical preacher has become so ingrained in our consciousness that actually playing that role must be very difficult. I imagine that it's similar to being an actor who's asked to recreate an iconic character from a well-known film. His audience will expect to see certain mannerisms and to hear his lines delivered with the familiar cadence and inflection. If he fails to capture the essence of the original performance, moviegoers will walk away disappointed for having been subjected to an inferior version of something they've come to cherish. If he succeeds too well, his performance descends from acting into impersonation or, even worse, unintentional parody. I pity the poor soul that takes the role of Vito Corleone in the 2022 remake of *The Godfather*.

Wainwright's delivery was the opposite of caricature. Watching him was like getting a look at the model that all of the other preachers were trying to imitate, or at least should have been trying to imitate. He managed to convey the biggest ideas without seeming hyperbolic. Urgency was communicated without histrionics. His language was eloquent, but accessible. Technically, his pacing and enunciation were flawless. Even the pitch of his voice was ideal, a perfect baritone. He could have stood up there and recited a list of names from the phone book and I'd have been perfectly happy to sit and listen to him.

As it happened, the topic of the sermon was the parable of the prodigal son, as told by the Apostle Luke. Despite having attended church only sporadically throughout my life, and not at all in recent years, it was a story that I'd heard more than once, and with which I was still pretty familiar. Even so, Wainwright's presentation gripped me from beginning to end. He focused on the proportionality of the father's reaction to the return of his younger son. It was one thing to let his mistakes slide and to accept him back into the fold, but did he really need to slaughter the fatted calf and throw such an extravagant party? Of course he did, because his son had come home, and that trumped everything else. So it was with God, also. He might be keeping tabs on billions of souls, but that doesn't diminish His joy when just one who has been lost finds his way back to Him. Wainwright veered from Luke's Gospel into Matthew's: "How think ye? If a man have an hundred sheep, and one of them be gone astray, doth he not leave the ninety and nine, and goeth into the mountains, and seeketh that which is gone astray? And if so be that he find it, verily I say unto you, he rejoiceth more of that sheep, than of the ninety and nine which went not astray."

Given the fact that Wainwright had personally asked me to attend the service, I had to wonder if he had picked his topic with me in mind. He understood that I'd drifted away from Christianity, so maybe he wanted to let me know that God's door remained open. He was also aware that I was very focused on thoughts of inheritance those days. If I wasn't his specific target, it was an awfully coincidental choice on his part.

As he wound down, I glanced at my watch. He had been going for just under an hour, but the time had flown past. I joined the congregation in standing and reciting the Lord's Prayer, but I didn't know the words to either of the hymns that followed, so I watched silently while everyone else belted them out. They passed around a collection plate and I threw in a few bucks, more to avoid an awkward moment than out of any sincere desire to contribute. Shortly after that, Wainwright delivered the benediction and the crowd started to trickle towards the door.

It took quite a while for the hall to empty out. Many members of the congregation made their way to the front of the room to have a word with their minister before they departed, and Wainwright made time for all of them. He stood to the left of his podium, exchanging handshakes with his flock as they filed past. Most of the time, he wore a welcoming smile, but every now and then I saw him adopt a more solemn expression, presumably in response to someone sharing graver news. His last few conversations were the longest and, judging by the look on his face, the weightiest. I guess that those with the heaviest burdens had hung back and waited for everyone else to clear out, in hopes of getting more of his attention, and less of everyone else's.

I stayed in my seat until the room was empty save for one last congregant. While he and Wainwright spoke, I made my way to the end of the third row of chairs, which was as close to them as I felt I could get while still maintaining a respectful distance. After a few more minutes, they shook hands and the man went on his way. Three-quarters of an hour after he'd said the benediction, Wainwright and I finally had the room to ourselves.

As I approached him, he flashed me a warm smile and offered me his hand. "I'm very glad that you came this morning."

"Thanks for the invite," I replied as we shook.

He gestured toward a door on the wall behind the podium. "Come with me while I change out of this robe?"

I followed him out of the hall and into a kitchen, where seven or eight men were busy tallying up the take from that morning's collection. There must have been at least five grand sitting on the stainless steel countertop, divided into neat stacks of small bills. As we passed through the room, the men looked up from their work and smiled at Wainwright. Several of them complimented him on his sermon. He acknowledged them with a nod and thanked them in a soft voice without breaking stride.

After passing through the kitchen, we wound up in a small, square room, which was empty save for a card table and a couple of folding chairs. Wainwright's suit jacket was hanging from a hook on the wall near the door, and I watched as he deliberately removed his black robe and placed it on a hanger before zipping it into a garment bag that he'd taken from the card table. Also on the table were a Bible, a spiral-bound notebook, two pens and a half-empty bottle of water. He removed his jacket from the hook, and replaced it with the garment bag.

Rather than putting on his coat, he draped it over the back of one of the chairs and continued in his shirtsleeves, taking a long pull from his water bottle. As he replaced the cap, he remembered himself and gave me a sheepish look. "I apologize," he began. "I don't have another bottle to offer you. You're welcome to have a drink from mine, if that sort of thing doesn't bother you. Or we could check the kitchen and see if..."

I stopped him. "No worries. I'm not the one that's been talking for the last two hours straight."

He laughed. "Occupational hazard, I guess." He motioned toward the chairs, and we both sat down. "So," he asked, "what did you think?"

I took a moment to choose my words. "I thought that your sermon was excellent."

"Thank you. And what did you make of the crowd? More than you expected?"

The question was a bit awkward, as I hadn't expected any crowd at all. I nodded slowly. "Yeah, I was surprised to see such a big group. I, uh, didn't know that you were still... still doing this kind of thing."

"I never stopped. Not really."

My instinct was to try to be delicate with my next question, but there was really no way to finesse it, so I just blurted it out. "And these people... they know about your... history?"

Wainwright answered without a moment's hesitation. "Of course they do. I think it's a wonderful example of the redemptive power of faith in Jesus Christ."

I shrugged. "I guess that's one way to look at it."

He learned forward in his chair. "It's the *only* way for a Christian to look at it. It's the whole point of everything we believe. Sin and then redemption through faith in Jesus... that's the way it works. If they didn't buy into that idea, they wouldn't have shown up here in the first place."

I considered pointing out that his first congregation had turned out to be considerably stingier when it came to forgiving his transgressions, but I held my tongue. It wasn't a complete shock to learn that a new batch of believers had embraced their imperfect pastor, especially after his flaws had been diluted by two and a half decade's worth of contrition. With enough distance, a troubled past can be a formidable asset when it comes to convincing others of the sincerity of one's beliefs. Would the younger George Bush ever have become president if we hadn't heard all about his youthful escapades? I guess we'll never know, but the voters sure seemed to embrace the narrative of the wild frat boy gone straight with the help of Jesus. Lots of people claim to be pious, but folks who sin spectacularly and then reverse course have a certain credibility that a run of the mill goody two-shoes lacks. Society tends to see the ability to reform in such a fundamental way as tangible evidence of a deep personal relationship with Christ. Maybe Wainwright was tapping into that impulse as well. Whatever dynamic was at work between him and his flock, it seemed pointless to continue discussing his past, so I simply replied, "Fair enough."

He chuckled again. "If you're going to work for me, I think we're going to have to give you a crash course in Salvation 101. Are you interested?"

"I'm always interested in salvation, wherever I can find it," I replied with a smirk.

"I was asking if you wanted to come and work for me."

"No beating around the bush, huh?"

"Well, you showed up this morning, right? I'm assuming you're here because you're interested in what I was saying the last time we spoke."

I held up both hands. "Slow down for a second. You invited me here today, and I came. Beyond that, I don't…"

He interrupted me. "Why did you come, then? You said yourself that you weren't much for going to church."

"I didn't know that I'd be going to church."

"What did you think a pastor would be doing at ten o'clock on a Sunday morning?"

"Like I said, it wasn't clear to me that you were a pastor anymore."

He paused for a few seconds before answering. "Fine. But you wanted to talk to me about something, right? You didn't come here without a reason."

I shifted in my chair. "My father came down to see me last week."

Wainwright nodded. "I see."

"I asked him a bunch of questions about my grandfather."

"And?"

"He never heard of you. And he pretty much laughed me out of the room when I suggested that Grandpa might have come to Jesus before he died..."

"But?" the old man prodded.

"But," I continued, "you were right about my grandfather wanting to leave me something in his will. It seems that my father talked him out of it."

He leaned back in his chair and folded his arms across his chest. "So, you see that I was telling you the truth, right?"

"All I can say for sure is that you talked to my grandfather. I still don't know about him getting religion and all of that..."

"He did," Wainwright interjected.

"I'm inclined to take your word for it," I replied, honestly.

He flashed me a broad smile. "Aren't you excited about the idea of picking up where he left off? He'd have been thrilled to see you getting involved."

"You know, I might be more excited if I knew what you were trying to get me to do."

He looked amused by this last statement, as if the very premise of it was absurd. I couldn't tell if he thought that he'd already told me the details, or if he saw them as so self-evident that only a fool would have failed to discern them on his own. Still, he humored me and explained. "I'm building a church."

I gestured back over my shoulder in the direction of the main hall. "Looks like you've already got one."

He sighed. "For years, we've been meeting in places like this, scheduling our services around pancake breakfasts and ice cream socials. It's time this congregation had a real home."

"Didn't Jesus say something about Him being there whenever two or three gather together in His name? It shouldn't matter where, right?"

"You and your Bible quotes," he muttered, before continuing in a stronger voice. "That's right, of course. We are a true church, wherever we meet, but we could be so much more with a proper facility." He paused as if give me a chance to absorb that thought before expounding on it. "People would have a place where they could feel the Lord's presence any time, day or night. A place to hold Bible studies, youth group meetings, weddings, funerals… all of the things that a church should do outside of those few hours on Sunday mornings when we rent this place. It could serve as a beacon to attract others in the community whom we haven't yet reached."

I stopped him. "I hear what you're saying. That all sounds great, really… but I don't see how I can help you."

He smiled. "I'm not asking you to write sermons or baptize babies. I've got that part covered."

"OK, but… I'm sorry if I seem dense, but I'm still not sure I understand what you're asking."

He thought for a few seconds before he answered. "As much as we strive to focus on God's kingdom, we can't change the fact that everything we do in this world is subject to earthly constraints. Money needs to be raised, and managed, and accounted for. We have to buy land and hire architects and contractors. Zoning boards, local governments, the IRS... all of them have rules that we have to follow, permits that we have to get... It's a little overwhelming for a simple pastor."

I took the self-effacing bit with more than a grain of salt. My limited interactions with Wainwright had shown quite clearly that he saw himself as anything but a simple pastor. Still, everything he'd said made sense; I just couldn't see where I fit in to any of it. I shook my head and looked at the floor. After a few moments of silence, he prompted me. "Well... what do you think?"

"My grandfather would have been perfect for that kind of stuff. He could have really helped you out."

"And now you can help."

I interrupted him. "Or my father, really. This is right up his alley."

"If he wants to get involved, I'd certainly welcome his contribution."

I laughed. "My father's not in the business of making contributions without getting something back. He'd expect to be well-paid for his services."

"I'm afraid he'd be disappointed with what I could offer him on that front. This project wasn't conceived with profits in mind, at least not material ones."

"Unfortunately, those are the only kind that interest him."

The old man nodded and paused for a moment before continuing. "But I'm not asking him to get involved. I'm asking you."

I laughed again. "I appreciate the thought, but I don't think I'd be of much use to you."

"When we talked the other day, you kept insisting that you were a smart guy, didn't you?"

"All I said was that I wasn't an idiot."

"Here's your chance to put your money where your mouth is."

"I just meant that I've read a few books. That doesn't make me qualified to... to do much of anything, really. You need an accountant, a lawyer, a tax advisor... maybe a real estate guy... someone that knows about construction... a little public relations expertise probably wouldn't hurt... I'm happy to hear that I've made a good impression and that you've enjoyed our conversations, but I am none of those things. Not even close."

I was expecting to see disappointment on his face, but he maintained his cheerful demeanor, despite my best efforts to convince him that he was barking up the wrong tree. "Your grandfather told me that you spent some time working for his bank in New York. Surely you must have learned one or two..."

"I made spreadsheets for a few months. Not really all that educational."

"We might be able to use some spreadsheets," he chuckled.

I slid my chair away from the table and stood up. "I don't want to waste any more of your time. Even if I wanted to help you out... if I thought that I could... I can't stay down here, anyway."

The old man kept his seat and looked up at me in silence for a few moments before asking, "You got a better offer somewhere else?"

"My dad sold the house. I have to be out in three weeks."

"Where are you going to go?"

I shrugged. "Home, I guess."

"Is that what you want?"

I stared at the floor again and tapped the linoleum with my left foot. "Maybe my father's right," I mumbled. "I should start doing something with my life."

"You gonna go work for him?"

I shook my head. "I doubt it."

"Well, what'll it be, then? Another company? Back to school, maybe?"

"I don't know," I replied, irritated at facing this question for what felt like the millionth time. "I'll find something."

Wainwright leapt out of his seat and pounded his fist on the card table. "You're not listening!" he yelled. After a moment, he lowered his voice a few notches and went on. "Here," he began, spreading his arms, "*Here* is something. I'm waving it right in front of your nose and you won't see it."

"I just don't think..."

He cut me off. "Just listen! Do you really think that whatever you can find in some cubicle in New Jersey, or on some trading desk in New York... do you think that's actually going to be more interesting, or more rewarding, than what I'm doing here? We're building something, something bigger than ourselves. Think about that and then tell me that you want to run away and become some middle-management stooge-in-training."

His exhortations hit home. I still didn't think that I'd be able to live up to the expectations that he seemed to be harboring for me, but I was absolutely sure that I wasn't ready to go home and embrace the sort of future that would have suited my father. Frankly, it was nice to be made to feel wanted. For once, someone was talking about my future without focusing on my limitations.

As seductive as it was to find myself being recruited, the practical difficulties at hand prevented me from getting too carried away. "You're probably right," I lamented, "but none of that matters if I'm homeless, does it?"

He smiled. "If you have some faith, you might be surprised at what the Lord can do for you."

"God's gonna pay my rent?"

"Come to my house tomorrow morning at eleven."

I sighed. "I feel like we're going in circles here. This just isn't going to..."

"Don't say anything else. Just come by tomorrow. You can give me your answer then." He extended his hand, and I took it. "See you tomorrow," he reiterated.

"OK," I agreed, before turning and walking out the door.

Chapter Fourteen

When Wainwright escorted me back to his office the next morning, I was surprised to find another man sitting in my usual seat. He stood when we entered the room, and Wainwright introduced him simply as "Peter." We shook hands before he resumed sitting, and I lowered myself into a wooden chair that Wainwright had moved from its home along the wall to a spot in the center of the room. The pastor made his way around his desk and parked himself across from us.

The three of us sat in an awkward, silent triangle for a few moments, looking at one another. Peter appeared to be a bit older than Wainwright, and not nearly as well-preserved. He was almost completely bald, and what little hair he had left had turned the color of cigarette ash. His skin was pallid, marked here and there with red blotches and deep wrinkles, and he somehow managed to look unsteady, even though he was sitting down. I saw his left hand trembling as he held it against his body, and the look on his face suggested that he was annoyed. I wondered what he could possibly have to do with me.

Wainwright stirred first and plucked a sheet of paper from the top of his desk and handed it to me, without saying a word. It was an advertisement for a house available for rent. In fact, I had come across a listing for that very house just a few days before, while I'd been surfing the internet in search of a new place to live. All of the images I'd scrolled through had started to blend together in my mind, but I was pretty sure I remembered this property. If I was right, it was a really nice place. It only had two bedrooms, but the kitchen was quite big, and newly updated, as was the master bathroom. There was beautiful patio out back, along with a pool, a gas grill and, for good measure, a tiki hut.

The flyer mentioned enough of these details to confirm that it was indeed the place that I thought it was. After a minute, I passed it back to Wainwright. He seemed to be waiting for me to react, but I wasn't sure what I was supposed to say. Finally, he prompted me. "Well? What do you think?"

"About… the house?"

"Yes, of course!"

"It's, uh, lovely."

"A satisfactory place to live, then?"

"I'm sure," I mumbled, still in the dark about where he was heading with all of this.

"So you'll take it?"

I looked across the desk at Wainwright, who was staring back at me with a huge grin. I stole a glance at Peter as well, whose expression hadn't changed at all since we'd sat down. I shook my head. "I'm not sure I understand."

"It's not complicated." He picked up the flyer and waved it at me. "I'm asking if you want to live in this house."

His playful demeanor was starting to annoy me. "You know damn well that I can't afford that place," I snapped.

He shrugged. "How do you know? I haven't told you the price yet."

"I've seen this listing before. They're looking for something like eighteen hundred a week, I think."

Wainwright turned to the stranger. "Was that the asking price, Peter?"

"Eighteen fifty," the older man growled.

"See," I announced as I pointed at Peter. "He says so as well."

The preacher nodded. "And he should know. He owns the place." I looked back at Peter, who acknowledged this last revelation with a quick nod. "And I know for a fact that he's willing to cut you a much better deal than that," Wainwright continued.

I turned to address the stranger sitting next to me. "I really appreciate the gesture… but I gotta tell you up front that I can't get anywhere near that price."

Wainwright jumped back in. "Peter is prepared to let you stay in his house, free of charge, for as long as you're here helping us. Isn't that right, Peter?"

"Uh huh," the older man grunted.

I sat back in my chair, dumbfounded. I studied both of their faces, looking for some sign that would confirm my suspicion that they were having a chuckle at my expense. I allowed at least half a minute to pass in order to give them opportunity to reveal their deception. When I was finally satisfied that neither of them were about to break into laughter, I repeated the punch line. "For free?"

Both of them nodded, so I continued. "That's incredibly generous, but I can't accept…"

Wainwright interrupted me before I could finish. "I seem to remember you sitting in this very room, not long ago, and telling me that you weren't too proud to take anything from anyone that was prepared to give it to you."

"It's not a question of pride," I replied. "I mean, we're talking, what, more than seven grand a month in lost rental income? I can't ask someone I don't even know to give that up on my account."

Peter shifted in his chair, and I thought I saw a look of relief flash across his face. Before he could say anything, though, our mutual friend spoke on his behalf. "Peter is more than happy to do this for his church."

"Why?" I murmured, hoping that Peter would answer for himself this time.

Again, Wainwright interceded before he could do so. "Peter's been very blessed. He owns several properties in the Keys, and he has a beautiful, loving wife." The preacher paused as if to let that sink in. "He just wants to share some of God's bounty with the church that's served him so well in navigating life's path."

"Thanks, John, but I'd like to hear it from him, if it's all the same to you."

Peter squirmed in his seat before he spoke up. "That's right. Just like John said. I'm, uh, happy to help." He was still wearing the same sour expression on his face, but since it was the only look I'd ever seen from him, I wasn't sure whether it had anything to do with the idea of me living in one of his houses for free. Maybe he was just upset because he was old and felt like shit. For all I knew, he'd been pissed off for the last fifty years.

I was struggling to accept his offer at face value, but I didn't have much else to go on. Before I had a chance to devote any more thought to it, I noticed Peter straining to pull himself out of his chair. I stood and offered to help, but he ignored my outstretched hand and managed to rise on his own. Once he was up, he reached into his pocket and pulled out a set of keys, which he dropped onto Wainwright's desk. "There you go," he announced as he turned and started toward the door. I noticed that he actually seemed to move well enough once he had gotten himself going. He paused when he reached the door, and turned back to face me. "My number is on that flyer, if you need to contact me."

Before I had a chance to reply, he'd already disappeared through the doorway. "Thanks," I called after him, anyway. All I heard in response was the sound of his steps on the hardwood floor, steadily receding as he made his way down the hall.

I looked back at Wainwright, but before I had a chance to say anything more, he hopped up from his chair and grabbed the keys and the flyer from his desk. "I want to show you something," he said, as he brushed past me and out of the room. When I didn't follow quickly enough, I heard his voice from the hallway, encouraging me. "This way!"

He led me a short distance to the end of the corridor and then around a corner to our left, where he opened a door and gestured for me to look inside. Judging from the room's size and location, I guessed that it was supposed to be a bedroom, but there was no bed inside. Instead, the small, square space was cluttered with cardboard boxes and unruly piles of papers. Three antique-looking floor lamps stood unplugged against the wall to my left, and wedged into the far right corner I saw a tall, empty bookcase. Its color implied that it was made of cherry, but from that distance I wasn't able to tell if it was real wood or a Wal-Mart special.

"I was thinking that we could use this as your office," he ventured. He must have taken the expression on my face for one of disappointment rather than the pure befuddlement that I was feeling, because he quickly added, almost apologetically, "We'll clean all of this up, of course. I have a nice table downstairs that you can use as a desk, and..."

"It's fine, it's fine," I told him. "I'm just not sure..."

I guess he figured that preventing me from getting a word in edgewise would keep me from turning down his offer. Before I had the chance to express another round of misgivings, he threw his arm over my shoulder and started steering me back toward the front of the house. "Of course," he interjected, "you'll want to go and see your new place right away." With that he handed me the keys and the flyer. "The address is on there."

He kept up a steady chatter until we reached the front door, but I found myself unable to focus on anything that he was saying. Before I could fully comprehend what was going on, I was standing at the top of the steps that led down to the driveway, and Wainwright was closing the door behind me. I stood rooted to that spot for several minutes, unsure of what I was supposed to do next. Part of me was inclined to walk away from all of it. It would have been easy enough to go back inside, politely but firmly return the keys, and go on my way. As I considered doing that, though, it dawned on me that there was no real reason for me to bail out at that point. All of the risk in our proposed arrangement seemed to fall entirely on Wainwright and Peter. If they eventually decided that I was less useful than anticipated, what was the worst that they could do? Kicking me out of my rent-free digs wouldn't render me any worse off than I was to begin with. All that I stood to lose were however many days or weeks might pass before they lost interest in me. It wasn't as if I was sitting on a surplus of alluring opportunities that I would have to forsake in order to play this one out. Turning down a perfectly good place in the Keys in order to go to the one place on earth where I was absolutely sure I didn't want to be seemed the height of foolishness.

That realization, and a sense of appreciation for all of the efforts that Wainwright had made on my behalf, convinced me that I should, at the very least, go and see the house. As I made the fifteen minute drive back to Marathon, I chided myself for having been so hesitant. I had always held myself out as the kind of person who was comfortable with uncertainty. It was a part of my identity to which I clung dearly, mostly because I needed it in order to justify so many of the choices I'd made. It seemed cool to steer clear of real work so long as I couched it all as an ongoing quest to find something interesting. Now that something interesting had fallen into my lap, I couldn't very well turn my back on it just because it was a little peculiar.

As if the universe had been eavesdropping on my thoughts and had decided to test my resolve, things got even weirder once I got to the house. As soon as I opened the door and stepped inside, I heard a woman's voice call out, "Hello! I'll be right there!" Completely unprepared to find anyone waiting for me, I froze in my tracks and waited for her to reveal herself, which she did a few moments later. "You must be James!" she said as she entered the living room. I just nodded and watched while she paused to remove a pair of oversized yellow rubber gloves. After she'd set them down, she walked over to me and extended her hand. "I'm Barbara."

"James," I replied, mechanically returning her handshake without the faintest understanding of who she might have been.

"It's nice to meet you. I'm so glad that you decided to stay and work with Reverend Wainwright!"

I would have guessed her to be around my age, and I found her appearance completely unremarkable. She was dressed for housework, so it was hard to get a good sense of her shape, but she looked neither fat nor thin. Her hair was a very light shade of brown, and frizzy, which I could see despite the fact that she wore it pulled back into a tight pony tail. I found her cute enough, I guess, but I doubt that she would have turned my head if I'd passed her on the street. Her presence in my new living room, though, paired with the fact that she seemed to know more about my immediate future than I did, had certainly grabbed my attention.

As I stood pondering all of this, it occurred to me that I had forgotten myself. "Nice to meet you, too," I blurted out, hopeful that I hadn't waited too long to reply. "I'm, uh, sorry if I seem a little confused… I just didn't expect to find anyone else here."

"Well, I wasn't expecting you quite so soon. I was just trying to do a little cleaning so the place would be ready when you got here." She gestured over her shoulder toward the gloves that she'd left on the table. I also noticed a bucket and a mop leaning against the wall.

"I, uh, really appreciate that." After a few moments, I went on. "John didn't mention that the house came with a maid."

She started laughing. "No such luck, I'm afraid. I'm your new landlord."

Once again, I'd lost the plot. "I'm definitely a little confused," I stammered. "I just met a guy… an older gentleman named Peter. I thought this was his…"

"Peter is my husband."

"Oh! I had no idea. I'm, uh, really sorry. I didn't mean to insult you by asking if you were the maid. I hope that I didn't offend..."

She interrupted me with her laughter again. "Don't worry about it."

Despite her evident lack of concern, I felt compelled to add, "They never mentioned you when we talked this morning." Of course, that wasn't entirely true. Wainwright had listed Peter's loving wife as evidence of the favor that the Lord had shown him. I had assumed that he was talking about someone closer to Peter's age, with whom he'd shared his entire life, but now I understood what the preacher had really been trying to say. Since God had seen His way clear to pair him with a woman four decades his junior, then the least that Peter could do was to lend the church one of his houses for a few months.

"Don't worry," she repeated. "Let me show you around a bit."

Before joining her for a tour, I needed to tell her one more thing. "I, uh... I just want to make sure you know about the deal I made with your husband. You know that I'm not going to be paying any rent here, right?"

"Yes, of course," she replied. "Reverend Wainwright explained all of that."

"And you're OK with it?"

"The reverend says that you're going to do some very important work for us."

"He didn't mention what, exactly, he expected me to do, did he?"

I watched her brow furrow. "You mean, you don't know?"

"Not really, no."

If that revelation troubled her at all, she got over it quickly. She simply shrugged and said, "I'm sure he'll explain soon enough. He's a brilliant man, you know."

"You're not the first person who's told me that," I replied, recalling my long ride with Liz and the effusive, if vague, praise that she'd heaped upon the old evangelist throughout.

"You'll see it for yourself, I'm sure."

I shook my head. "I just don't want to disappoint everyone. John – I mean Reverend Wainwright – has been so... persistent... in trying to get me to stay... and you and your husband so generous in giving me a place to live... I'm just afraid that I won't be able to live up to..."

She cut me off. "If our pastor believes in you, that's good enough for me."

I was glad to hear that at least one of us had faith. My immediate challenge was to find some of my own, if not in God, then at least in myself. For the moment, I let those thoughts go and tried to enjoy the guided tour of my new home. It was even nicer than I'd expected, with a very modern, open floor plan and plenty of very thoughtful decorative touches. I concluded that they'd been selling themselves short by asking only eighteen fifty a week. Based on other listings I'd seen, I would have thought that they could have gotten a bit more for it. Of course, my presence made that point moot, at least temporarily, and I felt another pang of guilt when I reminded myself of that fact, but I shook it off easily enough. I had given everyone involved fair notice of my shortcomings. If, after hearing all of my disclaimers, they still wanted to keep me around, that decision was squarely on them.

Chapter Fifteen

I couldn't believe the extent to which my new boss had failed to embrace modern technology. He kept names and phone numbers on index cards, which he didn't even file away alphabetically, and his financial records, to the extent he kept them at all, consisted of shorthand entries in an old set of black and white composition notebooks. It was a wonder that he managed to keep track of anything.

I took it upon myself to drag him into the twenty-first century, and my first order of business was convincing him to shell out a few hundred bucks for a laptop computer. Once we got it set up, I started entering data. At the very least, I'd explained to him, we needed to be able to keep track of his parishioners, their contact information and, most importantly, their donations. If we were really going to start spending those contributions on a construction project, we were going to have to figure out a way to record our expenses as well.

Wainwright never asked me to do any of that. In fact, he never gave me any direction at all. I just showed up and did what I thought would be helpful, and the old man seemed content to let me run with it. None of what I did amounted to anything more than mindless make-work, but I found it strangely satisfying. I'd driven all the way to the edge of the map in order to avoid being made to populate spreadsheets in some corporate cubical, but yet there I was, sitting in front of a cheap computer entering a never-ending list of names into an Excel file, and enjoying it. It was funny how the world worked out sometimes.

It helped that I wasn't exactly killing myself. Most days, I went over to the house around mid-morning and stayed until late afternoon, but I usually spent at least some of that time just chatting with Wainwright about his sermon for the upcoming weekend. Our discussions were usually the high point of my day, and I looked forward to them. The old man had a great talent for making theological inquiry seem like a collaborative effort, even though I'm pretty sure that none of my thoughts ever actually influenced his final Sunday product. For the first time in a long while, I felt engaged and useful.

After six weeks of this, we had what I felt like was a pretty good church membership list, as well as the beginnings of a workable accounting system. For my next project, I'd decided to try to build him a website. I went to his office and explained how handy it would be for communicating with the congregation, finding new members, and fundraising. I thought that we could even start recording Sunday services and podcasting them, as a start toward getting Wainwright the sort of broader exposure that he hadn't had since his television days. My website designing skills were rudimentary at best, but I assured him that I could use a template to get us going and that we could hire a pro to clean it up later.

He listened without saying a word, just flashing me an occasional half-smile or nod to show that he was paying attention. When I finished, I expected him to laugh and send me on my way, as he had after I'd explained each of the other tasks that I'd created for myself. When he said, "That sounds like a good idea," I started to stand up, but I froze in my tracks when he continued. "But I actually had something else that I wanted to ask you."

"Sure."

"It's, uh... more of a personal thing."

"OK," I replied, sitting down again.

He leaned forward and placed his hands on his desk, and hesitated for a moment before going on. "I'm not sure how to explain this, so I'll just say it. I have a daughter."

"A daughter? Really? I had no idea..."

"Does that surprise you?"

"Well... yeah. You've never mentioned her before."

He looked down. "Our relationship has been... it's not something I'm proud of."

"How old is she?" I asked.

"A couple of years younger than you."

"Why are you telling me this now?"

"I thought... I hoped... that maybe you could help me out... with her."

"Help you out? How?"

He took a deep breath and exhaled slowly. "The last time I spoke to her... it was years ago. I want to see her again."

I nodded. "Of course... but what does that have to do with me?"

"Maybe you could try to talk to her... convince her to give me another chance."

"You ever try calling her yourself?"

"She won't take my calls."

I shook my head. "I'm not sure I can help you with this."

"I know it probably won't work. I don't expect her to forgive me, but I've got to try, and I think sending you might be my best chance."

"What happened between you two, anyway?" I asked.

"I was never there for her, or her mother, when they needed me. Like I told you before, I've made a lot of mistakes in my life, but not being a father to my girl is the one that I regret most."

I had no idea what I was supposed to say to that. No one had ever asked me to help put a family back together, and I felt singularly unqualified for such a task. "Why do you think she'd listen to me?"

"Well, I *know* that she won't talk to me, but at least there's a chance that she might hear you out..."

"But she doesn't even know me."

He shrugged. "So she won't have any reason not to trust you, right?"

The whole thing sounded crazy, but I had the sense that he wasn't going to let it go, and there didn't seem to be any harm in humoring him. "OK. You want me to give her a call?"

"I think it would be better if you talked to her in person."

"Whatever you say. Where can I find her?"

He smiled. "She's in Las Vegas."

"Vegas? You're telling me that you want me to go Vegas to talk to her?"

"Yes, if you're willing to make the trip. I'll pay your expenses, of course."

Wainwright's proposition had just become a whole lot more appetizing. I started laughing. "Sure, I'll go to Vegas for you."

Chapter Sixteen

I detest airplanes. As if the cramped quarters, stale air and inedible food weren't enough, I'm susceptible to periodic panic attacks, during which I become absolutely convinced that my plane is about to tumble out of the sky. During those episodes, I'm reduced to seizing both armrests with a death grip and devoting all of my energy to preventing myself from disintegrating into a blubbering mess. My sense of terror rises and ebbs over the course of a flight, so it's not like I'm at my worst the entire time, but spending even a fraction of a day in that state tends to make it difficult to enjoy anything afterwards. Having been through that wringer enough times, I've learned not to make ambitious plans on days that I fly. I like to get wherever I'm going, maybe grab a bite to eat, and keep to myself until bedtime. It takes a good night's sleep before I feel ready to face the world again.

The one destination where my usual rules don't apply is Vegas. Like always, I struggle with the flight, but when the plane starts its final approach into McCarran, I can almost feel the malaise being flushed away by a fresh tide of adrenaline. The sight of the city sprawling across the desert below me is like a Pavlovian trigger. By the time I pick up my bags, whatever morbid thoughts I'd had at thirty-five thousand feet are long gone, and I'm itching to find a casino so that I can get my hands on some cards.

I've made the trip at least a dozen times, but I still feel that rush whenever the Strip first comes into view. It's funny, because I'm pretty sure that anyone who's ever seen me out there probably wouldn't have guessed that I was enjoying myself all that much. Some guys flip into spring break mode as soon as they touch down, bouncing between casinos and nightclubs on a seventy-two hour bender fueled by cash, Red Bull and casual sex. I've done it that way as well, but I always felt like the party component of Vegas was a waste of my time. There are plenty of places in New York where I can find an exorbitantly expensive bottle of vodka and a room full of good-time girls. Jean-Georges, Mario Batali and Thomas Keller serve dinners every night in Manhattan. What I can't do back home, at least not without going out of my way, is play games of chance for money. That's the thing that makes getting on that plane to Nevada worthwhile.

So, if you see me in Vegas, odds are that I'll be wearing my usual khakis and sitting at a game of some sort. The stakes and the venues might vary wildly, depending on who I'm with, how much of a bankroll I'm able to put together, and the way my luck runs. I've played blackjack in the high-limit room at the Bellagio with Silicon Valley millionaires, sat in late-night $2-$4 Hold 'Em games with off-duty dealers at the Orleans, and pretty much everything in between. Sometimes, I experience the whole spectrum over the span of a few hours. Finding a good game with the locals can often be more fun than rubbing shoulders with the high rollers.

Although I felt that familiar excitement as my flight from Miami rolled to its conclusion at the end of the runway across from Mandalay Bay, I understood that this trip was going to be different. For the first time, I was there on account of someone other than myself. I had been charged by Wainwright to act as his emissary, and my instructions were clear. Any gambling I might do this time around would be strictly incidental. Of course, I still planned to play a little. It wasn't like Wainwright had asked me to abstain. I just had to make sure that whatever I did didn't interfere with the task at hand.

That might not sound like much of a challenge, but as someone who has a history of getting so engrossed in poker games that I forget to eat for fifteen or twenty hours at a stretch, I felt it necessary to remind myself of my priorities. I'd never mentioned my predilection for gambling to Wainwright. I'm not sure that he'd have sent me out there if I had. My fear was that I'd have to go back to Marathon and explain that I hadn't been able to connect with his daughter because I'd been too busy riding a hot craps table at Caesars. As I rode in the cab from the airport to my hotel, I resolved, once again, not to put myself in that position.

Wainwright hadn't made anything easier by handing me three thousand dollars in cash before I left. His intentions, of course, had been good. The money was meant to reimburse me for my airfare and hotel and, most importantly, to buy a plane ticket for Wainwright's daughter once I'd persuaded her to return to Florida. I understood all of that, but I'd used frequent flyer miles for the flight, and I still had enough juice from previous visits to rate a complimentary room at the Wynn, so all of that cash was still in my pocket. In the name of better business practices, I'd been trying to break the old man of his habit of handing out wads of bills and get him to start writing checks instead, but he'd been slow to adapt. I debated the idea of giving him a piece of the upside if I wound up in the black. It seemed like the least I could do if I was going to gamble with his money. If I lost, I could always throw his daughter's plane ticket on my Amex and worry about paying the bill later.

It was a little after two when I got to the Wynn. After checking in and grabbing lunch, I sat down at a twenty-five dollar blackjack table on the Encore side of the casino. It was a comfortable spot with a friendly dealer, and things went well right off the bat. After forty minutes or so I had turned three hundred dollars into nine hundred. Predictably, I spent the next hour and a half giving most of my profits back to the house, but I caught one more lucky streak and walked away with seven hundred when I called it quits around six o'clock.

My plan was to show up at Jill's place around seven. Wainwright had given me a cell phone number for her, but it had proved to be out of date. The only lead I had was a street address, and I wasn't sure what I would do if that turned out to be stale as well. The old man had seemed pretty confident about his daughter's living arrangements, so I hoped to find her without having to get too creative.

I showered and changed before hopping into a cab and giving the driver the address that Wainwright had provided. The cabbie seemed a bit surprised at my directing him to a residential neighborhood, but when I explained that I was visiting a friend he seemed to accept it. Our trip took only fifteen minutes, and after I paid him I found myself standing in front of a row of low-rise condominiums. There was nothing luxurious about them, but they looked decently maintained. When I peered around the edge of the last unit, I could see a large swimming pool and a cute, little playground around back.

The complex fronted onto an ample parking lot, which was only about one-third full. I couldn't tell whether that was due to the condos being vacant, or if their occupants all happened to be out. It seemed equally likely that they just had more parking spaces than they needed.

I found the apartment and rang the doorbell. A moment later, I was face to face with a tall, thin redhead wearing sweatpants and a t-shirt. I put her in her early twenties, and I could see that she was very attractive, despite her disheveled appearance. "Jill?" I ventured.

"No," she shot back, without volunteering any additional information.

"I'm, uh, looking for Jill. I was told that this was her address…"

"You a friend of hers?" she demanded, at least confirming that I was in the right place, but not offering any encouragement beyond that. Her tone had a bit of an edge to it.

"A friend of her family's," I replied with a smile, hoping to disarm whatever suspicions she was harboring. "Is she around?"

"Nah. She's at work."

"Will she be back anytime soon?"

"Not 'til late."

I shifted my weight from one foot to the other. This woman seemed disinclined to tell me much, and I suppose that I had no right to expect her to. Still, I decided to try my luck. "Can you tell me where she works?"

She said nothing, initially, and it seemed like she was ready to slam the door in my face. To my surprise, she answered instead. "Sapphire."

"Sapphire? You mean the, uh… gentlemen's club, Sapphire?" I asked. When she nodded, I went on. "So she's… a stripper?"

"We prefer 'dancer.'"

"Sorry. She's a dancer, then?"

"Yup."

"Thanks. Thank you so much," I said, as I turned to leave. "Maybe I'll stop by Sapphire and see I can find here there."

I had taken four or five steps toward the parking lot when my new redheaded friend called after me. "Ask for Arianna."

"Arianna?"

"She's Arianna at the club. If you ask for Jill, nobody will know who you're talking about."

"Thanks again," I replied, as she shut the door. I had to call a cab to come and fetch me, and as I sat on the curb and waited, I lit a cigarette and considered what I'd just learned. Wainwright had neglected to share the fact that his daughter was a stripper. I wondered if he even knew. Assuming he didn't, was I supposed to tell him? Maybe that depended on how things went once I met her. I was certainly more intrigued by that prospect than I'd been ten minutes before. For once, I wasn't itching to get back to a casino. As I climbed into my taxi, I announced my destination. "I'm going to Sapphire, please."

Chapter Seventeen

There's no shortage of hyperbole in Las Vegas, and it's easy to dismiss the vast majority of it. I enjoyed the $7.99 prime rib special at the Four Queens, but I'm pretty confident that it was not the Best Prime Rib in the World. My mattress at the Wynn was not the most comfortable surface on which I've ever slept, and none of the singing and dancing and magic extravaganzas on the Strip were ever quite as wondrous as advertised. In a city full of superlative claims, visitors quickly learn to discount most of them.

Sapphire purports to be the biggest strip club in the world. Now, that's exactly the sort of typical Vegas bullshit assertion that I'm talking about, but, in Sapphire's case, I'm inclined to believe them. I can't think of another city where a seventy thousand square foot gentlemen's club would even be possible. Only Vegas has the blend of well-heeled tourists and limitless desert real estate required to make such a thing viable.

I'd gone there two or three times on previous trips. Some of my friends complained that it was too big, but I'd always rated its size as a positive. The sheer number of dancers on display guaranteed a varied selection, and I enjoyed mixing it up. No matter what your specific tastes might have been, the odds were decent that you'd see something you liked while you were there.

The place looked exactly as I remembered it. There was a small stage, complete with the obligatory pole, near a massive bar, and then row after row of tables and booths arrayed across a few tiers of varying elevation. The space was so big, and so dimly lit, that I couldn't even see the back wall from the front of the room. The only thing that seemed strange this time was the lack of customers. I was used to visiting strip clubs after midnight, when they're typically packed with men. Since it wasn't even eight o'clock yet, the hordes still hadn't shown up. There were a few guys huddled around tables, here and there, and another handful parked at the bar, but they were easily outnumbered by the dancers. A few of the girls flitted amongst the occupied tables, trying to work the small crowd, but most were just standing around in small groups, chatting with one another and, I assumed, waiting for more money to walk through the door before they opened for business in earnest.

The paucity of listeners didn't seem to dissuade the disc jockey, who continued to fill the cavernous space with impossibly loud music. Even at the front door, I could barely hear the bouncer. I eventually gathered that he wasn't going to charge me a cover because it was so early, but he wanted me to sit at the bar. When I asked for a table instead, he demurred until I handed him a twenty dollar bill. He walked me to a seat on the lowest level, to the left of the stage, and far enough away from it so that it wouldn't be a distraction. It was a good spot, and I thanked him. Before he could walk away, I motioned for him to lean in and held out another twenty. "I'm looking for a girl named Arianna," I said, loudly enough to ensure that he would hear me over the music.

He shrugged. "I don't know the dancers' names."

I went to my wallet for another bank note and pressed forty bucks into his palm. "Whatever you can do to help me find her, I'd really appreciate it."

With a quick nod, he shoved my money into his pocket and went on his way. I wasn't convinced that he intended to do anything other than enjoy his next meal at my expense, so I decided to enlist more help. When the cocktail waitress arrived a few moments later, I made the same request of her, and slipped her an extra twenty as well. I hoped that at least one of them would point Jill in my direction.

No sooner had the waitress returned with my gin and tonic than I was approached by my first prospective entertainer of the night. I guessed that she was Vietnamese, or maybe Cambodian, and on the wrong side of thirty. She was very attractive, but obviously no relation of Wainwright's, so I passed on her offer to dance for me in the hope that Jill would soon make an appearance at my table.

She didn't. Over the next forty-five minutes, four or five other girls stopped by to try to sell me lap dances. Each of them helpfully introduced themselves when they sat down, so I was spared the awkward task of trying to guess whether any of them were Wainwright's daughter. Some were more intriguing than others. I was particularly drawn to a black woman with a Caribbean accent who must have been as tall as me, at least in her high heels. A couple of the others were less visually stimulating but more insistent, especially a black-haired Russian who didn't seem capable of taking "no" for an answer. I turned them all away, though, reminding myself that I was there for a very specific purpose and determined not to flush my bankroll on a diversion that I knew would ultimately lead nowhere.

My resolve finally crumbled when a stunning creature named Patricia sidled up to me and threw her arm around my shoulders. I don't know that she was objectively any better looking than the others that had paraded by before her, but there was something about her that drew me in. She was a blonde, which usually wasn't my thing, but she came off as intelligent, and she radiated a kind of fun energy that I found quite appealing. We chatted for about ten minutes before she even suggested a dance, and when she finally did, I found myself unable to resist.

I let her grind against me for two songs, and she seemed a bit disappointed when I cut her off after that. As I handed her fifty dollars, she leaned in and whispered in my ear. "We could have some more fun in the back room, if you're up for it..." As she pulled away, she ran her hand lightly over my crotch.

I smiled and shook my head. "You're very beautiful, but I really can't..."

"Aw, c'mon. This is Vegas. Live a little."

"It's not that," I said quickly. "Another time, maybe, but I'm actually looking for someone tonight."

"And you've found someone, baby," she purred, grabbing my hand and playfully trying to pull me out of my chair.

I gently pulled my hand back. "I'm sorry. I'm trying to find another dancer here... a girl by the name of Arianna?" I could see the annoyance on her face as she stepped back to grab her dress from the chair where she'd tossed it. As she stepped into it and wriggled it over her hips, I continued. "I came all the way out from Florida to find her, actually."

"Is she your ex?" she asked, coolly.

"No, no... nothing like that. We're, uh, family friends and I was really hoping to catch up with her." It was about as close to the truth as I could get without going into far more detail than our circumstances would have permitted.

My experience with strippers is that they tend to get very territorial with their clients. They do, after all, operate in a highly competitive marketplace. Every dollar that goes into another girl's g-string is a dollar that they'll never see. Some of them tend to work in pairs or small groups and will throw business to others in their circle, but generally they're not keen on steering men toward their rivals. They always seem much more inclined to try to convince a customer to stick with them exclusively until his wallet runs dry.

I was surprised, then, when the next thing that came out of Patricia's mouth was a promise to send Arianna my way if she saw her. I thanked her profusely before she walked away, and considered trying to find her again once I'd had my talk with Jill. I knew that I'd probably wind up pissed off if I spent a ton of money, but the idea of hanging out with her in the back room was too tempting to dismiss out of hand.

After she left, I ordered a refill and renewed my vigil. Another half an hour passed, but I only had to deflect two more propositions. It was as if the word had gotten around among the dancers that approaching me was a waste of their time. That was fine with me, if it spared me from having to keep turning them away.

I had just started thinking about how much longer I should stay before giving up for the night when I noticed another dancer heading in my direction. I detected an air of tentativeness in her approach, which contrasted noticeably with the aggression displayed by the others. She stopped about ten feet from my table and stared at me for a few seconds before coming the rest of the way. "Hi, I'm Arianna," she announced as she lowered herself into the chair beside mine.

"James," I replied, offering her my hand.

As she shook it, I could see her wheels spinning, obviously trying to figure out if she was supposed to recognize me. I took the opportunity to check her out as well. She was on the tall side of average, with brown eyes and dark brown hair that hung all the way down to the small of her back. Not surprisingly, her body was fit and toned and more than worthy of any man's fantasy. Her skin was a little too suntanned for my taste, but that's really just picking nits. She was a beautiful young woman, by anyone's standards. When she spoke, she sounded as sexy as she looked. "Patricia said that you were asking about me?"

Even though this was the moment that I'd been waiting for, and I understood, generally, the message that I was meant to convey to her, I hadn't thought through the precise details of what I would say. As I sat there, nodding silently, I realized that that had been a mistake. If I had spent some time choosing the right words, maybe our first conversation might have gone a little better. As it was, the only approach that came to mind was a clumsy, direct one, so I blurted out, "Your father asked me to talk to you."

The expression on her face transformed from one of friendly curiosity to a look of piercing anger, with maybe a quick note of confusion thrown in along the way. Even allowing for the likelihood that she'd been feigning whatever amiability I'd perceived, it was jarring to witness such an abrupt change in her countenance. I braced myself for a confrontational response, but it never came. Instead, she simply stood up and said, "I think you've got the wrong person," and started to walk away.

Before she had taken her fifth step, I called after her. "You're real name is Jill, right?" When she stopped in her tracks, I added, "And your father is John Wainwright."

She turned back to face me, and stared me right in the eye before answering. "He's never been a father to me." She kept staring after she'd said it, almost daring me to contradict her.

I understood that if I was to have any hope of continuing our conversation, I would have to compose my response very carefully. I nodded slowly, and began. "He understands..."

That was as far as I got before she cut me off. "Who the fuck are you, anyway?" she demanded, as if the fact that she was talking to a complete stranger had only just then dawned on her.

"I'm, uh... I'm trying to... your father and I have been helping each other..." I stuttered.

"Go fuck yourself," she replied, before turning on her heel and starting to walk away again.

"Wait!" I yelled. She stopped. "Please... just hear me out."

She retraced her steps until she was standing directly in front of me. "Do you want a dance?"

"Uh, no... I don't think that would be... I really just want to talk. Can we just talk for a couple of minutes? Hear me out and I'll leave you alone, I promise."

She shook her head. "This is a strip club. I'm a dancer. If you want a dance, then you can pay me and I'll dance. If not..." She shrugged her shoulders.

As if on cue, right as I opened my mouth to reply, the DJ dropped a massive bass line to signal the start of a new song. I stood up and leaned toward her so that she'd be able to hear me over the din. "We can't really talk here, can we? When do you get off?"

"Late," she replied.

"I'm sure I can stay awake," I laughed.

The thumping of the speakers receded a bit and I found myself able to hear her again. "Not gonna happen. You want a dance or not?"

I shook my head and she turned to leave, but I had one more card to play. "Your father," I announced, "asked me to give you some money."

It was a crass maneuver, I suppose, but it proved effective. I could tell that she was intrigued, and she confirmed my impression when she quickly asked, "How much?"

"A decent amount."

"Well, give it to me and maybe we can talk."

"I don't have it on me," I replied. When I saw the skepticism on her face, I waved my hand in the direction of a nearby group of girls. "I was afraid I'd spend it if I brought it in here." When she didn't say anything, I continued. "Tell me where I can meet you later tonight and I'll bring it to you then."

She looked me up and down for a few moments before she finally gave me the name and address of a late-night diner, off the Strip and out of the way, and told me to be there at four thirty in the morning. I promised to meet her there, thanked her and handed her fifty bucks. "For wasting your time when you could have been dancing for somebody else," I explained, in response to her quizzical expression. She shrugged and slipped the money into her garter before walking away without saying another word. I settled my tab with the cocktail waitress and headed outside to get a cab back to the Wynn.

Chapter Eighteen

It was just after five o'clock when I finally accepted the fact that I'd been stood up, and I felt like an idiot for ever believing that Jill was going to meet me at that diner. I'm sure I wasn't the first guy to try to arrange an off-premises rendezvous after seeing her at the club. Most had probably spent a small fortune on dances before they popped that question. I'd only given her fifty bucks and an unwelcome reminder of her absentee father. In hindsight, it was pretty obvious that she was never going to show up to continue our conversation.

That realization made it even harder to swallow the idea that I'd been so easily deceived. Only a hopeless sucker or a delusional egomaniac would have expected to score a date, platonic or otherwise, with a Vegas stripper that he'd only just met and to whom he hadn't given any money. I should have recognized that she was blowing me off when she agreed to meet me, but the thought never crossed my mind. Since I wasn't being driven by prurient motives, I'd allowed myself to forget that, from her perspective, I was just another asshole who was probably trying to get into her pants.

I guess it could have been worse. She'd been considerate enough to send me to a decent place for my wild goose chase. If she'd been more mean-spirited, I might have spent the morning at a truck stop out in the desert, or in a rougher part of town. At least I got a nice bowl of grits out of the deal, and it was easy enough to make my way back to the Strip once I abandoned any hope of her joining me for breakfast.

I tried to sleep when I got back to my room, but I wound up lying awake and thinking about Jill. Leaving her alone would have been the smart play. I had two days left in Vegas, and I had better things to do with them than stalk a stripper who wanted nothing to do with me. It would have been easy to amuse myself until the time came to head back to Marathon. Without even having to lie, I could have told Wainwright that I'd talked to his daughter and she'd made it clear that she wasn't interested in reconciliation. I wasn't a fucking social worker. How could he have blamed me for not having been able to explain away twenty five years' worth of his bad parenting over a couple of drinks at a strip club? Even if I were inclined to give it another go, there was no reason to think that I'd do any better the second time.

As reasonable as that seemed, I found myself unwilling to walk away. For whatever reason, I couldn't live with the thought of disappointing Wainwright. It wasn't that I was afraid that he'd be pissed, or anything like that. I just felt a strange compulsion to do my best to make him proud. In a couple of months, the old preacher had achieved what my father had failed to do over a lifetime. I felt an almost filial duty to see my undertaking through.

Unfortunately, simply deciding that I wanted to take another shot at Jill didn't get me any closer to figuring out how to go about it. I considered going back to the club that night, but I'd already failed there once, and I was afraid that she wouldn't humor me with small talk next time. I fully expected to be manhandled to the curb by a couple of goons if I insisted on bothering her at her place of business again.

The other option was to try to catch her at her apartment before she left for her shift. There wouldn't be any bouncers standing ready to throw me out, but it was hard to imagine her doing anything other than slamming the door in my face. Any show of persistence on my part after that would probably end with her calling the cops. Spending a few hours sharing a holding cell with a bunch of sloppy drunks and unlucky johns was definitely not an outcome that appealed to me.

Neither alternative looked particularly promising, but they were the only choices that I could see. I stared at the ceiling of my hotel room for a couple of hours, trying to find a reason to prefer one over the other, but I couldn't commit to either of them. Frustrated, I decided to fall back on my usual Vegas routine. I convinced myself that shoving my dilemma aside and concentrating on poker for a while would free my subconscious mind to figure it all out and reveal the proper course of action. I just needed a distraction so that my instincts could take over.

So, I made my way over to the poker room at the Bellagio with twenty five hundred bucks in my pocket and high hopes of finding both profit and enlightenment at the tables. I staggered out almost twelve hours later with neither. Maybe I'd been too distracted by Jill to play good poker, or too focused on the cards to figure out what to do with Jill. Honestly, I thought I played pretty well. It's hard to cling to a belief like that after you've been separated from your last chip, but sometimes you just have to accept that it wasn't your day.

Probabilities are only so useful when working with small sample sizes. In every other game in the casino, that was the fact that made winning possible. Blackjack, when played without counting cards, is a losing proposition in the long term. Over an infinite number of hands, the house keeps at least two cents out of every dollar wagered.

Lucky for us players, we don't have to play an infinite number of hands, and over the course of a few hours, or a few days, it's possible to beat the odds. If you toss a coin a million times, you'll wind up with something very close to an even split between heads and tails. Over the course of those million flips, though, there will be stretches when sixteen out of twenty come up heads. The longer the stretch, the more likely it becomes that results will start reverting toward the mean, but it's exactly that sort of uneven distribution that makes it possible to make money on blackjack, or craps, or roulette, or even slot machines. As the ancient wisdom says, the key to winning is quitting while you're ahead.

Poker is a fundamentally different proposition because it's not structurally rigged against the players. You have the ability to choose whether to bet or fold, and if you're good enough at making decisions based on incomplete information, you can limit your exposure when the odds are against you, and maximize it when the situation is favorable. The existence of a class of professional players who reap steady profits in card rooms is proof that it's possible to achieve a meaningful statistical advantage over less proficient opponents.

Of course, everyone who sits down at a poker table believes that they're the one with the advantage. They can't all be right, but even the ones that are will still be vulnerable to the vagaries of fortune. In the long run, you'll do well if you keep making bets that have a sixty percent chance of winning, but you'll still lose four times out of every ten. Some nights, those less probable outcomes just keep piling up. When you're watching the dealer shove the pot toward the other guy, it's cold comfort knowing that you'd taken the better end of the wager. Logically, you understand that you just need to keep doing what you're doing, but sometimes you run out of chips before you can collect your karmic reward.

When I walked out of the Bellagio, I was feeling the usual blend of exhaustion, regret and defiance that follows getting busted in a marathon poker session. The one silver lining was the fact that the decision about where to chase Jill had been taken out of my hands. Since it was pushing midnight, the window to catch her at her apartment had long since closed. Once again, I found myself asking a cabbie to give me a ride to Sapphire.

Chapter Nineteen

Even though only twenty-four hours had passed since my last visit to the club, I was confronted with an entirely new cast of characters the second time around. Not only wasn't I approached by any of the same girls that had tried to sell me dances the night before, but I didn't so much as catch a passing glimpse of any of them. I suppose that was a testament to the diversity of entertainment on offer. Under different circumstances, I would have welcomed the seemingly limitless supply of eye candy, but the multitude of scantily clad women only served to camouflage the one that I was trying to find. It would have been hard enough to recognize anyone in such low light, but filling the room with dozens, if not hundreds, of women all wearing variations on the same skin-tight dress made the task damn near impossible.

It wasn't just the dancers whose numbers had increased, as I had to contend with a prime time crowd of customers as well. Such was the size of the place that I doubted whether it was even possible to fill it to its capacity, but it had to have been getting close. Instead of asking for a table, I took a seat at the bar. Still smarting from my beating at the Bellagio, I was resolved not to piss away any more cash than I had to, and I hoped that sitting alone on a stool would make me a less inviting target for solicitation.

That strategy seemed to work, but the bar was a lousy place to be if you wanted to see what was going on in the rest of the club. My view was limited to the handful of tables in the front row. Beyond that, individual forms melded into a mass of flesh which seemed to undulate in time with the pulse of the music. Occasionally, I was able to focus on a dancer writhing against a customer, or a cocktail waitress trying to shepherd a tray of drinks through the chaos, but it took only the slightest lapse of concentration to lose them in the crowd again. I felt a powerful urge to leave and take my last few hundred bucks to a blackjack table somewhere. Winning back my poker losses seemed like less of a pipe dream than finding Jill in that mob.

Even without shelling out for lap dances, I found myself out forty dollars after just two drinks. Before ordering a third, I decided to head into the crowd to see if I could somehow stumble across Jill. It seemed a hopeless undertaking, but after about twenty-five minutes of jostling and begging pardons, I spotted her. She and another girl were dancing for a pair of young, professional-looking guys, while two of their buddies sat across the table and looked on. I recognized her instantly, but suppressed my inclination to march over and announce myself. Instead, I worked my way toward the nearest wall and tried to find a spot where I could watch and wait.

I spent an awkward few minutes trying to keep an eye on Jill without looking like I was staring her down. In that respect, I benefited from the fact that there was no good place to stand and gawk at her. I tried to hug the wall, but the tumult of the club proved inescapable. Once or twice, my line of sight was obscured by passersby, and I nearly panicked at the thought of her disappearing back into the swarm, but each time the obstruction cleared and I found her dancing away in the same spot.

Of course, watching her at that moment meant getting an eyeful of her body, which was completely exposed save for the few square inches concealed by her tiny thong. I had obviously anticipated the possibility of seeing her that way, but my reaction to it was complicated. Once I'd learned that she was a dancer, I'd tried to talk myself into thinking of her as my little sister. After all, I was there on her father's dime. The least I could do was to try to find a way to keep his daughter out of my masturbatory fantasies.

Initially, I deemed my exercise in self-persuasion effective, because, like any older brother would, I wanted nothing more than to grab the guy for whom she was dancing and beat him within an inch of his life. As I continued to watch her, though, I realized that my rage wasn't attributable to any sort of fraternal instinct. It was simple jealousy, fueled by lust. No matter how much I wanted to embrace the idea of viewing Jill as a sister, it wasn't so easy to stifle my fundamental instincts. Her job was to get men aroused to the point that they'll happily agree to spend five hundred dollars on a thirty dollar bottle of champagne. As I watched her grind her pelvis into her companion's crotch, it became clear that she was very, very good at it, and that I was as susceptible to her appeal as anyone else.

As breathtaking as the sight of her body might have been, it was the look of barely controlled ecstasy on her face that really got me. It was exactly the face I would have wanted to see looking back at me if I'd been having sex with her. I fantasized about switching places with her customer and holding her hips as she rode me, and I could almost hear her moaning in my ear.

Abruptly, the song ended and I snapped out of my pornographic reverie. I watched her lean in toward her guy and whisper something in his ear. I assumed that she was trying to sell him another dance, and I tensed up at the thought of having to continue watching her from afar or, worse, the possibility that she might lead him off to a private room somewhere. I exhaled when she stood up and started getting dressed. Apparently, the fellow had passed on whatever she'd offered.

She lingered at the table for another minute before giving him a peck on the cheek and turning to leave. As soon as she made her first movement away, I sprang from my spot and followed, anxious not to lose sight of her. She hadn't taken more than a few steps before I was right behind her, tapping her on the shoulder. "Missed you at breakfast this morning," I declared, loudly enough to make myself heard over the surrounding din.

When she turned to face me, I expected to find a look of annoyance on her face. At best, I was hoping for confusion. Instead, I saw a friendly smile, which shockingly didn't evaporate even after I was sure that she recognized me. "Sorry. Just couldn't make it," she laughed.

For a fleeting second, I thought that she might have been sincere, but before I could reply, she turned and started walking away. "Hey," I shouted, "I still want to talk to you..."

She stopped again, and when she turned back toward me, her expression was colder. "You really can't take a hint, can you?"

I tried flashing a grin of my own. "I guess not. I just really think that you might want to hear..."

She cut me off. "Do you want a dance?"

Afraid that she would walk away for good if I refused, I nodded. She grabbed me by the hand and led me toward the back of the club until we found an empty chair, where she parked me until the start of the next song. As it began, she stood before me and gently spread my legs so that she could stand between them, gyrating and rubbing her hands along my thighs as she deliberately peeled off her tiny red dress. By the time she dropped it onto the floor beside my chair, any thoughts of seeing her as my long-lost younger sibling had been completely obliterated.

I gasped as she climbed into my lap and pressed her breasts into my face. I wanted to figure out a way to start a conversation about Wainwright, but it was hard to concentrate on anything other than the flesh dangling so tantalizingly close to my lips. When she leaned back, I stammered out the beginning of a half-assed pitch on behalf of the old man, but she pressed her index finger gently against my lips before I had a chance to say anything of substance. It seemed that our chat would have to wait until she finished with me.

Before I knew it, the music had stopped and she was asking me if I wanted another dance. I nodded and she kept right on going, all the way through the next song and straight into another after that. After that third one, I didn't think I'd be able to stand another three minutes of teasing, so I pulled away and politely declined a fourth. She dressed quickly and sat down next to me. "How much for those?" I asked, as I pulled out my wallet.

"Sixty, hon."

I pulled out three twenties and held them out toward her. As she reached for them, I pulled them back and held them against my chest. "Any chance we're ever gonna have that talk?"

She leaned in and pried the money from my grasp. After she slid it into her garter, she stared at me for a moment before asking, "How much money did he give you?"

"What?" I replied, unsure of what she was asking.

"Him... Wainwright... how much cash did he send?"

"Oh... uh, three grand," I told her, honestly.

"You have it on you?"

I shook my head. Again, I wasn't lying.

She pondered for a few seconds before she nodded and said, "OK."

"OK?"

"I'll meet you after I get outta here tonight. Same place I told you before. I'll be there at four."

"For real?"

She nodded and stood up. As she started to walk away, she turned back and said, "Just bring the cash."

I didn't say anything else.

Chapter Twenty

I was about two-thirds of the way through my breakfast when Jill arrived with two companions in tow. As they piled into my booth, I recognized the tall redhead that had answered the door at Jill's condo. I hadn't seen the other woman before, but it was pretty obvious that she was a stripper, too.

The sound of spoons clinking against coffee cups was drowned out by shouts and giggles, as the dancers' arrival injected a surge of energy into the sleepy restaurant. It seemed like everyone else in the place was marking the end of an adventure, trying to sober up and rationalize whatever damage they'd done to their bank accounts or their relationships before catching a few hours of sleep. Some were probably making plans to do it all over again the next day, while others would get on planes and head back to their real lives. Jill and her friends were in a different place. They had more money than they'd started with at the beginning of the night, and, having spent their evening indulging the fantasies of others, they looked ready to have some fun of their own.

Jill sat down next to me and her pals clambered into the bench across from us, falling all over each other as they went. "I think you already met my roommate, Lauren," Jill began, and as I reached out to shake the redhead's hand, she continued. "And this is our friend Cristiana, from Brazil."

"Nice to meet you," I said, as I extended my hand toward the Brazilian. She was drop-dead gorgeous, with short, blonde hair that framed a pair of brilliant green eyes that shone like emeralds set into the smooth, olive skin of her face. If she'd been seven or eight inches taller, she could easily have been a high-end runway model. Milan's loss was Vegas' gain.

"Hello!" she replied in a sing-song voice as she took my hand. Once everyone was settled, I tried to ask them if they wanted to order some food, but I wasn't able to get a word in edgewise. The women went right on with their conversation as if I wasn't there, even though they were talking about me. I was flattered to hear that I'd been deemed "cute" and "nice," but the whole experience was a bit overwhelming. Occasionally, they would address me as if to encourage me to join in, but each time they continued talking without waiting for my reply. They were going a mile a minute and I could barely follow the plot, let alone contribute.

Everything about the way that they were acting made no sense until it dawned on me that all three of them were blasted out of their minds on cocaine. I didn't know it for sure, but once the thought occurred to me, I would have been willing to wager on my diagnosis being correct. If you've ever spent time with people on blow, it's not hard to recognize the signs. It certainly explained the scene at my table better than any other theory that I could come up with.

Suddenly, Jill turned and grabbed me by both arms. "Hey! You wanna get outta here? We're going to a party! You wanna come? Let's get outta here!"

The torrent of conversation instantly dried up, and I glanced around the table and saw three beautiful, young faces anxiously awaiting my response. They seemed inexplicably keen for me to go with them. I'd like to believe that I was too attractive to resist, but I attributed their zeal for my company to the drugs and the money I'd mentioned. Cocaine has a way of infusing even the most insignificant desires with disproportionate earnestness.

I shoved the remnants of my breakfast toward the middle of the table and started to say something about getting the check, but before I had a chance to flag anyone down, Jill was dragging me out of the booth. Before she pulled me all the way to the door, I broke away and found my waitress taking orders at another table. Mumbling an apology, I handed her a twenty and hurried away to catch up with the girls on the sidewalk just outside.

They led me to a midnight-blue, new-looking BMW 3-Series sedan, which was considerably nicer than the Honda that was waiting for me back in the Keys. Lauren drove, Cristiana rode shotgun, and Jill and I sat in the back. The dancers had resumed their chatter, and I listened while they discussed strip club gossip and speculated about the guest list at the party. We'd only gone a couple of blocks, though, before Jill abandoned the conversation, turned to me and blurted out, "You got that cash, right?"

I shifted in my seat. "Well... I, uh... I don't actually have it any more..."

"What the fuck does that mean?" she demanded. "It was all bullshit? The money was all bullshit?"

"No, no... The money was real. No bullshit. But I, uh... I lost it. I'm really sorry."

"I don't understand. You 'lost it'? How?"

I pointed out the window toward the neon outlines of the casinos that lined the Strip, and laughed. "The usual way, I guess. Bad luck."

She shook her head. "You're a degenerate gambler. I can't believe he gave the money to a fucking degenerate gambler."

I interrupted her. "I don't know if I'd use the word 'degenerate...'"

"Dude, you just lost three grand that wasn't even yours. I'd say you qualify."

I paused, searching for an excuse, or at least a clever response, but I thought better of starting an argument. I simply said, "Fair enough," and hoped that she wouldn't kick me out of the car then and there.

"You gonna tell him about that when you see him?" I was relieved to see a hint of a smile creeping across her face as she asked the question.

I shrugged. "Don't know. Would the money have made a difference?"

"Hell yeah! Three grand would have paid my rent for six months."

"No... I mean, would it have made a difference between you and him?"

The smile faded from her face and she stared out the window in silence for a few moments before she replied. "Nah. Not really. Fuck it."

"Then I probably won't mention it."

"Maybe I'll tell him," she suggested with a mischievous grin.

"Perfect! If that's what it takes to get you to talk to him, right?"

"Don't hold your breath," she snorted.

We rode without saying anything else for five minutes or so, but one thing that she'd said had stayed with me, so I finally asked her about it. "Were you really gonna use that cash to pay your rent?"

She nodded. "Rent... car payments... whatever."

"Hmm."

"What?"

"You wouldn't have been tempted to throw it into a slot machine somewhere? Or whatever game you like to play..."

"I don't gamble."

"At all?"

"Never."

I couldn't get my head around the idea of living in Vegas without gambling. People generally didn't move to New Orleans to not eat, or to Nashville to not listen to music, but those were organic, fully-formed cities. I could think of other reasons to spend time in places like that. Vegas, on the other hand, is a mirage, a fabrication in the middle of the desert. If you took away the gambling, would anyone care if the whole thing just sunk back into the sand?

"Are you, uh, religious, or something? You don't believe in gambling?" I ventured.

"I don't believe in throwing money away," she replied. After a few seconds, she added, "I work too fucking hard for it."

Just then, the car pulled over to the curb. "Here we are!" Lauren announced. She and Cristiana seemed completely oblivious to our conversation in the back seat, which was just as well. It was awkward enough without trying to include them.

I followed them out of the car into a nondescript residential neighborhood. I think that we were somewhere east of the city, but I wasn't sufficiently familiar with the suburbs of Las Vegas to divine our precise location. The street was lined with modest, single-family houses, one of which was surrounded by parked cars. As we approached the front door, I heard the muffled sound of dance music emanating from within. The girls opened the door without knocking, and I followed them inside.

Chapter Twenty-One

Being at a house party reminded me of being in college, but this one was a good deal swankier than the ones I remembered. On any given night at an elite university, you can find the scions of the nation's wealthiest, most powerful families gathered in dingy basements, wading through a putrid swill of dirt, spilled beer and God-only-knows what else. Their entertainment consists of a loop of disco hits, '80's standards and whatever's currently popular, all blasted through outdated speakers at maximum volume. They drink the cheapest beer they can find and jump about until they puke, hook up, or get into a fight. On a good night, they do all three, but not always in the same order.

The gathering to which Jill had brought me was also in a cellar, but that was pretty much where the similarities between it and a typical college party ended. The vibe was completely different. The basement was much bigger than one might have guessed by looking at the size of the house above, and it was set up more like a nightclub than a frat house. It was dark, but once my eyes adjusted, I saw three plush couches and two small tables arranged along one wall. In the corner nearest the stairs, there was professional-grade DJ set-up, complete with a professional-looking DJ. The space in front of him was kept clear, presumably for use as a dance floor, and in the opposite corner a sleek bar was lined with top-shelf booze and a good variety of mixers. The biggest distinction, though, between the scene there and the ones I remembered from my younger days was the fact that the hosts, whoever they might have been, weren't trying to cram three hundred guests into a space built to hold sixty. A few people were dancing, and a few more lounging on the couches or just milling about, but they all seemed relaxed and comfortable. The volume of the music, while suitably loud for a festive occasion, was several notches below what I would have called oppressive.

If I'd been anywhere other than Vegas, walking into a place like that at four-thirty in the morning would have been bizarre, but out there it seemed normal, somehow. I couldn't tell if the party had been going all night or if it had only just kicked off. Strippers seemed well-represented, or at least that was the impression I got after a quick look around the room. I surmised that a fair number of them had just gotten off work and wouldn't go on the clock again until the following evening. Partying until morning and then sleeping the day away seemed like a reasonable approach for them.

As soon as we got downstairs, my companions fanned out and left me to navigate the festivities on my own. Lauren and Cristiana joined a group sitting on the couches, and Jill struck up a conversation with a pair of women near the DJ's table. I lingered at the base of the stairs for a few minutes, hoping that one of them would return and introduce me to at least one other person, but once it became apparent that they were ignoring me, I decided to explore. I wandered over to the bar and fixed myself a drink, and eventually found my way to a door that led to the back patio. There was an entirely different scene out there, with a handful of people sitting on lawn chairs and smoking cigarettes while two men and two women relaxed in a hot tub. There was a pool as well, but no one was swimming. The yard was landscaped such that the pool appeared to have been carved out of a dramatic rock formation, with the Jacuzzi set back into an intimate grotto. Submerged lights lent the water an eerie luminescence, while rays from floodlights hidden amongst the boulders reflected off of its placid surface. The whole thing gave the impression of having been very painstakingly designed and constructed.

I lit a cigarette and struck up a conversation with a pair of fellow smokers. It turned out that they were musicians. They were also waiters. Our chat was interesting, as it gave me a little taste of the crowd I'd stumbled into, although they confessed to not really knowing the hosts, either. According to them, there were quite a few aspiring rock stars in attendance, but none of them had progressed to the point where they were making enough money to quit their day jobs. They also vouched for the bona fides of the DJ, who was apparently a big deal in the underground scene and ready to make the leap to the bigger clubs. That made me feel a bit better about the fact that I didn't recognize any of the songs that he'd been playing, since I could attribute my unfamiliarity to his place on the bleeding edge of his genre. I tried to listen with an open mind, but his set only served to confirm the fact that electronic dance music is not my thing.

After my smoke, I headed back inside, promising my new friends that I would keep an eye out for their next gig. That was a bit insincere, but my hopes for their future success were genuine. Not only did they seem like a couple of very nice guys, but I thought that it would be cool to someday be able to tell people how I'd partied with them before they were famous.

Lauren and Cristiana were still parked on their couch, chatting with the crew they'd joined when we arrived. I didn't see Jill right away, but while I was at the bar pouring myself another drink, she appeared beside me and tapped me on the shoulder. "Hey," she greeted me. "I didn't see you around. Thought maybe you bailed..."

"No, no... I, uh, just went outside to smoke."

"Cool."

"Have you been out there? They've got a pool and a hot tub... and these rocks... it's pretty wild."

"Yeah, I've seen it."

"Pretty cool."

She nodded and we stood by the bar for a few awkward seconds before she spoke again. "Do you, uh... do you wanna go somewhere and talk?"

"Definitely. I'd love to talk." My thoughts were jumbled as I followed her across the empty dance floor toward the stairs. Talking to her was, of course, the whole point of the exercise, but I'd already given up hoping that it would happen. Nothing that she'd said in any of our brief exchanges had indicated any sort of willingness to discuss her father. I was shocked that she'd actually bothered to show up to meet me at the diner, but when I saw that she was with her friends and that they were coked up, I assumed that she'd just come for the cash that I'd dangled in front of her. Even though they still took me with them after I failed to deliver any money, I never got the sense that my inclusion was rooted in Jill's desire to continue our conversation. It felt more like they were just fucking with me somehow.

As we climbed out of the basement, I tried to compose my thoughts, at least to the point where I might be able to start a conversation, but the relentless electronic beats and flashing lights made it difficult to concentrate. I blinked as we emerged into the lamplight of main floor, and stuck close behind Jill as we snaked through a small crowd that had gathered in the foyer. She seemed to know where she was headed as we made our way past the kitchen and then down a long hallway. When we reached the end, she opened a door to our right, ushered me into a room, and closed it behind us.

Chapter Twenty-Two

"Whose place is this, anyhow?" I muttered as I looked around. The space was dominated by a king-sized bed, but otherwise empty save for a small nightstand next to the headboard and a leather armchair in the far corner. All of the furniture was jet black. A flat-screen TV hung directly across from the bed, the only thing that interrupted the barrenness of the bright white walls that surrounded us on all sides. The room's lone touch of color was supplied by the bedcovers, which looked like the inside of a blood orange. "It's cool that we're in here?" I asked, feeling a bit self-conscious about having stumbled into some stranger's bedroom.

Apparently not sharing my inhibitions, Jill hopped onto the bed and kicked off her shoes. "Two guys that Lauren knows," she said, in response to my first question. After a beat, she added, "They're gay. Does that bother you?"

"Not at all. I just feel a little weird about being in their bedroom."

"This is a guest room. And they don't care."

"You've met them?"

"Uh huh. A few times. They like to have parties."

"A lot of the girls here look like dancers," I ventured.

She shrugged. "Gay guys and rock stars... our kind of crowd."

I smiled and walked over to the armchair, but as soon as I sat down, she chided me. "I don't bite." She patted the spot on the bed next to her. "Over here, silly."

I hesitated for a moment, but did as I was bid, stepping out of my shoes before taking a seat. We sat silently for a few seconds, with our legs dangling over the side of the mattress, before she spoke again. "How well do you know him?"

"Your father? Honestly, not all that well. We met a few months ago."

"What did he tell you about me?"

"Just that he was worried about you."

"Did he tell you I was a dancer?"

I shook my head. "He didn't mention that."

She smiled. "So, you didn't think that you'd see quite so much of me, did you?"

I could feel my cheeks reddening, and I stared straight down when I answered. "No. Wasn't expecting that."

She repeated the question she'd asked in the car, after I'd told her that I'd gambled her money away. "You gonna tell him about it?"

I shrugged without taking my eyes off of the hardwood floor. She reached out and touched my chin, gently lifting my head until my eyes met hers. "Did you like what you saw?"

"Yes... of course..." I stammered. "I mean... you're a very beautiful woman."

I was still fumbling for a better answer when she pushed me over onto my back and, in one motion, swung her leg across and straddled me. Before I could react, she'd pulled her dress over her head and tossed it to the floor. She wasn't wearing anything underneath, not even the skimpy thong that she'd sported at the club.

I was feeling shocked, guilty and aroused all at once, but it seemed like the shock would win out. Lying there, staring up at her naked body, I found myself incapable of saying or doing anything. She leaned down and whispered some encouragement. "You're allowed to touch now."

I let my hands drift down the outside of her thighs until they got to her ass, gently stroking her smooth skin with the tips of my fingers as I went. I kept at it for a few minutes, not moving from beneath her, while she rested her head on my left shoulder. She seemed to enjoy it.

When she planted her hands beside me and pushed herself up so that her face hovered just above mine, I started to say something about maybe slowing down, but she cut me off by sticking her tongue into my mouth. While we kissed, I felt her hand unbuckling my belt. When our lips parted, she whispered in my ear again. "I wanna fuck you."

Those five words eradicated any lingering thoughts of restraint, and I grabbed her by her hips and threw her onto the bed beside me so that I could get my pants off. There was no foreplay. As soon as my trousers hit the floor, I was on top of her. And then she was on top of me. I wasn't going to last more than a few seconds with her bouncing on me like a wild animal, so I stopped her mid-ride, carried her to the chair and bent her over an armrest, reaching my hand around so my fingers slid between her legs and rubbed her there until her gasps sent me over the edge. I hoped that she'd felt the same intense release that I had.

Everyone wants to be good at sex. The faces and the noises that Jill made during our encounter made me feel like I was doing something right, but, having just seen that same blissful expression as a part of her strip club act, I couldn't help doubting whether she'd truly enjoyed it. I was also self-conscious about not having lasted longer with her. Our sex was certainly vigorous, but I'd be stretching it if I claimed that it lasted more than five minutes. As soon as it was over, I was already regretting not having taken my time.

As I stared at the ceiling and questioned my performance, I hoped that she'd be up for another round once I'd had a chance to catch my breath. When I saw her hop up and start to gather her clothes from the floor, I rolled over onto my stomach and propped myself up with my elbows. "Hey... what's your hurry?"

She stepped into her dress and pulled it over her hips, working her arms into the sleeves. "Let's get back to the party."

I reached out, took her wrist and playfully pulled her toward me. "I, uh... I hoped that we might hang out a little bit more..."

She withdrew her arm and bent down to pick up her shoes. "Why?"

The coldness that she managed to convey with that single syllable left no doubt that her interest in me, which had manifested itself so passionately only moments before, had completely dissipated. Confounded by her sudden change in demeanor, I sat up on the edge of the bed. "We never even got a chance to talk," I murmured.

"That was our talk. You can go back to Florida and tell Mr. Wainwright exactly what happened. Tell him everything."

"So, all of this..." I asked as I gestured toward the rumpled sheets on the bed, "all of this was just some crazy way of saying 'fuck you' to your father?"

She shrugged. "Call it whatever you want." After a second, she added, "You think you're the first goon that he's sent chasing after me?"

I tried to imagine the others who'd travelled that path, and I wondered if she'd given any of them, or all of them, the same treatment that she'd just given me. The idea stung a bit, but maybe not as much as it was meant to. I liked her, but it wasn't as if we'd developed any sort of deep, emotional bond, and I already understood that I hadn't gone to bed with a Vestal Virgin. I wasn't wounded as much as I was just confused by the bizarre chain of events that had kicked off once we'd found our way into that bedroom.

At that moment, it occurred to me that I was having a conversation with a fully-dressed woman with my dick hanging out, so I stood and retrieved my boxers, and then my khakis. As I buckled my belt, I started laughing out loud.

That seemed to irritate her. "That's right," she muttered. "It's all a big fucking joke, isn't it?"

I shook my head. "No... sorry... It's just that no one's ever called me a 'goon' before."

"If the shoe fits..."

Her disparaging characterization bothered me, so I piped up. "You know, I actually went to Princeton... studied philosophy..."

I couldn't tell if she was intrigued or put off by my revelation. Either way, I wasn't prepared for her next question. "So... what are you?"

"Huh?"

"People go to college so that they can be something, right? Like a doctor, or a scientist, or whatever... You say you're not a goon, so what are you?"

"You've been talking to my father, haven't you?" I muttered.

"What?"

"Nothing... Forget it. I'm, uh... I guess I'd say that I'm just looking for something interesting to do with my life."

"So, you work for my father?"

"For now, yeah."

"What do you do for him, other than chase me?"

I shrugged. "Whatever needs doing. He's... we're... working on building a church."

"Of course you are," she sneered. She paused, as if she expected me to defend the legitimacy of Wainwright's project. When I didn't, she went on, in a milder tone. "How did you wind up with him, anyway?"

"It's kind of a long story," I replied, pointing to the bed. She hesitated at first, but then we both sat down, and I proceeded to relate the entire history of my relationship with the old man. I told her everything, from that first encounter in Bob Baker's office and my ensuing trip to Miami, all the way through the sermon in the American Legion hall and the work that I'd been doing ever since. I may have omitted some details here and there, and I didn't say much about my family, but it was a pretty faithful account of my life since I'd gotten to Marathon. Jill listened to the whole story without interrupting even once.

Once I reached the end, I tried to gauge her thoughts, but her expression didn't give me much to go on. She sat and mulled over what she'd just heard, without comment or reaction, for several minutes until my curiosity finally got the better of my patience. "Well?" I prompted her.

"Well what?"

"What do you think?"

She looked down at the floor, and then up at the ceiling. I took her hand and tried to encourage her. "It's OK. Just tell me what you think. I'd really like to hear it."

She pulled her hand from mine, shifted in her seat, and exhaled before she pronounced her judgment. "I think that you should get your money back from Princeton because you're the biggest fucking idiot I've ever met."

That wasn't the first time that words to that effect had been tossed in my direction. On previous occasions, they'd come from friends or relations with Ivy League degrees who were troubled by my lack of professional ambition. My choices may have befuddled those people, but I was pretty sure that their disparagement of my intellectual capacity wasn't meant to be taken literally. In fact, I'd always assumed that they'd been trying to convey the opposite message. When my father called me an idiot, he was really telling me that I was too smart not to get with the program and be successful. It was just another tactic designed to get me off my ass.

Jill's assessment provoked an altogether different reaction, because I got the impression that she'd meant exactly what she'd said. It's quite jarring to be adjudged an idiot, in earnest, by someone you don't know. When that verdict is delivered by a person who covers herself in glitter and rubs her tits against strangers for a living, the impact is amplified to an uncomfortable degree.

As shocked as I was by Jill's response to my story, I didn't take offense, at least not at first. "Don't hold back," I joked. "I wanna know what you really think."

She didn't smile. "I'm sorry... but I mean it. He's using you for something and you don't see it."

"Look... I appreciate your concern, but I'm a big boy. I can take care of myself."

"I'm not so sure about that," she sighed.

I appreciated that she'd dropped the caustic tone, but I detected a whiff of pity in its place, and that was almost harder to stomach. "What, exactly, do you think he's using me for?" I asked, doing my best to make it clear that I was patronizing her.

She shrugged. "I have no idea. But if you don't see that..." Her voice trailed off.

If she was trying to get under my skin, it was working, and I shifted from patronizing to defensive. "Nope. I don't see it. But since you seem to know so much, maybe you could give me a clue."

She pursed her lips in an expression of disdain. "Because hidden pirate treasure is so fucking believable," she said in a soft voice.

Once again, I was caught off guard by her frankness. "Yeah. Of course. I mean, sure... I guess. But it seemed genuine enough... I mean, he showed it to me."

"And you checked it out? Or you just knew that it was real?"

I looked down at the floor, unable to answer for myself. Now that she'd raised the question, the whole thing seemed ridiculous. "I don't know," I blurted out. "It all made sense at the time." After another second, I added, "Besides, even if it was bullshit, I'm not sure I see the harm in it."

She rolled her eyes. "Let me make sure I get this straight. You went to Miami and collected thirty grand from this guy, and a week later you brought him a young girl.... Do I need to spell it out?"

"Yeah, maybe you do. You're not suggesting that we somehow... sold Liz, are you?"

"Not 'sold,' exactly. But my father has been in the business of arranging marriages for a long time. Usually between rich old men and pretty young girls... and the old men are always grateful enough to make a nice donation to his church."

I felt a chill as I thought not of Liz, but of the conversation in Wainwright's office where Wainwright had encouraged Peter to give me a free place to live. At the time, I'd noted how Wainwright made mention of the church's role in Peter's marriage, and of course I'd been struck by the age gap between Peter and his wife. In light of what I'd just heard, I wondered if I'd discovered another example of the sort of matchmaking that Jill was talking about.

Even with those thoughts swimming around my head, it seemed like a pretty big leap to go from doubting the provenance of a gold medallion straight to human trafficking. I composed myself and started to dismiss her allegations. "OK. You're right. The story about the treasure does seem pretty far-fetched, but I don't think that means..."

She cut me off. "It does. That's the one thing I am sure of."

I shifted in my seat on the bed. "I know that you don't think much of your father, but..."

"I know him. This is what he does."

"You said yourself that you didn't know what he was up to..."

She shook her head. "I don't know what he wants with you, but I'm telling you what happened to your friend. Some old man gave my father a lot of money, and you took her to him."

"What makes you so sure?"

Jill stood and started pacing back and forth along one side of the bed. She must have made four or five round trips before she finally stopped and, in a voice that barely registered above a whisper, said, "Because he tried to do it to me."

Completely unprepared for that revelation, I sat speechless while I tried to make sense of it. After a few minutes, I sputtered out a question. "But... I thought that you guys hadn't been in touch..."

"Not for years, now," she replied. "But we were. I lived with him for a while."

"He never told me that."

"That doesn't surprise me."

"What happened?"

She resumed pacing again, and I could see that she was struggling to hold herself together. Without breaking stride, she took a deep breath and started in on her story. "My whole life, it was just me and my mom. It was hard..." Her voice trailed off, as dormant memories of an impoverished childhood were re-awakened to inflict fresh pain on their bearer. She took a moment to gather herself before she went on. "It was just us. I never saw my father, never heard from him at all, until I was eighteen." She stopped pacing, sat back down, and continued. "About two months after I graduated from high school, he just showed up."

"Just like that? Out of the blue?"

"Yup. I came home one afternoon and there he was, sitting at the kitchen table."

"What did he say?"

"Everything you'd expect. There were lots of tears and talk about mistakes and regrets and how he never went a day without thinking about me... It went on for hours."

"What did your mom think?"

"She didn't wanna hear it." Jill stopped for a second and smiled. "She told him to go fuck himself."

"And you?"

I could see the tears welling up in her eyes, and she had trouble answering. "At first, yeah... I was pretty pissed off. I cried, and yelled, and asked him where he'd been when I needed him... and cried some more..."

She broke down completely at that point, so I put my arms around her and let her wail into my shoulder for a while. When it seemed like the worst of it had passed, I handed her a handkerchief from my pocket and watched her dry her eyes before she continued. "He begged me to give him a chance... asked me to come and stay with him for a while."

"And you said 'yes?'"

"I was eighteen," she replied. "I was eighteen and I was pissed at my mom. Pissed that we lived in a trailer park and fought all the time, and that I was waiting tables at Chili's... I guess I just wanted to hurt her." She said all of this while looking straight at the floor.

"So you went?"

"Uh huh. Off to Florida the next day."

"And then?"

"For a while... weeks... months... it was great. He had this big, old house. There was a beach. He didn't make me get a job, or pay rent. I felt like I won the lottery or somethin'...."

"And you guys got along?"

She nodded. "He seemed like he was really sorry for everything... like he was really trying to make things right. We got to know each other."

"That all sounds pretty good," I observed.

No sooner had those words passed my lips than I saw her countenance deflate. "It didn't last," she said, once again fighting to hold back her tears.

"What happened?"

"Well... you know how he is with religion, right?"

"Uh huh."

"It was great at first. I mean, my mom took me to church when I was a kid, but it was never very... deep. When I met him, he starts teaching me about the Bible and it's so... personal. For the first time in my life, I felt like it had something to do with me. I wanted to learn about Jesus." I nodded, and she went on. "But, after a few months, it turned weird."

"How?"

"He just started talking all the time about how God has a plan for each of us, and how he was special because God talked to him, and told him about His plans for certain people..."

"Definitely weird," I interjected.

She continued. "We always had people over at the house... just reading scriptures, talking, praying... 'Christian fellowship,' he always called it. He never seemed to care if I participated or not, but then he started pushing me to show up. There was one man that he really seemed to want me to spend time with..."

"An old man?" I guessed.

"He had to be in his '70's, at least. He had a little oxygen tank that he used to wheel around behind him."

"Good times," I joked.

Judging by the look she flashed me, it's safe to say that she didn't appreciate my attempt at levity. "He seemed like a nice guy. He always came as part of a group, in the beginning. My father asked me to look after him, help him out. I thought I was just being kind."

"But he had other ideas?"

"He started showing up more and more, and not just for group meetings. A lot of times it was just the three of us, and my father always pushed me to hang out with him. And then after he'd leave, we'd talk about surrendering to God, putting ourselves in His hands and letting Him guide us through our biggest decisions... like marriage. This went on for months before he finally spelled it out."

"He asked you to marry this guy?"

"Yup. Told me straight out that he'd had a revelation and that he was certain that God wanted me to marry him."

"What did you say?"

"Whaddya think? I said 'no.'"

"What happened then?"

She shrugged. "Nothing, really. More of the same. The guy kept coming to the house, and I kept hearing about how I should trust in the Lord..."

"That must have been hard for you."

"Not that hard... I mean, it was weird... and kinda annoying... but I figured he'd just give up, sooner or later. I wanted to give him a chance. I knew he was a very religious man and I was trying to respect that. I wanted him to keep being my father."

I felt myself growing angrier with Wainwright with each passing minute. It was one thing to know, in the abstract, that he had an estranged daughter, but it was quite another to watch her break down as she recalled their brief time together. At the very least, he should have told me the whole story before he sent me to find her.

Jill continued. "One night, the old guy came over, like usual, and we all prayed together. I was gonna go out, so after a while I slipped away and left them alone. But before I left the house, I overheard them..." She started sobbing again before she could finish.

I gave her a minute to collect herself before I encouraged her to go on. "About you?"

She blew her nose into my handkerchief. "Yes. The old man was complaining about things taking too long. My father promised that he could get me to marry him, but that it was going to be more expensive than what they had agreed. He said that it would cost fifty thousand."

"Wow," I muttered, unable to come up with anything more profound in the moment.

"I completely lost it," she continued. "Lost my shit and ran into the room, screaming at both of them. My father tried to calm me down... tried to say that I didn't understand, that it wasn't what I thought... but I left. I grabbed my stuff and left and I haven't seen him since."

I sat in silence for a couple of minutes, not sure of how I was supposed to respond to what I'd just heard. I'd never met anyone whose father had tried to sell them into marriage before. Without saying anything else, I got up and started putting on my shoes.

"Are you leaving?" Jill asked, with a trace of disappointment in her voice.

I turned to face her. "I owe you an apology... a very big apology. I hope you know that I would never have agreed to come here if I'd known any of this. I am so sorry for putting you through that."

"You didn't know."

"He should have told me. I can't believe he sent me to find you and didn't tell me why you'd left." I paused for a second, before adding. "He and I are going to have a long talk when I get back to Florida."

"Please don't."

"I have to. I can't let this go. Not after everything you just told me."

She sighed. "No one should waste any more breath on my relationship with him. It's over. Just leave it at that."

"You don't have to worry about it. It's between him and me."

"Fine... but can't you stay here, for now?"

I shook my head. "I'm sorry, but I gotta go."

She took me by the hand, and flashed me a hint of a smile. "Maybe," she said, as she nodded in the direction of the bed, "we can have a little more fun..."

I'd always been inclined to doubt the credibility of any story in which a guy turns down sex with a beautiful woman because he's not in the mood, but the events of that night demonstrated that such an outcome was in fact possible. After hearing that poor girl's story, the last thing that I wanted to do was have sex with her again. I pulled her toward me and embraced her. "I better go," I whispered.

"You need a ride?" she asked.

"I'll call a cab. Thanks, though."

"Wait," she commanded as she backed away, and I stood still as she snatched her purse from the floor and fished out a pen. Leaning over the nightstand, she jotted something on a scrap of paper before handing it to me. "My number... in case you ever want to call." I thanked her and gave her my number in return, and one last hug. "Be careful," she admonished me. "He's up to something."

"I can handle your father."

"He's a bad guy. Just remember that."

It seemed like the last thing on Earth that I needed to be reminded of.

Chapter Twenty-Three

I was back in Marathon for three days before I was able to bring myself to go and see Wainwright. I found it strange that he never reached out to me during that stretch. I would have thought that he'd have been curious to learn about my trip. Of course, since I'd found out about his family history, I imagined that he couldn't have been very optimistic about his chances of reconciling with Jill. I guessed that he didn't feel any pressing need to track me down just to get bad news more quickly.

That may have explained his lack of urgency, but it begged the question of why he'd bothered to send me to Vegas in the first place. It seemed like a strange thing to do, if he'd really known that there had never been any hope of getting his daughter back. I had other questions as well, after my talk with Jill. Had Wainwright really tried to sell his daughter to a sickly old geezer? What about Liz? And Peter and his wife, Barbara? The idea that I'd been working for a cut-rate version of Warren Jeffs nauseated me.

185

As disgusted as I was with Wainwright, I still felt ashamed about having had sex with his daughter. After three days of stewing, I still hadn't decided whether I was going to share that fact with him. If I was prepared to criticize him for not being honest with me, it seemed hypocritical to keep a thing like that under my hat. On the other hand, I'd been operating under his aegis for months. How could I tell him that I'd fucked his daughter without it coming across as some sort of cruel taunt? I debated whether the old man's sins justified a breach of loyalty on my part, but, of course, I had gone to bed with Jill before I'd learned about any of that. No matter how I tried to parse things, it was hard to find a way to feel good about what I'd done.

My emotions were complicated by the fact that I couldn't stop thinking about Jill. After she revealed how damaged she was, I felt like shit for sleeping with her. I hated the idea that she'd only seduced me because her father had scrambled her brain, and I regretted having inserted myself into a fraught relationship in which I had no proper place. Despite all of that, I found myself feeling more and more drawn to her with each day that passed. She was so different from the sorority girls and society heiresses that I'd grown up dating, and it wasn't just her looks. I'd met my share of attractive rich girls with issues, but Jill's blend of vulnerability and raw, self-destructive energy was unique, and intoxicating. I very much wanted to see her again so that I could talk to her on my own account rather than on behalf of her father. If I could have somehow had a fresh start with her, with everyone's cards on the table, I felt like we might have been able to build something between us. At the very least, I wanted to try.

I kept her phone number on the dresser in my bedroom and stared at it quite a bit those first three days back in the Keys, but there was no way that I could call her before I talked to Wainwright. Any conversation that Jill and I were going to have was going to have to address her father and my role alongside him. Besides, I'd promised her that I'd sort him out when I got back to Florida, and I didn't want to make myself into a liar. She seemed to have had enough of those in her life already.

All of these thoughts were bouncing around my head when I finally made my way to Grassy Key. As I pulled into Wainwright's driveway, I still hadn't settled on what I was going to say to him. I resolved to allow my instincts to guide me and to let the chips fall where they would.

He greeted me warmly as I entered, but he didn't say anything about Vegas. I acknowledged him, but only in the most minimal fashion, before heading straight down the hall to my room and shutting the door. Thinking that my reticence would goad him into following, I braced for a confrontation. I sat at my desk for almost an hour, imagining the various directions in which our encounter might have gone, before it dawned on me that he wasn't coming. Flabbergasted by his apparent disinterest and unable to wait any longer, I wandered back toward his office and stuck my head in the doorway.

I found him perched in his usual spot behind his desk, reading a newspaper and looking perfectly serene and untroubled. He glanced up when I peeked in. "Ah, Malcolm," he began, as he'd apparently anointed himself as the second person in the world entitled to address me by my given name. "I want to hear all about Las Vegas. Come in and tell me everything."

"I will," I replied as I stepped over the threshold, still not certain as to how much of "everything" I was prepared to share. After I closed the door, I turned to face him and waved at the chair. "Mind if I sit down?"

"Of course. Have a seat. Did you have a good trip?"

I sat, and tried to pick my words carefully before answering, "It was… interesting."

"Uh huh," he replied. "You managed to talk to Jill, then?"

I nodded. "We actually talked quite a bit."

His face broke into a broad smile. "That's great. I'm very glad to hear that. I didn't know if you'd be able to catch up with her." His smile faded. "Do you think she'll come and see me?"

"No. I, uh… I don't think she's gonna come."

"I don't mean today," he added. "But I was hoping that maybe she'd at least think about it. Did she say she'd think about it?"

I shook my head, and repeated my conclusion. "I don't think she's coming."

He sighed. "I can't say that I'm surprised, although I'd hoped that she might listen to you."

"Why me?" I asked. "I mean… why would she listen to me?"

He shrugged, and smiled again. "You're a very charming fellow, aren't you?" I didn't know how to respond to that, so I let it pass. After a few seconds, he went on. "So… what did she say when you talked to her?"

I hesitated, debating whether I should relate all of the details of my conversation with Jill and launch straight into an interrogation. I decided it was better to wait and see if he gave anything away, so I simply replied, "She told me some pretty crazy things."

His response surprised me. "Well... she lives a pretty crazy life, doesn't she?"

"What do you mean?"

"Taking her clothes off for all of those men," he scoffed. "It's no wonder she's a little... off."

I felt a surge of anger welling up within me, and I wanted to scream that maybe she wouldn't be doing what she was doing if her daddy hadn't fucked her up, but I held my tongue and asked a question instead. "You know what she does out there... for a living?"

He looked at me as if I were a fool. "Of course I know. I didn't think she was selling make-up at the mall."

"You might have told me about that before you sent me to meet her."

"I wanted you to keep an open mind."

I started to say something back to him, but thought better of it. "Whatever... but that's not what I was talking about."

"What, then? What kind of 'crazy' stuff did she tell you?"

It seemed that the old man was never going to reveal anything unless I challenged him, so I took a deep breath and dropped what I thought was the first of several bombshells. "She mentioned that she lived with you for a while."

"She did," he confirmed, in a very matter-of-fact way, "for about a year. She was just out of high school."

Disappointed not to have provoked more of a reaction, I tried turning the screw. "She also told me about an old man... the one with the oxygen tank."

"What about him?"

I remained unable to detect even the slightest indication that Wainwright was troubled by the tenor of our conversation. It was awkward to have to spell it all out, but that seemed to be the way he wanted to play it, so I obliged. "You tried to get her to marry him because he paid you to make it happen."

The old man let my words hang in the air as he spun his chair to the right and stared out the window. I studied his face, anxious to catch a glimpse of the crestfallen expression that I was certain was about to overtake his countenance. What I saw, though, looked nothing like remorse. If anything, he seemed to have a sort of wistful air about him when he murmured, "If she'd have listened, she'd own half the commercial real estate in Key Largo by now."

"What?"

Wainwright squared himself to his desktop again. "Mr. Johnston – that was his name, by the way – died... I think it was three... or maybe four, I can't remember... three or four years ago. If Jill had been his widow, she'd have been quite well off." He was as calm as ever as he told me of his acquaintance's demise.

The incongruence between the conversation that I'd expected to have and the one that I was actually having was mind-blowing. I thought that I was calling Wainwright out for trying to do something monstrous, but his response was to lament the fact that he hadn't been successful. I struggled to spit out another question. "You're... you don't feel... you're not... sorry... at all?" I stuttered.

"What should I be sorry for?" he asked, as if he truly had no idea what I was getting at.

"Man... it's your daughter... and you tried to push somebody onto her... like that...for money."

For the first time, I sensed a touch of defensiveness creeping into his voice. "I don't think that a father needs to apologize for trying to help his daughter into an advantageous marriage."

"Listen to yourself!" I admonished him. "She was just a kid. You could have given her a chance to find somebody... to fall in love."

"Isn't that romantic?" he sneered.

"It's the twenty-first century!" I shouted. "You should marry someone you love."

"For you, maybe," he shot back. "Maybe in the world you live in, that's all you need to worry about. But for the rest of us..."

I cut him off. "Bullshit! Don't try to turn this into some sort of class thing."

"Easy for you to say, when everyone that you know goes to college and does something with themselves, and whenever you're finally ready to settle down, you know that you'll have a bunch of nice, successful girls to choose from."

"This isn't about me."

He ignored me and went on. "Do you know where I found Jill?" He answered his own question before I could respond. "In a trailer park." He paused, as if to let that sink in, before continuing. "She was in trailer park, waiting tables at Bennigan's."

"I think it was Chili's," I interjected.

"Whichever. She'd barely graduated from high school. What kind of men, exactly, was she going to meet on her own?"

"That's not the point. It's her choice... it should have been her choice."

"It's exactly the point... and besides, she always had a choice. She had a choice and she made it and look where she is now... whoring herself out in Vegas."

"Take it easy!" I snapped.

He shook his head. "We have to call things what they are. It doesn't do anyone any good to bury our heads in the sand." I just stared at him. Before I could say anything, he went on. "I don't need you to tell me that I was a lousy father. I know that. I was never there for her when she was a kid, and whatever you think you know about me, you can never understand how much that haunts me, even now."

I nodded, and I could feel my outrage starting to ebb as, in that instant, his defiance was replaced by a sort of melancholic vulnerability. The moment proved fleeting, though, and when he spoke again, he veered away from contrition and back toward justification. "I should have done more for her. I know that. But if you're asking me to apologize for trying to find her a better life... for trying to keep her from the path that she's on now... that's never going to happen."

I had to hand it to the old guy for somehow managing to make me feel like I was the asshole in the room. I guess I hadn't appreciated quite how hard it would be to take a shot at his parenting, no matter how deserving of opprobrium he might have seemed. When he sat across from me and told me that he'd only ever wanted to help Jill, I almost believed him, and I felt a growing sense of self-doubt about having appointed myself as his judge. I had to remind myself that this man had tried to sell his own daughter, and that whatever discomfort our conversation was causing him paled in comparison to the pain that he'd inflicted on her.

And Jill wasn't the end of the story. I wanted to discuss the other girls as well, in the hope that shifting the focus away from his immediate family would make him more willing to confess his sins. "How's Liz?" I asked, trying to sound as casual as I could.

For a passing moment, he seemed taken aback, but he composed himself in an instant and responded in his usual assured manner.

"She's doing well. I had a letter from her not long ago." He paused before going on. "Why do you ask? Have you heard from her?" As good as he was at masking his anxiety, I was pretty sure that the idea of me being in touch with Liz was making him uneasy.

I had half a mind to lie and tell him that I'd talked to her, just to see how he reacted, but I didn't. "Nope... haven't talked to her since I gave her that lift to Georgia... just curious is all."

"Well, I'll certainly tell her that you asked about her. She'll appreciate that, I'm sure."

I ignored his attempt to brush me off and continued. "I was wondering... about Liz... if she was married..."

He nodded. "She is. Happily, it seems."

"To an older fellow?"

Given the direction of our conversation, Wainwright had to have understood the point that I was trying to make, but he nevertheless affected an air of puzzled innocence while he pretended to ponder my question. "He's younger than I am," he finally responded.

"But older than she is?" I guessed.

"He's in his early fifties, I think. Nothing wrong with that, is there?"

That was a loaded question if ever there was one, but I ignored it. "At least he's younger than our friend Peter, right?"

"What do you mean by that?"

I shrugged. "I'm just sayin'... I met Peter's wife... Barbara, right? I met her and she was quite a bit younger than him... like, forty years younger..."

Wainwright rolled his eyes. "If you've got something you want to ask me, you can just ask me, you know."

"Fine," I shot back. "I'm wondering if you're in the business of arranging marriages."

"Not sure that 'arranging' is exactly the word I'd use…"

"But you're involved?"

He started laughing. "It's kind of part of my job."

I glared across the desk at him. "I don't think it's funny."

Instantly, the smile left his face and he adopted a grave expression. "No. Marriage is one of the biggest decisions that a person, any person, has to make in their lives. People often look to their pastor for guidance, and I've always done my best to give them the best counsel that I could."

"But, it's not right… putting all of these young women with these old men…"

He interrupted me. "I've married a lot of couples. Sometimes they're the same age, sometimes they're not. Age means nothing. Besides, I've never "put" anybody into a marriage that didn't want to be there. I offer my advice and people are free to take it or leave it." After a second, he added. "Jill didn't get married, did she?"

I shook my head. "If you're saying that these girls wanted to marry these old men…"

The preacher cut me off again. "Like I said, not everyone has the luxury of living in a fairy-tale. There are lots of reasons to get married…"

"Money?" I interjected.

He nodded. "Sure, sometimes…"

"No. I mean money for you. The old guys pay you, right? To set them up with younger women? That's the deal, isn't it?"

For the first time that morning, one of my arrows seemed to hit home, and I could hear the indignation dripping from his words when he answered. "That is not the deal. Not at all."

I pressed my point. "So these guys never gave you any money? Never made a donation to the church?"

He shook his head. "Donations are a different question. If you're asking if anyone that I've ever married in the church has ever made a contribution, then I'm sure the answer is 'yes.'"

"Of course they have," I muttered.

"I don't like what you're implying."

"If the shoe fits..."

We sat in awkward silence for a few moments, until the old man posed a question. "You ever give money to a politician?"

"Nope."

"How about your father? I bet he's made some campaign contributions, hasn't he?"

I shrugged. "I guess. Probably."

"But he's not in jail for bribing a public official, is he?"

I understood the point that he was trying to make, but I couldn't quite believe what I was hearing. I stared at him, incredulous, for a few seconds before I blurted out, "I can't believe I'm having this fucking conversation."

He ignored me and ploughed ahead. "In some ways, the church is a lot like a political campaign. People support us because they believe in our goals and our philosophy. They think that their lives will improve if we're successful in our mission. But there are no guarantees when it comes to individual requests. God doesn't work that way. Not all prayers are answered, you know. Everyone understands that."

I stood up. "Here's a piece of advice," I began. "If you're trying to convince somebody that you've got integrity, you might want to avoid comparing yourself to a congressman." I started walking toward the door.

He chuckled, as if we'd just shared a joke. I turned back toward him and shot him an icy glare. "I'm leaving," I announced, before continuing on my way.

"Will you be around later? There are a couple of things that I wanted to…"

I cut him off as I reached the doorway. "I'm not sure I'll be back at all. Ever." I paused at the threshold to wait for his reaction.

The smile left his face and his eyes narrowed as he stared hard at me for several seconds. Finally, he just shrugged his shoulders and simply said, "Suit yourself." With that, he snatched his newspaper from his desk and went back to his reading. I hesitated for a moment to see if anything else was coming before turning on my heel and walking out.

Chapter Twenty-Four

I started packing as soon as I got back to the house. In my mind, I was done with Wainwright, and my first instinct was to clear out of the accommodations that he'd arranged for me. Leaving under my own steam seemed more dignified than getting kicked to the curb by the old man.

As I went through the place trying to round up my small collection of stuff, I found myself getting increasingly worked up over the idea of returning to my parents with my tail between my legs, trying to explain yet another half-assed, failed adventure. There wouldn't have been any point in even trying to describe my experiences with Wainwright to my father. No matter what I told him, all he'd hear were the bits that reinforced his view of me as a lazy, impractical quitter. Frankly, it was getting harder and harder to come up with arguments as to why he should see me in any other light.

Of course, by then I'd learned that the idea of having an argument, or even just an adult conversation, with my father about my life was a pipe dream. I knew that he wouldn't actually tell me what he thought; I figured that he wouldn't say much of anything at all when I told him about my stay in Marathon. I was sure that he'd convey his feelings indirectly, like he always did: a dismissive shake of his head here, a smirk there, maybe the occasional condescending tone embedded in an otherwise innocuous phrase. He had an amazing ability to make me feel like shit even when we just talked about the weather.

After about forty-five minutes, I realized that I wasn't packing any more. I was just pacing from room to room, envisioning various hypothetical interactions with my parents, none of which were particularly pleasant. In an effort to break the cycle, I made my way to the kitchen, grabbed a beer, and retreated to the couch.

As I sat and mindlessly flipped through the channels on the television, I began to talk myself out of an immediate departure from Marathon. As galling as the idea of Wainwright evicting me might have seemed, it wasn't half as exasperating as the thought of slinking back to my parents' place. Maybe that outcome was inevitable, but it occurred to me that I didn't need to be the one to speed up the timeline. For the moment, I still had a perfectly nice free house. If they'd have thrown me out, it would have been a different story, but until that happened, I was happy to sit tight.

As I pondered all that, I also realized that returning to New York wasn't necessarily inevitable. I'd only have to head home if I couldn't think of anywhere else to go. Just because Wainwright was no longer offering an alternative didn't mean that I wouldn't be able to come up with another. After all, I'd been in Marathon for months, and I thought about trying to find something new down there. I even considered giving Bob Baker a call.

Even if Marathon didn't work out, there were other places. I had classmates all over the place. I could always get in touch with some of them and arrange some visits. I'd been meaning to get out to California, anyway. Maybe the Silicon Valley guys would appreciate my talents more than the Wall Street set had. A fresh start out West seemed just the thing for me.

I got kind of excited by the vague ideas swirling around my head, but I didn't actually bother to do anything about any of them. I didn't think about specific places where I might have moved, at least not in any kind of practical way, and I didn't reach out to any of my friends. I didn't even call Bob Baker. I was so keen to avoid my parents that I went through the exercise of creating the illusion of ambition, but it was nothing like ambition that kept me from moving out of that house. It was spite, pure and simple. I was pissed off at Wainwright for queering our arrangement, so I decided to squat in his friend's house for as long as I could.

I say that it was spite that kept me there, but I suppose that I was also clinging to the hope that Wainwright and I might reconcile. Despite everything, I still harbored some affection for the old man at that point. He'd shown more interest in me than my own father had in years, and there was something about him that drew me toward him. Deep down, I wanted him to explain everything away so that things could go back to the way they'd been before my trip to Vegas.

I spent the rest of that day, as well as the next two, more or less rooted to the couch, waiting for Wainwright, or Peter and Barbara, to show up and tell me to get lost. I understood perfectly well that it was time to figure out the next step and move on, but it was like I couldn't bring myself to do it until someone compelled me. I needed somebody to show up and kick me out of that house.

No one ever did. That shocked me at the time, and I speculated quite a bit as to why things went down the way they did. Maybe, I thought, Wainwright hadn't understood when I'd told him that I was leaving, or maybe he hadn't believed me. I supposed that he could have been hoping that I would change my mind, and that he was just giving me space so that I could reconsider and find my way back into the fold in my own time. I figured that the most likely explanation was that the old man didn't think about my living arrangements at all. It wasn't his house, and I doubted whether the selfish prick would have spared a thought for Peter and Barbara and the rental income that they were forfeiting by putting me up at his behest.

After barely moving for three days, I could feel myself starting to go stir crazy. I did a couple of loops around the city's par-three public golf course the next day, and I went swimming at Sombrero Beach the morning after that. Both activities reminded me of everything that was great about living in the Keys, but it was hard to enjoy them. As pleasant as it was to lie in the sand, I knew that I couldn't make a life out of it. Sooner rather than later, I was going to have to find something else to do, and it was clear that I wasn't going to rest easy until I came up with an idea.

By the time I got back to the house, I was almost craving a visit from Wainwright. If only he would have shown up and told me to hit the road, I could have gotten on with things. It was just hard to jump back into the real world if no one was pushing me.

That explains the strange thrill that I felt when my afternoon lounging was interrupted by a loud knock at my front door. I set the remote down on the coffee table, and stood up and brushed the crumbs from my snack of potato chips and pretzels off of my chest. I suppose that I was hoping not to look like a bum when I got evicted, but that ship had sailed when I'd decided to pair a Red Stripe Beer t-shirt with some old lacrosse shorts. Accepting the fact that my look didn't radiate dignity, but at the very least no longer covered in salty remnants, I strode to the door.

At that moment, I was one-hundred percent certain that I'd find either Wainwright or my landlords waiting on my front step when I answered the knock. Even if I hadn't been expecting one of them to come and throw me out, the simple truth was that there weren't many other people in Marathon that were likely to show up at my house. Beyond those three, I'm not sure that anyone else even knew I was living there.

I took one last deep breath before I turned the knob and threw open the door, fully expecting to get my marching orders. My mind, which had already wandered into thinking about next steps, took a moment to process the reality that the person I found looking back at me was not one I'd been expecting. I stood dumbfounded in the doorway and stared until I was able to sputter a feeble greeting, which was really more of a question. "Jill?" was the only word that I could manage to say.

Chapter Twenty-Five

As soon as I'd gotten that one word out, Jill flew across the threshold and into my arms. "I had to see you again," she began, holding me tight around my torso. "It's OK that I came, isn't it?"

"Yes! Yes! Of course! I'm so glad you're here," I responded, so emphatically that I was more or less yelling.

"You never called me," she whispered.

I pulled back from her embrace, keeping my hands on her shoulders at arm's length. "I wanted to... I was going to... it's just..." I paused, my head swimming, still not recovered from the shock of finding Wainwright's daughter on my doorstep. After a moment, I found a bit of composure and finished my thought. "I wanted to sort things out with your father before we talked."

She frowned. "I told you not to bother... to forget about him."

I shook my head. "I couldn't leave it like that."

"So you talked to him?" she asked, trying to affect an air of indifference. When I nodded, she prompted me. "And? What did he say?"

I hesitated for a second before I answered. "I think I know everything I need to know about him now." I didn't want to spoil our reunion with any more talk of Wainwright, so before she had a chance to question my cryptic pronouncement, I added, "Let me take this for you," as I released my grip on her and reached out to grab the oversized red suitcase that she'd left in the doorway.

I dragged her bag into my living room and shut the front door behind me. I'm pretty sure we didn't open it again for four days. Jill and I withdrew into our own, self-contained universe, and it was fantastic. We talked each other's ears off, like old friends who hadn't gotten together for twenty years. I was anxious to learn all I could about her, and to share everything that she might have wanted to know about me.

In the end, we wound up talking more about me than her. At bottom, I've always been a self-centered person, and when I have license to talk about myself... well, let's just say that you don't need to drag the words out of me. Jill was a bit more reticent, which I suppose wasn't all that surprising, given the nature of her experiences. Even so, I felt like I got a pretty good sense of her life's story. After she stormed out of Wainwright's house all those years ago, she'd wound up back with her mother in Georgia. She hadn't been there long when she met a guy and moved to Miami with him. That fell apart pretty quickly, though, and the sudden need to start paying rent on her own place was what led her to make her first foray into dancing. She bounced from relationship to relationship and place to place, with stops in Tampa, Chicago and L.A. before she got to Vegas. It sounded like she drifted in and out of dancing, as circumstances dictated, but she always seemed to find her way back into the clubs when she needed to support herself.

I was genuinely interested in her story, but I didn't find any of it particularly surprising. It included all of the elements that our pop-culture stereotype of strippers would have led me to expect: a disadvantaged socio-economic starting position, a broken home, a fractured bond with her father, and a string of failed relationships with a series of less-than-ideal suitors. Her roster of ex-boyfriends could have come straight from a Hollywood list of stock deadbeat characters: there was the cocky, athletic muscle guy, the shady club promoter/part-time drug dealer, and the older, married sugar-daddy. When writers invent backstories for exotic dancers, they usually end up with something that sounds a lot like the one I heard from Jill. Maybe that should have aroused my suspicions, but I didn't think anything of it. Everything I heard was exactly what I would have expected to hear, and I never gave it a second thought.

The substance of Jill's biography may not have thrown me off, but the way she told it sure did. I found her to be remarkably articulate, to the point that I found it harder and harder to believe that I was talking to a stripper who had barely finished high school. I hadn't picked up on that when we'd met in Vegas, but I guess we hadn't really talked all that much out there. Over a couple of days' worth of conversations, though, the signs were unmissable. She had an expansive vocabulary, her grammar was consistent and proper, and she made references that I wouldn't have expected from someone who hadn't been to college. More telling than all that, though, was that she demonstrated the quickness of thought that I've come to see as the most reliable signal of intelligence. It's hard to explain, precisely, how that manifested itself. I just feel like I can sense whether I'm talking to a bright person or a dim person, and my conversations with Jill emphatically demonstrated that she was the former and not the latter.

The incongruity between her seemingly well-educated manner and the story that came with it only increased her appeal to me. I already knew that Jill was beautiful; once I figured out that she was smart, I felt like I'd won the lottery. The deepest thought I had on the subject was to lament the unfairness of the world. If Jill had been born into a family like mine, and if she'd had the opportunity to attend the sorts of schools that I had, who's to say that there would have been any limits on what she might have achieved?

Of course, my ability to think critically about anything at all was significantly diminished by the sheer volume of sex in which Jill and I indulged over the course of those few days. She had only been at my place for a couple of hours before it kicked off. Once again, she initiated things, and I was a bit tentative at first, but after that it was as if the floodgates had been thrown open. It was like living on the set of a porno movie that never ended. I think we used every piece of furniture in the place: my bed, of course, but also the shower, the bathroom sink, the kitchen counter, the dining room table... pretty much anything in that house that could support her weight became a prop in our un-filmed skin flick.

Before I met Jill, I'd always considered myself to be a sexually adventurous person, but a few days with her demonstrated how vanilla my previous experiences had actually been. Very few of the other women I'd slept with were anywhere near as comfortable with their bodies as she was. Most of them insisted on doing the deed with the lights out, and they were hesitant about trying new positions and letting loose. Jill had clearly found a way past those sorts of inhibitions, if she'd ever experienced them at all.

Whatever misgivings I'd had about my performance in Vegas were wiped away, and then some, by our Marathon escapades. My personal favorite was turning the back yard hammock into a sex swing in the middle of the night. I loved how I could just stand still and pull her out of midair and onto me, without having to hold her up. It felt like we were fucking in outer space. The darkness protected us from prying eyes, but Jill got so loud that I was sure that my neighbors were going to call the cops. Luckily, they embraced the *laissez-faire* spirit of the Keys and let us do our thing without complaint.

That was the way we lived for four whole glorious days: deep, fascinating conversations bracketed by raw, dirty sex, an endless parade of stimulation, both physical and mental. My euphoria reached its apex on the third day, after a particularly vigorous session in my bedroom. After we finished, I headed out to the back patio for a cigarette, which turned into three cigarettes, as the warm air and gentle breeze combined with my post-coital bliss to render me immobile for about twenty minutes. When I finally peeled myself out of my lawn chair and made my way back into the house, I found Jill in the living room, wearing my bathrobe and standing in front of the small bookcase that stood against the room's east wall. She was thumbing through one of the volumes, and without looking up, she asked, "Are these yours?"

"Nope. I didn't bring any of my books down here. Those were my grandfather's." They were pretty much the only things I'd taken from his house when I moved out. The thought of Burt trashing them to make way for his sixty-inch TV had turned my stomach to the point that I actually took the trouble to box them up and bring them along to my new digs.

"Some really good books here..." she murmured.

"Uh huh," I replied. I certainly didn't disagree with that assessment, but I was surprised to hear it from her. My grandfather's collection veered heavily toward non-fiction, mostly Greek and Roman history, and what novels there were all could have been fairly described as "classics." If I'd have been forced to pick a word to describe his literary tastes, "heavy" would have been the one that came to mind. I didn't think that there was much on that shelf that would have appealed to a young woman. I'm guessing that even my grandfather didn't stick his nose into Caesar's *Commentaries* all that often.

Jill sure seemed intrigued by whatever she was holding, so I took a peek over her shoulder. My heart leapt when I recognized the first page of Robert Penn Warren's *All the King's Men*. "That's my favorite book!" I blurted out.

She angled her head back and looked up at me. "Mine too."

"Really?" I shot back, without much of an attempt to conceal my incredulity.

"Don't act so surprised," she replied, admonishing me with a wounded look. "It's not like I'm illiterate."

"No... I didn't, uh... that's not what I meant..."

She smiled. "It's OK. You didn't think a stripper would read books like this, did you?"

"I'm sorry. I shouldn't have assumed..."

"I'm just fucking with you," she laughed.

"So... you haven't read *All the King's Men?*"

"I actually have. And it's great."

"Good for you," I replied, realizing as soon as I said it that it must have sounded patronizing. Thankfully, she let me off the hook and we started talking about the novel. We spent two hours discussing it, and other books and movies. As with most of our conversations those days, that one eventually transitioned into sex, right there on the living room couch. After we finished, as I reclined with her head resting in the crook of my elbow, I was pretty sure that I was falling in love with Jill Wainwright.

Chapter Twenty-Six

I'm not sure we would have ever left that house again if we hadn't run out of food. As much as I wanted to keep living in our little, exclusive world, I had to accept the fact that we wouldn't be able to sustain ourselves forever on half a box of Frosted Flakes. We didn't even have any milk left to pour over them.

Jill seemed enthusiastic when I proposed that we venture out to lunch before making a stop at Publix to re-stock our larder. We'd been so checked out from reality that the idea of putting on proper clothes and running mundane errands seemed like a grand adventure. When we walked out to the car, with me in my golf shirt and Jill in a cotton sundress, we were almost giddy.

I took her to a seafood joint on the water, which was a pretty normal set-up down there; given the geography of the Keys, it's probably harder to find a place that's not near the ocean. She was chatty on the drive over, but once we got to the restaurant, our conversation dried up. At first, I attributed her silence to a desire to look without distraction on the blue sea stretching out endlessly under a cloudless sky, a sight which I imagined would have seemed quite striking to someone who'd just arrived from the landlocked desert wastes. After we ordered a couple of beers, I tried to rekindle our banter, but I couldn't get any traction. She brushed two or three of my forays aside with one-word answers, staring out at the ocean all the while.

After our waiter delivered our drinks, I reached across the table and stroked her cheek with the back of my hand. "Hey," I began. "A penny for your thoughts?"

She turned her eyes toward me and cracked a smile. "That's a nicer proposition than I'm used to hearing." She ran her finger back and forth along the rim of her glass. "Guys usually offer me more than a penny, but it's not my thoughts they're interested in."

I lowered my hand to the table and laid it on top of hers. "You don't have to worry about that anymore."

She flashed another smile, but I could tell that it was forced. I winced when I realized that I was probably not the first guy who had promised to take care of her, and how infantilizing that must have felt. After an awkward pause, I went on. "My offer is genuine. Tell me what's on your mind."

Jill drew her hand back from mine, took a sip of her beer, and fidgeted in her chair before answering. "I don't know... I'm just... just thinking about my father is all..."

I interrupted her. "Forget about him. He doesn't matter. We'll go somewhere, away from here, and we won't ever need to worry about him again."

"He's up to something," she murmured.

"I'm sure he is. And I don't want any part of it. That's why we need to..."

She cut me off. "He'll get away with it. He always gets away with it."

I shrugged. "Not our problem."

I had barely gotten those words out when she slammed her hand down onto the table top and exclaimed, "Fuck him!" in a voice loud enough to turn the heads of an elderly couple eating lunch three tables away.

I flinched, stunned by her outburst, before trying to respond. "I know it sucks, but I'm not sure that there's anything that you and I can do about it."

She shook her head, still animated with anger. "Why the fuck does he always get to win? He runs his bullshit scams, and he doesn't care who gets hurt, and he always gets away with it."

I leaned back in my chair and spoke softly, trying to calm her down. "Look... we don't even know what he's up to..."

"Exactly. We don't know anything. Don't you wanna find out?"

I shook my head. "Not particularly."

When I looked at her face, I saw the same look of disdain that she'd given me in Vegas when I'd first told her of my involvement with her father. "How long did you say that you've been working with him?" she asked.

"A few months."

She shook her head. "For all you know, you're knee-deep in whatever he's got going. If I were you, I'd want to know what I'd gotten myself into."

"I'm not worried. I haven't done anything."

"Of course you haven't," she replied, smirking.

"I'm serious."

"Uh huh." She eyeballed me for a few seconds before going on. "So, he just went out of his way to find you, gave you a bunch of cash, gave you a place to live... I guess he did all that because he likes your looks?"

"I've been told that I'm easy on the eyes."

She ignored my attempt at humor. "My father is not a charitable man. If he gave you anything, it's because he expected something in return. I guarantee it."

I shrugged. "I don't know what to tell you. I didn't give him any money. I haven't done anything out of the ordinary..."

She interrupted me. "That's the trick. You may have helped him somehow without even knowing it."

I started to laugh. "Well, then he overpaid for my services, because nothing I did for him could have been worth all that much." I stopped laughing, reached for her hand again and said, "It's OK. Trust me."

We sat silently, her hand resting in mine, for about thirty seconds before she pulled away. She snatched her beer from the table and leaned back in her chair. After she took a sip, I heard her mumble, "You don't know him," as she stared at the miniature waves slapping against a nearby pier.

I was starting to feel some exasperation at Jill's unwillingness to move on, but I was mindful of her sensitivity when it came to her father, and I was determined not to show my impatience. I decided to try a different approach. "Even if we wanted to," I began, "I can't see how we'd figure out what he was up to. I mean, last time I talked to him, we didn't part on the friendliest of terms. I don't think I can just drop in and ask."

"We'll go through his papers and figure it out," Jill countered, so quickly that I could only assume that she'd already given the question some thought.

"I've been through his papers. Haven't found anything yet." After a second, I added, "Sorry to disappoint you," in the hope that she'd drop it before the waiter delivered our grilled fish.

I clung to that hope for a few seconds while she stared back at me, but it dissipated as soon as she opened her mouth. Rather than a tone of reluctant acceptance, I heard only incredulity. "You've seen *all* of his papers?"

I nodded. "Uh huh. That's what I've been doing over there for the last few months. He wanted me to help him get organized, so I've been going through his stuff, sorting it out, getting it onto a computer..."

"I can't believe he showed you everything."

"He did. I've been in his office dozens of times and..." My voice trailed off before I could finish my sentence.

I must have gotten lost in my own thoughts, because I remember being jarred back into the moment when I heard Jill's voice. "And?" she prompted me.

I took a deep breath and exhaled. "Actually... there's this one small file cabinet in the corner of his office..." I held my hand out, about four feet above the floor. "It's about this tall... three drawers. He always keeps it locked and I'm not sure what's in there."

"That's it!" she announced. "We need to get into those files." The thought seemed to infuse her with a fresh supply of energy.

I held up my hand. "Whoa... slow down for a second. It's not like we can just walk in there and..."

She blew right through my attempt to express reservations. "We need to see those files," she repeated, with her tone leaving no room to doubt her resolve.

"OK... but just how are we gonna do that? Like I said, that cabinet is always locked."

"Any idea where he might keep the key?"

I shrugged. "I think it's in his desk drawer, but I'm not a hundred percent..."

"Perfect. That should be easy."

"How do you figure?" I asked. "We can't just pull it out of his desk while he's sitting there, can we?"

She looked at me as if I were ten moves behind her, which I suppose I was. "We'll get him to leave for a while and we'll go in there while he's out." She presented this in such a simple and matter-of-fact way that I found myself embarrassed over having raised the question in the first place.

"How? He pretty much never leaves the house, except for Sunday mornings, and that wouldn't leave us a whole lotta time..."

"There's one thing that he'll definitely leave the house for," Jill said in a calm voice.

"What's that?" I asked.

"Me," she replied.

I started to stutter out some more misgivings, but she cut me off. "He's gone through a ton of trouble trying to track me down, hasn't he?" I nodded, and she went on. "You really think he'll say 'no' if I call him and tell him to come and meet me somewhere?"

I couldn't argue that point with her. Based on everything he'd told me, I was sure that Wainwright wouldn't turn down a chance to see his daughter. Even so, I wasn't thrilled about the idea of sneaking into his house while he was out, and I said as much to Jill.

She was unimpressed with my lack of gumption. "What are you worried about? You think he'll call the cops on you?"

"Uh, yeah. I don't particularly want to go to jail."

"You won't get caught. And even if you did, he's not gonna call the cops on you. Trust me, the last thing that John Wainwright wants to do is get the police involved in his affairs."

I took a pull from my beer. "Easy for you to say. You're not the one that's gonna break into his house."

"You won't get caught," she repeated. "I'll meet him somewhere out of town. If we start for home earlier than planned, I'll just text you. You'll have plenty of time to get outta there before he gets back."

At that moment, our waiter arrived with the entrées. I clammed up until he'd set them down and walked away. Once we were alone again, I made one last half-hearted objection. "I don't know," I said as I prepared a bite of fish with my fork. "I just don't want to get involved."

"You're already involved," she shot back as she tucked into her lunch, "whether you like it or not."

I nodded. I hadn't intended anything by the gesture, but Jill apparently took it to signify my acquiescence to her proposal. She immediately launched into specifics. She wanted to do it the very next day, and she was thinking about Islamorada or Key Largo as potential spots to which she could lure her father. Her ideas and questions came at me so quickly that I barely had time to get a word in. Maybe she should coax the old man down to Key West, or all the way up to

Miami? Should we wait a few days so that we could get our plans in order?

I spent our entire meal trying to figure out a way to let her know that I wasn't on board, but every time I came up with words to that effect, they disintegrated when I tried to move them into my throat. Whenever I caught a look into her eyes, I saw how earnest she was in her desire to get back at her father. The further that she went in spooling out the details of her scheme, the harder it became to stomach the idea of pulling the rug out from under her. Eventually, I just decided to play along. I told myself that if this half-assed plan would bring her some closure with the old man, it would be worth it. I knew that she'd been through a lot. I guess I just hoped that I would make her happy if I helped her out.

Besides, I didn't think I'd actually find anything. I had every expectation of telling Jill that the files were full of mundane church records, and then forgetting about the whole thing. It seemed a small price to pay to give her some peace of mind before I whisked her away to wherever we were headed next.

Chapter Twenty-Seven

We waited a few days before setting our plan into motion, but I'm not sure that it benefited from the extra time spent on its development. It was so simple, really, that we didn't wind up adding much to what we'd discussed over lunch. More than once, I considered calling the whole thing off, but Jill managed to suppress my cautionary instincts with regular doses of physical intimacy. It was hard to disappoint anyone who was so committed to making me feel good.

I raised only two practical questions about the break-in, neither of which seemed to trouble my partner. First, since our entire operation was contingent on Jill calling her father and setting up a meeting, it occurred to me that Wainwright not having a phone might have been a problem. When I raised this to Jill, she once again looked at me like I was an idiot and reminded me that it was 2012. She assured me that the old man did indeed have a phone, and that she knew how to contact him. I related the fact that I'd been unable to get a number out of him in all the months that I'd known him, and that more than once he'd cited his aversion to phones as a reason for never having called me. This provoked nothing more than a laugh. I pressed the question a bit further, but once Jill promised to share his phone number with me, there wasn't much else to say about it. Apparently, calling Wainwright wasn't going to be as difficult as I'd imagined.

The second issue was slightly more perplexing. I realized that I didn't have a key to the house. That one seemed to stump her, and we spent about ten minutes brainstorming alternative methods of entry before she grabbed me by the arm and smiled. She remembered that the old man had always kept a spare key in a small toolshed alongside the house. Of course, she hadn't been around in years, but she was sure that I'd find it there. Wainwright, she assured me, was a creature of habit. She also told me that she was confident that I'd be able to discover a way in, even without the key. I didn't love the idea of attempting to climb through a second-floor window, but it was clear that she wasn't going to see that as reason enough not to try. In the end, I let it go and prayed that I would find that key.

Finally, we felt ready enough to go ahead, and in the middle of the afternoon we sat down at the dining room table with Jill's phone. I was a bundle of nerves, but she looked steady as she dialed and held the phone up to her ear. I could only hear one side of the conversation.

"Dad? It's Jill."

There was a long pause after that, and I could only speculate as to whether the old man had been struck dumb by the shock of hearing his daughter's voice, or if he'd managed to muster one of his usual smooth responses. He must have come up with something, because Jill's next words sounded like an answer to a question. "I'm OK," she said. After another beat, she added, "Yeah... it's been a real long time... yeah, I'm still living in Vegas."

There was another delay while the old man spoke, and I got the impression that Jill was growing impatient, looking for an opportunity to jump in and move the conversation along. Finally, she got her chance. "Well... that guy you sent out to find me... yeah... after I talked to him, I thought a lot about you..."

She had to pause again, presumably to listen to her father's expression of joy at learning that my mission to Nevada had been a success. What he heard next surely made him even happier. "I was hoping that I could see you. I'm actually in Miami right now."

That disclosure must have triggered an invitation to Marathon, because Jill immediately had to parry it. "No... no... I can't. I can't come down there. I'm, uh, flying out tomorrow night." It was time for the big question. "I was thinking that maybe you could come up here? We could have lunch tomorrow before I leave... if you can make it..."

I felt my heart pounding beneath my shirt as I studied her face during the seemingly interminable silence that followed her offer. When I saw her lips curl into a smile, I exhaled, although I can't say that I felt relieved. I realized that I'd been harboring some hope that our scheme would somehow collapse before we could take it any further. She extended her right hand toward me with her thumb pointing toward the ceiling, signaling that Wainwright had given her the answer for which she'd hoped. Her words confirmed as much a second later. "Great! I'm at the Delano. Can you meet me there at twelve-thirty?" She stood up and walked around to my side of the table. "Uh huh," she went on. "That's perfect. Twelve-thirty at the Delano. See you then."

With that, she hung up, dropped the phone onto the table, and jumped into my lap. After giving me a long, firm embrace, she sat back and looked me in the eye. "We're all set!" she announced, with an exuberance that suggested that she wanted the whole world to know of our triumph.

I pulled her close to me again. Even though breaking into Wainwright's house wasn't something that I was excited about doing, it was hard not to feel a bit of a thrill. Jill's enthusiasm was infectious, and I got caught up in it. If nothing else, it would be an adventure, and it was making her happy. That was all I needed to know.

In the aftermath of the call we were filled with kinetic energy, and the two of us scurried around the house in circles as we rehashed our plot, straining to discover a critical point that we'd overlooked. Sure enough, we found one. We had always figured on Jill heading up to Miami early the next morning, but it struck me that maybe she should actually get a room and stay the night. That way, there wouldn't be any risk of her getting delayed on her way to the meeting, and it would spare her from having to lie if Wainwright asked her anything about the hotel, or how she'd spent the previous evening. Since the only thing that we cared about was getting Wainwright out of Marathon for a while, I'm not sure that those concerns were rational, but in the moment, they seemed worth addressing. I called the Delano and booked a room for Jill. I winced when they told me that they were charging my Amex $489, but I reminded myself that I was doing it for her, and that it was a small price to pay for a happy girlfriend. Besides, I'd be lying if I said I hadn't gotten at least a little curious about what Wainwright might have been hiding in his office.

We couldn't think of anything else that needed to be done, so Jill packed a small bag and I gave her a lift over to the car rental place. There was no one else there when we arrived, so we had the keys to a late-model Chevy Impala in hand within minutes of our arrival. As we walked across the parking lot with Jill's bag slung over my shoulder, one last question occurred to me. "Hey," I ventured. "I just thought of something."

"What's that?" she replied, without breaking stride. I'm not sure that there was anything I could have said that would have slowed her down.

"It's just that I... uh... what am I gonna do with whatever I find? I mean... should I take the files? Do we care if he notices they're gone?"

We stopped walking once we reached Jill's rental car. She pondered my question for a few seconds as she stood next to the door, before she just smiled and shrugged. "I don't know... maybe take pictures with your phone, or something like that. You'll figure it out." Before I could say anything in response, she opened the car door, took her bag off my shoulder, and threw it onto the passenger seat.

I nodded and simply said, "OK." I didn't think that I was going to find anything worth taking, anyway.

"See you tomorrow night," Jill said as she wrapped her arms around me and gave a long, passionate kiss. As she released me from her embrace, she slid her right hand down my torso and grabbed my crotch. She looked me in the eye. "Rest up! We'll have some fun when I get back."

I wished her good luck and watched her get into the car and drive off. After she'd gone, I stood there for a few minutes longer before heading back to the house, grinning like an idiot at the thought of the reward coming my way upon her return.

Chapter Twenty-Eight

I figured that Wainwright would need to leave Marathon by nine in the morning in order to be sure of making it to the Delano before twelve-thirty, and he struck me as the kind of man who'd want to be punctual for a meeting with his estranged daughter. Even so, I waited until ten before heading over to Grassy Key. When I arrived at the house at about quarter past, everything was reassuringly quiet. When no one responded to my five minutes' worth of pounding on the front door, I was satisfied that I had the place to myself.

I made my way down the stairs and around the side of the house, where I found the toolshed. It was made of wood and painted dark green, and about twice the size of a portable toilet. The door was fastened with a simple latch with no lock, and it swung open easily when I gave it a gentle pull. To my right there was a narrow set of shelves, and on the top one I found a small oilskin purse, sitting in the precise spot that Jill had described. I loosened the drawstring and reached in. Sure enough, I found a key. I replaced the pouch and stepped back outside, closing the shed door behind me.

Now that I was really about to let myself into Wainwright's house, my stomach began to seize up, the way a teenager's does when he's getting ready to pull something over on his parents. More than anything, I hoped that I would never have to look Wainwright in the eye and explain myself.

I lit a cigarette to try to calm my nerves, but that turned out to be counter-productive. As I paced back and forth alongside the house, I kept staring toward the driveway, as if I expected to see my father come walking around the corner and catch me in the middle of taking a drag. Annoyed at having somehow managed to dredge up the anxieties of my fifteen year-old self, I threw the half-finished cigarette into the grass and crushed it with my heel. I started walking back toward the front of the house, but after about ten paces I thought better of leaving evidence of my presence in Wainwright's yard. I retraced my steps, retrieved the cigarette butt and moved it to my car's ashtray.

When I finally opened the front door and went inside the house, it was about ten-thirty. Even if Jill's lunch with Wainwright lasted only an hour and he started for home right afterward, he couldn't possibly make it back to Grassy Key before four o'clock, and that was an unrealistically cautious estimate. That left me with at least five and a half hours, but I had no intention of lingering anywhere near that long. I planned on leaving as soon as I was able to confirm that there was nothing interesting to see. My guess was that I'd poke around for twenty or thirty minutes and then be on my way.

I started down the hall, hyper-aware of each creak of the floorboards beneath my feet. I wasn't tip-toeing, but I was trying to move as silently as I could. No one was there to hear me, but keeping quiet just felt like the right thing to do under the circumstances.

Before delving into the task at hand, I decided to take a peek at my workspace. I was curious to see if Wainwright had cleaned it out, but I found everything exactly as I'd left it. I wondered if the old man was still hoping that I'd return, or if he'd simply forgotten about me. I stood in the doorway for a few seconds, pondering that question, before I dismissed it as irrelevant. Once I finished my explorations, I had no plans to return to that house, or to see Wainwright again.

I wandered back toward Wainwright's office and took a seat in his chair. As I opened his desk drawer, another powerful wave of guilt washed over me. I recalled a traumatic moment from my childhood, when I'd stumbled across a box of condoms in my father's nightstand. I realized later, of course, that there wasn't anything untoward about that, but at the time, I was mortified at the thought of my parents' relationship having a physical component. For months afterward, I was uncomfortable around both of them, and haunted by the understanding that I'd brought the whole thing onto myself by sticking my nose into a place where it shouldn't have been.

Not for the first time, I felt compelled to remind myself that Wainwright wasn't my father. Whatever mischief that I was about to cause him was no more than he deserved. "Fuck him," I muttered, as I started pawing through his desk.

It didn't take long to find three bronze-colored keys, hooked to an unadorned ring. They were sitting beneath a few loose sheets of paper in the top drawer, but I didn't get the impression that the old man had taken any pains to conceal them. I doubted that he would have expected anyone to come looking for them.

I marched straight across the room and tried the first key in the file cabinet. It yielded no joy, but the second one slid smoothly into the lock, and when I turned it I could hear the bolt pop loose. I opened the top drawer and started thumbing through its contents.

The first papers that I found were all related to real estate purchases, which I didn't find especially surprising. Wainwright had always been clear about his desire to have his own church, and the first step toward that goal was the acquisition of land on which he'd be able to build. As I flipped through the pages, I could tell that the files related to more than one property, but it wasn't clear how many purchases were documented there. The drawer was about three-quarters full, but each transaction seemed to entail a decent amount of paperwork. I guessed that the whole set represented maybe three or four deals.

I pulled out the first contract that I could find so that I could take a closer look. The sellers looked to be a husband and wife, whose names I didn't recognize. The buyer was Wainwright, apparently in his individual capacity. That may have been a little on the sketchy side, but it didn't shock me. I'd helped him set up a limited liability company, explaining that he'd be better off doing the church's business through it rather than in his own name, but I knew that he'd mostly ignored my advice. I'd warned him that sooner or later the IRS was going to have some questions about the way he kept his records, as would his flock if they ever found out that he was commingling ecclesiastical and personal assets. He smiled and nodded every time I brought it up, but he just kept on doing things as he always had. Absent any other signs of wrongdoing, it didn't strike me as scandalous enough to report back to Jill.

Wainwright had purchased a plot of undeveloped land from the couple for fifty thousand dollars. Lacking any familiarity with the local land market, I had no way of knowing whether that price was high or low. As I continued to shuffle through papers, I found an appraisal, a title insurance policy, a mortgage arranged through a prominent regional bank, copies of surveys, deeds... pretty much everything you'd expect to see whenever anyone buys real estate. I chuckled when I noticed that Wainwright had used Bob Baker as his legal counsel. I'd never heard of Baker holding himself out as a real estate lawyer, but I imagined that he'd have done just about anything so long as someone was willing to pay his fee. I hoped for Wainwright's sake that he'd caught his attorney on one of his relatively lucid days.

I set that pile aside and searched the drawer until I found another transaction, which turned out to be very much like the first: another purchase of land from an unfamiliar seller, evidenced by another set of innocuous-looking paperwork. A quick glance through the rest of the drawer led me to conclude that it was filled with more of the same.

I took a few minutes to wedge all of those documents back into their places, doing my best to arrange them in the order in which I'd found them. I'm sure that my filing was imprecise, but it wasn't as if they'd been all that well-organized before my intrusion. Confident that my machinations would go unnoticed, I pushed the top drawer closed and moved on to the one just beneath it.

That's where things started to get interesting. It took me a good ten minutes before I was able to get a sense of what I was looking at, but I eventually figured out that the entire drawer was filled with geological surveys. Most of it was incomprehensible to me, an endless parade of color-coded maps littered with annotations and numbers. Their scale was such that I couldn't identify the locations that they covered, and they didn't include roads or place names that might have helped. There was a box in the bottom-right corner of each page which contained what I thought were GPS coordinates, right below the words, "PRIVATE AND CONFIDENTIAL – GREEN SUMMIT UPSTREAM EXPLORATION, LLC."

I was pretty sure I'd heard of Green Summit, so I stopped, pulled out my phone and Googled them. As I'd thought, they were a big natural gas outfit. They'd started out in Oklahoma in the early Nineties, but by 2012 they were running fracking operations all over the country. I couldn't imagine what Wainwright would have been doing with a pile of their maps.

I must have gone through seventy-five pages before I found a cover letter that mentioned a town called Immokalee. I couldn't remember ever having run across it in my travels around the Middle Keys, so I went back to my phone and learned that it was in Florida, but nowhere near Marathon. It was on the mainland, northeast of Naples. As best as I could tell, if there was a middle of nowhere in South Florida, Immokalee had to have been pretty close to it. Wainwright having a drawer full of geological surveys centered on a place like that, which had to have been at least three hours' drive from his home, seemed totally bizarre.

I kept turning pages, but nothing I read enhanced my understanding of the situation. In fact, I found myself feeling increasingly frustrated by my inability to grasp the significance of the data that I was holding in my hands. Given the involvement of Green Summit, I had to assume that the maps documented the presence of natural gas... unless they proved its absence. I wondered how rich this land was, if it was rich at all. Without a clue as to the meaning of the colors, I had no way of knowing.

Once I'd shuffled through the entire drawer without finding anything more revelatory, I pushed it shut and stood up. I made my way back to Wainwright's desk chair and reclined, staring at the ceiling and hoping for inspiration. The only thing that occurred to me was that I should step out for a cigarette. I started toward the door, but before I got there, I was struck by the idea of taking a second look at those real estate purchases, so I returned to the cabinet and pulled out the first set of papers. Looking at them with a fresh eye for detail, I immediately noticed something that I'd missed the first time around. The lot that Wainwright had bought was located in Immokalee, Florida.

I felt like kicking myself for not having noticed it before, but I quickly shunted those thoughts aside and began to speculate about the old man's game. He'd always told me that he was going to build his church in Marathon, and he'd even described the specific part of town that he'd chosen. When I saw the real estate contracts, I'd just assumed that he'd been buying land locally, but when I looked through the rest of the drawer, it was clear that all of his acquisitions were in Immokalee. Buying all those lots on the mainland sure seemed like a funny way to go about building a church in the Keys.

Of course, all those geological surveys suggested that Wainwright wasn't interested in building a church at all or, at the very least, that he had other priorities as well. I forgot about my cigarette break as my mind churned through the possibilities suggested by what I'd discovered, but the simple act of opening the third drawer spared me from having to continue to guess at his intentions. It was only about half-full, but its contents were unambiguous. Everything was laid out in a chain of correspondence between Wainwright and an employee of Green Summit named Lawrence S. Donovan. Mr.

Donovan's stationary identified him as his company's Vice-President of Resource Acquisitions, and the substance of his letters demonstrated that he was working hard to fulfill his mandate by purchasing properties in the Immokalee area from Wainwright.

A cursory look through those files was enough to confirm that the project was systematic and ongoing. The prices varied from sale to sale, depending on the amount of acreage being acquired; I noted that one plot went for a hundred and fifty-thousand bucks, another for a hundred and eighty, and a third for two-hundred grand. There looked to be maybe three or four more. Some of them had already closed, while others looked like they were still pending.

I stepped away from the cabinet and started pacing in a crooked loop around the old man's office. I understood that Wainwright was in the business of flipping real estate, but what did that mean? After all, there wasn't anything criminal about buying low and selling high. In my father's world, guys who managed to implement that approach with any kind of regularity were deemed worthy of the highest praise and showered with riches. It seemed unfair to revile Wainwright simply because I'd discovered him to be a practicing capitalist.

But revulsion was exactly what I felt, and it wasn't hard to come up with justifications for it. Most obviously, I suspected that Wainwright had raised the capital for his scheme by deceiving his parishioners. For years, he'd solicited their donations with the promise that he would use the funds to build God's house. I could only imagine how his followers would have felt if they ever learned that the bills that they tossed into the collection plate every Sunday had found their way into a down payment for a speculative real estate investment halfway across the state.

And what about the other end of those deals? How exactly, I wondered, had Wainwright managed to insert himself as an intermediary between his sellers and Green Summit? If the frackers were willing to pay top dollar for that land, then why didn't they just pay it directly to the original owners and be done with it? I could only assume that Wainwright had used some nefarious tactic to wedge his way into those transactions, although on some level I understood, again, that such a conclusion was unfair at that stage. My father employed a skyscraper full of traders and salespeople whose explicit task was to talk other people into taking the shitty ends of deals. Their entire existence was premised on the idea of buying an asset for X dollars, and then selling it for X+Y dollars. In that equation, the "Y" represented the bank's spread, or the amount by which the original seller was underpaid, or by which the ultimate buyer was overcharged, as a consequence of not doing business directly with its "true" counterparty. A banker would have explained that there were legitimate reasons for their involvement, and that their spreads were proper reflections of the value that they added to transactions. I'm not sure if I completely bought into the logic behind their business model, but the simple fact was that I didn't despise my father and his colleagues for being middle-men.

Maybe it wasn't the specifics of Wainwright's dealings that stuck in my throat so much as what I perceived to be his hypocrisy. For months I'd listened to him drone on, in private as well as in public, about the primacy of God's kingdom, the meaninglessness of earthly wealth, and the perils of greed. Even though I'd learned to discount his sincerity, it was still jarring to discover that the man who'd said all those things had been slashing and burning his way through the real estate market for months in search of a quick buck. My father may have had his flaws, but at least he'd never claimed that his elbows were anything other than sharp.

All of those thoughts were swirling around my head, but they were crowded out by the question that Jill had posed in anger a few days before: "Why the fuck does he always get to win?" I didn't have to understand all of the details of the scheme to know that the old man was making money. He was winning, and it rubbed me the wrong way, maybe just because I knew how much the idea of it would have pissed off his daughter.

That's when I started to panic. Jill had sent me to her father's house to find something and, much to my surprise, I'd actually succeeded. Now that I had, I realized that she was going to expect us to do something about it. She hadn't driven all the way to Miami and endured her father's company just so we could get in on his joke. I was pretty sure that her intention was to spoil his party, to make him feel, for once, what it was like to lose. I certainly didn't begrudge her those feelings, but I had no idea what I was supposed to do next.

What if she demanded that we call the police? That was a nonstarter for me. As a matter of principle, I had a real problem with ratting anybody out, but there were practical considerations as well. I didn't see how I could avoid facing a bunch of awkward questions about my role over the previous few months. Even if those didn't prove problematic, I wasn't keen on the idea of explaining how I'd deceived the old man into leaving his house so that I could break in and rifle through his papers. It didn't seem like a stretch to think that I'd be the one who wound up in handcuffs if the cops got involved.

I took a deep breath, aware that I was getting ahead of myself. I was worrying about the police, but I wasn't even sure that anyone had broken the law. In order to figure that out, I'd have to try to match up buys and sales, figure out how much profit he was making... maybe go through the mortgage documents and try to figure out where his money was coming from... talk to people in Immokalee and see how he'd gotten them to sell him their land... the list went on. I looked over at the file cabinet. I was sure that it contained the answers to at least some of my questions, but there were thousands of pages in there. It was only twenty-five after eleven, but there was no way that I was going to put everything together in four or five hours.

My mind jumped to another possibility: maybe we could somehow tip off the people with whom Wainwright was doing business. If we could just get them to start asking questions, maybe the whole thing would unravel under its own weight. That sounded great, but I quickly realized that I didn't know enough to be a whistle-blower. Who was getting ripped off here? Wainwright's congregation? The folks that were selling him their land? Green Summit? Unless I could answer that question, I had no idea whom to approach, or what to say.

I stopped pacing and went back to the cabinet. Everything I needed to know was in there. All I had to do was take the time to go through it. I pulled out a small batch of papers and started reading, line by line.

I only made it through a page and half before I realized that I wasn't absorbing anything. I'd already convinced myself that I didn't have enough time to do what I wanted to do, and it had become a self-fulfilling prophecy. I couldn't focus on anything beyond an unbearable awareness of the minutes slipping away.

I dropped the documents onto the floor in disgust and retreated back to Wainwright's desk, where I rested my head in my hands and massaged my temples. I considered simply taking all of the old man's papers back to my house, but I hated the idea of tipping him off to the fact that someone was on to him. Beyond a general sense that our goals, whatever they turned out to be, would be better-achieved if Wainwright's guard stayed down, I was also concerned for Jill. Wainwright wasn't an idiot. If he returned from Miami and found his files missing, his suspicions were going to land squarely on his suddenly-communicative daughter. The last thing I wanted to do was to bring heat on her because I'd made an impulsive decision.

I was weighing all of that in my mind when I was struck by an inspired thought: why not make copies? I might not have had time to read all of Wainwright's papers before he got back from Miami, but my gut told me that I could have them all photocopied and put back before the afternoon was out. My phone's internet confirmed that there was a shipping/printing shop that made copies on the Overseas Highway, not far from the grocery store. I looked at my watch and tried to work out the timing. I wanted the printer to be done by three, so that I'd have plenty of time to return the originals to their proper places without having to worry about Wainwright walking in on me. Assuming I could get everything over to the shop by noon, I was thinking that they'd have about three hours to make the copies, which seemed reasonable enough.

My intention was to haul the whole file cabinet down to my car, but that was before I discovered it to be a relic from a bygone age, when even inconsequential things were made out of steel. I had to strain as hard as I could just to lift it an inch or two off the floor. Without two or three more guys, there was no way that I was getting that thing out of Wainwright's office.

I scanned the room in search of anything that I might have used to carry the files, but it was fruitless. The old man always kept his office tidy. I, on the other hand, had never taken any such pains with my workspace, and as soon as that thought occurred to me, I ran out the door and down the hall. As always, my office was cluttered with cardboard boxes full of papers. I dumped the contents of three of the bigger ones onto the floor before taking them back to the file cabinet. Loading them didn't take long, even though I was trying my best to keep everything in order. I simply grabbed the largest stacks I could manage and placed them into the boxes one after another, a separate box for each drawer. When the drawers were empty, I carried the boxes down to the car one by one, trying not to jostle them too much as I went.

It was ten minutes past noon when I burst through the door of the copy shop and dropped the first box onto the counter in front of me. The clerk started moving toward me, but I didn't wait for his greeting. "How ya' doin?" I panted. "I've got a rush job here... very urgent... this box and two more just like it. I need all of it photocopied as quickly as possible."

It wasn't until I'd made my request that I took a second to assess the man looking back at me, and my heart sank when I did. He was a white guy, maybe a little younger than me, with dreadlocks that hung down to his shoulders. Nothing about his appearance suggested that he was capable of mustering the level of urgency that my situation demanded. True to my expectations, he hesitated for what seemed like an eternity before he said anything at all. When he finally responded, it was clear that he was working off of a script.

"Sir, our standard turnaround time for a bulk print job is next business day. We can have these for you by five o'clock tomorrow..."

"No, no...tomorrow doesn't work for me. Any way I can get them today?"

He rolled his eyes, subtly but still perceptibly, as if to rebuke me for cutting him off before giving him the chance to finish his recitation. Composing himself, he went on. "But if you're interested, we can offer you same-day pick-up for an additional thirty-five dollar fee."

His voice was nasal and whiny, not quite what I'd expected from someone with a hairdo like his, but I got over it as soon as I heard the words "same-day." "Yes!" I shot back, like I was worried about the offer being withdrawn if I gave myself time to blink before accepting it.

The clerk smiled. "Great. If you could just fill out this order form..."

I snatched the paper from his hand and a pen from the counter and began checking boxes and providing my contact details. I had gotten about halfway through the form when I looked up. "So, when, exactly, will these be ready today?"

"You can pick them up any time after five. We're open until..."

I didn't let him finish. "After five! I'm sorry, but that won't work for me. I really need these by three, at the latest."

I saw his dreadlocks brush against his shoulders as he shook his head. "Can't guarantee that. Our same-day service only means they'll be ready this evening."

I rested both hands on the counter and leaned in. "I understand that... I was just hoping, maybe, that you could do it right away. I mean, I know what the policy is, but maybe you could help me out? I'd really appreciate it."

"I can't make any promises. We have a queue of copy jobs, and I can't say for sure that we can get to yours immediately."

I pulled out my wallet and saw that I had forty bucks. I set it on the counter. "Man... this is all I've got on me... but is there any way that you can get me to the front of the line?"

The clerk threw furtive glances to either side, which seemed ridiculous because the store was tiny and it was pretty clear that he and I were the only people in it. He must have satisfied himself that he was in the clear, because he grabbed the money and shoved it into his hip pocket. "OK. I'll have these ready in three hours."

"How about two and a half?"

"Yeah, probably, but three is all I'll promise."

I nodded. "Good enough. I really appreciate this, man." I turned and went out to the car to fetch the other two boxes.

Chapter Twenty-Nine

I may not have had warm feelings about my whiny-voiced, dreadlocked friend, but I'm pretty sure that he thought even less of me by the time the afternoon was over. I suppose that his aversion was understandable, given that I loitered in front of his shop window for two hours, staring in at him while I chain-smoked and checked my watch every few minutes. I had intended to go and eat while he labored away on my behalf, but I found that I didn't have much of an appetite. Once I gave up on lunch, though, I realized that I didn't have anything to do other than wait it out. The guy probably thought that I was some sort of weirdo, baking in the sun on the sidewalk in front of a strip mall while I waited for my photocopies.

Whatever I might have thought of that clerk, my dealings with him proved satisfactory enough. At about quarter to three, he waved me back into the store and presented me with six boxes full of papers. He even helped me carry them out to my car. I appreciated that gesture at the time, but once I considered the fact that he'd charged me almost two hundred bucks on top of the extra forty that I'd thrown him, I felt like it was the least he could have done.

It was after four o'clock by the time I finished putting everything back into its place at Wainwright's house. Afraid of him walking in on me, I worked as quickly as I could, but that only served to convince me I'd done a half-assed job. I felt compelled to triple-check every room before I left, but I finally satisfied myself that all was in order. Once I pulled out of the driveway without having seen the old man, my tension instantly began to dissipate.

By the time I got home, I was feeling pretty pleased with myself. I couldn't wait to show Jill how much I'd done with the time that she'd bought for us. As I sat on my couch and rewarded myself with a beer, I tried to imagine her reaction. A couple hundred bucks in duplicating charges was a small price to pay for the smile that I expected to see when she walked in, and I was happy to imagine the various other ways in which she might have expressed her gratitude.

As I patted myself on the back, it occurred to me that Jill would be even happier if I could at least begin to explain what it was that all of those papers meant. I pulled one of the boxes up onto the dining room table and started removing its contents, laying everything out in neat piles. It felt like I was starting in on a jigsaw puzzle, and I wouldn't be able to start putting pieces together until I'd separated all the edges and corners.

I got sucked into the process of sorting and organizing, and I lost all track of the time until I was snapped out of my trance by a knock at the door. I glanced at my watch and was shocked to see that it was pushing six-thirty. Given the time, I assumed that it was Jill, back from Miami. I strode across the room and opened the door with a flourish, thrilled by the prospect of announcing my accomplishment to my very hot and soon-to-be very grateful girlfriend.

I wish that I could say that my face didn't betray my shock at the identity of my visitor, but I'm sure that my jaw fell too far to go unnoticed. Instead of being face to face with my beautiful lover, I found myself on the receiving end of her father's broad, toothy grin. "Malcolm! I'm glad I caught you. I've got some good news and I wanted very much to share it with you." With that, he took a step toward the door, as if to make his way inside.

Bitterly aware of how stupid I would have felt if Wainwright had discovered copies of his files spread out across my dining room table only hours after I'd gone through all that trouble to steal them without detection, I quickly shifted my body across the doorway to block his path.

It was almost funny to see the look of confusion spread across his face once he grasped that I didn't mean to let him into my house. His usual eloquence deserted him, and the best he could do was to sputter, "You're not letting me...? I mean, can I, uh...? Can we maybe talk inside?"

I shook my head. "I, uh... I have company right now."

That seemed like a decent excuse and I was proud of myself for coming up with it on the spot, but Wainwright blew right through it. "That's OK," he replied, having gathered himself. "I'll just be a few minutes. You can introduce me..." Once again, he made like he was getting ready to go through the door.

His nonchalance made it clear that the time for subtlety had passed, so I extended my arm and grabbed the frame of the door, leaving no way in but through me. As I did so, I explained, quietly, "I'm sorry, John. I really don't want to be rude here, but we're trying to be discrete about this." I nodded over my shoulder, in the direction of my imaginary houseguest, and lowered my voice even further. "I promised her that we wouldn't tell anyone that we're seeing each other, so..."

The old man's face brightened, and he gave me a knowing nod. "I understand," he said. He took a small step backwards, as if to emphasize the point, before going on. "I just wanted to let you know that whatever you did out in Vegas, it worked."

"Huh?"

"I saw Jill today... in Miami. She reached out to me after you talked to her. I just wanted to thank you for that."

"I'm, uh, really glad to hear..."

He interrupted me. "The way we left things... between you and I... I felt bad about that, and I wanted to talk to you anyway... but then this happened, and I'm just so happy that I wanted to run right over here and tell you about it."

Regardless of what I thought I knew about the old man, in that moment, it was hard to see him as anything other than what he appeared to be: a father who was thrilled to have another chance to repair his relationship with his child. Knowing that it was all a part of our ruse turned my stomach. All I could do was look down at the ground and nod.

Wainwright didn't seem to notice my unease, and he went on. "I really can't thank you enough. There's nothing I want more than to bring Jill back into my life."

The more he expressed his appreciation for my help, the more wretched I felt. After a few seconds of silence, I looked back up at him. "I, uh, hope it works out for you."

"It's a first step, at least," he replied, his tone infused with hope. Again, I just nodded, and he continued. "I do hope that we can talk sometime. Maybe you can come by the house? Or to services on Sunday?"

"Sure," I said, eager to end our conversation. "I'll stop by sometime."

"Soon, I hope?"

"As soon as I can."

"Well, I'll see you soon, then. Thanks again." He offered me his hand, and after I shook it he turned and walked back toward the street. I stood and watched until he'd gotten into his car and driven out of sight. When I finally released my grip on the door frame, I noticed that my hands were shaking.

Chapter Thirty

Jill called about forty-five minutes after her father left, and I picked her up at the car rental place. It wasn't anything like the triumphant reunion that I'd envisioned earlier that day. I was still shaken by how close Wainwright had come to finding his files in my house, and I felt like a scumbag for using his relationship with his daughter to manipulate him. For Jill's part, she spent the whole ride back to the house sullenly staring out the car window. I tried to tell her about the day's achievements, but I wasn't sure that she absorbed any of it.

When we got home, I marched straight to the dining room table and started to walk her through what I'd learned. I'd only gotten about a minute into my spiel, though, when she buried her head into my shoulder and started sobbing. I placed a stack of geological surveys back down onto the table and guided her over to the couch, where I held her without saying anything for about five minutes. When it seemed like she was starting to pull herself together, I drew back, took her by the hand, and asked, "What happened?"

She used the collar of her shirt to dab the tears from her cheek, and she kept dabbing after they were gone, like she was trying to put off having to answer my question for as long as she could. Finally, she let go of her shirt and took a deep breath. "Nothing," was all she said.

"You can talk to me," I said, as I rubbed my fingers along the back of her hand. "You can tell me anything."

She acknowledged my invitation by giving my hand a quick squeeze, but she didn't take me up on it. "It was nothing, really," she repeated.

"C'mon," I prodded her, trying to look her in the eye as I spoke. "You were giddy when you left for Miami last night, and now you're...." I was going to say "a mess," but I thought better of it and chose "all upset" instead. I paused for a reaction, but when she didn't say anything, I added, "So something must have happened."

Jill shrugged. "I don't know... I can't explain it... it's just... him."

"Did he do something? What did he do to you?"

She shook her head quickly. "No, no... nothing like that. It's just that he always makes me feel like shit."

I smiled. "Yeah, well, he's good at that."

"I'm serious! I want to be mad at him... I should be mad... but whenever I talk to him, he always makes me think that maybe I was wrong. Maybe I should give him another chance...."

"Fuck that. You don't owe him anything. He's good at making you think that you do, but you don't. Don't let him fuck with you." It was funny to hear myself counseling her that way, because I was still struggling with the guilt that the old man's most recent visit had stirred up within me. Seeing his effect on another person made it easier to remember that the guy had a long track record as a con man.

My words of encouragement seemed to work a little, and over the next couple of days, Jill regained her appetite for our plot. It helped that we were able to figure out precisely what Wainwright was up to. Not only was it satisfying to put all the pieces together and solve the puzzle, but it also reminded us that the good reverend was serving Mammon with a zeal that any truly pious man would have found quite unsettling.

It took hours to wade through all of those papers, but Wainwright's scheme proved unambiguous. It was about as simple as it gets, really. He was buying land in Immokalee for about fifteen-hundred dollars an acre, and then selling it to Green Summit for more than three times that price. In the first deal I'd come across in his office, he'd bought thirty acres for $1,666.67 per acre by putting up ten grand in cash and borrowing the rest. When he sold it a week later and paid off the mortgage, he scored a hundred grand in profit. It was the sort of return on investment that guys like my dad could only have wet dreams about, unless they were willing to go to jail. Nobody made that much money that quickly unless they were ripping somebody else off.

The essence of Wainwright's transactions turned out to be exactly as I'd assumed, but having time to go through everything gave me a chance to appreciate the finer points of his scheme. The documents covered purchases from six different sellers, and six corresponding sales to Green Summit. Five of them were completely done, and the old man had already cleared over half a million dollars all together. It looked as if he'd closed them in ascending order of price, so that he'd been able to use the proceeds from one to fund the down payment for the next. The only time that he'd been forced to dip into his own pocket was for the initial ten thousand bucks that had gotten the ball rolling.

He was saving the best for last. There was only one deal that was still open, and it was much bigger than any of the others. This time, Wainwright was buying three hundred and fifty acres, and he was looking at a $1.25 million gain when he flipped it. I admired the old man's killer instinct. However he'd managed it, he'd tapped into a very lucrative revenue stream and he was squeezing it for all that it was worth. I couldn't honestly say that I wouldn't have been inclined to do the same.

Of course, nothing that I'd seen constituted evidence of Wainwright having committed a crime. If convincing people to make bad deals had been illegal, then everyone who'd ever worked at a bank would be rotting in prison, right alongside all the car dealers and the guys that charged six bucks for a cup of coffee. Predictably, though, when I tried to convey this to Jill, she scoffed at the idea that her father's dealings might have been above board. I explained Wainwright's scheme by walking her through a matching purchase and sale, and I could sense her outrage building as she began to understand exactly how well the real estate market had treated the old man. No sooner had I gotten to the punch line than she started firing questions at me. They were the right questions, too. I guess you didn't need an Ivy League degree to understand that we were looking at something shady.

"Why on earth," she began, "would these people sell their land to my father for fifty thousand dollars when they could have sold it to Green Summit for a hundred and fifty?"

"Or," I countered, "why would Green Summit buy it from your father for one-fifty when they could have gotten it from the original owners for fifty grand?"

She nodded. "Right. Exactly. Why would anyone do that? Do any of these papers explain it?"

I shook my head. "They're just contracts. They don't say why people decided to sign them."

"What do you think? Can you think of a reason?"

As it happened, I'd given that question a good deal of thought, and I was happy to share my conjectures. "I don't know. There had to be some reason why the sellers and Green Summit either couldn't or wouldn't do business directly with each other... maybe he bought from a bunch of environmentally-friendly types who wouldn't have sold to a fracking company, and he promised to keep their land unspoiled..."

"Could be," she shrugged.

I went on. "Or maybe the sellers were True Believers who weren't inclined to sell their land at all, until your father told them he was gonna use it to build some sort of evangelical wonderland..."

"That would be illegal, wouldn't it? I mean, if he flat out lied to them..."

"I'm not a lawyer. It probably depends on what he told them... what he promised... if he signed anything... who knows if that's even what happened?"

"I'm sure it's something like that," she announced, with more conviction than her view seemed to merit.

I shook my head. "Not necessarily. Maybe there's something we're not thinking of...it could have been anything, really. That guy at Green Summit might be in on it. He could be working with your father, stealing from his bosses by overpaying your dad for the land and then splitting the profits with him."

"That's gotta be a crime, right?"

"Sure, if that's what they're doing... but we have absolutely no proof of anything like that. We're just guessing here."

She seemed to deflate as my words sunk in. I understood how earnestly she believed that her father was up to no good, and I was inclined to agree with her, but we just didn't have the sort of evidence that we needed to expose him to the world. Her shoulders bowed forward and I could hear the resignation in her voice. "It's too late, anyway, I guess. I mean, he's got the money now..."

I shrugged. "Yeah, he's got a bunch... but not quite all of it."

"What do you mean?" she shot back. "I thought you said that he already sold the land to Green Summit."

I pointed toward the files scattered across the table. "There are documents for six different deals here, all of 'em just like the one I just showed you... your father buys land from somebody and sells it to Green Summit for a big profit..."

"I understand that."

"Six deals," I repeated, "but only five of them are done." I let that sink in for a second before I went on. "And the last one is the biggest by far."

She looked back at me with a blank expression, but her lips curled into a smile as she realized that she might have still had a chance to throw a wrench into her old man's plans. "How big?" she asked.

"He stands to make over a million... a million and a quarter, actually."

Her eyes widened when she heard the number. "When?" she murmured.

I picked up a stack of papers and shuffled through them until I found the date I was looking for. "He's supposed to close the buy a week from tomorrow, and he'll sell it on to Green Summit a week after that."

"A week!" she shouted. "That doesn't leave us much time!" The idea of having a deadline must have triggered some sort of manic response in her, because she suddenly lost the ability to stand still. I watched as she circled the table three times in rapid succession.

Part of me wanted to just stand there and count how many loops she'd make before she ran out of gas, but I felt like I should try to slow her down before she went too far down whatever rabbit hole she was getting ready to jump into. "Time for what?" I asked.

She stopped dead in her tracks. "To stop him!" she announced, as if it were the most obvious thing in the world.

"Uh huh," I replied. "And how, exactly, are we gonna do that?"

Her expression made it clear that she wasn't going to let a little thing like not having a plan deter her. "I don't know." She paused and smiled before adding, "You're the one that went to Princeton, right? You can come up with something, can't you?"

I chuckled. "I think I might have been absent the day they taught us how to blow up other people's land deals out of spite. Maybe I'll call one of my classmates and see if they can send us the notes from that lecture."

Jill wasn't amused by my attempt at humor, a fact she made clear be calling me a "dick." I reached out and took her by the hand. "I'm sorry," I began. "I shouldn't have made this into a joke, but I'm not sure that we should get involved in this."

She pulled her hand back. "So you're OK with him getting away with it?"

"Are we even sure that he's getting away with anything?"

"He's making all that money. Doesn't that drive you crazy?"

I shrugged. "People make plenty of money every day, and a lot of them are dirtbags. From what I've seen, the biggest assholes usually make the most money. It's not my job to stop 'em."

She just stared at me for a few seconds, apparently stunned by my inability to muster an appropriate amount of vitriol against her father. There really was a disconnect between the two of us on that point, I suppose. After everything that Jill had told me, I certainly didn't harbor much affection for Wainwright, but any ill will I felt toward him was purely vicarious. It wasn't like he'd done anything to me. As much as I appreciated where Jill was coming from, I didn't feel it on a personal level the way that she did. All I really want to do was move on and forget about the old man altogether.

I took a shot at steering her in that direction. "I understand. I really do," I began. "I just think that maybe we'd be better off if we didn't get tangled up in your father's bullshit. I mean, let's just get out of here and go live our lives, like we talked about..."

She interrupted me. "I don't even know what that means. Where are we gonna go? What are we gonna do? You keep saying that we should run off together, but you never tell me where... or how..."

"I don't know," I said, stung by having been reminded of my inability to sort out my life. "But I don't see how screwing your dad over is gonna help us figure it out."

"Maybe not," she replied, "but it'll make me feel better."

I nodded and walked over to the refrigerator and grabbed myself a beer. After I flipped the bottle cap into the trash, I turned back to face Jill. "OK," I announced. "Let me think about it. I'm gonna go outside for a smoke."

"You'll think about it?" she asked.

"Unless you'll just forget it, like I said..."

"No, no... I wanna do something."

I wandered outside and parked myself in my lawn chair, where I stayed until I'd finished my beer. The plan that I formulated didn't require much in the way of ingenuity. My only goal was to keep our involvement in Wainwright's affairs to a minimum, while still satisfying Jill's itch to have a go at her old man.

When I returned to the living room, I found Jill sitting on the couch. I sensed that she was anxious to hear my thoughts, but she kept her impulses in check and didn't say a word. I stopped at the fridge and swapped my empty beer for a fresh one before sitting down next to her. "OK. Here's the deal. Tomorrow, we'll make an anonymous phone call to the seller. We'll say, 'we work with John Wainwright,' or something like that, and then we'll spill the beans about Green Summit. We'll tell him exactly how much money your father's making on the deal. That should be enough to make him reconsider his decision to sell his land."

Jill flashed me a smile. "That's all I want to do."

"Good," I replied. "But I want you to promise me that you'll let this go once we're done. I mean, we'll tell the guy what we know, but after that it'll be up to him to do whatever he wants to do. Once we tell him, we're done."

"Sure."

"I'm serious. I don't wanna waste any more energy on this. If your father still manages to do his deal and make his money..."

"I understand," she said, nodding.

I smiled back at her. "OK, then. We're good?"

"We're good." We sat silently for a few moments before she asked, "What do we do now?"

"Now," I replied, "we eat some dinner. You want a steak?"

She nodded, and I headed back outside to fire up the grill.

Chapter Thirty-One

Whatever tensions that Wainwright's papers had stirred up between us seemed to dissolve over dinner, washed away in a tide of butter and animal fat. In an ideal universe, I'd have opened a nice Cabernet to go with our steaks, but I was short on wine. A couple of cold, domestic beers had to suffice, and they proved more than worthy of the task.

I knew that all was well between us when our post-dinner lounging turned intimate. It was the first time we'd made love since Jill had gotten back from Miami, and it was a relief to get back into our groove. By the time we fell asleep in my bed, our limbs still entangled, I'd pretty much forgotten about Immokalee.

The good times kept right on rolling the next morning, when I awoke to the indescribable sensation of Jill going down on me. I propped my head against a pillow and just watched her take me in, trying to sear the image into my memory. It's tempting to veer into hyperbole when discussing this kind of thing, and I try to avoid it, but I honestly can't remember anything, before or since, ever making me feel as good as she did that morning. It was one of those moments that I wished would have lasted forever.

We didn't quite make it to forever, but I couldn't complain about what came next. After that long, slow build-up, Jill swung her leg across my body and started to ride me. It wasn't the sort of wild, animalistic sex that I'd experienced with her before; this time, it was like she was moving in slow-motion, determined to keep us from careening into a premature ending.

She had an amazing sense of just how far she could go without pushing me over the edge. Whenever I was on the brink of not being able to take any more, she would break her rhythm; a couple of times, she stopped moving entirely and we just stared into each other's eyes until it was safe to go on. Things went on that way for almost twenty minutes, but I eventually reached the point where no amount of patience was going to delay things any longer. Once we were finished, she curled up alongside me and whispered "Good morning."

Still overcome by an all-encompassing wave of bliss, the only response I was able to manage was a subdued, "Umm hmm." We just laid there for a few minutes after that, with Jill's head resting on my shoulder and her fingernails gliding gently across my chest.

I'd almost drifted back to sleep when she broke the silence. "I was thinking…" she announced.

"Uh huh," I answered, mostly just to prove that I was still awake.

"About all this stuff with my father," she went on. "About calling that guy today."

I opened my eyes and let out a sigh. This was not a topic that I was eager to revisit, and certainly not while I was still straining to cling to my contentment for as long as I could. I tried to cut her off. "Yeah, I haven't forgotten. Give me a little time to get myself together... maybe get a cup of coffee, or something. After that we can start in on figuring out who we need to call."

"Well, I was thinking..." she repeated. "I was thinking that maybe we shouldn't call this guy after all."

After all of our back and forth the previous day, that was the last thing that I expected to hear, and I was thrilled by the prospect of her having taken my advice to heart. "That's, uh... that's great!" I stammered. "I think we'll be much better off if we stay away from all this. We'll just do our own thing and forget about it."

For a fleeting moment, I thought that I might have disentangled myself from Jill's cold war with her father, but my relief proved to be short-lived. I'd barely gotten those last words out when I saw her shake her head. "No... that's not what I meant. I thought maybe, uh... we could try something else."

Whatever she had in mind, it was clear that she was hesitant to share it with me. In light of everything I'd said the previous day, I suppose that made sense. Still, if we were going to have any kind of lasting relationship, I wanted her to feel like she could approach me with anything that was on her mind. I pushed myself up to a sitting position, and took her by the hand. "Tell me about your idea."

She flashed me a smile. "OK. But promise me you won't laugh, all right?"

I nodded. "I promise."

"Even though this is gonna sound a little crazy..."

"I promise," I repeated. "I won't laugh."

She took a deep breath and exhaled. "What if *we* bought the land?" When I didn't respond right away, she went on. "We don't just ruin his deal... we take it from him. And we make all that money for ourselves." She paused again before concluding, "He gets screwed while we get rich."

I sat silently for about ten seconds, trying to process what I'd just heard, before I broke into a fit of laughter. Jill looked pissed. "Fuck you! You promised!"

I tried to compose myself. "I'm sorry. And I understand where you're coming from, I really do." I shook my head. "But I just don't see any way for us to pull that off."

"Why not?" Jill demanded, hotly. "My father's doing it, isn't he? He's nothin' but a bullshit con artist and he's gonna pull it off. Why can't we?"

Under different circumstances, I would have dismissed such a ridiculous question out of hand, or at the very least answered it in such a way as to make my disdain apparent. At that point, though, I understood that Jill had raised it in earnest, and it was clear that she wouldn't have appreciated a flippant retort. I tried to tread as lightly as I could. "Well, I mean, we don't have relationships with any of these people. The seller... Green Summit... they don't even know we exist."

"Green Summit won't care who they buy the land from," she shot back.

"Even if that's true, the seller's already signed a contract with your father. We'd have to convince them to back out and deal with us instead. Hard to think of a reason why they would listen to someone they've never even met...."

She shrugged. "We could tell the guy a bunch of bad things about my dad. We wouldn't even have to lie."

"You're assuming he'll even talk to us."

"Or we could just offer him a little more money. That usually gets people's attention."

I nodded. "I think you just identified our biggest problem."

"What? Money?"

"Yup. Even if we could somehow convince these guys to do business with us, we just don't have enough cash."

"You said my father was borrowing from the bank. Can't we do the same thing?"

"The bank takes time. Weeks, at least, to get approved for a mortgage. Your father is ready to put money on the table next week, and what are we gonna say? We *might* have a mortgage sometime later this summer... if the bank says 'yes,' which they won't."

"How can you be so sure? They give loans to all kinds of assholes, don't they?"

"I don't know... the fact that neither one of us has a job..."

"I might still have a job in Vegas. If not, I'm sure I can get another one."

"So we'll just tell our loan officer that I'm unemployed and you're a job-hopping exotic dancer? I'm sure he'll just sign that check as soon as he hears that..."

"Money's money, isn't it?"

I shrugged. "Even if we could make it work, which is a big 'if,' the bank won't finance the whole thing. They'll expect us to put up a down payment." I paused to let that sink in, and then I asked, "How much cash can you get your hands on?"

"I don't know... maybe, like, six or seven grand. Maybe a little more."

I shook my head. "A bank's gonna want twenty percent. If we did the deal at the same price that your father's paying, that's a hundred thousand bucks."

"You have any cash?" she asked.

"Nothing like a hundred grand."

I expected the conversation to continue in the same vein, but my last answer seemed to have stymied her. Without saying a word, she stood up, threw on a robe, and left the room. I flopped backwards onto my pillow and stared at the ceiling, exasperated at the fact that she seemed to be annoyed with me. What the hell had she expected me to say? It wasn't like I had a spare half-million dollars stashed under the bed. She was the one who'd cooked up a crackpot idea, and it hardly seemed fair to punish me for not wanting to jump on the bandwagon.

Still, the thought of her resenting me drove me crazy, so after a few minutes I dragged myself out of bed and went into the kitchen to try to make peace. I got a chilly reception once I got there, as Jill went about emptying the dishwasher and stacking plates without so much as a nod in my direction. The way that she was banging things around made it pretty clear that she was irritated.

Without saying a word, I made myself some coffee and sat down, hoping that she'd realize that I wasn't the one who deserved the blame for whatever it was that she was feeling. When I got about halfway through my cup without seeing any encouraging changes in her demeanor, I decided to rekindle our conversation. "Hey," I began. "Are you pissed off at me?"

She stopped in her tracks, placed her dishrag on the counter in front of her, and turned to face me. There was an awkward silence before she finally answered. "No," was all she said, with a palpable lack of conviction.

"That's good," I replied. "But it kinda seems like you are."

Again, a few moments passed before she responded. "It's not you," she said, shaking her head. "It's just... this whole thing... I thought maybe we could really do something with this."

"Look, I know how badly you want to burn your father's ass, but..."

"It's not that... well, yeah, of course... but it's not just that. I just kept thinking that this could solve all of our problems at once. We coulda used that money to set ourselves up somewhere... it's stupid, I know..."

"It wasn't stupid," I admonished her. "We'll come up with something."

She walked over to the table and sat down next to me. "I know we will, but this woulda been a sure thing. I mean, if we coulda pulled this off, we woulda made all that money, right?"

"Yeah, I guess..."

"We just need money. If we had the cash, I know we could do it."

"Maybe. There's a bunch of other things we'd need to figure out."

She brushed my reservations aside with a dismissive wave of her hand. "It's just the money. We could do the rest."

I shrugged. "I guess we'll never know, because we're never gonna get our hands on that kind of..."

She interrupted me before I could finish. "How about your family?"

I probably shouldn't have been surprised at her bringing my family into it. In hindsight, it seems obvious that she was always steering our conversation in that direction. At the time, though, it felt like it had come completely out of left field. "What about my family?" I mumbled.

"You said they had a lot of money, right?"

"Yup."

"Well, maybe they could lend you some?"

It was my turn to be dismissive. "That's never going to happen," I replied, as I stood up and walked my empty mug to the sink.

I had intended the gesture to put an end to any further discussion along those lines, but Jill either didn't pick up on it, or chose to ignore it. "But we only need the money for a week... then we could pay 'em back, no problem. They wouldn't even miss it."

"My father would never go for that."

"Why not? He sounds like a guy that likes to make money."

I shuffled back over to the table and resumed my seat. "He definitely likes to make money."

"So what's the problem?"

"For starters, we'd be the ones making the money here. Not him."

"We can give him a cut."

I started laughing again, this time without feeling guilty about it. "Give him a cut? Of his own profits? You definitely don't know my father."

"Fine. We can split it with him, then. There's plenty to go around. Even if we just got half of it, we'd still be..."

"We'd be lucky if he threw us a few cents on the dollar as a finder's fee. More likely, he'd just take us to dinner and buy us a bottle of wine."

"We can work something out with..."

I cut her off. "No. We can't. All this talk," I said as I waved my hand, "is beside the point. It doesn't matter whether we could talk him into splitting the money with us, because there isn't going to be any money. He'll never agree to get involved with this, no matter how much we promise him."

Jill didn't say anything right away. She just sat and stared at me for what seemed like an eternity before she looked down at the table and shook her head. "Your dad really doesn't trust you, does he?"

I was flabbergasted by her inability to grasp, or her unwillingness to admit, the impossibility of what she was asking me to do. "We're not talking about asking him to let me take his Mercedes out on Friday night..."

"Yeah, but you'll never know unless you ask, right? What's the worst that can happen? You afraid he'll laugh at you?"

Funny enough, that was pretty much exactly what I was afraid of. My old man's opinion of me was low enough as it was. I didn't see how approaching him with some half-baked, get-rich-quick revenge plot was going to enhance my standing in his eyes. "Sometimes you know the answer before you ask the question," I said.

"I still don't see the harm in..."

"'Cause I don't want to look like an asshole! That's the harm!" Without another word, she stood up and walked back to bedroom. I followed her and watched as she threw off her robe and changed into a pair of shorts and a t-shirt. As she knelt down to put on her shoes, I asked, "Where ya' goin'?"

"Gonna go for a run," she answered, without looking up.

"OK... Well, uh, I was actually thinking about going and hitting some golf balls today..."

"Fine."

"We can talk later?"

She shrugged. "Sure," she replied, as she brushed past me and headed toward the front door. I watched her through the window as she walked through the front yard. When she reached the sidewalk, she turned right and started jogging, and within seconds she was out of sight.

Chapter Thirty-Two

When I was eleven, or maybe twelve, I carved up my right leg pretty badly when I tried to jump my dirt bike over a rocky creek bed. It was a stupid thing to do, because I always knew that I was never going to make it. Even without having studied physics, my understanding of the laws of motion was sufficiently developed to inform me that my attempt was doomed from the start. In the end, I suppose I wound up being pretty lucky. The blood and the large flap of skin hanging off of my shin were unpleasant, but at least I didn't break anything.

Given that I was pretty sure that I was going to hurt myself, you might wonder why I went ahead with it at all. The simple answer is that I did it because Scott Macmillan called me a "pussy" for hesitating. As soon as my friend threw down that gauntlet, I couldn't launch myself onto those rocks fast enough. I might have been an idiot, but no one was going to call me a pussy.

I don't imagine that this is a particularly unique story. Most boys, at some point in their childhoods, have done things that they otherwise wouldn't have because they didn't have the fortitude to resist peer pressure. This incident stands out in my memory, but I'm sure that it wasn't the first time it happened in my life. I think that everyone would agree that such things are a normal part of growing up.

Of course, characterizing any behavior as a typical part of the maturation process implies that, eventually, we're supposed to grow out of it. When a twelve-year old boy attempts a hopeless trick on his dirt bike in order to get his buddies to stop taunting him, he's just being a regular kid. When a thirty-year old man does the same thing, he's a damned fool.

I'm happy to say that I've never been goaded into another Evel Knievel moment, but I can't really claim to have figured out how to handle peer pressure. Since high school, this failing has mostly manifested itself when I drink. On my own, I think I can appreciate that there's never any reasonable justification for finishing those last few shots of whatever rotgut bourbon happens to be in front of me on any given night, but if I happen to be with someone who might question my manhood, all that good sense goes out the window. That bottle always winds up empty.

I always felt like I should have stopped caring so much about what other people thought of me, but I was never quite able to tune them out and do my own thing. Anyway, it's not like it ever did me any real harm. I suppose I've puked a few more times than I otherwise would have, and suffered through some avoidable hangovers, but that always seemed a small price to pay for immunity from questions about my masculinity.

All of that explains, at least as well as anything else can, why I found myself sitting in a conference room in my father's office building on a Friday afternoon, four days before Wainwright was slated to close his final land buy. After Jill had jogged off in a huff over my unwillingness to solicit a capital contribution from my family, her words had continued to gnaw at me. She certainly hadn't been wrong. I hadn't wanted to ask my father for money because I was afraid that he'd laugh at me. Whatever other reasons I might have had, it pretty much boiled down to that.

About half an hour after she left, I hauled myself over to the driving range, in the hope that spending a little time with my long irons would take my mind off of everything. As it turns out, isolating oneself from the world with a bucket of golf balls tends to promote introspection rather than discourage it. I found myself spraying shots all over the range while I replayed my conversation with Jill, too distracted to properly do the thing to which I'd turned in search of distraction.

Her calling me out for cowardice triggered all of my usual angst, and I'm sure that those feelings were amplified by my inability to define our relationship. Was she my girlfriend? Would she stick around if she thought that I was afraid of my dad?

Beyond that, there was something else that she'd said that I found myself unable to ignore, the bit about my father not trusting me. That really got under my skin, because by then I was completely convinced that my father was never going to approve of the way I lived my life unless I toed the line and did things his way. At some point, I just wanted to him to accept the fact that I was as much an adult as he was, and to at least entertain the possibility that I might be capable of finding my own path. I understood, of course, that asking him for half a million dollars was a different question entirely, but in my mind it was all connected. I was thirty-one years old, for Christ's sake. How long would I have to wait for him to start treating me like a grown-up?

Once I started going down that road, it was just a matter of letting my frustration build, which it steadily continued to do as I smacked ball after ball down the range with my four-iron, barely taking time to take a proper stance before I whacked away. The exercise surely didn't do much for my golf swing. What was supposed to have been a focused practice session had devolved into an aggression-burning workout. I might as well have been pounding away at a punching bag.

When I got back to the house, I dumped my clubs in the doorway and marched straight to the bedroom, where I found Jill fresh out of the shower, wrapped in a towel and brushing her long hair in the mirror. Without even giving her a chance to get dressed, I had her follow me back to the dining table, where I parked her so that she could watch and listen while I called my father. As I waited for him to answer, I turned on my phone's speaker and set it on the table between us.

She had a front row seat, then, as I explained the situation to my dad and asked for his backing. Honestly, I thought I did a pretty good job of presenting things, without getting into any of the sordid details that might have put off a man like my father. I began by reminding him that we'd discussed Wainwright on his last visit, and then explained that my association with him had led to my getting wind of an appealing business opportunity. I walked him through the deal, and outlined the massive return that he was sure to see on his investment. At the end, I told him that I needed half a million dollars in order to take advantage of the opportunity, and then I held my breath.

I didn't have to hold it for long. My fear had been that my father would laugh me off the phone when I asked him for five hundred grand. As it turned out, the reality was even worse. Instead of laughing, he just swatted my request aside, taking the same tone that he'd used whenever I'd asked for too much dessert as a child. *You've already had two cookies tonight, Malcolm. You know better than to ask for a brownie sundae as well.*

When I pushed back and tried to get him to take a few seconds, at least, to think it over, the only concession that I could draw out of him was an offer to have his people look it over, "if this is a real thing." I saw that as a ray of hope, but as soon as I reminded him that our timeline would preclude any kind of extensive analysis, he reverted back to his original flat refusal. After a couple of rounds of asking didn't yield the faintest sign of progress, I thanked him for his time and hung up.

I held my palms up and looked at Jill, who looked damp and dumbfounded by what she'd just witnessed. "See what I mean?" I prompted her. "I told you that there was no way in hell he'd go for it."

She shrugged. "At least you tried."

I took a deep breath, and shook my head. "I told him about your father before... before I even met you," I began. "He was down here, not long after I met your dad, and I told him a little bit about it. He was suspicious, convinced that your father was glomming onto me because he knew about my family's money. I'm sure he thinks that this whole thing is me getting played by Wainwright."

"That's ridiculous! My father doesn't even know that you know about..."

I held up my hand, chuckling. "I know, I know... but I'm not the one you need to convince."

She gestured toward the stacks of Wainwright's papers that were still piled high on the other end of the table. "What about all that? Doesn't that prove that this is real?"

"Doesn't much matter if my father never looks at..." I stopped in the middle of my sentence and started laughing.

"What? What's so funny?"

"That's it," I murmured.

"What's it?"

"My father needs to see these papers."

Jill looked confused. "You think you can get him to come down here? Like, tomorrow?"

I shook my head. "That's never gonna happen. I gotta take 'em to New York."

"How are you gonna...?"

"Frequent flier miles, baby!" Not for the first time, I was grateful for all of that post-college travelling that my family had funded. Before Jill could say another word, I grabbed my phone, stood up and announced, "I gotta go make some calls." I headed for the back patio, leaving Jill alone in her towel.

Chapter Thirty-Three

The door to the conference room swung open and my father burst through it, wearing a look of concern that I perceived to be genuine. "MJ!" he cried, using the nickname by which he'd called me when I was a boy. "Is everything OK? Janet told me that you were here and I was worried. Are you OK?"

I nodded. "I'm fine. Everything's fine." I could see Janet, who had been my father's secretary for as long as I could remember, standing in the hall behind him. I gave her a quick wave, which she returned before my father shut the door behind him.

When he turned back to face me, I could see that his concerned expression had evaporated, replaced by one of unadulterated confusion. "Well, uh, I'm glad to hear that. I was worried," he repeated. After a pause, he went on. "Obviously, I'm surprised to see you here."

"I really need to talk to you."

"Are you back up here now? I thought that you were still in Florida..."

"I'm still down there. Just in town for the day. I wanted to talk face-to-face."

He didn't seem to know how to respond to that. "So," he sputtered, "you came... you flew all the way up here... just to talk to me?"

"Yup."

He shook his head. "You coulda just picked up the phone."

I shrugged. "I tried that the other day and I didn't get very far."

He just stared at me for a few seconds, furrowing his brow and pursing his lips together, before he began slowly shaking his head. "James, I'm really busy here today. I wish you would have called first." I noticed that he'd gone back to calling me by my grown-up name.

"I understand that, and I'm sorry. I just thought..."

He cut me off. "Janet pulled me off of a conference call to bring me down here. I had four lawyers on the phone who charge me a thousand bucks an hour, each."

"Sorry," I repeated. "At least it won't cost you anything to talk to me." I flashed him a quick smile.

"Somehow, I doubt that," he muttered, without showing the slightest sign of being amused.

I leaned forward against the table and gestured toward the chair next to me. "Just give me thirty minutes. Hear me out and then I'll leave you alone."

"Half an hour's a long time..."

"Twenty minutes?"

"If this about me giving you money for that scheme you told me about the other day, I can give you my answer right now..."

I held up my hand. "Just wait. I'm asking you to please hear me out before you say anything."

He shrugged. "You know my answer's not gonna change, right?"

"C'mon, Dad... I flew all the way from Florida to have this conversation. Humor me."

He took a deep breath, exhaled slowly, and took a seat in the chair next to me. "Fine. Say what you came here to say."

"Well," I began, "I didn't tell you the whole story on the phone." From there, I launched into a complete history of my association with Wainwright, leaving nothing out. I told my dad all about Liz, Peter, and, of course, Jill, including the stories behind our meeting in Vegas and her torturous relationship with her father. I disclosed the fact that we'd been living together since her return to the Keys, and I even explained how we'd conspired to break into the old man's house and steal his files. I knew that I was taking a big risk by going with the truth, but it seemed just crazy enough to maybe work.

After telling him all of that, I paused, eager to try to gauge his reaction. To his credit, he'd made a good show of at least seeming interested while I'd shared my story. For all I knew, he'd only feigned engagement out of courtesy, but I wanted to believe that my tale had sucked him in. For as much as he gave the impression of being an active listener, though, his demeanor offered no clue as to what he was thinking. I tried not to read too much into that; after all, he had forty years' worth of practice when it came to keeping a poker face while people sat across from him and tried to persuade him to invest in their enterprises.

After what seemed like an age had passed, he finally spoke up. "I'm not sure what to say."

"Hell of a story, isn't it?"

He paused for another beat before answering. "That's one way to put it, I guess." A few more seconds passed before he added, "Why on Earth would you tell me all of that?"

I felt like I'd prepared myself to answer any number of questions that he might have thrown at me, but that wasn't one of them. I felt my stomach seizing up as I fumbled for a response. "I, uh, just wanted to be honest with you," I stammered. "I wanted to make sure that you understood that all my cards were on the table when I asked you for this."

He took another deep breath, and I could see that the look of concern had found its way back onto his face. "I appreciate that, I guess, but hearing all this... it worries me. Your judgment... it just seems... I mean, you can understand why I'm worried about you, right? You do see that, don't you?" I opened my mouth, but he went on before I was able to get a word out. "All this stuff about arranged marriages, and envelopes full of cash... you shacking up with a stripper..."

"I know."

"And then you broke into his house! Have you thought about that, James? You're lucky you're not in jail."

"You're right," I admitted. "It was crazy... all of it. I knew it was crazy while it was happening, but there's an opportunity here, regardless of how we got to it."

He shook his head. "After everything you just told me, I don't see how I can..."

I didn't wait for the punch line. "When I first told you about Wainwright, when you were down in Marathon... you were worried that he was out to rip us off somehow, right? You got pissed off when I didn't take your warning seriously enough. Remember that?" He nodded, and I went on. "I had to tell you this whole story to show you that he's not playing me. He doesn't even know that we know about this deal."

"OK... but that doesn't necessarily mean that I'm gonna..."

I cut him off again. "And this explains why Grandpa was hanging around this guy, doesn't it?"

"What do you mean?"

"It's obvious. Grandpa must have gotten wind of what Wainwright was doing and he was trying to get in on it."

My father didn't say anything, but I could tell that this last statement had gotten his wheels spinning. I knew that he'd never bought into the idea of my grandfather suddenly finding religion before he died, because that outcome seemed completely at odds with everything that my father understood about his old man. Introducing money into the equation, though, must have made it all much easier to process; Grandpa spending time with an evangelical preacher made a lot more sense once my father was able to attribute it to a quest for earthly rather than heavenly rewards.

I sensed that invoking my grandfather had bolstered my credibility with my dad, so I tried to run with it. "This is for real," I said, softly. "Grandpa must have understood that." When my father didn't say anything right away, I reached for the first of several piles of documents that I'd taken from my bag and set on the conference room table prior to my father's arrival. "Let me show you..."

I expected him to stop me before I could get into the show-and-tell, but he didn't. He let me walk him through the paperwork for Wainwright's first land deal, and he even asked a few questions along the way. The more I sensed that he was finally taking me seriously, the more assured my presentation became. I took a glance at my watch. We'd been talking for thirty-five minutes.

I explained that Wainwright had already completed four other deals similar to the one that I'd just shown him, and then I turned to the big one, the one that we still had a chance to take for ourselves. I grabbed another set of papers and started guiding my father through the details. We looked at Wainwright's contract with the seller, the geological surveys, his correspondence with Green Summit... Once again, he let me get all the way through my spiel without cutting me off.

Once I was finished, I sat back and waited for a reaction, but my father just stared silently at the papers on the table in front of him. When I couldn't bear it any longer, I prompted him. "So... what do you think?"

He picked up his hands and fiddled with his wedding ring for a few seconds before he spoke. "Looks like these guys already have a deal. How do you know they'll even talk to you?"

I smiled. This was a question that I'd most definitely anticipated. "I've already talked to them."

"You have?"

"Yup. The seller was easy. I called him up yesterday and told him that I was working with Wainwright and asked if we could meet on Monday, supposedly to discuss logistics in advance of his closing. Once I get into the room with him, I'll get him to make a new deal with us. I figure he'll listen if I offer him another fifty grand or so..."

"What if he doesn't go for it?"

I shrugged. "Then the money stays in our pocket and we won't be any worse off than we are now, right?"

He nodded. "OK, I guess. But what about your buyer? If they back out, this whole exercise will be for nothing."

"That was a little tougher," I admitted. "When I got him on the phone, he didn't want to talk to me... didn't want to admit that he knew anything about it. It took a while, but once he figured out that I knew exactly what was up, he came around."

"What did he say?"

"At the end of the day, Green Summit doesn't really care who they buy the land from. If we're the ones that wind up with it, and our title is good, they'll give us the same deal that they would've given Wainwright."

"He said that?"

I pointed to the speaker phone in the middle of the table. "You want me to call him again, from here? You can hear it for yourself."

My father shook his head. "No. No need. I think we might be getting a little ahead of ourselves..."

Hearing that took the wind right out of my sails. "If you want to take some time to think about it, I understand, of course, but we've got to move fast."

"James... I know that you understand, at least a little, how these things work. There are certain procedures... processes... hoops that we jump through in order to get comfortable before we make an investment."

"I'm not asking for the bank's money," I reminded him.

"I take a similar approach when I invest for my own account. It's simply a matter of prudence."

"I get that. I really do. I wouldn't have brought something like this to you unless I was sure..."

He interrupted me. "Look... I can't say that I approve of what you've been doing... Honestly, I'm still having trouble getting my head around it. But this..." He paused, and gestured toward the papers that covered the table. "You've obviously put some real thought and effort into this. Guys come in here and pitch me on investment ideas every day, and most of them aren't half as articulate as you. If you could take that energy and devote it toward something real..."

He left the rest of his sentence unsaid, as if to invite me to complete it with whatever dream I hoped to realize. "You've been telling me that I need to get out there and make something happen for myself, right?" I asked.

"This isn't exactly what I had in mind."

"Me neither, but this is what I found, and I thought it was worth taking a shot."

After that, we just sat and looked at each other for a few moments before I stood up and started gathering my files. When I was done, he asked, "Are you going to see your mother?"

I shook my head. "Not this time. I gotta get back."

"You should visit her sometime. She worries about you."

"I know. I'll come back up here soon and see her."

"Good."

I zipped my bag shut, set it on the floor next to me, and offered my father my hand. As he rose to shake it, I thanked him.

"I'm sorry that I wasn't able to help you," he said, sounding sincerely disappointed.

"You heard me out. That's all I wanted."

"Should I have Janet call you a car?"

"Nah. I'm gonna grab a bite, and then I'll hop in a cab. Thanks, though."

With that, I opened the conference room door and started heading toward the elevator. I was about halfway down the hall when I heard my father call after me, "Take care of yourself!"

I paused and turned back toward him before replying. "You too, Dad."

Chapter Thirty-Four

As it turned out, I should have taken my father up on his offer to get me a car to the airport. I don't imagine that the two slices that I had at the nondescript pizza joint around the corner from his office were any better than the fast food I could have grabbed in the terminal, and I wound up paying fifty dollars for a cab to LaGuardia about twenty minutes after I left the conference room, anyway. I had a couple of hours to spare before my flight, but I didn't have the energy to drag my suitcase all over Manhattan just for the sake of killing time.

Waiting at my gate, I'd already gotten through an issue of *Sports Illustrated*, a bottle of water and a Cinnabon when my phone rang. I brushed the crumbs off my lap and fished it out of my pocket, and saw that it was my father, calling from his office. "Hey, Dad," I answered.

"Glad I caught you before your flight."

I checked my watch. "I think we still have another fifteen minutes before they board us. What's up?"

"Five percent," he replied.

"What?"

"Five percent."

"I heard you. I just don't know what you're talking about... what's five percent?"

"If we do this deal, I'll give you five percent of the profits. That's sixty grand."

My heart rate immediately accelerated, and I had to struggle to get my next breath. I couldn't believe what I was hearing. "You still there?" he asked.

"Uh, yeah... I'm still here. I just don't know what to say."

"Just say we have a deal."

"I don't understand. I thought you said that you were..."

"Just call it a hunch," he replied.

"That's fantastic!" I said. "I just can't believe that you're actually gonna do this. Thank you!"

"So you're OK with five percent?" he asked, for the third time in less than two minutes. I had to hand it to him for keeping his eye on the ball.

"Actually, I was hoping for a little more even split..."

"Uh huh. What did you have in mind?"

I hesitated for a second, but decided to throw it out there. "I was thinking more like sixty-forty... your way, of course."

He laughed. "That's a mighty big ask from somebody that's not putting up any capital."

"Yeah, but I'm the one who found this deal, and I'm the one doing all the work."

"Maybe you'll be able to find another investor that will put a higher value on your contributions. I hope it works out for you."

"You know that there won't be any other investors."

"Exactly." I pictured him sitting at his desk, looking as smug as could be. He had me over a barrel, and we both knew it. Five percent of one-point two million was a hell of a lot better than a hundred percent of nothing.

I decided to try a different argument. "I know that you give those hedge fund assholes twenty percent of your upside, and you're not even related to them."

"They're professional money managers."

"They're clowns. Half the time, they can't even beat the index."

"Those guys have put in their time. They've earned the right to charge what they charge. Not sure your track record matches up."

"I'm just sayin' that their job is to come up with investment ideas, and that's what I did. It just so happens that my idea is gonna triple your money in a week. I'll put that up against their ROI any day."

"So," my father responded, after a long pause, "you're saying that you want twenty percent?"

"How about twenty-five?"

"Don't push your luck."

I did a quick bit of math in my head, which confirmed that, at twenty percent, I was looking at two-hundred and forty thousand dollars. It was a lot of money, and I was pretty sure that it was as good as I was going to do. "OK" was the only thing I said.

"OK," my father repeated. "We'll split the profits eighty-twenty. The funds will be in your Citibank account on Monday morning."

"Thank you," I murmured, still dumbfounded at the turn that events had taken. It still didn't feel like it could possibly be real.

My father gave me some final instructions before we hung up. "Keep me in the loop."

"Sure... of course. Anything else?"

"Don't fuck this up."

That summed up my marching orders about as well as anything could, so we said our goodbyes and ended the call. I noticed that they'd started calling rows for my flight, so I gathered my stuff and started making my way toward the boarding door. Before I got there, I dialed Jill's number and left her a quick voicemail.

"We did it!" was all that I said, right as I handed my ticket to the gate agent and walked onto the jetway.

Chapter Thirty-Five

By the time I touched down in Miami, I had two voicemails waiting for me. The first was Jill's ecstatic response to the message I'd left for her. I was already fantasizing about how she'd react when I delivered the good news in person, and hearing the excitement in her voice got me even more amped up. I was so anxious to get on the road back to Marathon that I broke into a jog on my way to the baggage claim area.

Unfortunately, all that euphoria drained out of me when I listened to that second voicemail. Jill had left it about ninety minutes after the first one, and as soon as I heard her voice I knew that something had shaken her. Apparently, she'd gotten a call from Georgia. Her mother had had a stroke, and was in the hospital fighting for her life. She said that she was leaving for Valdosta right away, and that she'd call me when she could.

I had already slowed to a walk, but when I got to the end of the message, I stopped moving altogether. I just stood in the middle of the terminal, staring at my phone and trying to make sense of what I'd just heard. The timing was unbelievable, and it wasn't like we had any flexibility with what we were trying to do.

At that moment, I caught myself, and I felt like a massive asshole for turning my thoughts toward anything other than Jill's well-being. I knew that she'd drifted apart from her mother in recent years, but the fact remained that this was the person who'd taken care of her throughout her entire childhood. I couldn't fathom what must have been going through her mind. When I dialed her number, it went straight to voicemail, which made sense when I realized that she was going to have to drive through the night. I just wanted her to know that I was thinking about her.

It was after one in the morning by the time I made it back to my dark, empty house. I noticed that Jill's red suitcase was gone, which shouldn't have been surprising, given that it was the only piece of luggage that she'd brought out from Vegas. Still, the absence of her things seemed to amplify my loneliness. Taking her away from me just as I felt as if I would burst at the seams for want of someone with whom to share my adventures seemed like the cruelest of pranks.

I'd traveled at least twenty-five hundred miles that day, but that felt like small potatoes compared to the width of the chasm that my father and I had suddenly managed to bridge. Getting his backing had left me ecstatic, but also terrified. That combination apparently trumped physical exhaustion, and I spent most of the night lying in bed awake, staring at the ceiling and fighting the urge to vomit. I must have drifted off eventually, because I awoke just after nine o'clock on Saturday morning, drenched in sweat and disoriented by the bright sunlight that had filled the room. Apparently, I'd neglected to close the curtains before crawling into bed.

When I retrieved my phone, I found a text from Jill waiting for me. Her message was brief, simply saying that she'd arrived safely at the hospital and repeating her promise to call me when she got the chance. I sent her a short reply, just to let her know that I was thinking of her, and resolved not to pester her until she was ready to talk.

Ninety minutes later, I found myself dialing her number, and leaving her a voicemail. I knew that I should have given her some space to take care of her mom, but I couldn't contain myself. I wound up leaving six other messages on her phone over the course of the weekend. As worried as I was about her and her mother, it was my own selfish desire to talk to her that drove me. I hoped I didn't annoy her too much, but I counted on the fact that people don't usually get dumped for being *too* communicative during a crisis.

Without anyone around to talk to, Saturday and Sunday blended into one unbearably long purgatory. When I wasn't pining for Jill, I was freaking out about the fact that my father was going to put half a million dollars into my bank account in less than forty-eight hours, with the expectation that I would triple his investment in a week. I kept going over my plan for Monday, convinced that I'd overlooked something obvious that would wind up sinking me. I found myself hoping that I'd find a reason to call the whole thing off, but in spite of all my obsessing, I wasn't able to come up with one. I suppose that should have made me feel better, but my sense of foreboding only seemed to increase as the minutes crawled by.

By Sunday night, I was a total wreck. I'd barely slept since getting back to the Keys, and I'd only managed to choke down a few bites of food over the course of the whole weekend. It was as if every fiber of my body was trying to talk me out of moving forward with our scheme. All I had to do was sleep in on Monday, and then wire the money back to my father when I woke up. No harm, no foul.

The problem was that nothing had changed since Friday. My plan was as sound (or as unsound, as the case might have been) on Sunday as it had been two days before. After flying all the way to New York and selling my father on it, I couldn't very well abandon it because I'd gotten cold feet.

Of course, I also had to consider Jill's feelings. She'd been the one driving the boat on all of this, and I didn't want to disappoint her, especially in light of what she was going through. I was sure that our plan was the furthest thing from her mind at that moment, but it felt like it was the one thing that I could do that would put a smile on her face. The fact that she might not feel like enjoying it right away didn't make it seem any less worth doing. If anything, her circumstances made me even more determined to make something good happen for us.

It was just before eight on Sunday evening when I heard my phone ringing, and when I saw that it was Jill, I snatched it from the coffee table and answered. "Hey! I'm so glad you called. I've been so worried about you... and your mother. How ya doin'?"

"I'm, uh, OK, I guess. Hangin' in there."

"How's your mom?"

She paused for a moment before she answered. "We still don't know... can't get a straight answer from anyone here. I mean, it seemed like she might have been showing some positive signs, but the doctors are so cautious about saying anything. We just have to wait and see..."

"Well, that sounds like it could be encouraging... maybe..."

"We just have to wait and see," she repeated, like she was trying to inoculate herself against any unwarranted optimism.

"I'm so sorry... about everything. I wish that I was there with you."

"You've got plenty to do on your end," she replied. "Tell me about your trip to New York."

I felt guilty about shifting her attention away from her ailing mother, but I was so anxious to share that I jumped into it without hesitating. I told her everything that had passed between me and my father, including the financial arrangement upon which we'd agreed. If she was troubled by our share being less than she'd anticipated, she didn't show any sign of it. When I got to the end of my story, her only reaction was to say, "It sounds like your father really does believe in you."

I wasn't sure that I'd ever heard anyone say that before, at least not since I was a child. I downplayed it with a quick "I guess so," but hearing it really touched me.

"Thank you," she went on, in a softer voice.

"Don't thank me yet," I laughed.

"No... I know how hard it was for you to go to your father... and that you did it for me."

"I did it for us," I corrected her.

"Thank you," she repeated. "It means a lot."

"I was thinking that maybe after I got done in Immokalee tomorrow, I would drive up to meet you."

"Don't," she shot back.

"But I really want to be there for you..."

"The best thing that you can do for me right now is to take care of this business for us. By the time you're done, I'm sure my mom will be better and we'll celebrate then."

"I just thought that maybe I'd have some time after tomorrow, before we sell..."

She cut me off. "Let's just get through tomorrow first, OK?"

"Yeah... OK."

"You ready?"

"Uh huh." That was the furthest thing from the truth, but I didn't see how giving voice to my misgivings would have helped either of us at that point.

"You got this," she said.

"I hope so."

"You got this," she repeated. "Call me when you're done tomorrow?"

"Of course."

"I love you," she announced. It was the first time that a woman had ever said those words to me.

"I love you, too," I replied, instantly.

After that, we said our goodbyes and hung up. Just like that, all of my concerns melted away. I was invincible.

Chapter Thirty-Six

As wonderful as it was to hear Jill profess her love for me, the one thing that it didn't do was help me fall asleep that night. If anything, adding a dash of ecstasy to the already potent cocktail of emotions that was sloshing around my system made it even harder to shake the insomnia that had plagued me for three nights running. I tried sipping on a glass of bourbon before bed, but it didn't seem to have any effect beyond making me feel like my body temperature had gone up a few degrees. Once again, I stared at that ceiling for hours, sweating through my sheets while my mind pulled me in a thousand different directions at once.

When morning finally came, I tried telling myself that never having fallen into too deep of a sleep might have been just as well. I was supposed to meet the seller in Immokalee at ten, which meant that I needed to be on the road by six, at the latest. Under normal circumstances, I would have had concerns about oversleeping, especially without another person around to act as a fail-safe for the alarm clock. As it happened, though, spending the night half-awake made it easier to get out of bed, and I wound up hitting the road a little before five-thirty.

I picked up a couple of Red Bulls on my way out of town, but that was more a precaution than a reaction to anything that I was feeling. Now that the day had finally arrived, adrenaline had taken over and I wasn't struggling with the exhaustion that should have accompanied a sleep deficit like the one I'd been racking up. The scenery didn't hurt, either. Watching the sun climb out of the Atlantic was an exhilarating sight, no matter the circumstances. By the time that dawn had fully broken, I was almost to Key Largo.

I approached Immokalee from the south, along Route 29. It was the sort of road that doesn't even exist in the northeastern part of the country: perfectly straight, impossibly flat, and just about devoid of human activity. According to my map, it ran along the edge of a wildlife preserve, but I never caught a glimpse of any of the resident panthers. Other than the blue sky and the narrow ribbon of grey asphalt that extended out to the horizon in front of me, the only visible color was the green of the thick, low vegetation that covered the ground for as far as I could see to either side.

I had to have gone at least ten miles before I saw my first building, a ramshackle gas station that may or may not have been defunct. After that, it was back to nature. Immokalee was about twenty miles off of I-75, and it's hard to imagine a more desolate stretch anywhere on the East Coast. I considered how terrifying it would have been to walk it after dark. Some people are afraid of big cities, but I would have gladly strolled through the roughest neighborhood in Detroit if it meant avoiding the swamp people and the gators and whatever else prowled the night on the outskirts of Miles City, Florida. I could almost hear the voice-over guy from the movie trailers in my head: *On Route 29, there's no one to hear you scream...*

Zipping by at seventy miles an hour in the bright sunshine, though, made it all seem innocuous enough, and after fifteen minutes I noticed the first heralds of civilization: an uptick in the frequency of the road signs, and then another gas station, and, eventually, some cultivated fields. These were followed by a handful of produce warehouses, and then, around a bend to the left, some houses and an elementary school. Before I knew it, I was smack in the middle of a town.

There didn't seem to be a whole lot to it. At the corner of Main and 1st there was a sign pointing toward the courthouse and the sheriff's office, and also toward the local Seminole Indian casino. I thought about following that arrow and finding a roulette wheel where I could throw the whole half-million on the "second twelve" bet. I knew that I would lose that wager slightly more than twice as often as I won it, but at least I understood those probabilities. I had sold this real estate flip to my father as a sure thing, but now that I was only a few minutes away from putting it all into motion, I had to confront the fact that I really had no clue about the odds I was up against.

I took a deep breath, thought about Jill, and smiled. I didn't need to gamble on a bouncing ball or a deck of cards. We had it all figured out. Buy low, sell high, simple as that. I'd come too far to chicken out.

I followed Route 29 around a sharp bend to the right, where it stopped being Main Street and turned into North 15th. Once I passed the Burger King, I started paying attention to the addresses. According to the directions I'd pulled from Google, the place I was looking for should have been on the left, about a quarter-mile farther down. I missed it the first time, but when I turned around and made another pass, I spotted the number on a building and pulled into its tiny parking lot.

I was supposed to meet the seller at his office, but this place didn't appear to be much of one, even by local standards. It was the simplest of structures, nothing more than a white, rectangular box onto which someone had slapped a red tile roof. There were two windows facing the street, and a door which opened into the parking lot on one side. I didn't see any signage that would have alerted passersby to the nature of the business being conducted inside, and my car was one of only two in the lot. I assumed that the other belonged to the man whom I was there to see.

Only when I got out of the car and approached the door did I find a small placard hanging on the wall, letting me know that I was, in fact, about to enter someone's place of business. "JOS. M. SMITH," it read, and then, just below that, in smaller type, "Insurance Brokerage." Nothing about the building or the sign seemed permanent.

That impression was reinforced when I pushed the door open and stepped inside. The lights were on, and the room appeared to be furnished, but everything was covered by a white drop cloth, as if someone were in the middle of painting the walls. "Hello?" I called out.

I heard rustling through the wall, followed by a man's voice: "Coming!" Seconds later, one of the two doors leading out of the main room swung open, and a short, slight man walked through it. He looked to be maybe fifteen or twenty years older than me, but he was dressed like a refugee from a northeastern prep school: flip-flops on his feet, Madras pants, a blue and white striped Oxford with the sleeves rolled up to his elbows. "I'm Joe Smith," he announced as he held out his hand. I thought that I detected a hint of an English accent when he spoke, but I wasn't sure.

"Nice to meet you," I said, as I shook his hand after introducing myself.

"Sorry about all this. We're right in the middle of moving to a new office, just down the street." He paused and gestured vaguely toward the road. "But they're still setting everything up over there. I didn't want to get in the way, so I figured we'd just meet here. I hope you don't mind the mess."

"Not at all," I said, more concerned with trying to place his accent than I was with the state of his offices. I'd decided that he wasn't English. He might have been Australian, but I wouldn't have been willing to wager on it. Wherever he'd come from, he'd apparently been in the States long enough to erode all but the vaguest hint of his origins.

"So," he continued. "You work with John?"

I nodded. "I've, uh, helped him out with one or two projects over the last few months."

"Uh huh. Well, I have to say that I was a bit nervous when I heard from you..."

"Nervous?"

"We're all set to close this deal tomorrow, and then you call to schedule this last-minute meeting... makes me wonder if there's a problem..." The way he pronounced the soft "ch" in the word "schedule" gave him away as a foreigner.

"Not really a 'problem,'" I murmured. "I just hoped that we could discuss one or two things..."

"I knew it!" he roared, raising his voice so suddenly that it made me flinch. "I'm calling John right now!" He turned and marched back through the door from which he'd come.

I followed right behind him. "Hold on! There's no reason to call John."

"Like hell there isn't!" he replied, without breaking stride. We'd gone into what I assumed was his office. The only furnishings left in it were a desk and couple of chairs, but at least they weren't covered by tarps. The desk was empty save for a few sheets of paper and a telephone. Smith parked himself in his chair and reached for the receiver.

"Wait! Just hear what I have to say before you make that call."

He shook his head. "You're here to stall. I can feel it. When I made this deal with John, I was very clear about the timing. I need to get this settled. If he's not ready to do that, then he and I need to talk…" His voice trailed off after that, but I was pretty sure that he muttered something about Wainwright not having the balls to come himself.

"I never said that Mr. Wainwright wasn't ready to close," I announced.

That seemed to grab his attention. "So, we *are* all set for tomorrow, then?"

I shrugged. "As far as I know, John's still expecting to close tomorrow, sure."

Smith sat back, eyeing me as he crossed his arms. He looked ridiculous, with his jumble of clashing stripes and plaids hanging off of his stick-figure body. After a moment, he spoke, his voice lowered once again to a normal conversational volume. "But you didn't drive all the way here from the Keys just to tell me that, did you?"

There was my opening. I paused and took a deep breath. "What would you say if I told you that I wasn't here on John Wainwright's behalf?"

"Is that what you're telling me?"

I nodded. "I'm here because I hoped you'd be willing to listen to a better offer for your land..."

He cut me off. "It's a bit late for that now, don't you think?"

"That's up to you to decide. But I'm willing to pay you more than you're getting from Wainwright."

"How do you know what I'm getting?"

"I know that he's agreed to pay you five-hundred thousand dollars tomorrow." Smith obviously tried not to react, but he had a lousy poker face. If I hadn't already been sure about Wainwright's price, his seller's expression would have confirmed it beyond a doubt. I went on. "I'm prepared to offer you a ten percent premium on top of that."

"Fifty thousand more?" he asked, maybe forgetting that his calculation served to verify the fact that I'd gotten the price right.

"Yup."

For a moment, I thought that I might have piqued his interest, but when he spoke again, he tried to shoo me away. "I wish you'd come earlier, before I signed papers with John. I don't think that I can just breach my contract with him."

I unzipped the briefcase that I'd carried in from the car, pulled out a copy of the agreement between Smith and Wainwright, and tossed it onto the desk. "You mean this contract?"

He sat quietly for a few moments, flipping pages and looking confounded. Once he got to the end, and saw his own signature on the last page, he set it back down. "Yeah, that's the one... how in blazes did you get your hands on that?"

"I'm a close friend of the Wainwright family." I wasn't lying to him. After all, Jill was a member of the Wainwright family and we'd gotten pretty damned cozy.

He hesitated before going on, but if he was thinking about asking another question about my relationship with the old man, he must have thought better of it. Instead, he just shook his head. "Doesn't really matter where you got it from, does it? Doesn't change the fact that I signed it."

"If you're worried about Wainwright suing you, don't."

He started laughing. "I'll bet you're going to explain exactly why I don't need to worry about that, aren't you?" I opened my mouth to oblige, but before I could get a word out, he continued. "But even if you could convince me, I'm afraid you're wasting your time."

"Why's that?"

"Like I said, you're too late. I don't have time to go through all this again. I need the money tomorrow."

I smiled. "I'm ready to close as soon as we can get the papers signed. We can do it today, if you want."

"That's not how it works," he snapped. "Have you ever bought land before?" This last question seemed intended to make me feel like a child.

"I have," I replied, deploying my first out and out lie of the day. "And I'm ready to close."

"I'm sure. And your bank will just give you a mortgage this afternoon, just like that?" he asked, snapping his fingers for effect.

"I'm ready to pay cash," I replied, coolly. "No mortgage. No bank."

Smith raised his eyebrows and shot a glance at my briefcase. "You have half a million in that bag?"

"I don't have the cash on me, no... I just meant my bank is ready to wire it to your account, as soon as I give them the word."

"Uh huh," was all he said, and I was pretty sure that it was his way of letting me know that he thought that I was full of shit. Still, he continued to humor me. "That's nice," he went on, "but there are some other things you'll need before you can close: contract, survey, appraisal, title search...." Again, he sounded like he was trying to explain the workings of the world to a twelve-year old kid.

I just grinned, picked up my bag and started pulling out papers and setting them on his desk. "I've got it all covered," I announced.

He pawed through the documents in silence for a few moments before he murmured, "All of this was prepared for Wainwright."

"No need to reinvent the wheel," I said, still grinning.

"You said you were his friend?"

I shrugged. "Acquaintance might be a better word."

"'Thief' seems more like it."

"Definitely not the word I'd pick." I wasn't smiling anymore.

"You *did* steal this stuff from him, didn't you?"

"I wouldn't call it 'stolen,'" I replied, weakly.

He smirked. "What would you call it?"

"The free market at work," I replied, anxious to try to shift his focus away from the provenance of the documents in my briefcase and back toward the money that I was trying to dangle in front of him. "John never mentioned that there might be other parties interested in your land?"

"Must have slipped his mind."

"Well, I'm glad I got to you in time." After a beat, I added, "That extra fifty grand will get you some nice furniture for that new office."

Again, I was pretty sure that I detected a flicker of interest in his eyes, but he wasn't on board yet. "And if I were to do this," he asked, "what's to stop our friend Mr. Wainwright from turning his lawyers on us?"

"If he sued you, he'd have to open himself up to questions, and I can guarantee you that he's not gonna be willing to do that."

"What makes you so sure?"

I paused for a few seconds, searching for the right words. Finally, I settled on, "John Wainwright is not what he appears to be."

"What the hell does that even mean?"

"It means he won't want to answer questions under oath about where he gets his money."

He sat and stared at me with his elbows on his desk and his chin resting on his interlocked fingers for what seemed like quite a long time. When he finally spoke again, I was disappointed. "This is ridiculous," he muttered as he extended his right arm in the direction of the phone. "Let's call John right now and see what he has to say about all this."

"I'd really rather not…"

He tried to brush my protest aside. "You've said some nasty things about the man… only seems fair that we give him a chance to defend himself." When I failed to immediately acknowledge the logic of his suggestion, he added, "I made a deal with him, after all."

I nodded, to try to convey the fact that I was sympathetic to his situation, but my sympathy only went so far. "I appreciate that, but I didn't come here to get into a bidding war. If you dial that number, my offer's off the table."

My threat had the desired effect in that Smith pulled his hand back from the phone without placing his call, but it also seemed to piss him off. He pushed himself back from his desk and stood up. "I don't like being strong-armed."

I stayed in my chair and adopted the most innocent tone that I could muster. "No one's strong-arming anybody here. I'm trying to give you *more* money for your land, remember?"

I watched him walk slowly over to the window. He lingered there, staring out at the street, for a few seconds before he said anything. "You keep saying that, but my gut tells me that I should have thrown you out of here ten minutes ago."

"And yet I'm still here," I observed.

He turned back to face me. "It doesn't add up. You want me to believe that Wainwright is a shady character, but you're the one that shows up out of nowhere with half a million bucks burning a hole in your pocket. Where does a young guy like you get a hold of that kind of cash?"

I mentioned the name of my father's bank, and asked him if he'd heard of it. When he said he had, I explained that my father was a very senior managing director there, which only seemed to confuse him.

"So," he ventured, "your father's bank wants to buy my land?"

"No, not the bank... just me and my father. I only mentioned the bank to show you..." I hesitated for a moment, searching for the right words. "I just wanted you to know that I wasn't some sort of criminal... or just a punk. My family's had money for a long time." As soon as those words left my lips, I regretted them, but I'm not sure that there's a way to say what I was trying to say without sounding like an asshole.

I stood up and joined Smith at the window, where I held my phone so he could see the screen as I Googled my father's name. Sure enough, all the search results mentioned the bank. Then, I pulled out my wallet and showed him my driver's license. "See?" I asked. "Same last name."

He shook his head. "Not a particularly uncommon one. That certainly doesn't prove anything."

I opened up a new window and let him watch while I logged into my bank account and pointed to the balance on display: $553,000 and change. "You believe Citibank?" I asked.

"How do I know that's not some bullshit trick you just played on your phone?"

"When I wire you the money, your bank will confirm receipt. I can't fake that, can I?"

He wandered back over to his desk and sat down, rubbing his temples with his hands. "What makes all you guys so keen on this property, anyhow? I mean, why is a posh New York banker like your father interested in my little patch here in South Florida?"

"Actually," I corrected him, "this is my deal. My father is providing some of the financing, but I'm the one who's interested."

"Why you, mate?"

I shrugged. "Same reason as Wainwright, I suppose. I see it as an attractive investment opportunity."

"Maybe I ought to just hold onto it, then."

My heart sank, but I tried not to let it show. "Maybe you should," I said, simply.

He continued to rub his head. "My daughter," he announced, "starts university next month."

"Congratulations," I replied, thrown off by the sudden turn toward the personal that our conversation had taken. "Where at?"

"Wake Forest, in North Carolina."

"I know it, of course. Good school."

"Not cheap," he shot back. "First tuition payment is due next week."

I had to suppress the urge to smile. Smith needed liquidity. He was going to sell his land one way or the other.

He went on. "That extra fifty thousand could cover a whole year, just about."

"Just about," I repeated. I had been thinking about pointing out that very fact before he spared me the trouble by bringing it up himself. I sensed that he was coming around.

He straightened himself up in his seat and folded his hands together in front of him. "I'm scheduled to close with Wainwright at one o'clock tomorrow afternoon."

"Uh huh," I replied, waiting for the punchline.

"So if I don't get the money from you by noon, our deal will be off and I'll go ahead and sell to him. Understood?"

I nodded. "So we have a deal?"

"One other condition," he said. "When we're all done, you're the one that has to call Wainwright and let him know."

I walked toward him with a broad smile. "Gladly," I replied, as we shook hands.

Chapter Thirty-Seven

Getting to "yes" in our negotiations proved to be a double-edged sword. Almost instantly, it felt like someone had opened a valve and released all of the anxieties that I'd been hauling around ever since Jill and I had cooked up our crazy plot. There were still a ton of moving parts, but I felt like I'd just cleared the toughest hurdle. We were in the deal. From there, we just had to execute the game plan, and our reward would be there, waiting for us. The thought of it infused me with a feeling of weightlessness.

Unfortunately, the spigot that drained my tensions also seemed to have tapped into my reservoir of adrenaline, and I could almost feel it seeping out of me. Finally, my body was starting to rebel against my poor use of it, and it conveyed its displeasure by shocking me with intermittent pulses of extreme fatigue. When these were coupled with the peaks of elation that my brain was still trying to surf, it made for a pretty disconcerting sensation.

My cause wasn't helped by the fact that my moment of triumph was followed by a dispiriting period of inactivity. Right after we'd shaken on our agreement, Smith had dialed his lawyers and instructed them to prepare the documents necessary to effect our new arrangement. When he got off the phone, he told me that it was going to take them a few hours, at least, to get everything teed up. This was disappointing news, as I'd assumed that they'd merely take the papers they'd already prepared for the sale to Wainwright and insert my name in place of his. When I said as much to Smith, he just shrugged his shoulders and flashed me a half-smile, wordlessly bidding me to accept the futility of demanding anything more expeditious from people that got paid by the hour. I didn't say anything else about it.

Smith looked at his watch and suggested that I go get something to eat, and return around one o'clock. Having nothing better to do, and thinking that my body might appreciate some nourishment, I readily agreed. I'm not sure if my fried chicken value meal made me feel better or worse, but at least I made sure to suck down a couple of Diet Cokes for the caffeine. Those, combined with the coffee I picked up at a donut shop on the way back to Smith's office, guaranteed that I'd spend half the day standing in front of a urinal, but that seemed preferable to falling asleep in the middle of our closing.

I'd been back from lunch for almost an hour when a woman pushed her way through the door, with a briefcase slung over her right shoulder and two oversized file folders tucked under her left arm. She seemed oblivious to my presence as she brushed past me and dumped everything onto Smith's desk, tossing a terse greeting in his direction as she did so. He thanked her for responding to his call so quickly and introduced me.

She had blonde hair, but when she turned toward me to shake hands, I could see that her roots were dark brown. She wore a grey skirt and a plain white blouse. I think that the ensemble was meant to be topped off with a matching jacket, but in that part of the world, it seemed excessive to expect anyone to parade around in the heat of the day in full dress uniform. I didn't find her unattractive, but there was something off-putting about her expression. Her face was too thin and her features too angular, which made her look like an angry bird. The softness that would have come with the addition of a few extra pounds would have done her a world of good, I thought.

By the time I'd drawn that conclusion, she'd already turned away and started pulling papers out of her briefcase and arranging them in neat little piles on the desk. Smith and I watched her without saying a word. Finally, she ran out of papers, and she set the empty folders on the floor and turned back toward me. "You ready to buy some land?"

"Yup."

"Pull up a chair, then," she said, as she pointed to a spot alongside the desk. As I made my way across the room, she reached into her briefcase and pulled out a handful of black pens and dropped them beside one of the piles of papers.

I lost track of how many times I signed my name over the course of the following hour. There were a lot of documents, and she had us sign all of them in triplicate. She explained each one in turn, but I stopped paying attention after the first few. I felt like she must have sensed that I was tuning her out, because every now and again she stopped and asked me if I understood what I was signing, and if I wanted to get a lawyer. Each time she asked, I assured her that I was good to go, and each time I told her that, she hesitated for a moment, as if she didn't believe me. Whatever doubts she may have had, they never stopped her from moving on to the next set of documents.

About halfway through, she passed me a letter and said, "Here is where you'll indemnify Mr. Smith for any claims that might be asserted against him by Mr. Wainwright."

"What?"

"It means that you'll be responsible for any cost that Mr. Smith incurs as a result of…"

I cut her off. "I know what an indemnity is. But we didn't discuss…"

Smith jumped in. "If you're so confident that Wainwright won't sue us, you should be willing to…"

I held up my hand. "Fine," was all I said, as I slid the papers toward myself and signed the first copy. I was confident that Jill and I would be able to handle her father. All I wanted to do was finish with Smith and get on my way.

By the end, I was signing papers as quickly as she could put them in front of me. When the assembly line stopped, I looked up, anxious to keep the ball rolling. It took me a few seconds to realize that there wasn't anything left to sign. I looked at the attorney, and then at Smith, and then back at the attorney, waiting for one of them to hand me another document. When neither did, I sat up straighter in my chair and asked, "Is that it?"

"That's it," the attorney replied, flashing me her first smile of the afternoon.

I stood up slowly. "So… we're done?"

"Well, there is one last thing…" she began.

"The money," Smith interjected.

"Oh… yes… of course," I stammered. I asked him for his bank account information before excusing myself and going back into the front room so that I could make a call. Over the weekend, my father had emailed me a contact in the private banking group at Citibank (as it turned out, it was actually the head of the private banking group). I should call this fellow, he explained, when I was ready to wire the money, and it would go much smoother than it would if I went through the regular retail banking channels. Sure enough, when I got him on the line I learned that my father had already reached out to him, and he'd been waiting for my call. I simply gave him the instructions and he promised to take care of it.

It took another fifty minutes for Smith's bank to confirm receipt of the funds. Once the word came, we all stood up and shook hands. The lawyer had already prepared complete sets of closing documents for each of me and Smith, and as she placed mine on the desk, I repeated my earlier question. "We're done, right?"

She nodded. "The land's all yours. You just need to record the deed with the Collier County Clerk."

"I think I saw a sign for that on my way into town."

She shook her head. "That's just the town clerk. The county clerk's office is in Naples."

"How far's that?"

"About forty-five minutes." She must have seen the frown on my face, because a few seconds later, she continued. "I can send a paralegal from my office over there to take care of it for you, if you'd rather."

"Really? I mean, that sounds great, but shouldn't I do it myself?"

She patted the folder. "You have everything you need right in here. If we don't file it, you can always go back and file it yourself. I just thought it would be more convenient for you if..."

I didn't even let her finish before agreeing to let her handle it. It might not have been best practice, but the last thing I wanted to do was drive forty-five minutes in the wrong direction before starting for home. I thanked her profusely before turning back to Smith. He gestured toward the phone. "I think you should break the news to our friend now."

I'd almost forgotten about my agreement to call Wainwright. I asked Smith to read out the number, and my hands shook as I dialed. When it started ringing, my heart was beating so hard that I swore that I could see my shirt moving when I looked down. My mind went blank, and I realized that I had no idea of what I would say when he picked up. Luckily, he never did. I wound up leaving him a halting voicemail, asking him to call my cell phone about an urgent matter. After I hung up, I shook everyone's hand one last time before I gathered up my documents and headed back out to the parking lot.

Chapter Thirty-Eight

I'm not sure when, precisely, I began to suspect that some-thing was wrong. It certainly wasn't the day I bought Smith's land. My spirits were soaring when I pulled out of his parking lot, and I only drove a couple of blocks before I paused to share the good news with my co-conspirators. My first call was to Jill, but she didn't answer. After I left her a voicemail, I tried my father, who picked up on the first ring. That fact alone showed me something, since he almost always let Janet answer my calls.

I walked him through my entire conversation with Smith, and he listened, for once, without interrupting me. The only time he chimed in was to express reservations about my promise to indem-nify Smith, but after we discussed it for a few minutes, he agreed that it had been a concession worth making in order to close the deal. When I got to the end of the story, he showered me with con-gratulations. I couldn't remember the last time I'd elicited such an unreservedly positive reaction from him.

We talked for about twenty minutes, and if I hadn't cut him off, I think he would have been willing to stay on the line and re-hash my negotiating strategy for another hour. As nice as it was to have piqued his interest, I needed to get home. I ended our call with a promise to update him after I contacted Green Summit, and then I cracked open one of the Red Bulls that had been sitting on my passenger seat since the morning and started back toward the Keys.

Along the way, I pondered my next steps. I longed to connect with Jill, but either way I planned to reach out to Donovan at Green Summit the next day, to let him know that I'd be the one selling him the land, and to schedule our payday. My deepest anxiety arose from the prospect of Wainwright returning my call, but I tried not to obsess over it. Sooner or later, he was going to find out what Jill and I had done. That was sort of the point of the whole exercise, after all. I figured he'd spit some vitriol in my direction, and then I'd tell him to fuck off. In an ideal universe, he'd comply with my request at the first time of asking; at worst, I'd have to endure a few more rounds of abuse first. I was confident, though, that he would just fuck off, eventually. I couldn't really see what other choice he had, no matter how angry he was.

When I got back to Marathon, I tried calling Jill again, without success. I parked myself on the couch with a beer and flipped on the ballgame, but I didn't make it through the sixth inning before I drifted off to sleep. Sometime in the middle of the night, I woke up enough to stumble from the couch to my bed. I never even bothered to undress.

That explained why I was roused from my slumber the next morning by a vibrating sensation against my left thigh. My phone, still in my pocket, was ringing. Disoriented, I struggled to untangle myself from my bed sheet so that I could reach it. After a few seconds, I managed to fish the phone out of my pants and lifted it to the vicinity of my head. "Hello," I mumbled, as I pressed the button to take the call.

A familiar voice thundered back at me. "Then one of the twelve, called Judas Iscariot, went unto the chief priests, And said unto them, What will ye give me, and I will deliver him unto you? And they covenanted with him for thirty pieces of silver. And from that time he sought opportunity to betray him."

After a few seconds of silence, I replied. "Hello, John." When he failed to acknowledge my greeting, I added, "I take it that I'm supposed to be the Judas in your story, right?"

"The lowest level of Hell is reserved for traitors, Malcolm. Remember that."

"Well, in order for me to be Judas, you'd have to be Jesus..."

The old man sighed into the phone. "How could you, Malcolm? How could you?"

"How could I what?"

"I was always good to you, wasn't I? We were going to build something together..."

"The only thing you were building was your own fortune," I snapped.

"My... transactions... in Immokalee were completely separate from our work with the church."

"No shit," I interjected.

"If you had concerns," he continued, "you could have just come to me and asked."

"'Cause you always gave me a straight answer, didn't you, John?"

"When did I ever give you a reason not to trust me?"

Now, there was a loaded question if ever there was one. I paused, ready to launch into a long-winded diatribe outlining all my reasons for not trusting him, but I stopped myself before I began, and instead simply said, "You should ask your daughter."

"What does Jill have to do with any of this?" he demanded.

"This whole thing was her idea."

"What do you mean?"

"Exactly what I said."

"You and her... you're together?" he asked.

"Yup. Ever since Vegas."

This revelation seemed to take the wind out of his sails. I braced myself for a tongue lashing, but it never came. In fact, he didn't say anything at all. After a while, I felt compelled to ask if he was still on the line. "I am," he grunted.

"So where does that leave us?" I asked.

"How do you mean?"

"Well, our mutual friend, Mr. Smith, was worried that you might sue him..."

"I'm not going to sue anyone, Malcolm, but I expect you already knew that."

"I was sorta counting on it."

"You think you're so damned smart," he hissed. "Let's see how it works out for you."

"Pretty fuckin' well, so far," I snarled. "But I'm guessing this is the part where you explain how you're gonna get back at me..."

"Dearly beloved, avenge not yourselves," he recited, calmly, "but rather give place unto wrath: for it is written, Vengeance is mine; I will repay, saith the Lord."

"So, you're gonna leave it up to God, huh?"

"It's always up to God, Malcolm, whatever you and I might think, and in my experience, people usually get what's coming to them."

"I'll take my chances." After that, our conversation dried up once again. About ten seconds passed in silence, and it seemed like as good a time as any to try to get off the phone. "I'm not sure there's anything left to say..."

He cut me off. "One last question, Malcolm."

"What?"

"Was it easy for you?"

I began mumbling something about how hard it had been to raise the money, but he stopped me. "No," he said. "That's not what I meant. I was asking if you thought of me as a friend... if you hesitated, even for a moment, before you..."

"Not really," I replied, half-lying. An honest answer would have been much more complicated than that, but it didn't seem like the time to get into it with him.

When he spoke again, it was another recitation, but not from the Bible this time, at least not the King James Version:

Facilis descensus Averni:
Noctes atque dies patet atri ianua Ditis;
Sed revocare gradium superasque evadere ad auras,
Hoc opus, hic labor est.

"I'm sorry... my Latin's a little rusty. Is that Horace?"

"Virgil," he replied. "It means that the descent down to Hell is always easy, but once you make the trip, it's hard to get back up."

"Uh huh," I replied, unsure of what I was supposed to say to that.

"Good luck, Malcolm."

I was still mulling over why he might have wanted to wish me luck when I heard a click. Apparently, Wainwright had hung up. As it turned out, those were the last words I ever heard him say.

Chapter Thirty-Nine

I'd barely put the phone down before it started ringing again. I assumed that Wainwright had thought better of letting me off without further insult, so I braced myself and answered without even looking at the screen. Instead of an old man's bitter rant, though, I got an enthusiastic greeting from my father.

"Upbeat" probably isn't a strong enough adjective to describe his mood. He spoke in short bursts, telling me things, asking me questions, but mostly, I think, trying to convince himself that everything was under control. There was one update from his end: he'd had his lawyers contact the Collier County Clerk's office and they'd confirmed that a deed had been recorded in my name. I was glad to hear that Smith's attorney had lived up to her promise.

He seemed satisfied when I laid out my plan to call Green Summit and tee up our sale. I also told him that I'd spoken to Wainwright, and confirmed that the old man wasn't planning on suing anyone. That qualified, in my dad's estimation, as "good news," and we patted each other on the back a few more times before he rang off.

It was the first time in days that I'd felt unrushed, and I wanted to enjoy the sensation a bit before getting back to business. I threw on a pair of shorts and set up camp in my lawn chair, with newspaper in hand and a thermos full of coffee next to me. Another call to Jill went straight to voicemail, but I took it in stride. Soon, I figured, I'd have even more good news to share with her.

It was half-past eleven when I finally made my way back inside and laid everything out on the dining table in anticipation of my call to Mr. Donovan. My heart was in my throat as I dialed his number and it started ringing on the other end. I took a deep breath. Five rings. Ten rings. No one picked up. I must have let it ring twenty-five times before it occurred to me to hang up. I immediately tried again, with the same result.

That was surprising, since the only other time I'd called him, a secretary had picked up instantly. Still, I didn't think much of it at the time. Maybe they were just away from their desks. Maybe their voicemail was down. These things happened.

I left the phone on the table and moved to the couch, determined to wait twenty minutes before I tried again. I tried to distract myself with television, but as soon as my self-imposed waiting period had run, I was back at the table, dialing. If anyone was near the phone on the other end, they continued to demonstrate a remarkable capacity to ignore my attempts to summon them into conversation.

That cycle repeated itself roughly every thirty minutes for the rest of the afternoon, until my father called at four o'clock, looking for an update. My not being able to get Green Summit on the phone was apparently not the story he was looking to hear. "What do you mean you haven't been able to get through?"

"I've, uh, been trying his number all day... no luck."

"Have you left him a message?"

"No. Haven't been able to. No one ever picks up."

"Voicemail?"

"No voicemail, either. It just rings and rings. I'm wondering if their phones are down or something."

"Try their main number," he commanded.

As obvious as that sounds, it hadn't even occurred to me. Buoyed by the prospect of finally getting Donovan on the line, I promised my father that I'd get right back to him. I hung up and Googled the main number for Green Summit.

"Good afternoon, Green Summit," came the greeting when I dialed it, from a woman who sounded much happier than I would have thought anyone in Oklahoma City had a right to be.

"Uh, hi," I replied. "I'm trying to reach Larry Donovan."

"Please hold for one moment." I was treated to fifteen seconds of an elevator-music version of a Steely Dan song before she came back on the line. "I'm sorry, sir, but we don't seem to have anyone here by that name."

I was convinced that she'd gotten it wrong. "Actually, his name is Lawrence, not Larry. Lawrence S. Donovan." I was reading straight from one of his letters on the table in front of me. "D-O-N-O-V..."

She interrupted me. "Sir, we only have one "Donovan" in the whole company. Are you trying to reach Eloise Donovan, by chance?"

"No. There must be some sort of mix-up. I'm trying to reach Lawrence Donovan, Vice-President of Resource Acquisitions. I know he's there. I spoke with him just the other day."

"Hmm," she replied. "I have the company directory right here, and I don't see any 'Lawrence Donovan.' Are you sure you don't mean Eloise, in Human Resources?"

"No," I replied, straining to contain my frustration. "I don't need anyone in H.R. Your company is buying my land. I discussed it with Mr. Donovan last week. I need to speak to someone who can help me with that."

"Just a moment, sir."

It was back to the Steely Dan, for a bit longer this time. When the conversation resumed, the receptionist's voice had been replaced by that of a man. "Hello?"

"Hello... Mr. Donovan?" I ventured.

"Umm, no," he replied. "I'm Bill Jacobson. Maybe, uh, I can help you with something?"

"My name's James Bennett," I announced. "I spoke to Larry Donovan last week about selling you guys a piece of land..."

"Are you sure you talked to somebody here? Could it have been another company, maybe?"

"It was definitely you guys." I went on to read the address off of Donovan's letterhead, right down to the zip code.

"That's us," he admitted. "But I'm afraid I've never heard of anyone named Donovan."

"I had a call with him last week," I repeated. Again, I read from the letter in my hand: "Lawrence S. Donovan, Vice-President of Resource Acquisitions." After that, there was nothing but dead air, which lasted long enough that I felt compelled to ask Jacobson if he was still on the line.

"I am," he murmured, "but I'm not sure what to tell you. There must be some kind of misunderstanding..."

"How so?" I asked, a knot forming in pit of my stomach.

"Well, uh... *I'm* actually the Vice-President of Resource Acquisitions at Green Summit... have been for the last six years."

"Who the hell is Larry Donovan, then?" I demanded, hotly.

"I have no idea."

That knot in my stomach ballooned to the size and weight of a bowling ball, and I had to lean against the table to keep from falling out of my chair. It was Jacobson's turn to ask if I was still there. A weak "uh huh" was the only response I could manage to squeeze out.

He asked where the land was, and when I mentioned Immokalee, he said he wasn't aware of the company looking at anything in that area. "How much were we supposed to pay you?" he asked.

"Five thousand an acre. For three hundred and fifty acres."

"I don't know what to tell you."

I took a deep breath, and tried to compose myself. "Well, it sounds like you're the right guy to talk to. Maybe we can still make a deal."

"I don't think so."

"But there's gas... or oil... or something. I've got copies of the surveys. It's all here..."

He cut me off. "In that part of Florida? They've been pumping oil around there since the Forties, but there's nothing new that would make us buy anything for anywhere near the prices that you're talking about."

"But these surveys..." I repeated, flipping through them as I spoke.

"They didn't come from us."

The conversation continued in that vein for a few more minutes, as I kept tossing out bits of evidence from Wainwright's files, and he kept denying ever having heard of any of it. Deflated, I finally let him go and retreated to the back yard to chain smoke.

I was on my third cigarette when my father called back. The first two hadn't helped me figure out what to tell him, but dodging his call seemed futile. I answered with a reluctant, "Hey, Dad."

He didn't bother with small talk. "Are we all set with Green Summit?"

"Seems like there's some confusion over there today..."

He jumped right on me. "Confusion? What confusion?"

"I'm having some trouble getting hold of Larry Donovan and..."

"Did you call the main number, like I said? Just call the main number and ask for..."

"I called the main number."

"And?"

"They didn't know who he was."

The line was silent for a few moments, before my father asked, "What did they say?"

"They said that no one by that name worked there."

"Who did you talk to?"

"A guy named Jacobson."

"Did he say anything else?"

I let that question hang in the air, not quite ready to send my father over the edge by relating the entire substance of my conversation. "Don't worry," I assured him. "Just a mix-up of some kind, I'm sure. I'm gonna track down Donovan."

"You better," he warned.

"I will."

"Call me back."

"Uh huh."

Whatever hope I'd been clinging to when I preached that optimism to my father was washed away over the course of the next hour. I started with another call to Green Summit, praying that a different receptionist would find a different company directory and magically put me through to Donovan. When that prayer went unanswered, I went back to the file and found the name of the lawyer that had handled Green Summit's previous deals with Wainwright. According to the documents, the closing of Wainwright's final sale the following week was supposed to take place at his offices in Naples. He was quite cordial when I got him on the phone, but he too professed ignorance of the deal, and of Wainwright.

No one, it seemed, was prepared to take my new property off my hands. Desperate to find someone, anyone, who would talk to me, I tried calling everybody that had any connection to Immokalee: Smith, his lawyer, Wainwright... even Bob Baker. I probably rang each of them a dozen times, or more. None of them ever picked up.

Eventually, I gave up for the night. The last call I made was to Jill, and it too went straight to voicemail. "Please call me back, baby," I said. "I think we might have a problem...."

Chapter Forty

I was hopeful when I found three voicemails waiting for me the next morning, but they were all from my father. I was out of ideas about what to do next, so I called him back and told him everything.

I knew, of course, that this was bound to upset him, but I was still unprepared for the stream of venom that followed. It was as if he was trying to bury every complimentary word that he'd uttered over the previous few days beneath a dozen disparaging condemnations. As he was berating me, I wondered whether he treated his employees the same way, or if he'd reserved those particular insults for me alone. I suspected the latter. He could always fire an under-performing banker, but he was stuck with me.

Once I gave him my summary of where things stood, he never let me get another word in. When he was done ranting, he announced that he would deal with the situation himself and commanded me to stay by my phone. He was still muttering something about letting grown-ups handle grown-up things when he hung up.

I felt compelled to do something, so I cycled through my list of phone numbers and tried them all again. The people that answered my calls still had no idea what I was talking about, and the ones that might have had a clue refused to pick up. Overwhelmed by a sense of impotence, I sank into my couch and closed my eyes.

I'm not sure how long I laid there before it hit me. Wainwright's house was only fifteen minutes away, and he wouldn't be able to ignore me if I went and stood in his living room. I threw on a pair of shorts and headed over to Grassy Key.

When my emphatic pounding on his front door went unanswered, I let myself in with the same spare key that I'd used on my last visit. I stalked from room to room, yelling his name and demanding that he show himself. I was so fired up that I didn't detect anything unusual about the house, but when I finally stopped and stood still for a moment, I noticed that something had changed. The timeworn furniture was still there, but the walls were bare. The photo of Wainwright with Reagan was gone, as were the others that had hung beside it.

I went straight to Wainwright's office and threw open the drawers of his desk. They were all empty. The file cabinet was unlocked, and its contents had been removed as well. I didn't see a single scrap of paper anywhere.

It was the same story in the rest of his house. There was no sign of the morass of documents that I'd left in the room where I'd worked; only a handful of empty cardboard boxes remained. In Wainwright's bedroom, the sheets were still on the bed, but his dresser and closets had been cleaned out. The old preacher had broken camp.

I felt the vibration of my phone against my leg. "Dad," I answered.

"Our money's gone." He sounded more resigned than angry this time.

"I don't understand..."

He sighed. "I called a friend of mine at Mr. Smith's bank, to try to get a line on what was going on. Turns out that those funds were wired out to an offshore account first thing yesterday morning, and Smith's account was closed."

"Wainwright's gone too," I chimed in.

"Gone?"

"I'm in his house right now, and it looks like he moved out."

"It's starting to look like we got taken, James."

By then, I already understood that, but hearing my father put it into words still sucked the air out of my lungs. I struggled to inhale. "Well," I stammered, "we've, uh, still got the land, right? Maybe we can sell it and at least recover our..."

He interrupted me with a loud, sarcastic cackle. "I haven't told you the best part yet. I had my attorneys take a closer look at that deed..."

His voice trailed off, and I had to prompt him to finish. "What about it?"

"It seems that you are now the proud owner of a third of an acre of prime Florida real estate."

"Bullshit!" I yelled. "I saw the papers. It said three-hundred and fifty acres."

"There was a decimal point. *Point*-three-five-zero acres."

"Dad, I swear... it wasn't there..."

He cut me off. "The locals told my lawyer that it's good land for growing tomatoes..."

"It was three-hundred and fifty..."

"Maybe we should go into the ketchup business..."

"There wasn't any decimal point!"

"Enough!" he roared. "I don't want to hear any more goddamn excuses!"

"What do you want me to say?" I shot back. "What are we supposed to do now?"

"You don't do anything. I'm gonna take care of this. Your friend ripped off the wrong guy. The Secretary of the Treasury takes my calls. We'll find Wainwright. I'll call you."

As unbecoming as his bluster may have been, it did make me feel a little better. If anybody had the resources to track down Wainwright, it was my father. As I drove back to Marathon, I imagined visiting the old preacher in prison and gloating about how he never should have messed with my family.

Chapter Forty-One

Two private detectives showed up at my door the next morning, courtesy of my father, and I spent the better part of the day walking them through everything that had happened since I'd gotten to the Keys. I understood the point of their investigations, but as the day went on, I found myself feeling more and more put off by their tone. When our conversation turned to my relationship with Jill, they didn't even try to mask their suspicion of her or, for that matter, of me. I couldn't help but wonder if my father was harboring the same doubts. The men left me their business cards and told me to contact them immediately if I learned anything new.

After they left, my thoughts stayed focused on Jill. I realized that, to anyone else, the timing of her departure would have seemed suspicious. All the people who'd ripped us off had vanished into thin air, and she seemed to have gone along with them. Even though she hadn't returned a single phone call since my trip to Immokalee, I refused to draw the obvious conclusion. She was taking care of her mother, and when she could, she'd come back and we'd figure everything out, together. I needed that to be true. I left her another voicemail, begging her to call me back.

That day blended into the next, and then into the one after that. I never left the house, never even bothered to shower or dress. Other than lobbing voicemails into Jill's phone, I did nothing at all. That's the way my father seemed to want it.

After three days of complete solitude, I couldn't bear it any longer. I dug out one of the detective's cards and called him. "Yeah," he answered.

"This is James Bennett."

"Uh huh. You got any more information for us?"

"No. Nothing new on my end, but I was wondering if you had any luck finding Jill Wainwright. I can't get her to return any of my calls and I'm worried."

"If we find her, we'll let you know."

"I know she's somewhere around Valdosta, so it seems like you guys should be able to track her down."

"Leave the investigation to us."

"Have you checked the hospitals?" I demanded. "Have you even looked?"

"We're looking into everything."

"You need to find her!"

"We'll take care..."

I hung up before he could finish putting me off again and immediately dialed my father. "Hello, James," he said, coolly.

"Dad... we need to find Jill."

"My people are working on it."

"Are they? I just talked to one of your guys and I'm not convinced."

"I asked you to stay out of this, didn't I? It's best to let our investigators handle it."

"It's been three days and I don't even think they've gone to Georgia to look for her! What if something's happened? I'm gonna call the police."

There was a long silence after that. "James," my father finally replied, in a very measured tone, "it's very important that you not involve the police at this time. Do you understand?"

"Why not? The more people looking for Wainwright, the better, right? How does that hurt us?"

"James, have you told anyone about this? Anyone at all?"

"Who am I gonna tell?" I muttered.

"Have you?" he demanded, raising his voice.

"No."

He paused for a moment before going on. "I need you to listen to me very carefully. If the... events... of last week... were to become public knowledge, it could be very damaging to the family." He spoke slowly, like he was trying to explain the laws of physics to a first-grader. "It's very important that we control this information until we..."

He droned on in business-school-speak, but he didn't need to. He'd made his priorities clear enough. When I thought about it, it all made perfect sense. My father had long since graduated from analyzing financial statements and crunching numbers. Whatever value he had as a banker arose from the fact that he had a rolodex full of CEO's, financiers and politicians, all of whom were willing to take his calls because they thought of him as a serious man. If word got out that he'd let himself get swindled by a fellow like Wainwright, then maybe those guys wouldn't want his advice any more. Every sage, old hand on Wall Street knows that they're always just one bad trade away from being a laughingstock, and Immokalee had been a pretty goddamned bad trade. A guy like my father should have seen red flags all the way, but he blew through them because he wanted to help me make something happen. That realization was enough to get me to agree to keep the police out of it. "OK. I understand," I told him.

"Good," he replied. "You'll keep this to yourself?"

"Sure, but I'm not gonna stop looking for Jill."

"Do what you have to do," he said. "But keep it discrete."

Chapter Forty-Two

Discovering that my father was more concerned with damage control than he was with tracking down Jill or his money at least served to re-instill some purpose into my days. Once again, I was back to playing at being a private detective.

I started by calling every hospital within thirty miles of Valdosta, trying to figure which one of them might have been treating Jill's mother. It proved a difficult question to ask, seeing as how I didn't even know her name. Even if I had, I'm not sure that anyone would have told me anything. Apparently, polite requests don't carry as much weight as federal privacy regulations.

My next call was to the general manager at Sapphire in Vegas. "These girls flake all the time," he laughed, when I tried asking him if he'd heard from Jill. I believed him when he went on to say that he didn't even remember her.

It was depressing to discover how little I actually knew about the woman I thought I loved, and who purported to love me back. I racked my brain for anything else that she'd told me that might have helped me find her, but her mother, her father and her job were all that I had to work with, and two of those three were dead ends. The only path that I could see pointed toward her mother.

All I knew about her was that she'd been one of Wainwright's followers back in Valdosta, so I went back to those old articles by Jerry Barnes in the *Times-Union* and started picking out names. Even a quarter of a century later, most of them proved surprisingly easy to locate. I bought a subscription to one of those background-check websites and just fed them in, one after another, and wound up with a list of phone numbers. The majority of the people mentioned in Barnes' piece seemed never to have left southwest Georgia.

Over the next few days, I talked to a dozen of Wainwright's ex-parishioners. I began by explaining that I was an associate producer at Fox News, and that I was researching a story about the history of the evangelical movement in America. As soon as people heard that it was for television, they opened right up. The years seemed to have mellowed them toward Wainwright, and many of them recalled their days on the compound with something approaching nostalgia. One or two were critical of Barnes for publishing his story, although even they admitted that their old pastor had been undone by sin. Several expressed their hope that he'd found his way back to the righteous path.

In that context, steering those conversations toward Wainwright's indiscretions came naturally, and no one balked at mentioning his lovers by name. In fact, they seemed quite keen to seize the opportunity to gossip about their former church-mates. The names of the two women who'd filed unsuccessful paternity suits against Wainwright were a matter of public record, and mentioning them drew responses that ranged from dismissive and lightly judgmental to downright nasty; the word "whore" was tossed around more liberally than I'd expected.

I had already assumed, of course, that neither of those women were Jill's mother; things only got interesting when I invited speculation as to whether or not Wainwright's ungoverned passions might have led to any actual offspring. No one knew anything for sure, but one name kept coming up: Betsy Miller. A couple of people recalled her and Wainwright having been especially close just before things fell apart at the compound, despite her only having been seventeen years old at the time. One person insisted that she was even younger than that. The consensus seemed to be that if Wainwright had had a child with anyone, then Betsy Miller was the likeliest candidate to have borne it.

Armed with Ms. Miller's name, approximate age, and hometown, I went back to work on the internet, which pointed me toward Elizabeth Louise Harper, née Miller, aged forty-five, from Moultrie, Georgia. According to a wedding announcement in the *Journal-Constitution*, she'd married Alan "Trip" Harper III in 1991, and the couple had settled in Alpharetta. It seemed as if they were still there.

The more I read about her, the more my heart sank. Based on everything that Jill had told me, I was looking for a poor, unmarried woman that had never made it out of her trailer park in Lowndes County, not someone that had been to college, married into money and moved to a posh suburb of Atlanta. Still, she was the best lead that I'd ginned up so far; if she'd been as close to Wainwright as the others suggested, then maybe she'd be able to point me in the right direction. I dug up a phone number and dialed it. She answered on the second ring, in a sweet drawl, "Hello?"

"Hello… Mrs. Harper?"

"Yes."

"Mrs. Harper, my name is James Bennett. I'm an associate producer at Fox News, researching a story about the history of the evangelical movement. I understand that you were a member of John Wainwright's church in Valdosta back in the early Eighties and I was hoping that I might ask you a few questions about…"

That's as far as I got before she hung up on me. That click turned out to be the most exciting thing I heard all day. I'd finally found someone who didn't want to talk about John Wainwright. My interest in Mrs. Harper immediately increased tenfold.

Chapter Forty-Three

Peter and Barbara never bothered to kick me out of their house. Looking back on it, I can't be sure that it even was their house. Either way, it wasn't mine, so I decided to leave, about a week after my first phone call to Betsy Harper. It wasn't as if there was anything keeping me in Marathon. Wainwright and everyone connected with him were long gone.

The lone exception was Bob Baker, whom I tracked down easily enough at one of his regular drinking haunts. I pressed him pretty hard about Wainwright, but he purported not to know anything about anything, and I believed him. It was hard to envision a canny operator like Wainwright confiding in such a pathetic drunk, and the fact that Baker was still around after everyone else had cleared out seemed to confirm his innocence. I even had a drink with him before we parted ways.

I loaded up my car and started north; coming from the Keys, it was the only direction available. Eventually, it would lead me back to my father, but I dreaded the idea of being in the same room as him. We'd been talking on the phone and his anger seemed to have cooled, but I was afraid that the sight of me would rekindle it. I was pretty sure that he wouldn't haul off and punch me, but anything short of that seemed like fair game. I imagined him simply slamming the door in my face when I showed up on his front step, without saying a word. The idea of him freezing me out stung more than any beating would have.

Home was dominating my thoughts, but New York wasn't my immediate destination. I was planning a stop in Atlanta first, to take one last shot at the only person who might have had a line on Jill's mother. I'd called her again, but she hadn't proved any more talkative at the second time of asking; she hung up before I managed to get ten words out. She must have noted my number on her display, because after that she just stopped answering altogether.

By then, so much time had passed without a word from Jill that I'd given up any real hope of ever seeing her again. Still, I continued to leave the occasional message on her voicemail, begging more for an explanation than a reunion. I felt like I deserved at least that much.

I didn't get on the road until the afternoon, so I spread the drive from Marathon to Alpharetta over two days. Betsy's house was in a newer development, and it was enormous. From the curb, I guessed that it easily covered more than five-thousand square feet. I paused next to my car to stretch my legs before I trudged to the front door and rang the bell. A moment later, the door swung open and I was finally face to face with Betsy Harper. "Can I help you?" she asked, after I let a couple of seconds pass without announcing my purpose.

I was too busy staring at her to answer. Looking at her was like looking at a distorted copy of Jill. There were one or two wrinkles under her eyes and a few more pounds around her midsection, but those cheekbones... that nose... the brown eyes and hair... it was all

Jill. "Mrs. Harper," I stammered. "I've been trying to reach you on the phone..."

Her eyes widened and she moved to slam the door on me, but I blocked it with my right arm. She raised her voice. "I thought I made it clear that I didn't want to discuss..."

"I need to talk to you about your daughter."

"I don't have a daughter," she replied, as the color drained from her face.

I shook my head. "She looks just like you, you know. Her name is Jill. Jill Wainwright..."

"You've got the wrong person," she said, her voice shaking as she tried to push the door shut while I held it open. "If you don't leave right now, I'm going to call the police."

"Please... just give me five minutes. Five minutes, and then I promise I'll leave you alone. I need to find her. I got mixed up with her father and he stole a bunch of money from me, but I don't care about that... not really. I just want to talk to her and make sure she's OK."

I felt her pushing hard against the door again, and this time I didn't resist. Once it closed in my face, I shouted, "I was in love with her!" straight into the wood before I turned and started back toward my car. Whatever Betsy Harper might have known, she'd made it pretty clear that she wasn't going to share it with me. I was about to get in and drive away when I heard a noise behind me, and I looked back and saw Betsy's head hanging out of the doorway. "Hold on," she called. As soon as I heard her voice, I turned and hustled back to her.

"I have a whole life now," she began. "Two boys... a husband... they can't find out about any of this. You understand?"

I nodded. "I'm not lookin' to cause you any trouble."

She looked me up and down one last time before she opened the door the rest of the way. "My kids will be home from school in an hour."

"I'll be gone," I promised, as I stepped over the threshold. The interior of the house was every bit as nice as the outside had suggested. I followed my host into her kitchen, a grand temple of granite and stainless steel with an island as big as a queen-sized bed for an altar. "You have a lovely home," I offered.

"Thank you."

"It's nothing like what Jill described."

"What do you mean?"

"She talked about growing up poor, living with her mother in a trailer park..."

"Uh huh," Betsy replied, gesturing toward a chair at the kitchen table. "Wait here."

I took a seat and watched her walk out of the room. A few minutes later, she returned with a large cardboard box and set it in front of me without a word. When I shot her a confused look, she pointed at the box and said, "Go on. Take a look."

Inside, I found photos, letters, newspaper clippings... an archive, it seemed, of a girl's childhood. It wasn't obvious at first, but once I got past the baby pictures, I realized that I was looking at images of Jill. My hands tingled as I stared at her teenaged face. "You *are* her mother," I murmured. That pronouncement didn't elicit any reaction at all, but that didn't curb my rising excitement. "You know where she is?" I asked, my voice rising. "If you can tell me anything... anything at all... it would mean so much."

She lowered her eyes. "This," she said, waving her hand at the box, "is all I have of her."

"What do you mean?"

She bit her lower lip, clearly struggling to get the words out. "I haven't seen Jill... not once... since she was four days old."

"I don't understand. She told me about growing up with you..."

Betsy sank into the chair next to mine and let out a heavy sigh. "My mother and father," she began, "were very devout. When John Wainwright came along and started his ministry, my father believed in his message, with all his heart. We went to the farm to help with the work he was doing..."

"Uh huh."

"I was just a kid," she went on. "And hearing him... talking to him... he was tall and handsome and he knew everything. It felt like I was talking straight to God."

"I'm sure."

"I wasn't the only one," she snapped. "A lot of the girls felt a calling to be close to him."

"So I've heard."

She shook her head. "I know it sounds ridiculous, but what he and I had... it was different. There was a connection."

It didn't seem like my place to disabuse her of whatever notions she had about her relationship with Wainwright, so I just smiled and nodded, and after a moment she continued. "I found out that I was pregnant just before... just before everything got turned upside down..." Her voice trailed off.

"What happened then?" I prompted.

"It was crazy. People that had been living together on the farm, working toward a common purpose, they just... they turned on each other, just like that. It got ugly."

"What happened to you?"

"I went to John and told him about the baby..."

"And he believed you?" I blurted out. When I saw the wounded look on her face, I scrambled to make amends for my insensitivity. "I'm sorry... I didn't mean to suggest... it's just that I know that a couple of other women claimed that he'd gotten them pregnant as well, and I know that he denied it."

"Those girls were liars. But he knew that I was telling the truth."

"What did he say?"

She shifted in her seat. "I would have followed him anywhere... would have done anything to stay with him... but I let him talk me out of it."

"How?"

"He told me that I was different from the other girls... that I could go to college and get married and have a good life... but not if I became a teenaged mother."

"What did you tell your parents?"

"Everything... well, it was really John who told them. And they agreed with him."

"They did?"

She nodded. "They sent me to Tennessee to live with my great-aunt until the baby was born. Told everyone that I'd gone on a mission trip to Africa. When I got back we all just pretended like it had never happened."

"So... who took the baby, then? Did Wainwright have another woman raise Jill?" This was precisely the question that I'd come all the way to Alpharetta to ask.

The expression on her face was an amalgamation of confusion and pity, a look that one might have expected to see from a woman who'd just realized that she'd been talking to a half-wit. She spoke slowly. "There wasn't anybody else. John came up to Tennessee and took Jill from the hospital, just like we'd agreed. He raised her himself."

After everything that had happened, I suppose that hearing that shouldn't have fazed me, but it did. I just couldn't get my head around the idea that nothing that Jill had told me, nothing that she'd claimed to have felt about her father, nothing that she'd made *me* feel about him... none of that had been real. I shook my head. "No... no... That's not right. It can't be right. She told me everything... about how she grew up with her mother... how her father abandoned them.... That can't be right."

Betsy gestured toward the box again. "It's all in there."

I lunged out of my chair and reached into the box and pulled out the first thing I could get my hands on. It was a letter, and as soon as I removed it from its envelope and unfolded it, I recognized Wainwright's handwriting:

August 10, 1995

Dear B,

We celebrated Jill's 10th birthday last week. She's a head taller than the other girls her age. You would be so proud of her. Her violin lessons are going wonderfully, and she is already learning algebra. I've enclosed a few recent pictures.

With affection,

J.

I tossed it aside and read another letter, and then two more, each in the same vein. The photos documented the milestones of a young girl's life: opening presents at her first Christmas, riding her first bike, wearing her leotard for her first dance recital, smiling through her braces before her first date... The only thing that had stayed constant as she'd aged was her bright-eyed smile. I set the pile on the table and sat back down. "Wainwright sent you all of this?" I asked, still not quite believing what I'd seen.

She nodded. "Three or four letters a year, like clockwork, until she turned eighteen. Less often since then, but once they grow up..."

"And your husband has no idea?"

She looked at the floor. "He thinks she's one of my cousin's kids."

I noticed a tear running down her cheek. "I'm sorry," I said. "I can't imagine how hard it must have been for you, all these years..."

She wiped her eyes with a napkin that she'd grabbed from the table. "When he took her from me, I didn't think that I'd ever hear anything from either of them again. I wasn't sure I wanted to, really. I thought it would be easier if I could just forget about her." She paused to dab her tears again. "When he sent me that first letter, I cried all night... But I was glad that he sent it... glad that he kept sending them. I was never going to forget her. Knowing that she was OK meant a lot."

I just sat there, without any idea of what I was supposed to say next. After an awkward minute, I started pawing through the box again, because it seemed easier than continuing the conversation. I stopped when I got to a newspaper clipping that featured a picture of a young, beaming Jill beneath the headline, "HOME-SCHOOLED GIRL SETS PERFECT MARK ON SAT, WINS SCHOLARSHIP

TO YALE." I held the sheet out toward Betsy. "He home-schooled her?"

"She was always a very bright girl," she replied, a flicker of pride cutting through the sadness in her eyes.

"But Wainwright... he taught her himself?"

She nodded. "People say a lot of terrible things about John, and Lord knows he deserves a lot of it, but no one can accuse him of being a bad father. Jill meant everything to him... always."

I dropped the newspaper clipping, bowed my head into my hands and rubbed my eyes. When I opened them again, I found Betsy staring at me. "What in God's name happened between you two, anyway?" she asked.

I opened my mouth to answer, but instead I pushed my chair away from the table and stood up. "I'm sorry," I blurted out. "I need to get going." Without waiting for her, I started for the door, mumbling thanks and apologies as I went. She followed right behind me, saying something, but I didn't hear a word. I practically ran out the front door, and didn't stop until I'd parked myself in the driver's seat of my car. I looked out the window and saw her standing in her doorway, staring at me, and I started laughing out loud. I laughed so hard that I started to cry.

Chapter Forty-Four

Back in college, I had a friend who had a theory that boys don't become men until they realize that their fathers are full of shit. He wasn't talking about adolescent crap, like that time you got pissed at your dad because he wouldn't let you shave your favorite team's logo into your hair, or that time you felt like a victim because he refused to let you spend the weekend at your buddy's beach house without a chaperone. He was talking about the moment when you looked at the grown-up things in your father's life – his job, his finances, his relationship with your mother – and you began to appreciate that he had no idea what he was doing. Once you stripped away that cloak of all-knowing invincibility, you understood that he was just a man. And so were you.

I'd spent the better part of a decade trying to convince myself that my dad was full of shit, but I never found any facts to support that hypothesis. In fact, all the evidence pointed in the opposite direction. The one and only time I ever saw him do anything dumb was in this affair with Wainwright, and that was entirely my fault. My father's biggest misstep had been allowing himself to indulge the belief that I might have been right about something. As it turned out, only one of us was full of shit.

He got over the loss of the money, I think. He never said so directly, and we never had a teary exchange of contrition and absolution to mark the occasion. That just wasn't who he was. Progress in our reconciliation was marked by subtler signs. When I moved back into the house, he barely acknowledged my presence. Gradually, his stare across the table became less icy, and the pointed silence between us was more frequently replaced by small talk. After a few weeks, we'd reached the point where both of us were more or less pretending the whole thing had never happened, which, in our family, was the preferred approach to dealing with unpleasant things.

My cause was helped by the fact that my father remained a rich man. I'm not sure that he would have forgiven me so easily if I'd lost enough of his fortune to turn him into a man of conspicuously more modest means, but I like to think that he'd have found a way. Sons are made to exasperate their fathers, and fathers will always roll their eyes and shake their heads before they do whatever they can to help their sons. The two of us were never going to be the pair who rewrote that script.

I knew that our relationship had returned to something close to its pre-Wainwright state when my father started to beat the drum of me finding a real job with his old vigor. If anything, he was more encouraging than he'd ever been. Despite the unfortunate nature of "recent events" – that was as close as he would get to an acknowledgement of our misadventures in Florida – he purported to have been impressed with certain qualities that I'd displayed. After all, I'd managed to talk him into investing in my scheme. He seemed convinced that I had what it took to carve out a legitimate career in business, and offered to help me find a proper place to start.

I really wanted to go along with him, to show him how much I appreciated his forgiveness and valued his counsel. It certainly wasn't my childish contrariness that held me back this time. I was ready to put myself in his hands, but there was one thing that I couldn't get over. It kept gnawing at me, never far from the surface of my thoughts, and I realized that I needed to do something about it before I'd be able to move on.

It wasn't the money. As my father had reminded me on numerous occasions, it hadn't come out of my pocket. If he could get past it, then so could I. And it wasn't the ignominy of having been the mark in Wainwright's long con. I kicked myself about that every day, but I knew that I hadn't been the first person to fall victim to the old preacher's charms, and I assumed that I wouldn't be the last. Sometimes, the guy across the table outplays you and the only thing you're left with is a lesson.

When I closed my eyes and tried to fall asleep at night, it wasn't Wainwright's face, or even Jill's, that haunted me. It was Liz's. Of all the things I'd discovered about Wainwright, it was the idea of him selling young women to old men that made me sick. At first, I tried to convince myself that it hadn't really happened. After all, Jill was the one who'd told me about it, and her word had proven less than trustworthy. As much as I wanted to dismiss it, though, I couldn't discount what I'd seen with my own eyes. There was Liz, wide-eyed and chattering away as I delivered her to that truck stop in Georgia, and Barbara mopping the floor of a house that she co-owned with a man forty years her senior. And even if Jill had fabricated the story about her father trying to marry her off to the old codger with the oxygen tank, I knew that Wainwright had, at the very least, been willing to pimp her into a sexual relationship with me in order to further his money-making scheme. There was too much there to ignore.

The realization that Jill's father had ordered her into my bed so that he could make half a million bucks ensured that I'd probably never figure out exactly how I felt about her. She might not have been damaged in the way that she'd told me, but it was hard not to see her as having been used badly by Wainwright. Even so, I struggled to gin up the sympathy that her situation seemed to demand. I'd never been in love before, and learning that the whole thing had been nothing more than play-acting on her part stung. Fair or not, I found myself unable to put all of the blame on the old man.

Liz, though, was another story. I was the one who'd fetched Wainwright's money from Miami, and I was the one who'd taken her to Georgia and watched her get driven away in that silver Lincoln. It wasn't just a question of figuring out if Wainwright had done something terrible to her. Her predicament was on me as well. Before I could get on with my life, I was going to have to figure out what we'd done to Liz.

Chapter Forty-Five

After I'd been home for about a month, my dad's investigators told us that they'd tracked the Wainwrights to the Pacific coast of Nicaragua. Doing anything about them there would have required bringing a federal case, literally, and my father remained adamant about not taking things in any sort of public direction. He told me that he was going to call off his dogs and implored me to put the old man and his daughter out of my head.

Instead, I asked him to have his people help me find Liz. He demurred at first, as that part of the story always seemed to make him uncomfortable, but when I gave him my word that that would be the end of it, he relented. Even he must have understood my reasons for wanting to atone for whatever harm I might have done to that poor young woman.

I was shocked by how much more helpful the detectives became once they understood that my request came with my father's acquiescence. I gave them all the information I had about Liz, which amounted to her first name, her hometown, the approximate date and rough geographical location of her marriage, and the fact that she'd married a man who was much older than she was. Within forty-eight hours, a messenger brought me an envelope containing her photograph, along with copies of her birth certificate, high-school transcript and marriage license. More importantly, they also gave me her current address and phone number.

Two days after I dropped her on the side of I-75, Miss Elizabeth Silva became Mrs. Simon Dumont, and took up residence with her new husband on the outskirts of Albany, Georgia. Unsurprisingly, Wainwright had lied when he'd told me that the man with whom he'd matched Liz was younger than he was. Two weeks after their wedding, he'd celebrated his seventy-ninth birthday.

I called her right away, and she answered with a simple, "Hello."

"Hi," I began. "I'm trying to reach Liz." I knew it was her, but I asked anyway.

"This is Liz."

"Liz... Hi. This is James Bennett. I'm not sure if you remember me, but I gave you a ride from Marathon to..."

She cut me off. "I remember you."

"Uh, that's good. That's great. How have you been?"

"Fine."

Her minimalist responses didn't give me much insight as to her state of mind. "That's good," I repeated. "Glad to hear that..."

"Did John ask you to call?"

"John?" I sputtered. I'd been so focused on figuring out how to steer our conversation toward Wainwright that I found myself completely unprepared when she brought him up herself.

"Reverend Wainwright," she replied. "Do you have a message from him?"

"Umm, no. He didn't ask me to call you." Almost as an afterthought, I asked, "Have you spoken to him recently?"

"He used to write to me all the time, but I haven't heard from him for over a month. He's OK, isn't he? Please tell me nothing's happened to him."

"He's fine. I think he's, uh, traveling at the moment."

"Thank God. I was starting to worry about him." The relief in her voice sounded genuine.

"Trust me," I replied. "John Wainwright is the last person that you should ever worry about."

"What do you mean? Why did you call me?"

"I, uh... I just wanted to make sure that you were OK."

"Why wouldn't I be?"

"You got married so suddenly. And your husband is... Well, he's not a young man, is he? It just seemed like such an unusual match, and I was just wondering... I wondered if you were happy, that's all."

"What's it to you?"

"Well, uh, since I was the one who drove you up there, I just felt... I'd hate to think that I had something to do with putting you into a bad situation."

The words that followed came out of Liz's mouth, but they were pure Wainwright. "We find happiness when we do our best to follow the path that the Lord lays out for us. My calling is to be a good wife to Simon."

"Uh huh," I said. "What if we left God out of it for a minute? Are *you* happy? I'm asking how you really feel..."

She stuck to the script. "Following God's will makes me happy."

"But what if none of this has anything to do with God?"

"I have faith," she announced, before quoting from the Book of Hebrews: "Now faith is the substance of things hoped for, the evidence of things not seen."

I searched for a response that wouldn't offend her. "I appreciate your belief. I really do. I'm just concerned that you might have gotten some bad advice from your minister."

"John Wainwright is a true prophet. He's a teacher, a scholar..."

I completed her sentence. "A visionary, a great man... Yeah, I know. I've heard all that before. I can't tell you how many people have assured me that John Wainwright is a paragon of saintly virtue... but what if he's not?"

"What if he is?" she shot back. After a pause, she continued. "You think he didn't warn us about people like you, people who wouldn't see the truth?" She recited the words of the Apostle Paul: "Be ye not unequally yoked together with unbelievers: for what fellowship hath righteousness with unrighteousness? And what communion hath light with darkness?"

The amount of time that she'd spent with Wainwright had clearly twisted Liz's worldview, and I understood that I was going to have to tell her more in order to have any hope of getting through to her. "Look," I began. "There are some things about Wainwright that you should know, things that might be hard for you to hear." I half-expected her to hang up on me, but she didn't, so I went on. "About a week before I drove you to Georgia, I went on another trip, to Miami. I met the same guy who picked you up, and he gave me thirty thousand dollars to deliver to Wainwright." I paused for a second to let her process that, before adding, "He was paying for *you*."

The silence on the line implied that this had at least gotten her wheels spinning, and when she finally responded, she sounded a touch less assured than she had just a few moments before. "Simon is a faithful member of the church. He's made many donations over the years."

"You weren't the only one that Wainwright sold. It's uncanny how often God's blueprint called for young, attractive women to marry rich, old men."

"Reverend Wainwright would never do anything like that."

I took a deep breath. "I know that there's probably nothing I can say that will make you believe me, but the one thing I am sure of is that John Wainwright will do anything for money. Anything."

"You're right," she replied. "I don't believe you."

I was tempted to tell her the whole story about Immokalee, but I heard my father's voice in the next room and remembered my commitment to discretion. "I can't tell you the details, but I know for a fact that he recently stole a large sum of money."

"How?" she demanded. "From who?"

"From someone I know. I can't say more than that, but I know about it first-hand."

"I need to talk to Reverend Wainwright."

"Why do you think you haven't heard from him lately? He left the country so he wouldn't get caught. You'll probably never see him again."

"Do you know where he is?" she asked, softly.

"Nicaragua, maybe. I don't know for sure."

There was only silence after that, and when she finally spoke again, I thought I detected a trace of resignation in her voice. "It's hard," was all she said.

"What?" I didn't quite grasp what she'd meant by that.

"This... all of it... you asked me about my life and I'm saying it's hard."

I tensed up. "Is your husband cruel to you? Does he...?"

She didn't let me finish. "No, no. Nothing like that. He's just... old. And sick. It's just the two of us here. Sometimes I dream about what it would have been like to have a different life, with someone else. But then I remember God's plan."

I was struck by the gravity of what I'd done. For all I knew, Liz's confidence in Wainwright was the only thing keeping her afloat, and I'd just poked a hole in it. I felt like I should offer her a lifeboat. "If there's anything I can do to help you out, I'd be happy..."

"Help me? Help me how?"

"Well... if you, uh, ever wanted to leave your husband, I'm sure that I could..."

"You mean a divorce?"

"If that's what you wanted, yeah. And if you needed some money to get you on your feet afterwards, my family and I could..."

She started to laugh. "So, you're offering to pay me to leave my husband?"

"I'm offering to help you however I can. Just tell me what you need."

There was another stretch of silence before she replied. "We've got almost fifteen acres down here, you know."

"Uh huh."

"And a savings account and some investments."

"OK."

"I don't need your money. Simon provides for me, and I'll be taken care of after he's gone." It seemed like she'd rediscovered some of her conviction.

"What if he lives for another twenty years?" I murmured.

"Mr. Bennett, I hope you're not suggesting that I'm just waiting for my husband to die."

"No, of course not," I stammered, even though that's exactly what I'd understood her to have been trying to communicate with her recitation of their marital assets. I sensed that it was time to end our conversation. I wasn't sure that I'd done enough to assuage my guilt, but it wasn't like I could force her to leave her husband. At least I'd told her the truth and offered to help her. That seemed to be about as far I was likely to get on the road to redemption.

I decided that I could live with that, and I was just about to wish Liz the best of luck and say goodbye when she said something else.

"Maybe there is one thing that you could do for me."

"Name it," I replied, grasping for a chance to do something that might make me feel better about myself.

She corrected herself. "Actually, it's not really for me."

"What is it?"

"It's, uh... it's my sister."

"I didn't know you had a sister."

She ignored me and went on. "Her faith has never been as strong as mine, and without John around to support her, I'm worried. She's so young, you know."

"How old is she?"

"Sixteen."

Hearing that made the hairs on my arms stand up. "Sixteen?" I repeated.

"Yeah."

"Wait a minute... Are you telling me that Wainwright arranged a marriage for your sixteen-year old sister?"

"Not a marriage. Not yet, anyway. Sixteen is too young..."

"Goddamn right!" I interjected.

She went on. "It's a 'placement.' That's the word that John always used when the marriages couldn't happen right away. My sister was 'placed' with her future husband. They'll get married when she turns eighteen."

"Where is she now?" I demanded.

"I don't know. Somewhere in South Florida, I think. She was supposed to leave a couple of weeks after I did, but I haven't been able to reach her..."

"What does your mother have to say about all this?"

"She believes in John."

"But your sister is still a child!"

"My mother believes," Liz repeated.

I wanted to lash out and ask how anyone could stand by and let something like that happen to a sixteen-year old girl, but I knew there wouldn't have been any point. "Were there others, too?" I asked.

"What?"

"You said that John had a word for this sort of arrangement... he called it a 'placement.' Does that mean that your sister wasn't the first underage girl that he...?"

"There were others."

"My God," I muttered. Liz didn't say anything else until I asked, "What do you want me to do?"

"I was hoping that maybe you could find my sister and just check on her. Make sure she's OK."

I took a deep breath. It wasn't like I was gonna say no to that one. "And you have no idea where she is?"

"Like I said, I'm pretty sure she's in South Florida, but I don't know..."

"Know anything about the guy she's with?"

"Nope."

"Can you at least tell me her name?"

"Catherine. Catherine Silva."

"OK. I'll, uh, try my best. I'll let you know."

"Thank you."

I hung up with her and shuffled toward my father's study. When I pushed the door open, I heard my father on a business call. "That's not even a real offer," he sneered at whoever was on the other end of the line. "We had a deal at seventy-eight and a half and we expect you to honor that." He looked up and gestured for me to sit down in the chair across from him before he went on. "I know what fiduciary duty is, George... Yes, of course... My point is that there's no financing there... How can your board even...? Fine. Do what you have to do. Just know that we're not going to sit here forever while you shop our offer... Alright... we'll expect to hear from you by noon tomorrow, then." He leaned forward and set the receiver into its cradle before flashing me a smile. "That guy's been an asshole since boarding school."

I just nodded. "Dad, do you have a minute?"

"Sure. What's up? You look tired. Did you ever manage to track down that girl?"

"Uh huh."

"And? How did it go? Everything OK?"

I took a deep breath and exhaled, and then I shook my head and said, "It's worse than I thought." From there, I launched straight into a recap of everything I'd just heard from Liz. When I finished, my father just sat there, resting his chin in his hands. "Well?" I demanded.

He began to massage his temples. "I'm not sure what you want me to say, James. It seems that your friend was into some very disturbing business."

"He's not my friend," I shot back.

My father shrugged. "If only you could have realized that a bit earlier."

"This isn't about me, Dad, or your money. I'm asking what you think we should do now."

He didn't answer right away, and I studied his face while I waited for him to say something. He looked like he was straining to broadcast how seriously he was entertaining my suggestion, kind of like he'd done when I'd begged him to take me to Disney World when I was ten. After a healthy pause, he finally spoke. "You were exactly right, James, when you said that this isn't about you. I don't think we should get involved."

"I'm already involved."

"No, you're not. I know you feel some sense of responsibility, but you didn't do this. Wainwright deceived you as much as he deceived anyone else. You had nothing to do with these girls."

"But I did," I corrected him.

He stood up and walked around to my side of the desk and placed his hand on my shoulder. "Your heart's in the right place. I'm proud of you, actually. It shows your character. But it's important to recognize that certain things just aren't our business."

"Whose business is it, then?" I demanded, hotly.

He withdrew his hand, and as he lowered himself into the chair next to mine, he asked, "What, exactly, do you think we ought to do?"

"I don't know," I replied, shaking my head. "Call the police, I guess."

"Which police? Where?"

I hesitated for a moment before I answered. "Florida, I think."

"I thought you said the girl was in Georgia."

"She is, but her sister…"

"Could be anywhere, right?"

I shrugged. "Maybe we should call the FBI, then."

My father winced. "I don't think that's a good idea at all."

"Dad," I began. "I know that we agreed to keep this whole thing low profile, but some things are more important than your reputation."

He waved his hand. "I'm not worried about *my* reputation."

I laughed. "What? Are you worried about mine? 'Cause I don't think I'm risking much on that front."

He didn't crack a smile. "You're the one that accepted the money in Miami, right?"

"Yeah, but…"

"And you're the one that transported the young woman across the state line, aren't you?"

I blinked. "Are you suggesting that I could get into trouble?"

He held out his hands. "All I'm saying is that you'll have some explaining to do." After a beat, he added, "And for what? We already know that Wainwright's left the country. It's not like they're going to be able to arrest him."

I took a deep breath, ready to launch into an impassioned discourse about child abuse, the exploitation of women, and our responsibilities as members of the human race, but I wound up keeping all that to myself. I knew that whatever I might have said would have been futile. My dad had about as much appetite for getting involved with this as he'd had for the Magic Kingdom all those years ago. We wound up going to Paris that spring, and I can still remember my nanny dragging me around the Louvre while I whined about not being in Orlando. That may have been a trivial event in the greater scheme of things, but the lesson had stayed with me. Once my father decided he didn't want to do something, nothing that I could say was likely to change his mind. I had a better chance of convincing him to line up for Space Mountain behind twenty-five Nebraskans wearing neon yellow "Druckenmiller Family Reunion" t-shirts than I did of getting him to sign off on either of us spending any more time in John Wainwright's world.

My father was still talking, expounding on the importance of minding one's own business and covering one's own ass, but I'd tuned him out. I was just waiting for him to finish so that I could leave when I noticed a copy of that morning's newspaper, folded and sitting on the edge of his desk. As I stared at it, a fresh thought dawned on me. Maybe there *was* someone out there who'd be interested in digging up dirt on John Wainwright. I looked up and saw my dad staring back at me, apparently waiting for my reaction to whatever it was that he'd just said. I just thanked him for his time before I sprang from my chair and hurried out of the room so I could make another call.

Chapter Forty-Six

Four days later, I met Jerry Barnes for the first time. Even though I arrived at the coffee shop about ten minutes early, I found him parked at the counter, waiting for me. Judging by his half-empty mug, he'd been there for at least a few minutes.

After we shook hands and introduced ourselves, I took the stool next to him and ordered a cup for myself. The place was a throwback to the twentieth century, a reminder that there had been a time before espresso, steamed milk and flavored syrups. In this joint, fifty cents got you a cup of strong, drip coffee, with half and half and sugar on the side. It seemed exactly the sort of place that a newspaper man would pick for a meeting.

As much as the coffee shop played into my preconceived notions of a journalist's haunt, Barnes himself didn't fit the part of a grizzled, old reporter. For one thing, he didn't look old. If I hadn't known that he was pushing sixty, I wouldn't have guessed that he was a day over forty-five. He was short, maybe just a shade over five feet tall, and he still had a full head of dark brown hair. I wouldn't say that he wore it long; "unruly" is probably a better word for it, and it was the only thing about him that seemed even the slightest bit unkempt. His pale pink dress shirt was overlaid with a subtle pattern of tiny purple squares, and it fit him perfectly. Neither his red silk tie nor his grey wool pants would have been out of place in my father's offices, and his entire ensemble put paid to my expectation of a rumpled correspondent trudging around town in a mustard-stained trench coat.

Once I'd sweetened and tasted my coffee, I began. "Thanks for meeting me. That was quite a story you wrote about John Wainwright, back in Jacksonville."

"Thanks," Barnes replied. "My Pulitzer Prize must have gotten lost in the mail." He smiled and added, "Along with all my other Pulitzers."

I chuckled. I'd done some research on Barnes. He'd fashioned a respectable career for himself, working at a few decent-sized papers over the years, but he'd never gotten that call from the *Times* or the *Post*. I thought of him as a .300 hitter in Triple-A ball who'd never been given his shot at the majors. His self-depreciating quip made me think that he might have seen something similar when he looked in the mirror. Every newspaperman around his age had started out with the goal of being the next Woodward or Bernstein, but most of them never found their Watergate. "That Wainwright piece was quite a story," I repeated.

Barnes took a sip of his own coffee before he spoke again. "I have to say, I was surprised to get your call. It's gotta be twenty-five years since I've heard John Wainwright's name."

"So, you've never done any kind of follow-up on him?"

He shrugged. "There wasn't much else to say. After my story came out, the guy folded his tents and disappeared. No news there."

"Well, I think what I'm about to tell you would make a pretty good story," I began, before jumping right in and outlining everything I knew about Wainwright's brides-for-cash program. I must have talked for ten minutes straight, with Barnes saying nothing more than an occasional "uh huh" the entire time. When I'd finished, he waved the waitress over for a refill. He stared straight at me while she poured our coffee, waiting for her to walk away before saying anything. After she'd gone, he said, simply, "That's a hell of a story."

"You think you can write about it?"

He shrugged. "Maybe, but I have a couple of questions for you first, if you don't mind."

"Sure. Of course," I replied.

"Well," he began, "let me cut to the chase. I'm wondering why Frazier Bennett's son came all the way to Baltimore to talk to me about all this."

I fumbled with my spoon, and I could feel myself blushing. Barnes must have noticed, because he added, almost apologetically, "You had to figure I'd check you out, right?"

I nodded. "Fair question, I guess, but can we just say that I'm a concerned citizen and leave it at that?"

He chuckled. "C'mon. Your dad's one of the most powerful bankers in the country. When I hear that his son is mixed up with a guy like Wainwright, it sounds to me like there might be a story there."

"I never said I was mixed up with Wainwright," I protested.

"You sure do seem to know an awful lot about him."

I sighed. "You're right. I know him."

"And?" he prompted me.

"And what?"

"What makes you want me to tell the world that he's a pimp in preacher's clothing?"

"'Cause he is. He's a bad guy, and everyone should know it. Isn't that enough?"

His phone buzzed, and he fished it out and answered a text before continuing our conversation. "Sorry," he said as he slid the device back into his pocket. "I just want to know if there's some sort of beef between you and Wainwright."

"Nothing worth mentioning," I replied, lying through my teeth.

Barnes nodded. "If I called your father, he'd tell me the same thing, huh?"

"Why, uh… I don't really think… I mean, you're not gonna…?"

He mercifully interrupted my faltering attempt to talk him out of contacting my dad. "Your father doesn't know you're here, does he?" I shook my head, and he went on. "Now I'm really curious."

"Why do you have to make this about me?" I asked, trying to convey an air of irritation. "Or my father? We certainly weren't involved in any of the stuff with the girls. Why can't you just write a story about that and leave us out of it?"

"Maybe I can," Barnes replied. "But if my source has an axe to grind, I need to know about it. Journalism 101, my friend."

His request was neither unreasonable nor unexpected. I'd hoped that Barnes would let me keep my association with Wainwright to myself, but I always understood that he was likely to insist on getting the whole story. I glanced around the restaurant and leaned in toward the reporter. "OK," I said, lowering my voice so that our fellow patrons wouldn't be able to overhear what came next. "I'll tell you everything, but I've got two conditions."

"Which are?"

"First," I began, "everything I'm about to tell you is off the record. You can't write about any of it."

"I don't know if I can promise that. If it's part of the story, I'm not sure that I can leave it out."

"Then we'll scrap the story altogether. Your call. But what I'm about to tell you can't wind up in the papers."

"OK. What else?"

I swirled my coffee around in my cup. "I think I should tell you the story first. Are we off the record?"

"If you say so."

"Good," I replied, before I proceeded to fill him on everything that I hadn't yet shared. I told him all about my early encounters with Wainwright, my affair with Jill, the real estate scam in Immokalee and the promise I'd made to my father to keep quiet about the lot of it. Barnes seemed riveted.

When I finished, his face broke into a broad smile. "That," he announced, "is a hell of a story. I can picture the headline: 'Wall Street Elite Swindled by Televangelist Pervert.'"

I felt a rush of panic shoot through me. "Hey! I thought I made it clear that we were off the..."

He held up his hand and stopped me. "I know, I know. Off the record. Don't worry. I understand why your family doesn't want this to get out."

"So you're not gonna write about it?" I asked.

"I promised I wouldn't."

I felt some of my anxiety drain away. My father would have disowned me if he'd known that I'd spilled the beans to a reporter, no matter what guarantees I'd extracted beforehand, but I believed that Barnes would keep his word. "So," I went on, "do you think you can write the story about Wainwright without mentioning the stuff about me?"

He picked up his coffee cup. "I need to talk to my editor. See what he thinks."

"Will you talk to him?"

He hesitated for a moment before he gingerly placed his cup back on the counter. "Are you sure you want me to? I mean, in my experience, once you tell part of a story, the rest of it usually finds its way into the light as well. Even if we don't write it, I can't promise you that someone else won't stumble onto it if they start poking around. Could you live with that?"

That was the question that I'd been struggling with ever since I'd decided to reach out to the press. Barnes wasn't telling me anything that I hadn't already considered. I had enough common sense to understand that putting any part of this in the papers risked exposing me and my father, but I'd shown up for our meeting anyway. I'd hoped to hear something that would absolve me, to discover a way for me to have my cake and eat it, too, but Barnes threw the whole thing back in my lap. He made it clear that whatever happened would be on me.

I took a deep breath before I answered. "Fuck it. If it gets out there, it gets out there. It's worth it." As soon as those words cleared my lips, I felt like an asshole for betraying my father. Once again, he stood to suffer on account of one of my questionable decisions. For me, though, the game had changed once I'd talked to Liz. It was one thing to keep quiet when it was only about the money, but now there were bigger issues than the Bennett family's pride at stake. If the price of doing something was a little embarrassment on our end, then we would have to live with that. I was confident that we'd survive.

Barnes stood up and threw a five-dollar bill onto the counter. "OK. I'll talk to my editor. I'll have to sell him on it. I mean, it's not a local story, but I've written about this guy before, and the subject matter is pretty juicy..."

I interrupted him. "Hold on. I haven't told you my other condition yet."

He grimaced. "You're a real pain in the ass, you know that?"

I ignored him and continued. "I want to help you write the story."

Barnes smiled. "Of course. You're gonna be my main source on this. I'll need you to give me names, dates, places, contacts that can corroborate whatever you tell me... You're gonna be all over this."

"That's not what I mean. I'm saying that I want to *write* the story with you. And I want my name on it, as a co-author."

He stared blankly at me for a few seconds before dismissing my request. "That's not how it works."

Undaunted, I just nodded. "But that's what I'm asking."

He responded with a forced laugh. "Have you ever written anything before?"

"Uh, yeah. Of course I've..."

He cut me off. "Let me stop you right there, before you regale me with some bullshit about how you were the best writer in your freshman composition class and how, this one time, you wrote this really great term paper. I'm asking if anyone has ever paid you to write anything, if you've ever had anything published." I shook my head, and he continued. "No? Nothing? Magazines? Your school newspaper? I bet you've never even posted on a fucking blog, have you?"

"Nope."

"Then why on Earth would I share my byline with you? It's taken me thirty-five years to stake my claim to that space on the page. If you want a soapbox with your name on it, go out and get your own fucking column."

I stared down at the counter and mumbled something about being a bright guy and a quick learner. When Barnes spoke again, his tone was milder. "I know you're well-educated," he replied, "and I'm sure you're quite capable. It's just that... sources provide information, and journalists write stories. That's the way it is."

I nodded. Again, I knew that he wasn't out of line. I didn't really have a compelling argument as to why he should share a publishing credit with me, so I decided to tell him that only thing I could: the truth. "Jerry, I have no idea where John Wainwright is right now. Our best guess is that he's somewhere in Central America. I don't imagine I'll ever see him again, and even if we write this article, it probably won't affect him much. Most likely, he'll never even read it. But if he does see it, somehow, I want him to know... I need him to know... that it came from me."

Barnes stood there for a moment, studying my face, before he removed his jacket from the back of his stool and put it on. Without saying a word, he walked away. I don't know what was going through his head. Maybe he still harbored a lingering disdain for the old preacher, or maybe he just took pity on me. Whatever the reason, he stopped just before he got to the door and retraced his steps, until he was standing next to me again. Neither of us spoke until he gave me a slight nod and muttered, "OK."

I smiled. "OK?"

He shook his head. "I'll talk to my editor. I'll give you a call." With that, he turned on his heel and left.

Chapter Forty-Seven

Our story ran eight weeks later, and I'm pretty sure that I was the first one to see it in print. I couldn't sleep the night before it was published, so I camped out at a newsstand near my hotel and waited for them to deliver the morning edition. I snatched the top copy from the bundle and found the headline on the front page below the fold, just as the editor had promised: "THE FOR-PROFIT PROPHET." Right below it was the byline: "By Jerry Barnes and M. James Bennett." I bought twenty copies and carried them back up to my room.

As for the article itself, I just skimmed it to confirm that Barnes had kept his promise not to mention the real estate scam, and I was relieved to find that he'd been true to his word. I didn't bother to read any closer than that, since I already knew the story by heart. When Barnes agreed to share the writing credit with me, he made damn sure that he got his money's worth. I wrote every word. And then I re-wrote them. And re-re-wrote them. Now, I laugh when I remember feeling pretty good about the first draft that I'd handed to Barnes. He ripped it apart at the cellular level and sent me back to the drawing board. "We're in the newspaper business," he thundered. "We're not novelists, or fucking bloggers, where we can ramble on forever. Every word, every syllable, has to have a purpose."

My second effort wasn't much of an improvement on my first, and the stream of invective with which my co-author responded to my third draft let me know that I was getting worse as I went. I'm not sure how many versions of the story I wound up writing; the weeks that I spent living on coffee, fast food and four hours of sleep a night took their toll on my ability to keep track of the finer details of my initial foray into journalism. Gradually, though, Barnes stopped using words like "amateurish" and "hopeless" in his critiques, and drafts started coming back to me without having been completely defaced with red ink. After he read my final version, he just grunted, "We're good," and we sent it off to the editor. I can't remember ever feeling so proud of anything in my life.

I sat at the desk in my room and scrawled the last address the investigators had for Wainwright onto the front of a large envelope. I wasn't all that confident that it would ever reach him, even if he was still in Nicaragua, but I had to try. I slid a copy of the newspaper into the envelope, along with a piece of hotel stationary on which I'd handwritten a line from St. Paul's letter to the Galatians: "Be not deceived; God is not mocked: for whatsoever a man soweth, that shall he also reap." Beneath that, I signed the note, simply, "Good luck. MJB."

I also prepared envelopes to a handful of Nicaraguan government officials, including the Director General of the National Police, the Minister of Women, and the ambassador in Washington, D.C. I included a copy of the article in each one, along with a letter suggesting that they might want to take a second look at their recently-arrived American émigré.

I threw the other sixteen copies into my suitcase and checked the train schedule. I planned on heading straight to my father's office when I got back to New York. I'd already told him what I was up to, and even though he hadn't been thrilled about the idea, I was eager to show him the finished product. More importantly, I wanted to tell him that I was moving to Jacksonville. After all the criticism I'd endured as Barnes' sidekick, the last thing I expected was for him to encourage me to take up his profession, but that's exactly what he did. He still had quite a few friends at the *Times-Union*, and once he put in a word with them, they agreed to take me on as a junior reporter on their city desk. I'm sure that it wasn't exactly what my father had in mind, but it was a real job, and I figured that had to count for something.

Before I left, I paused to call Barnes. The phone rang six times before he finally picked up and mumbled, "Hello."

"Hey, Jerry. It's James. The article came out today. Have you seen it?"

"I'm still in bed. What time is it?"

I had forgotten that it wasn't even six in the morning yet. "It's, uh... pretty early. Sorry."

I braced myself for a tongue lashing, but it never came. Instead, he asked me how it felt to see my name in print. "Good," I replied. "Really good."

"I was the same way the first time I got published... couldn't sleep a wink, waiting for that paper to come out in the morning." He paused for a second before continuing. "Of course, now that I've been through it ten thousand times, I prefer to get some fucking sleep."

"Sorry," I repeated. "I'm about to head back to New York, and then down to Florida next week. I just wanted to say 'thanks' before I left."

"I think you could be a good newspaperman, James. Stick with it."

"Thanks," I said again.

"Let me know how it goes in Jacksonville."

"I will."

"One last piece of advice," he began. "Forget about Wainwright. Move on."

"OK. I'll try."

The line was silent for a few moments, until Barnes said, "Take care of yourself."

"You too," I replied, before hanging up and dragging my suitcase into the hall.

Epilogue

I have no idea whether Wainwright received my note, or if he ever read our article. I did get an acknowledgement from the Nicaraguan ambassador, which I'm pretty sure was a form letter, thanking me for my interest in his country and assuring me that his government would devote due attention to the issues that I'd raised. Upon reading that, my assumption was that they simply didn't care about the old man's predilection for underage matchmaking. Maybe that was the case, but about a month after our story hit the news, we got word that Wainwright and his daughter had left Nicaragua and were in the wind. Justifiably or not, I like to think that I played a role in screwing up his plans for a comfortable retirement on the beach.

We've still not managed to track them down. I imagine they made their way to another Caribbean hideaway, but for all I know they're back in the States, up to their same old tricks. Whenever my phone shows an unknown caller, a little part of me expects to hear the old man's voice on the other end. I'd be lying if I denied ever having fantasized about coming home from work and finding Jill waiting for me at my place, brimming with apologies and explanations. Deep down, though, I know that that's never going to happen. The Wainwrights aren't coming to visit just so I can get closure.

Our story burned bright across the media landscape for about a week. Jerry and I even got to go on CNN, where we shared a panel with a woman from Utah who had founded an organization that helped young girls escape from Mormon fundamentalist compounds. We wound up connecting her with Liz's sister, Catherine, who left her geriatric fiancée and moved out West. She's living in an ex-polygamist safe house, and I understand that she wants to devote her life to helping other women find their way out of coercive relationships.

Beyond that, I'm not sure that our reporting had much of a tangible impact. One or two police departments launched investigations into our allegations of underage matchmaking, but I haven't heard of any old men actually getting arrested. Liz and Barbara are still with their elderly husbands, as far as I know. Like most news, our story's grip on the public's attention proved fleeting. The world moved on.

I've been in Jacksonville for nine months now, and for the first time in my life, I feel like I'm actually making a go of something more legitimate than online poker. Like anything else, my new profession has its ups and downs. I struggled at first, but I feel like I'm finally settling into the rhythm of writing for a daily newspaper. My assignments so far have mostly been mundane, local stuff, but I've been uncharacteristically at peace with the idea of starting at the bottom. My editors seem to like me, and it seems like bigger and better projects are in my future. It helps that I talk to Jerry a couple of times a week. He still gives me a lot of shit, but somehow it always feels constructive.

I keep in touch with my father pretty regularly, as well. Most of our conversations center around him warning me about the dire economic state of the newspaper industry and urging me not to get too comfortable in my new vocation. He tells me it's wonderful that I'm so interested in media, but that I'm on the wrong end of the business. Why write for a newspaper when you can buy it, sell it, lend to it or liquidate it? The money is always going to be better on my dad's side of the table.

Given the frequency with which he emails me articles about the demise of this or that venerable daily, it's hard to argue with him. But I didn't get into journalism for the money. I guess I could get up on a soapbox and cite the noble history of newspapers, or explain how a functioning press is essential to a free society, but those aren't the things that motivate me, either. I just like to write, and I don't hate waking up every day and going to work. That's really all I was ever looking for in a job.

I can see how my choices must get under my father's skin. He spent years trying to get me to pick a career, and when I finally did, it happened to be in an industry that he honestly believes will become defunct before I'm ready to retire. I hope he's wrong about that. I want to keep writing. And I hope that my father will keep reading. According to our circulation department, he's the *Times-Union's* only subscriber who lives in New York. Every day, they Fed Ex him a copy of the paper, which he receives the following morning. It's enough to make me think that maybe, just maybe, he's proud of me after all.

ABOUT THE AUTHOR

Armed with degrees from Duke University and the University of Michigan Law School, Bob Waldner moved to New York City many years ago to seek his fortune. Not being an adept fortune-seeker, he started writing fiction. He published his first novel, *Peripheral Involvement*, in 2014, and his short stories have appeared, or are scheduled to appear, in *The Saturday Evening Post, theEEEL* and *Mulberry Fork Review.* He continues to practice corporate law in Manhattan, where he lives with his wife, Erinn, and his two daughters, Maureen and Madeleine. You can find him on the web at www.bobwaldnerbooks.com.

Made in the USA
Lexington, KY
03 December 2015